A DESERT IN BLOOM

William Landvoigt Bayne

First Printing 2025

ISBN 979-8-9913479-0-7
Library of Congress
Cataloging-in-Publication Data
is available upon request.
Thank you for supporting
independent authors
and publishers.

COYOTE FILMS EDITION
Press: info@adesertinbloom.net

Book Design by Averi Media

There is a place, not far from our memories,
where truth and legend meet.
When we are in that place nothing else matters,
not even the words we use to describe it.

\- WLB

for Jocelyn and Thomas

I CIRCLED THE OLD CABIN like I would a used car, peering through the tainted windows for any sign of life. The one-room shack sat behind a rusty barbwire fence, miles beyond the power lines. Perched on tree stumps and concrete blocks, the cabin walls were damp with the same rain that had soaked my shoes.

It was perfect.

I'd spent the last ten years making money and then hiding it, first from my ex-wife and then from myself, hoping to keep from pouring it out in a drunken binge on some blurry craps table. I convinced myself that what I really needed was a piece of land somewhere, so I could get away from all the unappreciative people in my life and the beast that raged inside my head.

My new girlfriend was resting in our car at the bottom of the hill. Even sick with the flu, she'd managed to push my impatient soul past the miles of muddy track to the hidden cabin. I'd wanted to give up and go home, but she had urged me to keep going, doggedly following the gritty map that some real estate agent had scrawled on a piece of scrap paper.

Three months later, I met Dave Bailey. My girlfriend had gone back to her husband, but I was still making a weekly pilgrimage to the cabin - army cot, sleeping bag and whiskey bottle in hand. On the way there, I saw a hand-painted sign on a broken sheet of plywood:

U-NAME-IT RANCH

Horses 4 Sale

The 4 was big and red and drawn in backwards.

Back in another life, I had a horse. I turned off the highway onto a gravel road and headed for the U-Name-it Ranch.

Dave's daughter took me out for a ride. There were two horses for sale, one palomino and a stocky Appaloosa. The palomino was pushing twenty-five, and the Appy had no brakes at all. When we got back to the house, I passed politely on the horses. Dave offered me a cup of coffee instead.

A healthy spoonful of creamer barely turned it from black to dark brown. Even sugar failed to mask the bitter aftertaste. I'd find out later that Dave never emptied the grounds in his weathered 'Mr. Coffee'. He would add to them instead, until they overflowed the tortured paper filter. When the filters ran out, he'd make do with a doubled-over paper towel.

We sat by the kitchen window, at a green Formica table with a chrome rim. We talked about horses, the countryside all around, and my new endeavor 12 miles to the west. He seemed pleased that I'd rejected the horses his daughter had for sale. I felt like I'd passed some kind of invisible test, designed to keep total imbeciles away from his kitchen table. I couldn't tell you how long I was there that day, only that time seemed to fade away with my reserve, and that more than one cup of coffee was involved.

Dave Bailey had come to Grass Valley as a young man, closer to a boy in fact, in a time when boyhood faded quickly under the sharp lash of the Great Depression. His family had settled there during the heyday of the big underground gold mines, when land was cheap, and California offered hope and promise to the wandering refugees of the Oklahoma Dust Bowl.

I asked him about his folks, and when he mentioned his dad, he broke out in a broad smile. He paused, took some tobacco out of a foil pouch and began to roll a cigarette.

"Like I say, he was a top mechanic, and there wasn't nothin' that he couldn't talk to you about. And I mean talk to you, and know what he was sayin' when he did." Dave sealed the cigarette paper closed with a stroke of his tongue. "Politics or whatever, he knew."

Dave pushed the thick round glasses back on his nose and lit his cigarette. "And Dad didn't have, but I think a year of college. Unlearned, but he was a book reader. If there was a book that told you how to do anything, well, Dee Bailey would read it. Then he'd try it out - and he improved on a lot of things."

"Dee?"

"Yessir. He was a David, too, like his daddy, like me. So, everyone called him Dee." Dave took a long look out the window and another puff on his cigarette.

"My Grandma Bailey used to say when he was a little-bitty boy, he would make his own light bulbs and batteries. He'd have lights all around, out in the yard and in the house, before electricity was even in that part of the country. Even in town, there was no electricity. Everybody would come out to the farm just to see those lights, and all the other crazy things that Dad could make…"

WHEN THE TRACTORS CAME, they carved the ancient prairie into long straight lines. Soft soil turned to hard angles, tall grass into bearded wheat and corn. The rains stopped in protest, and the wind came up like a punch in the gut, spat out in chunks of gritty brown dirt.

The droughts wore on for years, endless furrows turned to choking clouds of dust. Paint peeled from the storefronts and the farmhouses, from hay rakes and automobiles, bare metal left to rust in the hazy sun.

Day became night. Dark storms lashed the Great Plains all the way down to Texas. Coal-grey snow fell in New England, and the streets of Chicago were covered in dust an inch thick.

Even the rich fell poor, fortunes lost in a snare trap of ticker tape, greed and bankruptcy. Millions lost their jobs and their families. More went hungry and homeless in the shantytowns and tent cities across America. Banks failed, and for many, so did faith.

Some died a little bit at a time in soup lines, others all at once at the bottom of a tall building.

EROSION

AUGUST 1931
Yuma County, Arizona

THE BALDING FIRESTONES were barely holding their own against a swirling wind. Dee Bailey had overinflated them, hoping to add some traction and make another flat tire less likely. He doubted any part of his theory would hold true. The old Essex still swayed with every gust, and he'd already patched two inner tubes since they'd left the camptown.

He didn't like traveling in a high wind, but stopping could be just as dangerous, especially at night. The converted wagon they were using as a trailer didn't have any running lights, only reflectors. It wouldn't take much for someone to barrel into their little caravan, even if they were well off the path. At least their headlights gave the other cars a sense of where they were and where they were going.

All of the kids were asleep, and so was Floy. Dee glanced at his wife, grateful for her slumber. Four children, even in the big ragtop, could get to be quite a load. They'd sing for a while and do their letters and their numbers, but soon, the numbing sameness of the road would wear them down and the inevitable bickering would begin. Beno was the worst, always wanting to enforce her will on the younger ones. Velda Jean had a tendency to sulk, and Davey was hard pressed to listen to anyone. Thank God for little Wanda - she was the bright spot in the back seat. Passed around from sibling to sibling, her natural good humor brought everyone's spirits up. For such a long, hard trip as this, he was proud of his children.

He gathered his thoughts in the cooling silence. *We had to leave.*

The bank failures and the constant drought had ground Dee's hometown into dust. Oklahoma was twice cursed; what little the people had left was slowly being stripped away by the wind. His father-in-law had taken out ahead of them; John Cox had found work in a labor camp and sent word back to Floy. It was the final domino in a long line of them, and Dee had decided to make a break for it. Everything that they couldn't pack in the rubber-tired wagon was either given away or sold.

His father had been unusually supportive. Dee had refused any money - those left behind would need it more. Jacob David Bailey would never leave their family farm. He was hard as the land that bore him. "Godspeed," he'd said. "And look to John Cox for counsel."

His old man was right. It was Floy's father who had finally pushed them out of the labor camps.

"Look at your hands, Dee. You're a mechanic, not a ditch digger. Pretty soon those hands won't be good for anything but."

His father-in-law had pressed a few dollars into his hand. "For gas, and a little something for the children." Dee had taken it this time, knowing he was stretching the good will of the Lord, starting off with such little money and so few prospects. But John Cox was right. Camp life wasn't meant for families, not his or anyone else's.

Six weeks before, John had sent one of his sons out ahead to scout the way, hopeful that Irvon might find something better. But no one had heard from Floy's little brother in over a month.

It was his turn now.

He'd heard there was work to be had across the border in California, with talk of some great canal in the offing. If so, there'd be lots of heavy equipment, and a need for good mechanics. They'd left reluctantly, and there were more tears to go with the ones shed for Oklahoma. Like Irvon, he had promised to send word if he found work.

But damn, this trail was a weary one. Every day, they passed the crippled wrecks along the roadside. Broken cars and broken dreams, remnants of the great gypsy caravan that stretched from the dusty plains all the way to California. They stopped where they could to help, in exchange for what little the people had to offer. Most had even less than they did. Without unpacking the wagon and setting up shop by the side of the road, there was often little that Dee could do. But he had tried. And some of them Floy gave comfort to, or a little food, and he some fuel or a few cents.

Now, he'd come to the same sorry state. He reached down in his pocket, letting his fingers settle on the few coins that he found there.

One nickel and three pennies.

Eight cents left, and still over a hundred miles to California. Dee bristled. A hard choice, but he would have to sell his tools.

An oncoming ice truck crested the hill in front of him, and caught by its high profile in the wind, swerved into their lane, the bright beams raking Dee's eyes. Dee floored the Essex and veered off the side of the road. Avoiding the big truck sent their trailer fishtailing wildly behind them, and the sudden movement threw Floy across the seat into Dee's shoulder. She grabbed the benchback and pulled herself up, then looked behind to see that the children were still sleeping.

"God, Dee, you scared me half to death."

Dee eased off on the accelerator, braking gently to settle the trailer in behind them. It had taken a full day to load the wagon, and even though it looked like a great laundry basket on wheels, the weight was carefully distributed, its center of gravity as low as Dee could make it.

"Scared me worse, Mother. I'll be glad for daylight."

"Me, too, darling." Floy slid over on the seat, her body gathered up next to her husband. She lifted the blanket from around her knees and draped it over Dee's shoulder, letting her head fall against his chest.

"How far to California?"

Dee brought his hand back from the steering wheel and stroked her hair, running his fingers across her brow. "Not far, baby, not far."

Floy raised her head to look through the windshield, saw headlights on sand and nothing more. She closed her eyes. "Are we going to make it, Dee?"

"We'll make it, honey."

As they crested the next hill, Dee saw a dim line of lights spread neatly along the horizon. His fingertips fell to her lips, and he brushed her cheek, watching as the distant dots drifted into focus.

* * *

THERE WAS LITTLE LEFT TO DO but bank the stove for the night and lock up the store. Madeline Spain had finished her bookwork, carefully noting the litany of debits and credits that built the balance sheet of Wellton, Arizona. Other than the railroad depot, there was hardly any currency in town that didn't pass through her books in one way or another. Fifty years ago, Harlan Spain had drilled a well here, and the people and the money had flowed ever since. First, the railroad came, looking for water to fuel their steam engines on the long journey to the coast. Then came the engineers and the line hands, the farmers and the shopkeepers, all turning toil in the little tank town by the big well that Harlan Spain had dug in the sand.

Madeline had heard her husband tell the story at least a dozen times. How in 1870, Harlan's rig had broken down in the desert halfway to Yuma; how the old man had tested it right where it sat, right on top of the biggest artesian aquifer in Southern Arizona. The drill went down only forty feet, but the water shot up for a hundred, washing away years of spent dreams and hard labor. Harlan Spain capped the gusher, filed homestead papers at the Yuma Land Office, and made his fortune on the sweet water between the Colorado and the Gila River.

Madeline Spain closed the books on the Wellton General Mercantile, The Wellton Hotel, The Rosebud Cafe, and Spain's Safety Garage & Service Station. They'd turned another profit, not an everyday occurrence in such difficult times. Lawrence's father had invested wisely after Harlan died, and when Joseph passed away, he left more than a few going concerns to his only son. But the big well was the fountainhead, the source of all the tankage sales, the irrigation leases, and the lush, green fields of alfalfa they harvested every year. Fortunately, Lawrence had never been one to spend beyond his means, and except for the railroad right of way, much of the real estate in the little township of Wellton still belonged to the Spain family.

Ever since Joseph passed, Madeline had managed the family business. Her husband didn't like the idea at first, a testament to his considerable male vanity. He was more than happy to oblige, once he found out how much work was involved. Lawrence wasn't lazy, just a boy at heart, more interested in fast horses and airplanes than the day-to-day drudgery of ledgers and inventory. Madeline did all the shopkeeping, leaving him to tend the farm and his civic duties as Wellton's Justice of the Peace. It was a pleasant arrangement for the both of them; Lawrence fell headlong into his role as town patron and she was grateful for some diversion from the children. Her mother had kept a nanny, and her grandmother as well. Madeline was certain the young Mexican woman she had hired was equally capable of boiling bottles and changing diapers.

Now that the children were mostly grown, she enjoyed their presence more, and let her influence fall on matters more crucial, like manners and deportment. She was determined to see her two daughters off to finishing schools in the East, and that neither of her two sons would end up a farmer or a bartender.

Madeline stacked the ledgers under the cash box in the Wheeling Safe, spun the combination lock and closed the steel case. She took her hat from the tall stand by the door, and paused to look out the window of the General Mercantile. Lawrence should be here any minute now; he'd promised to take her into Yuma to see a picture show.

Outside, a green car and trailer had pulled up alongside the curb. There were children in the back seat; she could see their eyes pressed up close to the window glass. A striking man with straight black hair closed the old car's hood and wiped his hands clean on a small towel. He bent over to speak to a woman in the front seat. She could just make out their conversation, listening out of idle curiosity to pass the time.

"There's nothing but the jam left, and we've no bread, Dee."

"I've got fuel enough, I think," the man replied. "And they're hungry. Maybe I can get half-a-loaf, and we can at least make them a jelly sandwich." The blonde woman nodded, turning back to her children.

Madeline watched the man fold the towel neatly and place it in the back of the trailer. He straightened his shirt, ran his fingers through his hair and looked down the street. She could see his eyes take in the length and breadth of Wellton, almost as if he were somehow its first citizen, instead of yet another lost soul on the road to California. His gaze traveled up the street and back to the sign above her door, then down to the window where she was standing. She tried to avert her eyes, but he caught them for a moment; the small hairs along the nape of her neck tingled, and she turned away.

She busied herself tidying the counter as the man came through the door, flustered at the thought of being caught at the window like a small child. The man moved silently through the store, casually looking at the shelves, appearing for all the world to be in search of some perfect jewel, and not the half-loaf she knew he could barely afford. He stopped by the breadbox and looked down at the loaves the baker had left that morning. They were all unsplit, and the price she had stenciled above the case was twelve cents apiece.

The man took one of the loaves and brought it over to the counter. She looked up at him and was startled again, as his face betrayed no anxiety, only the steady calm of someone on an errand of some importance.

"I'd like to buy half a loaf, if I might."

In that moment, she would have given him the bread, given him her life, given him anything he wanted, but the moment passed like a hot wind, and she caught herself standing bolt upright and speaking as if he were a neighbor down the road, or her pastor on a Sunday morning.

"I don't see why not, let me slice it for you."

"Why, thank you." He smiled, and the thin lines surrounding his eyes curled up like long grass in the wind. "That's very kind of you."

Madeline turned away to the butcher block behind the glass case where she kept the fresh meats. She looked down at her trembling hands and the long bread knife. She feigned a casual lightness.

"Are you on your way to California, then?"

"Yes ma'am, we are. I've heard there's work to be had on the canal."

"So, you're an engineer, then?" She knew that he wasn't, but couldn't bear to place him as a common laborer in a ditch somewhere.

"No, ma'am... a mechanic. There's bound to be a few big diesels and they're prone to need a careful hand."

Thoughts spun like thin webs across her mind, shooting this way and that; her husband Lawrence, the woman in the car, her children, their empty garage and the foolish man that she had fired only a week before, for thievery and incompetence, how happy she was, and how happy she wasn't, and this quiet man with all the dignity she had never found in all her years with all her graces, and the madness of it all at once, on a night where nothing happens in a town where nothing happens.

Her hands shook as she cut the loaf in two. She wrapped it carefully in white butcher paper and handed it to the man. "That will be seven cents."

The man reached into his pocket and brought out a few coins, placing a nickel and two pennies into her hand. His fingers were rough and well formed.

"Thank you very much." He smiled softly and turned toward the door.

Madeline watched as he moved across the floor, silently counting his footsteps. "Sir?" She saw only his feet as he turned around. She looked up to face him squarely.

"Just how good a mechanic are you?"

"The best I've ever met, ma'am."

She sensed that he was telling the truth as he knew it, as he always did. "Stick around for a minute. I've got a proposition for you." She reached down to get the ledger for the garage.

There was no turning back now.

DAVEY WATCHED THE BIG SNAKE move across the rock, coiling and uncoiling in its slow dance with the shadow of the sun. It struck him that snakes moved like water flowing downhill, with no beginning or end to their motion. He wasn't at all sure if he liked them, but he was certain they had some special power, something that let them get from here to there without the benefit of arms or legs.

Grandpa Cox had told him never to touch one, no matter how pretty they were, 'cause they bit hard and sometimes they wouldn't let go. Momma said they were full of poison, and would kill you if you ever got bit, even if they just scratched you, and that it hurt for a long time, even worse than a beating. When he asked his Dad about them, he got one of his big books down from the shelf and showed him pictures of all the different kinds and pointed out the ones that could kill you. Davey wasn't sure if the one he was looking at was the kind that killed you, but he thought maybe it was.

Davey figured he could get a big stick and beat it to pieces if he had to, 'cause it didn't look like it could kill him, not if he didn't want it to.

Sitting under the footbridge, Davey felt pretty safe because he could see the snake real good, and he didn't think the snake even knew that he was there. Davey watched as it slid away again. He figured that the snake liked being in the sun, seeing as how it kept slipping out of the shadows. This time of year, it got pretty cool in the shade, but Davey had the big coat his Uncle Irvon had given him. He could sit under that footbridge for as long as he wanted.

He'd been coming to the dry wash for three days now, ever since he started skipping class at his new school. He didn't need to go anyhow, 'cause his mother had taught him to read already, and besides, if he wanted to get a beating he could always get one at home. All he had to do was talk back to his mom, or pick on one of the girls. That schoolteacher should know that.

Once, when he was only five, one of the kids at the big picnic said he was stupid, and that was OK, because it was just the two of them there, but when that other kid said it in front of the whole class, well, that's not OK, 'cause standing up in front of everybody makes it hard to do your letters, even when you're eight, and he would've got them all out if that big mouth hadn't call him stupid. He only hit him once or twice real hard; the rest of the time he was just letting him know that he could hit him two or three times before he could get up, 'cause Davey was fast, and Grandpa said to let them know what they're in for right away. But that ain't no reason to get beat with no buggy whip, that's for sure. Anyway, they could have their dang old school.

Davey pulled some gravel out of his pocket and tossed it at a dark hole across the wash. He practiced throwing until he used up all his rocks, and then he crawled down to the dry creek bed and got some more. On the way, he checked to see that the big snake was still where it was before, and it was, so he went back up under the bridge. He had a jelly sandwich in his book bag, and a big pear that his mother had given him for lunch. Davey ate the sandwich and half of the pear.

He threw the rest of the pear by the hole. He knew something lived in that hole, he just wasn't going to give it his sandwich. He was right, because a big packrat came out and took the pear. The snake saw the rat, too, and moved faster than Davey thought it could. It grabbed the packrat real quick and bit down hard. Grandpa was right. Davey didn't think that snake was gonna' let go.

It took all afternoon for the big snake to swallow the packrat whole, first unlocking its jaws, then sliding its muscles to allow the rat to pass, still moving, into its belly. Davey wondered if it could do that to him, too.

He noticed that the snake was moving real slow. This would be his best chance to find out. He searched out the biggest rock that he could lift, and hoisted it over his head. The big snake sounded like a hundred hornets as he approached, and waved its tail and hissed, but Davey didn't let it bite him, even though it tried. He timed the snake's movements as it moved from side to side, then dropped his weapon from above, crushing the diamond-shaped head below. Davey thought the packrat might still be alive, so he slit the snake's belly open with his knife to take a look. The rat was dead. He figured it was moving only because it hurt so bad to get swallowed while you were still alive.

Davey tossed the carcass in the dirt and made a face. He didn't like snakes any better than he liked school.

* * *

FLORENCE COX BAILEY gathered the blue gingham cloth at its edges and began her crossover stitch. She had almost seven yards of the checkered fabric left, all salvaged from a broken trunk that Dee had found in some abandoned wagon. With a little careful cutting, she'd removed the stained and moldy sections, tailoring the rest to fashion curtains for the kitchen window and a new dress for little Wanda's birthday. Back in Oklahoma, Dee had found the derelict wagon on one of his frequent foraging trips out on the prairie. She had hated to see him go, always worried that he might get lost or stranded, but he would just smile and tell her not to pay so much attention to the old Indian stories that her father used to frighten the children.

When times were better, she had scoffed at her husband's frontier expeditions, but lately, his careful scavenging of those pioneer wrecks had proved to be a godsend - spare parts and scrap iron for Dee and some handy household goods that they otherwise couldn't afford.

Those were the days made for dreaming, before the dust storms came and the stock market crashed. Dee would strike out in his airplane for the surrounding farm towns, his handbills drifting like paper rain from the sky above. They were bold like he was, big block letters proclaiming:

THE THRILL OF A LIFETIME!
See the future from the
WINGS of a MECHANICAL MARVEL!
- 5 Minutes for ONE Dollar -
It's a ride you will never forget!

And she never would. The first time he took her up in the clouds, she lost all sense of herself, the chill wind roaring by, the tiny world floating like a child's toy below. If it was only five minutes, they were the longest she had ever known.

Her daddy had given her the dollar and insisted that she go, but only after he'd made the trip himself. He waited patiently, seemingly unconcerned that her ride was so much longer than his own. She thought her father must have seen something of himself in the Bailey boy, all brass and confidence, his eyes set upon the great new world. Until that moment, she had never cared for Dee Bailey, though all the girls in Chandler turned their heads at his strong form and his fine head of straight, black hair. She had found him callous and too freethinking, with all his talk of machines and the changes they would wage upon their world.

And when that small town mechanic had somehow managed to trade himself into an old airplane, she'd thought that he'd explode, he was so full of himself. No one expected it to fly again, after it had crashed into a wheat field on the outskirts of town. But Dee had buried the pilot, and traded the angry farmer a new hay rake for the crumpled shell left broken in his windrows. It took him weeks to reconstruct it, but no sooner than he did, he was flying looping circles over the town square, playing daredevil for all the world to see.

She was smitten in that Curtis Jenny, a thousand feet above the farmland she had known as home, by his easy smile and his fierce dark eyes. They were married less than three weeks later, in the small church by the square, Father beaming and Mother weeping, laughter and dancing and all the children dressed like Easter, with the seed of her firstborn deep within her.

The first months were like a circus train, all color and excitement, both she and he up over the prairie, each new town slipping away into the next. Dee would carry the "cargo" and she would take the tickets and count the money, putting a little aside on each trip for the day when they might settle down. And every time they returned to Chandler, her mother would cry and her father would take Dee aside into the parlor, where they would talk for hours.

As the baby began to grow inside her, Dee made her stay behind, and no amount of longing or cajoling could make him change his mind. So she ached for him and sang to the baby in her belly, and made curtains like the ones she was making now, anything to pass the empty hours without him.

And then her Beno was born, so little and so frail, named for barely a bean's worth of space she took up on her blanket. Dee's flights became less frequent, the small house and the small child taking more and more of his time. There were motorcars to work on; her father had expanded the Cox Carriage House to carry automobiles alongside the horse-drawn wagons. "I never thought you could keep those damn things on the road," Daddy had said. "But you've changed my mind, Dee".

She had known better, of course. Even though the Dodge Brothers built a fine car, Dee could never get John Cox out of his old buggy. Everyone realized that the automobiles were added for his grandchild's benefit. Still, Floy could tell her father liked being first to sell the horseless carriages, confident in his livery's reputation, now that Dee Bailey was there to repair them. Sadly, no one could afford to buy a Dodge now, nor even a Ford for that matter.

Velda Jean was born next, almost two years to the day from little Beno; she was twice her size and ten times her constitution, always to be the steady one amongst the children. Dee was pleased, and more than a little bit relieved; he had feared for another rough birth. Each day had brought him closer to home, his barnstorming trips decreasing as his family grew larger. She could see him change, his freewheeling nature brought down to earth by the iron weight of fatherhood. He was home more, but she seemed to see him less. By the time Davey was born, there was a total end to the airplane sideshow. Dee sold the old Jenny shortly thereafter, to buy new tools for his shop. But she had saved his scarf and his flying goggles, and kept them in her cedar chest for the time when they might soar together again.

Floy lifted the curtains up to the window. They would fill the space nicely. For weeks she'd been refurbishing the little cabin, sprucing up their new family home. The girls were a big help, and even rough and tumble Davey took pride in swinging his broom like some knight in shining armor.

A thin layer of dirt coated the windowsill. Floy brushed it off in reflex. She had cleaned that same sill, only yesterday. It was getting harder and harder to keep up with the blowing sand; it seemed to be everywhere these days.

She looked out at the Spain's garage in the distance. She could hear Dee's hammer, guided by his one good eye in the failing light. The children were long since in bed; she'd kept his supper warming on the stove. The steel cadence of his labors ceased, and Floy grew hopeful for his return. She could see a lantern lit in the shop and his shadow by the window at his bench.

With a quiet sigh, she eased into the chair beside the kitchen table. Her needle freshly threaded, Floy Bailey began to sew once more.

THE ADOBE-WALLED SERVICE STATION was little more than a block-house with two gas pumps, but it was more than enough for Dee Bailey. The main road ran right in front of it, and there was plenty of traffic to and fro. Dee liked the steady flow of customers; it was a good mix of travelers, locals and long distance haulers.

Wellton's Main Street was a just a small part of Highway 80, laid over on the old east-west Butterfield Stage Route. It was rough going in places, especially across the steep pass into Yuma. At least once or twice a week, there was a break-down or a bust-up that Dee would have to see to. Lawrence Spain had given him an old abandoned Cadillac, and Dee had cut the back off, laid in a flatbed, and fit it with a pulley winch and a bumper crane. It wasn't exactly a Dodge, but it made a better tow truck than anything else in the long valley.

The Spains took all the profits from the pumps, but Dee kept his labor and half from all the parts he sold. Plus, his family had the use of one of the big vaca-tion cabins behind the hotel. Mrs. Spain had already promised him a larger house down the road, once Dee could get around to fixing the roof. All in all, a good deal better than the labor camp they had fled just six weeks ago.

He had never told Floy how desperate he was. Digging water holes was better than no work at all, but every shovelful of dirt wore on his mind as much as it wore on his back. He felt as though he were digging his family's grave, and there would never be a bottom to the pit, only a deep descent away from the sun.

But now he felt alive again; the rhythm of his labors were his own and full of promise for his family. In the first week, he'd torn out all the fixtures from the garage, refitting or replacing them with spares from the trailer. He rebuilt the lift, greased and packed the pumps, set his rack and forge, and built worktables for his machine tools. The parts bins were a shambles; he took each and every pin and bolt, sorted, cleaned and racked them, carefully keeping them separate from his own. Every night he would work until the dull haze of sleep fought to overtake him. There were times he didn't make it to his bed, falling asleep where he'd last leaned to rest, only to wake to the morning sun or Floy's hot coffee and mild reproach.

They had been lucky, and he knew it. Of the ten thousand men and women who traveled this dusty road, he'd found work and a place to stay, and some strange generosity that had given his family a second chance, in a time when there were few chances to go around. He'd already sent word to John Cox at the labor camp, and soon they'd all be together again.

His children were well fed and slept warm, with a hard roof over their heads, and his hands were full of purpose. Things had changed for the better, but they could change again. He knew that no matter what happened or whatever stood in his way, he could never let his children go hungry again.

The sharp tap of a car horn interrupted his reverie.

Dee looked outside. Lawrence Spain's big Chevrolet sedan was pulling into the pump island. Dee wiped his hands on a shop towel and walked out to greet him.

"Going to Yuma," Lawrence looked through the windshield and gestured to the west. "Need anything from the big city?"

"Not a thing, Mr. Spain."

"Try Sheriff, hey you, or even sumbitch, anything but Mr. Spain." He smiled and leaned across the seat. "Where you're concerned, Dee, I'd much prefer Lawrence."

"Alright, Lawrence." Dee nodded quietly and reached for the hand crank that pressurized the gas pumps.

"Don't need any, Dee. I'm off to pick up the Missus and head for the picture show."

"Well, have a good time."

"I'll do that," Lawrence grinned. "They're showing *Hell's Angels* - the Royal Flying Corps, Baron Von Richtofen and Jean Harlow. "How could I go wrong?"

Dee laughed. "I don't think you can." He and Lawrence had found a common bond in their love of airplanes, and Lawrence had even threatened to buy one, until Madeline Spain vetoed any such frivolous expenditure.

"Well, I'm off." Lawrence floored the accelerator pedal and the burgundy sedan spun out into the highway.

Dee stepped back inside the garage. Outside, he could see the fading taillights of the Chevrolet as it left town. His thoughts returned to the first night he'd seen the lights of Wellton, and the first time he'd met Madeline Spain. A sudden confusion twisted in his belly and he returned to his work, pressing himself into his lathe.

* * *

SAM KINGSTON crossed the Mercantile threshold at 8am, regular as clockwork. His mailbag was slung over one shoulder, more like an extra body part than a bit of baggage. As usual, he was whistling. Today's selection featured *The Sidewalks of New York*, his perennial hot weather favorite.

"Morning, Miz' Spain. Two letters, one package, and a fancy New York catalogue." The postman's mailbag slapped at the counter like a fat man's belly.

"Thank you, Sam." Madeline reached for an icy bottle of soda pop. She wedged it in the red cooler case to remove its metal cap. "Here you are."

Every morning, Sam Kingston would bring both the post and the weather report - the mail by conventional means, the temperature by his musical selection. Sam saved the 'east side, west side' lilt for the real scorchers.

"Looks like a hot one." Sam let most of the cool beverage barrel down his throat. He paused for a response.

"I'd say so," replied Madeline. She never ceased to wonder at the ritual of weather that so dominated discourse in the West. Eastern courtesy demanded 'How do you do?' and 'Fine, and thank you', but anywhere past the Rockies and 'Looks like rain' would pass for polite conversation.

Still, Sam was a welcome sight, often bringing news that was seldom heard from anyone else in her small town. She cultivated his visits with soda pop in the summer and hot coffee in the winter, knowing full well that the Post Office was only 300 feet down Main Street.

"Sheriff find anything?" Sam flashed his most sincere look.

Lawrence had left town early, on horseback with Bill Gale. Last night, the border patrolman had found a body out in the desert alongside the railroad tracks. She wondered how anyone else could have known; they'd left just before dawn, while most of Wellton was still sleeping.

She tempered her answer with the knowledge that Sam was the closest thing to a local newspaper the town had; any reply would soon be common knowledge all along his route. Her husband was sheriff of a town not too far removed from frontier justice. Its cemetery was dotted with unmarked graves filled by rumor and a rope in the last century. "If it's a stranger, we can take our time," Lawrence had said. "But if the corpse is local, then Katie bar the door. All hell's gonna' break loose."

"We'll just have to wait till he gets back, Sam."

"Probably some Mex', drunk on the tracks," Sam shrugged. "But thanks for the cold drink just the same."

Madeline frowned, barely containing her discomfort.

The postman hoisted his bag and shuffled across the worn wooden floor. "By the way, 'saw your new mechanic at the garage. Quite a feller, that one, eh Miz' Spain?"

The bell on the doorjamb jingled open. Madeline turned away, her face flushed red in the hot desert air.

"TEN YEARS AT THIS and I'll never get used to the smell." Lawrence Spain slid down off the big thoroughbred with a careful step. He knelt over the crumpled form laid out next to the tracks.

"Yep, he's ripe." Bill Gale stayed on his mount. Leaning back in the saddle, he sliced a wedge of tobacco from its plug. "That's a nasty gash he's got, too." Satisfied, he sent a long looping stream of brown spit into the center of the dead man's back.

"Watch your trail, Bill." Spain barely tolerated the border agent's lack of respect for any Mexican, alive or dead. He knew Gale as an honest man, even a decent one, but could never get past his cold-blooded nature.

"Gonna' get even sweeter, once that sun gets up some." Gale pulled the brim of his hat down. "I figure one of his amigos didn't like him near as much as his boots and ventilated him." After 13 years on the job, Bill kept a wary eye for bandits, most of whom he figured were Mexican government employees.

Gale had been part of Pershing's failed attempt to capture Pancho Villa; that's where he developed a taste for tequila, chile rellenos, and Mexican women. Once he'd left the Army, he stayed on the border. He liked being a government agent; what he didn't receive in salary was more than made up for by the freedom to do as he pleased.

Spain glanced at the body's bare feet. Gale might be right; it wouldn't be the first time. "This just how you found him?"

"Except for the bird's work."

Lawrence could see the vultures' path, up around the eyes where the skull was split, and near the calloused feet. He reached under the body and rolled it over on its side. The thin woolen serape surrounding it was faded from years of use, and too large for the small frame.

"He's just a boy, Bill."

Gale looked away and spat. "Don't make him any less dead."

Lawrence reached down and pulled the serape from around the boy's trunk. He opened the small leather pouch that he found there. Inside was a tiny cross worked from pot metal, and a single peso.

"Looks like your theory won't hold up…"

Gale shrugged as the sheriff examined the boy's hands, then watched as he paced the distance to the railroad tracks. Spain knelt to touch them.

Bill Gale liked this sheriff, even hunted with him, but damned if he'd ever understand the man. Wealthiest family in town, smart as a whip; Lawrence Spain could have had any woman he wanted. Then he up and runs off to Boston and marries a goddamn Mexican girl.

Spanish heritage, my ass. Damned peculiar, these rich folks.

Gale peered up at the sun and thought about all the whores he could buy if he had just half of Spain's money.

"Hot as a pistol and barely nine o'clock." Lawrence Spain tapped the long steel rail and turned toward the border. "Won't they ever learn?"

"Lawrence, what in the hell are you talking about?" Bill Gale was almost out of tobacco and losing interest. "They cracked his head, stole his boots, and left him for the buzzards. Now, let's get our butts back to town, 'fore we bake out here."

"Dammit, Bill, look at his feet. That boy never had a pair of shoes on in his life. He was hit by the train."

Spain bent down to raise the boy's arms. "See these hands. They're blistered. It takes something mighty hot to burn through a fieldworker's hands. Like an iron railroad car baking in the sun. My guess is he tried to hop a freight train and didn't think to wrap his hands first. Burnt 'em clean through." Lawrence held the boy's fingers up for effect. "Once the kid let go, he never knew what hit him."

"If you say so, Sheriff." Gale could see that Spain was right. He just couldn't understand why he spent all that time on figuring it out. The border patrolman spat again.

"Lord almighty, Lawrence, if I could count all the dead Mexicans I found out on this desert - hell, I shot half of 'em, myself."

Without a glance, Spain dropped the boy's arms and stepped over to his horse. He took the bedroll from his saddle and wrapped the boy in its folds. Roll ing his burden onto his shoulder, he draped the body over the cantle of his saddle and mounted. Sand flew as the thoroughbred bolted at the smell; Lawrence laid his spurs into the big horse's flanks, and it leapt into a canter.

Gale watched the town sheriff ride away at a pace his government mount could never hope to match.

Damned peculiar man.

"KEEP YOUR SHADOW off the water, Davey." John Cox didn't have to look up. The squish of bare feet in the mud told him that the boy had changed positions. *Fine boy, that Davey.*

"Grandpa, how come you knew I had a shadow?" Davey glanced back at his grandfather, still stretched out beneath the cottonwood, felt hat hung low over one brow. He'd thought that he was sleeping.

"Sun moves even if you don't." Cox smiled secretly beneath his hat. "That big fish you're looking for won't come anywhere near a moving shadow. Keep the sun in his eyes, same as a gunfight."

Davey nodded and repositioned himself along the pond's edge, carefully calculating the angle of the sun against the spot he'd figured for the big bass' hideout. He twirled his hook line gently, careful not to dislodge the dragonfly his grandfather had captured.

"Just the wrist, Davey." Content underneath his wide brim, John Cox was celebrating his recent liberation from the reclamation labor camps. Day after day, he and a hundred men had been digging giant water holes for twenty cents-an-hour. A decent wage in hard times, but he was grateful to be free from it.

No need to stir prematurely.

The boy stayed focused on his target, looking slightly past it as his grandfather had shown him. "Same with a knife, a gun or a hook," he'd said. "Find your spot, look past it for your distance, then let her fly."

Across the way, the same voice trickled out from under the hat. "And don't waste too much time aiming, she'll just move on you, and then where will you be?"

Davey released the lure, letting it settle alongside an old stump. Satisfied, he drew it rhythmically back to shore, simulating the skimming motion of a bug on water. The wall-eyed bass was convinced, and certain of its dinner, moved as one large muscle towards its prey. It broke the surface of the water like a rock on a mirror, lurching and diving to extricate the hook from its bowels.

The barb was set less by Davey's expertise than by the pure power of the animal's leap. As the great fish crashed again, the boy wailed with terrified delight at his accomplishment. "Grandpa! I got him!"

His words were more a gurgle than a cry - the bass had pulled the small boy off the bank and deeper into the pond. Thrashing about to keep his head above water, Davey cried out for help, half-smiling and half-choking, held fast in the grip of the giant fish.

"Grandpa! Grandpa! What'll I do?"

John Breckinridge Cox considered the moment in silence. He reckoned the child would survive this encounter with or without his advice. Some problems are best solved by experimentation. Still, good manners demand a timely answer to any question. Cox lifted his hat and leaned back against the tree.

"Well, Davey... I suppose that depends on whether you're going to eat him or ride him."

The boy strained to fathom the answer as the big fish towed him beneath the murky waters. The power of the bass was like a falling stone, the cord around his wrist an anchor chain. He felt his lungs about to burst and the sting of rushing water against his eyes. Davey arched his back in protest and gave a desperate pull. The big bass bolted towards shore, its insides stung by the edge of the barbed hook. Davey threw his body up into the light, gasping for air. Plunging his feet down deep into the mud, he braced himself and spat out his reply. "Eat him! Eat him! Eat him!"

Cox laughed out loud at his miniature Colossus - legs astride, jaw set with fierce determination. David Russell Bailey would never be a large man; his frame was small even for his years, but his singular grit would carry him twice as far. The old man doffed his hat in silent admiration. He held it like a bucket as he waded into the pond.

"Then fetch him in the hat, boy, and we'll make your momma proud."

Davey made the arduous journey of fish into hat, grinning all the while, not for the pride of his mother, but for the quiet approval of one old man. A still moment came in the splashing laughter and the blood of the great fish, an icy clarity that would rise sporadically throughout his life. But this was the first time, and the only thought that surfaced was for his father, that he might see him now.

WE WERE SOMEWHERE outside of Ely, Nevada, in a 1956 Ford Country Sedan. Ford called it a sedan, even though it was really a wagon, because it had four doors and a lot of extra chrome. This one had a 292 V8 with electric overdrive; when new, it came with branding irons embossed on the upholstery. The paint was two-tone, buckskin and cream, though years of sun had rendered it pink and white by any fair description. I bought it on a whim from a drug dealer in Vallejo, California.

Over the last two years, Dave Bailey and I had become good friends. I'd closed my business in the city and started to renovate the old cabin. My occasional visits to his little ranch had become a near daily ritual, always accompanied by coffee around the kitchen table. After a while, we ventured out into the world together. They were short trips at first, to see a horse or go to a tack sale, but as we grew closer, our journeys grew longer and more varied. Dave rarely left his ranch, but for some reason he would venture out with me, perhaps to see the countryside, or more likely to keep me from bad horses or worse behavior.

This time, the plan was to go all the way to Montana, to visit Dave's daughter. She had taken up with a plumber from Missoula. I'm not sure if Dave ever really liked the man; Dave's family always called him Doc - or Dave or even Pop, but this fellow had never gotten past 'Mr. Bailey'. Still, Dave wasn't the type to interfere. Once they were married and moved on, Dave and I decided we should take a trip to see them in the old '56.

I wondered where Dave had got his nickname, and like the old saw said, whether I should think twice about playing poker with him. After a while, even I caught the bug and called him Doc most of the time.

"You just go ahead, call me Doc," he said. When I asked him how and why he got the nickname, he gave me a grin. "That's a story for another time."

Doc and I had been on the road for almost a full day; we'd left Grass Valley and headed north through the foothills towards Lake Tahoe. Dave's little sister Wanda and her husband Tommy lived at the lake. I thought we might stop, but Dave had wanted to drive straight through.

"Let's just keep on driving. We'll stop there some other time." Dave spoke about Wanda and Tommy often, with deep affection. I wondered why we never went to see them.

Instead, I asked Doc about the first time he went to Montana.

He smiled, pushed the bent, straw cowboy hat back on his head, and pointed out the open window. His thinning grey-blonde hair was combed to one side and rippled in the highway breeze. "It was somewhere back in the '30's… this part of the country was empty as a beer can."

It was still empty, as far as I was concerned.

We'd made our way to US Highway 50, suitably called 'The Loneliest Road in America'. Cut across four hundred miles of desert mountains and alkali flats, it was broken up only occasionally by scattered ghost towns, a hard rock mine or the remnants of the Pony Express trail.

"You want to stop somewhere for the night?" I asked.

"Sure. Let's lay our head down."

A mining town named Ely lay up ahead in the empty distance. I figured on a cheap motel, a hot meal and a cool drink.

Maybe more than one.

THE HORSE CHILDREN

APRIL 1935

Gila River Basin
Arizona Territory

NAKI'ZAS WAS VERY OLD, old enough to remember the desert before the earth changed, before the dams took the cottonwoods from the riverbanks, and the Gila River withered into the shallows. Naki'zas was Apache, raised to manhood alongside Victorio. He was born Mescalero, in the land beyond the Big River, on high plains lush with flax and clover. As a young warrior, he walked in Chiricahua to the Eagle's Nest, where no white man had ever stepped. Naki'zas danced the Long Dance, ate sage buttons and the jimson weed, took a life and gave it without regret.

When his people were driven across the Rio Grande, Naki'zas settled at the headwaters of the Gila, there to fight or die. Twice he went to the reservation with Geronimo, and twice he escaped to the mountains. When the horse soldiers found them for the last time, his Apache were gone forever, wounded by the white men's knives and murdered by their words.

Geronimo took up the plow in the dust lands beyond the Navajo, never to see the Spirit Mountains again. Naki'zas took up his blanket and wandered, never to hear his name again.

Everyone he knew in the other life was dead now, even the white men. He was dead, too, because his name was never spoken. He had not heard Naki'zas, Two Snows, in as long as the buffalo were gone.

He lived alone for many years, following the dove and eating pinion berries. When the missionaries came, they called him Joe and taught him numbers, and gave him new blankets and a coat. They died too, drowned by the fever that had killed so many of his people. Joe buried them in the mission graveyard, in the way that white men fancied. He wandered west, until he came to a small town by a well tower, where he fell asleep behind a big barn next to the mesa.

The years passed like falling leaves, and his hate dried up with the waters of the Gila.

THE WELL TOWN was good to Joe. He worked here and there, shoveling mud and gathering fresh greens. He kept a small shack behind the dairy barn in exchange for doctoring boils and mending fences. It was uncomplicated work. Joe's only confusion came in tending to the farm animals. They seemed to take on the ways of their white masters, making them harder to know than their wild ancestors.

The Big Woman in town gave Joe a place to stay and traded for his medicines. She even paid him in whiskey, for tarbush extract or the bones of a saguaro. Joe was fond of the white man's whiskey - it was not so sweet as mezcal or sotol'ka, but it never brought ghosts to his dreams like they did, or make him wish for the Spirit Way and lance. The white man's whiskey was a warm blanket, numbing all thought and care, not good for remembering, but very good for forgetting.

Finding the tarbush took longer and longer each year; the canals and dams were changing the rhythm of the earth, and the healing floods had grown scarce in the springtime. Fresno scars dotted the landscape, and alfalfa fields checkered the mesa.

This time, Joe had been walking for two days. He had traveled many miles. His legs were tired; he stopped to rest underneath the shade of a honey mesquite, its twisted limbs almost as old as his own. He waited patiently for the boy to slip up behind him.

The old man spoke without turning.

"I have heard you for ten minutes, Coyote." Joe had sensed him only moments before, but he chose not to let the boy know how much his stalking had improved. The first time they met, he had listened to the boy rattle about in the desert for hours.

"Joe, how come you can hear so good, if you're as old as they say?" The boy sat down on the loose sand.

"Maybe I am not so old? Or maybe you walk like drum?" Joe put the plants he'd been gathering into his pouch and settled in beside the young boy.

"You talk funny, Joe."

"You listen funny, Coyote." Joe had given the boy a spirit name, because the boy was very good and very bad, all at the same time. The boy didn't know why he was called Coyote, only that he liked having a name that no one else could call him by.

"You must hear behind the words to know truth," the old man said. "White people talk too much."

"Some sure do." Davey pointed at Joe's leather pouch. "Are those more plants for Miz' Spain?"

The old Apache had already taught him about ironwood seed, about squaw-berries and sotol. Davey had even taken some of Joe's yucca fruit home to his mother. She had boiled them like Joe said; they tasted like sweet potatoes, only a little stringy and tough to chew.

Joe nodded and pulled some tarbush from his pouch. "This will cure the ache in your belly, when you eat the white man's food."

"Your food ain't so jake, all flat cakes and berries."

"Then I will keep the yucca." He knew the yellow-haired boy had a taste for the silky-sweet cactus pods.

"Aw, don't take it to heart, Joe." The boy stood up and pointed to the sack beside him. "I got some rabbits in my bag, you want some?"

"That is good." Joe had quit hunting many years before, after his eyes had lost the distance. He seldom had meat on his table. "Here, take this." He reached inside his pouch and removed some slender green branches dotted with yellow blossoms. "Make a poultice from the flowers to save the flesh from snakebite."

"Why, that's just broomweed." The boy looked disappointed.

"Makes a good sweep, too." Joe laughed and brushed his hand across the boy's blond hair. "My people take it when it has the flowers. They crush it, as a cure."

"I don't like snakes."

"Then they won't like you." Joe bent his wrist forward. "Good reason to take the medicine."

The boy took the branches, folding them into his pants pockets. "Do you like snakes, Joe?"

"My people say the snake ties the earth and the spirit world together." Joe closed his eyes. "They say you must walk on the snake to cross over to the other side."

"Have you ever been bit by a rattler, Joe? Did you ever have to use the broomweed?"

Joe rolled up his pants leg and pointed to a knotted area alongside his knee. "Here, once, a long time ago."

The boy leaned over to examine the old man's leg. The brown flesh was dry and withered all along one side. "You put that medicine on it?"

"Not for two suns... so my skin turns to paper." Joe looked at the boy and lowered his voice. "If the snake bites you and you want to live, there is one thing you must do."

"What's that?"

"Find shade."

"What's that supposed to do?" The boy looked puzzled.

"Find shade. Walk slow. Sit down." His dark eyes met the blue of the boy's and he whispered. "Be quiet like stone. Like water, like mountain. Do this, and your spirit is hidden. If you are still, the snake cannot find your heart."

The boy closed his eyes and grew very quiet, as if to try the cure before the sickness.

"That is good, Coyote."

The old man leaned against the rough shredded bark of the mesquite. The orange glow of the descending sun warmed him. He thought of cool mountain waters and the name he hadn't heard in so many years.

'I went to the lady's door,
to ask for a piece of bread…
She said no, no, no, son,
the baker is dead.'

'Hallelujah, I'm a bum,
Hallelujah, bum again.
Hallelujah, give me a handout…
to revive me again…'

I'M NOT SURE if either one of us was in tune, but we were loud. The front windows were open and the wind was ripping through the old station wagon. Our big Ford was careening down Highway 84 alongside the Snake River into Hells Canyon. Its ancient radio needed new vacuum tubes, so Doc and I were singing one of his favorites to pass the time.

"My mom used to feed the bums as they came through town. Dad said 'leave 'em be', but Mom would have none of it." Dave took the creased straw hat off his forehead and wiped the sweat from his brow. "They knew it, and passed the word on down the line. 'She's good for a sandwich, or a drink of lemonade', and she was, she wouldn't turn anyone away." He shook his head and gazed out the window at the passing stalks of Ponderosa pine and Doug fir.

We were on our way out of Idaho, bound from Paradise, Montana. I had heard that it never snowed in Paradise, and Doc and I had determined to find out if that were true, and if so, why. Sure enough, we were told - the high mountain passes above town intersected perfectly to cut off the big winter storms.

Despite the weather, we decided that the rest of the place fell somewhat short of its given name.

It was hot inside the canyon, steaming hot, and the warm roar of Betsy's V8 was pouring through the firewall, her insides relentlessly perforated by who knows how many do-it-yourselfers for the last thirty years. The dense heat crawled up through the cabin floorboards and radiated down through the steel canopy, its off-white roof barely reflecting the noonday sun. The deep canyon held fast to the bright glow, throwing the sunlight back on itself as it bounced off the two-lane blacktop like the walls of a blast furnace.

"Well, they sure knew what they were doing when they named this place." Doc smacked his lips. "Hotter'n a piss-ant in a pepper can."

I glanced over at Doc as he pulled his fixin's from his shirt pocket. He opened the glove compartment door, laid out the tobacco and began to roll a cigarette. The wind picked up his papers and blew them around on the front seat.

"Did your mom and dad ever fight?"

I was curious about his parents. Everything Doc had told me made me think there was something rare about their relationship. Me, I was 35, and I'd already blown through two marriages. Clearly, there was something awry in my relationships with women. I had reason to ask; my old girlfriend was back. She'd finally left her husband for good and moved in with me, but things weren't ideal. One reason I looked forward to my summer travels with Dave - it got me out of the house and away from the mounting pressure.

"Nope, they were like two lovebirds." Dave smiled in reflection. He cranked his window up halfway, hoping to keep the loose tobacco in his cigarette papers long enough to begin a roll. "They never fought, just quiet-like, talked about things." He held the papers with the fingertips of two hands, then drew it across his tongue with a twist, sealing the slim package.

"But yessir, don't tell Mom or Dad either one, you wasn't gonna' do something that they asked you to, or 'I'll do it later'. When they asked you to do something, you went and did it, unless they said, 'Hey, tomorrow I want you to do this'." Doc dangled the cigarette, reached in his pocket, and drew out a plastic butane lighter.

"But if they said go out and get some wood, or go out and feed the rabbits or go out and take care of your horse, or do something or the other, that's exactly what you'd better do. And I don't mean tomorrow, I mean now."

"What would happen if you didn't?"

"Mom would cut down a big salt cedar switch and give me what for." Doc spit out a laugh and lit his cigarette.

"Dad... he never did give me no lickin' or nothing. Y'know, he could just talk to me and make me wish that I was dead. I'd ten times rather he would've knocked me for a loop, doubled up his fist and sent me across the room, but no, he'd just sit there and talk to me." Doc pushed his index finger and thumb together tightly. "Made me feel like I was about this big."

We got quiet and listened to the old Ford descend into the canyon. I had reinforced the glove compartment latch with part of a plastic bottle to hold the door shut, but it still vibrated like a pendulum. The cloth lining in the window channels had worn away decades ago; the glass rattled with the sound of a proud body once well-built, but aging. Even the oppressive heat had a sound, a low hum that pummeled the beads of sweat off my forehead in a slow, steady stream.

I spied a turnout at the bottom of a switchback, alongside a small clearing that led down to the riverbank. The many cars that had pulled off there made a rough landing spot.

"I'm stopping." The big wagon swung easily into the turnout; dust flew as I braked to a stop in the clearing. A path led down to the river, about 20 feet below. "That water looks just right. I'm gonna' take a break and soak my head."

What I didn't say was, 'I'm a bit hung over'. The night before, we'd stayed in a small motel in Lewiston, one with a convenient watering hole next door.

Dave looked at me askance. "It's not that durn hot, and we want to make Oregon by dark. But you go soak your head, that sounds like a good idea."

"You may be an old desert rat, but me and Betsy could use a break." I figured Doc wouldn't begrudge the old Ford a rest, even if he knew I was nursing a hard night. He didn't care for my drinking - one of the few things we'd ever butt heads about.

The water ran fast and cold, cold as ice; I squealed as I dropped into it. With my boots and shirt off, I only lasted about 45 seconds. Out of the water and shivering, I saw Doc standing above me. He sported a wide grin.

"Fill up this jug, fresh water for the ride out." He tossed me the container, bent down into the stream, and cupped some water onto his face. Taking a kerchief from his pocket, he dipped it, soaked it, squeezed the bandana and tied it loosely around his neck.

"This is nice country," he said, getting up. "What you think it was like to be the first man down in this canyon? White man, anyway. You think ol' Lewis and Clark got all shake-ity, too?"

I grinned at him as I put my boots on, rinsing my feet as I went. I was trying not to let the little clods of mud stuck between my toes migrate into my socks, where they'd solidify as spiky pebbles.

"They had an Indian girl to guide them, Saka-ja-wea, I think. Kinda' like Pocahantas."

"Now, that was a damn stupid thing, I'll tell you."

Dave raised the water jug and took a deep drink. "Them Indians should've let the whole bunch of 'em starve. Or hung 'em up by their heels." He shook his head. "They just didn't see it coming."

I looked up, wondering. "Then you wouldn't be here, and neither would I."

"Hell, I don't know." He paused for a moment, as if to see his thoughts play out in the air.

"Back in Oklahoma, my daddy went with his daddy into the villages, met with the Chief and ate dog. And I knew 'em too, down in Wellton. Knew them pretty well."

Doc looked across the icy river and let out a deep breath.

"Nope, they just didn't see it coming." He dropped the jug in the sand and turned to head for the car.

MAY 1935
The Bailey House
Wellton, Arizona

"I BETCHA' I CAN throw that same as him."

"Betcha' can't." Huey Spain stood arms crossed, defiant in his adversary's dusty backyard. He towered over the Bailey boy by a full foot and outweighed him by at least twenty-five pounds.

"Wanda, come over here." Davey knew he was up to his neck, but that had never slowed him down before. His little sister stuck her head out of the cardboard box that made her playroom. She tossed her bright red hair, blue eyes sparkling in the desert sunlight.

"Wanda, Huey don't think I can do that movie trick."

"Which one, Davey?" Wanda Bailey popped straight up, and like a vaudeville magician's trick, a cloud of red dust rose all around her. Never far from Davey when he would let her, she felt proud to be consulted in a matter of honor.

Davey scowled. "Why that hatchet throw, where they cut something in two."

"He can do any old throw." Wanda was sure that he could, even though she didn't know what he meant by it. If Davey said he could do something, then he could do it. Or he'd die trying. And that's what she feared most, that someday, some terrible thing would reach out and take away her protector, her impossibly brave hero. "Dave can do anything," she said, with absolute conviction.

"Oh, I wouldn't go that far, little sister." Davey smiled. Sometimes, Wanda made him feel as though he could do almost anything. "But I can sure as Christmas throw that hatchet trick."

"Yeah? Well, let's see it."

Huey Spain was bound and determined to see Dave Bailey fail, and it didn't matter much to him at what. "Only do it just like they did, and put something on somebody's head. Put it on Wanda's head."

Davey felt a slow, sickening wave move through his stomach. "Huey, shut your mouth."

"I'll do it, Dave. Let me!" This was her big chance. She didn't know what the boys were up to, but she might get to help her brother do something really important.

Davey watched Huey flash the stretched out smile he always got when he thought he was better than anyone else. Better than the Baileys, better than anyone who didn't live in a fancy house.

"Yeah, c'mon Bailey, put up or shut up." Huey hated Dave Bailey, even though Dave had befriended him when no one else would, or perhaps because of it. Bailey reminded him of his big brother Freddy, always the perfect one, always his mother's favorite. "Do it, Dave, do it or you're yellow."

For a moment, no one spoke, and Wanda wondered if Davey would strike out, laugh or simply walk away, but his eyes betrayed nothing.

Davey speared Huey with a cold stare, then picked up a small hatchet from the kindling pile. He walked his little sister over to a salt cedar tree and carefully balanced a tall block of wood on the top of her head.

"Don't move an inch, Wanda." Wanda knew that he meant it. Still, she wasn't sure what else she was supposed to do. He was so serious. But then, David Russell Bailey was always serious underneath that easy smile. And that was something, something special that made her feel safe.

She watched her brother pace off ten steps and turn to face her. Her eyes caught his and they were on fire, wide open and burning. Not on her, but above her, on the space above her head, on the tall block of wood. His arm rose and the axe caught the sun, glistening sharp. She wanted to run, to bend, to turn, to cry out, but she could never be the one to fail him. Her eyelids fluttered as she drew in breath.

The sound was dull, like the crunch of an apple.

In the instant she heard it, she knew that she was all right. She heard the blade rush of wind and the echoed impact from the fractured wood above her head. Her eyes opened and she looked out, ready to share in his triumph. But when she saw him, she saw a sadness she'd never seen before, like a quiet end to some dense thought behind his eyes. He walked over to her slowly and pulled her out away from the tree where the axe lay embedded in the bark. Davey touched her face, and she laughed, but as he turned she could see his hands were trembling.

Huey Spain never did see Dave's hands. He felt only the crush of bone and the flow of blood as he lay face down, his nose broken and bleeding in the hot sand.

"NOW'S THE TIME." Wanda looked plaintively at her older brother. "And don't forget to ask if I can ride it."

"Let's get it here first." Davey was starting to get nervous; he could feel the troublesome knot lumping up in the back of his throat. He hated asking anyone for anything, especially his father.

They had gathered at the edge of the porch, a view of their father's chair unobstructed by the open window. Almost every night after dinner, Dee Bailey would retire to the overstuffed chair by the porch window, there to read one journal or another until it was time for bed. Momma and Beno and Velda would be clearing up the dishes and getting things set aside for breakfast. Davey and Wanda were supposed to do their schoolwork and get ready for bed, but supper was only just finished. This was the best chance at their father's uninterrupted attention.

"Do you want me to ask him?" Wanda offered her services with the utmost sincerity. "He's easy for me."

"Don't be silly, it's my horse."

"But you said you'd let me ride it." Wanda was sure her participation would be enough to carry the day.

"If I go telling him that, he's sure to turn me down."

"But you promised." Wanda's small voice began to rise. "You said I was going to get to ride it. You said so." She had her teeth set into this one and wasn't going to let go.

"All right, all right. You just sit here, and don't make any more noise." Davey got up and headed for the door. It was easier to face his father than to argue with his little sister. The knot in his throat was clearing.

Dee Bailey was studying screw threads and spirals in the *Advanced Shop Mathematics* series from the University of Wisconsin. He didn't bother to look up from his journal. His son's distinctive shuffling step had already warned him of some weighty issue requiring his attention. He hoped it wasn't more trouble at school. Dee noted his place alongside worm gear power transmission, and spoke without raising his eyes.

"What is it, David?"

"Dad, I think I found me a horse." Davey figured he'd get right to it.

"Really?" It was better than another school fight, but not exactly what he'd had in mind. Dee was having trouble pretending to read. "I wasn't aware that you were looking for one."

"Well, I wasn't exactly, but this real good deal come along, and I don't want to have to keep borrowing one, and I could get around quicker and faster, and besides, just about everybody else I know has a horse." It wasn't what Davey had planned to say, but words were always difficult with his father.

"I don't see what that has to do with anything, son." Dee closed his book and looked directly into the boy's eyes. *Time for the first line of defense.*

"Have you spoken about this with your mother?"

"No, sir, I have not. I figured this should be between you and me."

Dee Bailey let out a deep sigh, searching for the brake pedal. Davey's knack for finding trouble wasn't going to be reduced by any form of rapid transportation. "And how do you propose to pay for this horse?"

"With my own money."

His best shot had missed. Two down, one to go.

"That's all well and good, but buying an animal is not the same thing as keeping one. What about feed? You can't expect anyone else to help you take care of it."

Sometimes, Davey thought his father forgot he was almost twelve years old. "I'll cut buffalo grass and pack it down off the mesa."

His small son stood board straight and resolute. Dee grimaced.

This is how Goliath must have felt.

"That's a fine idea, but a horse eats a lot more grass than even you can carry."

"I won't be carrying it." Davey smiled triumphantly. "The horse will."

Outside, her head tucked up close to the window, Wanda heard her father's elusive laughter.

She smiled as he put his book away on the table beside him.

Davey would get his horse, and she would get to ride it.

WALKING WAS ONE OF THE THINGS Dave Bailey did best. He could walk for miles at a time, usually when he was in some sort of trouble at school, or sometimes just for the heck of it, to see how far he could ramble into the desert without losing his way. A steady pace felt good in his legs, and besides, he didn't have a horse anyway. Most of the white kids his age had one; Wellton was still mainly a farming town. The countryside was dotted with livestock. There were ranch strings, draft horses, carriage hacks, ladies' walkers, even a few thoroughbreds. Important men like the sheriff rode big, fast mounts, and around Fair time they'd hold races on Main Street, or run the quarter mile just to settle a bet.

Davey had walked ten times that far since breakfast, all the way to Copper Ridge, but he didn't plan on walking back. Old Sudlow had told him he wouldn't sell the horse to anyone else for a week, and today was only Sunday.

He'd beat the deadline by two days, even if he had to borrow fifty cents to do it. Audra Jean was happy to lend him the money, just like he knew she would.

Fifty cents wasn't even a drop in the bucket for a Spain. And besides, Audra Jean was sweet on him. Now, she'd get to ride up beside him whenever she wanted, even if it was only a three-dollar horse.

Still, a debt was a debt, and Davey had given it considerable thought before asking. He had two-fifty of it himself; he'd saved that much from odd jobs, and the nickel a day his father gave each of the kids for hard candy and soda. His sisters usually spent their nickel right away, but Davey knew money got better when you kept it around for a while; it had a way of adding up all by itself.

When he told his dad he'd buy the horse with his own money, it made him feel all grown up and responsible. But he hadn't said anything about the fifty cents he'd borrowed, and that's what was bothering him. Davey didn't like keeping secrets from his father, even if they hardly ever talked. "Learn to make do with what you've got, and you'll never need anything else," his dad would say.

Davey had never seen his father borrow much of anything, though he'd lent his fair share, some of it never to return.

But this here was different. He figured what was between him and Audra Jean was his own business, especially since he'd already kissed her and all.

Sort of like we're engaged or something.

Davey let the thought sink in and didn't like where it came to rest. He decided to tell his dad about the four bits, and let things work out whichever way they would. The matter settled, he increased his pace, his footsteps launching miniature dust clouds behind him.

He could just make out the blurry edge of Sudlow's barns across the riverbed when something else caught his eye. A long string of horses were moving along the edge of the dry bank at a gallop, almost a mile away. He squinted into the sun, bracing himself to focus out the distance. They were wild horses; he could tell by the number of mares and yearlings. There were no free-range domestic herds out this far; mustangs would snap them up as quick as you could say goodbye. The Spanish found that out a long time ago. He couldn't see what was driving them, but surely something was.

Davey started down into the valley at a slow jog, figuring to get a good look at the herd as they crossed the Gila where Sudlow's fence met the dry bank. John Sudlow had fenced his place just like everyone else in the Mohawk Valley, using bits and pieces of barbwire and mesquite post. His fence ran clear down to the river on one side, but he hadn't run it along the bank itself; no sense in letting it wash away. The river had stopped free flowing years ago, but every once in a while, when the thunderheads rose and the dams upstream were filled to bursting, you'd get a floodwater down the Gila that could burst the walls of Jericho. Besides, what water was left in potholes was too precious to let sit in the sun; when there was water in the Gila, you wanted your livestock to get a chance to drink it.

Davey figured that the horses had come from that big pothole upriver; it was one of his favorite hunting spots. You could just about guarantee good game within rifle shot, even an occasional pronghorn or mule deer. Mustangs would come there, too. They were tricky to catch sight of, as they'd spook at the drop of a hat. It was too far to go on foot, unless you had all day to get there - soon enough he'd fix that deal. Right now, he wanted to know what was driving that herd, and why they hadn't cut across the riverbed and up onto the mesa to get free of whatever it was that was chasing them. He slid the last few feet off the hillside, and knelt down to get a better look.

The answer was right in front of him. Just across the riverbed, there was a long strand of baling wire tied off to blackbrush, propped up with a stack of rocks, or looped around some cactus. It ran upriver for as far as he could see. Here and there, rags and pieces of string were tied to it; not enough fence to hold anything in that wanted to get out, but more than enough to keep a horse on a straight line, if you didn't press him too hard. The herd passed not fifty yards away from Davey, their pounding hooves and labored breath sounding in his ears.

Through the dust cloud that trailed behind them came a single rider, rope beating, his long coat flapping in the wind, driving the herd downstream. Davey strained to make him out, but couldn't place the man. He'd have known him for sure if he'd seen him before, even though the rider wore his kerchief drawn up around his face to block the blowing sand. There were only a few one-eyed men in the county, and none of them wore a patch like this one did. The horseman passed by Davey's vantage point without breaking gait, easing up on his mount as the small herd neared Sudlow's fences.

There he let the horses drop to their own pace, moving just along the outside edge of the string. At the end of the fence line, the rider let them settle and mill about, being careful not to send them up again, as they were only held at the corner of two fences, with nothing to keep them from curling out and around to head back upstream. The animals appeared grateful for the respite, some of them looking for graze, others rolling in the dust, spending the heat of their exertion. The rider turned his mount and stopped some hundred yards away.

Davey slowed his approach, as much in amazement as anything else. He couldn't figure why anyone would go to such trouble to box horses in a trap that couldn't hold a milk cow. The mustangs might be settled now, but as soon as they got the notion they'd be gone. It was one thing to drive them into a corner; the makeshift line the cowboy had strung along the riverbank was a neat trick. But it would take more than that for one man to hold them there, much less rope one, without sending them all bolting upriver.

He was in earshot now, close enough to hear the drover whistling to himself as he stepped down off his horse. He was a tall man, almost chest high to his horse's withers, and he seemed to carry as much weight as his large frame would allow. The drover tied his horse to a clump of greasewood and glanced at the herd. The line of the man's face marked him older than Davey had thought; he could see signs of it in the molasses way he moved.

The big man reached beneath his saddle and drew a rifle from its scabbard, cocking and mounting it to his shoulder in one fluid motion. His left hand passed up over his dead eye and flipped the black patch that covered it back on his forehead. Before Davey could reason the rifle or its purpose, the sharp crack of its discharge startled him, and one of the horses on the perimeter of the herd fell over into the dirt.

The other horses in the herd tensed, but didn't bolt, and Davey sensed the distance was calculated as much for that effect as for the ease of target. His stomach knotted as he watched two more drop, each as suddenly and finally as the first. Davey was used to a little blood; his recovery from buck fever was long ago and far away. Still, it was hard to watch these horses fall, for it wasn't the sick or the aged, but the best of the herd that caught the rifle's blow.

He knew it wasn't his business; he should just pass on by and take possession of the horse he'd walked so far to find, but something took him, and he reached down and scratched up the first handful of rocks that he could find. He tossed them defiantly at the gathered horses, shouting for them to break ranks and flee.

The big drover made a slow turn, rifle still in hand. His fingers slipped deftly across the cloth patch, bringing it back into place atop its withered socket. "Now, if a rifle shot's not gonna' spook 'em, what makes you think a couple of rocks will?"

Undaunted, the animals continued to mill about, oblivious to all but the wheatbrush and the sage. The drover motioned with the tip of his Winchester. "C'mere, boy." The big man's voice echoed under his breath, deep as a spring well.

Davey figured he'd stepped in it sure this time. You can't go messing about in other people's business and not expect to get some knocks. He moved forward gingerly, his head braced for the boxing that his ears anticipated. Under his breath he mumbled, "I'm sorry, sir."

"And what exactly are you sorry for, son?"

"For wrecking your sport." Davey focused on what he knew to be true. "If you want to kill a few mustangs, it's none of my business."

"Only a fool kills for sport, son." His one eye seemed to take in all of Davey and make him feel smaller than he really was. "Do I look like a fool to you, boy?"

Davey didn't like where the conversation was headed. Better to be absent. He moved off to the side, keeping a careful eye on the old cowboy and his rifle. "No, sir, you're as smart a man as I've seen all day."

The big man chuckled and dropped his rifle butt onto the ground. "You're an uppity little rascal, now aren't you?" With a deliberate flip of his wrist he cocked his thumb toward the mustangs. "Well, if you're so dang smart, tell me how come that dead horse is chewing on buffalo grass?"

Davey Bailey was seldom at a loss for words, even with his elders, but this time he had no fresh reply. One of the fallen horses had gotten up, a little wobbly at first, but now, it had slipped into a grazing rhythm with the rest of the herd.

"That's a crease, son." The old man lifted his rifle. "And I don't like to do it more than once, but since I've spent all my time jawing with you instead of getting down to business, I s'pose I'll have to." In a single moment, his eyepatch flipped back onto his forehead and he fired off another shot. The horse shuddered and rocked back down into the sand. "And they're not dead son, just a little discombobulated. You put your shot through the thick crest at the top of the neck muscle - shock of it knocks 'em out cold."

Sure enough, Davey could see the labored breath passing along the horse's ribcage. He felt a little bit like the mustang, knocked senseless, and none too quick to recover.

"Now, if you're through messing about, I'll excuse myself and get a rope on that bastard before he goes and wakes up again." The rifle was sheathed and the cowboy was back on his horse before Davey could respond. The big man rocked forward with a slight squeeze and his mount leapt into a lope, the dust from its heels kicking up in the boy's face.

"Well, I'll be." Davey stood, mouth wide open, as the drover's lazy whistle faded away into the herd.

"OH, THAT'S JUST JASPER MCCALL." Old Man Sudlow seemed singularly unimpressed with the boy's rambling reconstruction of the morning's events. "He comes round about every summer, last ten years or so." Sudlow was carefully counting the nickels, dimes and quarters that made up the bounty for Davey's new horse. "I let him use some of my corrals, and he sets his traps up along the riverbank."

"Have you ever seen him crease a horse?" Davey was anxious to get another opinion on the drover's strange alternative to a rope or a box canyon. John Sudlow was perched on his porch steps, the coins laid out beside him.

"Don't believe I ever have, Davey." Sudlow seemed to lose his place, and started counting all over again, restacking the loose change as he went. "But I know he does, and it seems to work well enough for him. I wouldn't try it with any animal I wanted to keep around though."

"What's he do with the horses?" Davey was marking time now, wanting to reach out and count the money himself, for Old Sudlow seemed to have started over yet again.

"Some I buy from him, some he breaks, and some he just lets go." Sudlow moved one stack aside and marked off a dollar, then started on the second stack, lost count, and began again. "I knew him when he had his own place, up around Tacna. He did pretty well with it, too. Ran some of the best stock in this country, 'til he lost his eye."

Davey struggled with his curiosity, knowing another question would cost him yet another count. He was determined to learn more about Jasper McCall. "What happened?"

"You know boy, I'll never get this done with you jabbering at me." John Sudlow put the second stack aside, and cocked his bald head towards Davey. "He was running mustangs up on Antelope Hill and got into a wreck. Came down flat into one of them 'guilla thorns - went clear through his eyeball. Doc Phillips had to take out what was left after it festered. Nearly died. Lost his place, too."

Lechuguilla was sharp as a knife. Davey had used the long rigid leaves to stake out rabbits when he didn't have a spit for his fire. He pictured the accident and had to clear it from his mind. He took on a whole new set of thoughts about Jasper McCall. "Where's he live, now?"

"Can't say as I know, Davey. He comes through pretty regular, but I never asked him." Sudlow started counting out the last stack of coins, paused for a moment, and leaned over to peer at the boy. "How much did I say for that horse?"

"Three dollars, Mr. Sudlow." Sudlow's memory was as stiff as his game leg.

"And just how much did you give me?"

"Three dollars, sir."

"Well, then let's go get your horse." Sudlow pocketed the loose change. He strained to get to his feet. "I don't know as we'd live long enough to see me tote up all this silver."

Sudlow reached for Davey's shoulder, using it for support as he walked down off the porch. For as long as Davey had known him, John Sudlow had walked with a cane. He'd always got around pretty good with it, but it seemed like the years might be catching up with him.

"Like I say, Davey, this is a good horse, but he's an old horse. In fact he's so old, I used to say he was born in the Civil War."

"I know, Mr. Sudlow." Davey had seen the horse before. "For three dollars, I don't expect no race horse."

Sudlow stopped and whistled for one his hands. "Pedro! Come get the black out of the barn and bring him here."

Sudlow waved his cane in Davey's face, punctuating every word. "Don't think you know so much just 'cause you're young, boy. That horse would probably outlast any mount in this county on a long run; he's just not a sprinter." Sudlow looked down at his withered legs and took a deep breath. "Horses don't age like we do, all bent up and twisted for their last days. That horse can still teach you a thing or two."

Davey realized for the first time that the black was John Sudlow's own horse, not just one of many bought or sold as stock. He watched as the big gelding was led out of his stall; he'd been curried and combed, maybe even by old Sudlow himself.

The horse was tall and thin, its withers exposed by the passing of the years. It nickered as Sudlow took the lead rope from his foreman, and nuzzled the grey sleeve on Sudlow's arm.

Davey wanted to say something, but he didn't know what it would be.

"Get him out of the barn, Davey." Sudlow ran his hand along the gelding's muzzle and up onto its broad neck. "Let him run."

The old man pushed the cotton rope into Davey's hands. He turned to limp away, his long cane scratching a thin pattern in the clay.

IT WAS THE MAGIC HOUR, the one Old Joe had told him about, when the trees would turn blue and then black, the sky gold into crimson. The sheen on the edge of the horizon would make the desert look like one long string of lakes, stretching out for as far you could see. The day birds were looking to roost for the night, and the creatures of the evening were slipping slowly out of the long shadows and into the half-light. The first stars would soon blink into existence and the air would cool, sometimes plummeting into chill.

The old Apache said this was the time that you could see the earth breathe, and sometimes Davey thought he did, at least he could see rolls and curls where he knew the desert was flat, and motion in the great rocks that bound the mountains together. He would listen for the wind, for the voices of the spirit world that Joe had told him about, for Sky Father and the Rain Woman. They never spoke to Davey like they did to Joe, but he listened all the same, feeling somehow closer to them than the distant saints and serpents in his mother's Bible.

King nickered as if to signal attention; he'd been standing rock still for nearly ten minutes. Sudlow was right; the old horse had plenty of life left in him, but one thing he didn't take to was standing in one place for too long. Davey suspected that King's old bones were partial to arthritis, for he surely liked to move more than sit still, and was sometimes a little stiff after a long whoa. Davey had spent nearly every waking hour with him, learning his moods and his ways, and teaching him his own, the sound of his voice and the feel of his hands.

He'd named the big gelding after Sgt. Preston's dog, the one in the radio show, for both the horse and the dog were a loyal sort, and Davey had always liked the sound of 'On King!'. He occasionally cried it himself, even though he was far from the Yukon and the sled dogs of the Royal Canadian Mounted Police. His sister had wanted to name the black *'Beauty'*, after the book, and the horse's fine dark coat did fit the bill, but Davey felt that too much of a girl's name and would have none of it.

When he brought the horse home, his father had simply nodded and said he seemed a good-tempered animal, and asked after his care and lodging. Davey built a stall out back of the house from the remains of a tin roof shed, blown over by the railroad tracks at the edge of town. For the first few days, that was all he did, work on the stall and work with the horse, even using King to drag the weathered wood for his own stable. King took to drafting right away; Davey had salvaged an old horse collar from the garage, tethering the gelding with two lengths of hemp rope and a section of chain his father had given him.

But the old horse was a hard ride, as his backbone laid up high above his withers; at a trot it seemed as if he'd split you in two. The sheriff saw Davey on him and offered the loan of an abandoned saddle, and Davey thought it was his lucky day, until he cinched it up and the old horse nearly crushed him, rolling over onto the ground. He'd tried a dozen more times, but for as long he had the horse, he could never get a saddle on him, for all he'd do was lay down.

Davey even thought to take him back to Sudlow and cry foul, but his mother asked what other faults the old horse had, and he could think of none, and his grandfather reckoned that the horse's back wouldn't fit any saddle with his withers up so high, and "better the young adjust to the old, than the other way around". So Davey took two gunny sacks and stuffed them with batting, and his mother stitched a strap to them for a bareback pad, and King took to it almost as well as Davey's backside.

When Old Joe saw the pad, he said that it was good, that white men didn't know their own horses, for they couldn't feel them under heavy leather, and that a horse would join with a man at the spine if he would let it, and something about a woman taking the spirit of the horse for her baby. Joe had said that this was so for Geronimo; that his mother had taken the horse spirit by entering labor on its back, and that was why the soldiers could never catch him or follow his trail. Davey didn't know much about that, but King did ride better with the pad than he ever did with a saddle, and sometimes, when he was at a gallop or in the midst of a long ride, Davey would feel the pad disappear, and then his legs, and he could understand the legends of men with the bodies of horses.

King lifted his tail and stretched out; the hot, steaming pulp from his bowels fell in quick succession, as if to make comment on Davey's deeper thoughts. The boy laughed and let him finish, then pushed the gelding into a fast trot, grateful that he wasn't joined at the waist with a horse, if only to save himself from passing the formidable volume of crap that they produced.

Davey turned King into the wind. He caught a passing whiff of fresh green manure. It was beginning to get seriously dark, there was no moon, and he wanted to make some headway on the journey home before the sky turned pitch black.

THIRTEEN RAILROAD CARS sat on the siding like a long line of beads on a metal string. The sun was rising directly to the east, shining a dull spotlight on the lead locomotive. A smaller line of tracks ran alongside, surrounded by men in grey hats and coveralls. They were hoisting a small, flat chassis with a heavy tripod onto the parallel track. Another group of men opened several large cases and assembled the biggest camera that Davey Bailey had ever seen. It was flat black, with a lens that looked like it might be a telescope. The workmen mounted it on the tripod dolly, adding wires and levers and seats and a wide umbrella to block the rising sun.

Men and women of every description were all around the coaches and the freight cars; some positioning large shiny boards, others changing clothes, some carrying cables or boxes, but all following the hoarse instructions of a bald man with a megaphone.

Davey and Wanda had come to Yuma all the way from Wellton on horseback, just to see the excitement. When Wanda heard the movie crew was in town, she'd insisted Davey take her there, and would have none of it when he resisted. "You'll take me and promise to stay as long as I like, or I'll never speak to you again."

She was shaking as she spoke, bursting with anticipation at the prospect of seeing her singing cowboy, and beside herself at the thought of not doing so. Yesterday, Wanda had overheard Sam Kingston telling their mother about the big movie star and the Hollywood picture show they were making at the Yuma stockyards. From that moment on, there would be no peace in the Bailey household until his little sister got to go.

Davey was happy to take her - any excuse to saddle up King and slip away from school. Lately, there'd been more trouble with some of the Mexican boys, so his mom didn't take much convincing. Wanda had enlisted their father in less time than it took to hop on his lap and flash her big blue eyes. Davey had figured what the heck, who knows, she might even get to see her matinee idol and his big, sorrel gelding in the flesh.

They left early, in the cold moonlight before sunrise. Wanda was slung up behind, their lunch bag packed with ham sandwiches, apples and chilled cucumbers. One of the apples had already passed the alarm to old King, waking him in preparation for their grand adventure.

The trail was well worn, a shortcut off the main highway through Telegraph Pass, made by the caravan of kids who went to Yuma once a month to see a picture show, to visit relatives or pick up groceries. Davey loved those expeditions; all the kids would leave their horses by the lettuce sheds and walk downtown to the movie theatre. Sometimes, Davey would just wander along Main Street and watch the big trucks on their way out to the Colorado. Since the reclamation began, there were dozens of the lumbering diesels going back and forth from the All-American Canal.

This wasn't the first movie company to come to Yuma; it had already doubled for the Sahara in *Beau Geste*. Rudolph Valentino had come as the silent *Son of the Sheik*, in long, white robes by a canvas tent. John Wayne had come, and Ronald Coleman and Gary Cooper, Fay Wray and Myrna Loy - whenever Hollywood required a vast desert only a day's drive away. The long dunes of southern Arizona had passed for Morocco and Mexico, for Hell's Island and the dusty trails beside the Rio Grande. Today, it would double for the Red River Valley, and Gene Autry would be the one to test his mettle against the sun and the sand.

Davey wasn't sure what to make of it all - so many people and a line of gawkers all along the side of the highway. But he'd seen famous folk before. Once, a few years back, a little man with a painted mustache had stayed at the Wellton Hotel. A young girl was with him; she took notes and carried his coat, but mostly he kept to himself. Mrs. Spain said he was a movie star named Charlie; Davey thought he was a little odd, with his funny voice and strange manners, but he turned out to be a pretty good egg. He would wander around town, mostly alone, just watching. Then one day, when a big wreck was out on the highway, he asked to go along on the tow truck and his dad had said, "Well, why not?".

So Charlie went with them to clear the twisted remnants of a head-on crash. Davey had closed his eyes and whispered 'Holy Moley', but Charlie got right in and helped, baggy pants and all, kicking glass off the highway, and tying up loose fenders with bailing wire. When they got back, Davey asked him if he was going to make a movie in Wellton, but he said he was just taking a rest, and didn't want to be around any crowds.

Down by the tracks, the man with the megaphone called out for quiet. Davey slid off King and led him around the far side of crowd, keeping Wanda high up on the horse so she could see above the onlookers. The film crew had been working for a week at the old territorial prison, its whitewashed walls doubling as the villain's hideout. Davey wished he could've been one of the townsfolk hired as extras; he'd heard that one fellow got paid a hundred dollars to take a punch and fall off the spillway up at the Laguna Dam. Today, they were shooting the big finish – a desperate fight on top of a boxcar.

The man with the megaphone called "Quiet!" and everyone hushed. Men in coveralls pushed the camera dolly alongside the boxcar as three men on top of the train fought mightily, their ax handles swinging like baseball bats. No one hit anyone with anything; Davey could see they missed each other by six inches or more. He thought he could do as much for a lot less than a hundred dollars. They repeated their mute battle four or five times, and then the bald man called out something with his megaphone, and everyone packed up and started to leave. Wanda cried out, almost in tears, and asked where Gene Autry was. The movie man must have heard her, because he laughed, and said that Mr. Autry wasn't here today, but his horse was, and asked if Wanda would like to see him.

Wanda squealed and said yes, and nearly put old King into a gallop by kicking his ribs, but Davey grabbed the reins and settled him down, and King nuzzled his neck for another piece of apple.

The bald man said, "Follow me," and walked them around the side of a big trailer. There was a horse car there, custom built right on the back of a Dodge truck. Painted all along the side was 'Gene Autry's Melody Ranch' in bright script letters.

The movie man spoke softly to a small man dressed in a red shirt and red suspenders; the groomsman opened the swinging tailgate to reveal the big sorrel gelding with the white blaze. Wanda jumped down and ran forward while King nickered, as if to greet an old friend.

"Pull your horse back and I'll let her climb up," said the man in red, and Wanda practically leapt into his hands. The groomsman lifted her gently up on the big gelding, and Davey was sure he could see his sister grow three inches taller.

"Tell your friends you got to ride Champion the Wonder Horse," said the movie man, smiling as he walked away.

She did so, over the years at least a thousand times, and as she did the horse grew even larger and more beautiful, and the day more electric, and the shirt and suspenders as red as any sunset. And six months later, when *Man of the Frontier* came to the Yuma Theatre, Wanda made her father take her early in the morning, and she sat in the front row for all three shows.

THE SUN was dropping fast as we crossed the shallow valley outside of Bakersfield. There was nothing more to see than a flat, orange haze smeared by dust at the horizon.

"I've seen prettier sunsets."

After so many trips cross-country, Pop and I had settled into a kind of rhythm; he would start to tell one of his stories - I would press him about some tiny detail or another, and then I would quietly pull out my little tape recorder and turn it on. Our old Ford station wagon would rattle and shake as we went, the years ebbing and flowing with the white lines on the highway.

"Right down here's where we should see that big cattle ranch..." Doc was looking out the window, quietly reflecting as he gazed to the south. Cattle and horses of various size and description grazed in the large pastures that lined the roadway.

We were headed for Wellton, Arizona - first through Bakersfield and Barstow to skirt the Mojave Desert, then a turn on Highway 95 towards Yuma. After years of cajoling, Doc had finally consented to a road trip back to his old hometown. He'd told me 'no' many times, that he didn't want to muddy his memories, that going there might take away from the pleasure of it all. I asked why, and he said that on his last trip to Wellton, it just didn't feel the same, and he wouldn't say another word about it.

Then one day, while I was pressing him about the layout of the old town, he said, "Get old Betsy gassed up, and we'll go." By then, we'd christened the '56 with a name of her own.

"Are you sure?"

"As sure as I'll ever be." He laughed and got up from his chair beside the kitchen table. "Besides, I'm tired of telling you everything I know about that place.

Time to go see for yourself."

I didn't hesitate, and one day later we were on our way.

The quickest route would have been straight down Interstate 5, then east on I-10 at San Diego, but Pop didn't want to go through LA or even populated Nevada, or on any Interstate at all, if we could avoid it. So, it was a long, slow trip on two-lane blacktop, but we always had plenty to talk about. I felt as if buried treasure lay just ahead, outside the boundary of my vision.

"Nothing like an old horse..."

"What, Pop?" I glanced in his direction.

"Ain't nothing like an old horse." He grinned. "No sir."

I'd wanted to go riding with Dave for years, but had never got the chance. In fact, I had only seen him on a horse once or twice, and then only for a few moments at a time. With his thick glasses, I wondered if his vision kept him from it, or just the natural passage of time. Then I found out he'd gone on a long trail ride into the Tahoe National Forest with his daughter and a few of her friends.

I didn't know for sure, but I'd heard that he took a liking to an old black horse that someone had traded for at the ranch, and his daughter had talked him into going along. As I understood it, he'd taken that horse 100 feet straight down off a switchback - sliding the horse on its back feet, rump down, all the way to the lake. No one seemed to know if Doc had done it on purpose, or just missed the trail and held on for dear life.

"Ol' Gene Autry has a horse that's 38 - 40 years old. Champion Number Three," he announced triumphantly.

"Number Three?"

"Well, he had just one horse for all his movies, or so they said. That was one hell of a horse - he could do tricks like nobody's business and then some. I saw that horse once, a long time ago."

Pop pulled a hand-rolled cigarette out of his shirt pocket. "But what he did was replace old Champion with ones that looked just alike. I read he still has Number Three, after all these years." He coughed and reached for the silver thermos and red cup that accompanied us on all our travels. "I wonder if he still rides that thing? Autry's got to be all of eighty years-old by now."

"Hasn't seemed to slow you down any."

The sun continued to dim, so I pulled out a dashboard knob to turn the headlights on. The big V8 swept up into the winding hills, and I thought about looking for a cheap motel, preferably one with a bar and a restaurant next door.

Doc lit his cigarette, softly illuminating the cabin. Tiny reflections danced off his thick lenses.

"Yep. It's a great life, if she don't weaken."

BLOOD CANDY

MAY 1936
Coyote Wash
Yuma County, Arizona

ERNESTO VASQUEZ could run faster than anybody in Wellton, maybe faster than anyone in all of Arizona. He never thought of himself as fast; for as long he could remember, he ran simply for the joy of it. When he was little, he would catch prairie chickens for his mother; as he got older, he could even catch the occasional jackrabbit, if he came upon one unawares.

When bothered, he would go into to the dunes west of town and run until he fell exhausted. Ernesto loved to push himself, far from his friends, till the ache in his legs turned from a slow burn to steaming coals in his calves, thighs and ankles. He savored the warm haze that came down through his head and into his legs, masking his pain with the hot syrup of exertion. Everything else would fade away in the distance, like the passing landscape beside him. He could just run, and all the hurt and the hate in the world would flow into the ground beneath his bare feet.

Today's run was finished. Even though he had pushed himself hard, he'd saved enough for a quick burst of speed if he needed it. And he might too, if El Blanco was about. Two times already, the bastardo had caught him out alone, but Ernesto was quicker than the big black horse El Blanco rode; twice he had sprinted through the dunes before they could catch up to him. How he hated the blonde one, but not for the usual reasons. Ernesto feared him, and he wasn't used to being frightened by a white boy.

He and his compadres were much respected before the gringo brutalized them; for years they had controlled the temper in the back alleys and the schoolyard. But lately, the blonde-haired boy had set out to punish them, and their reputation had suffered under his hand. Ernesto was keen to avoid the fate of his companions, so he kept a wary eye on the crest of the dunes.

Perhaps it would have been better had they not tried to hang him.

Artemio Cabrero had argued vehemently against it; Tomás had simply shrugged it off, saying they had pushed him hard enough already. But Ernesto wanted him humiliated, strung up by his own rope - no matter what the risk. The

Bailey boy would have to beg for his life; only then would they release him, fully compliant to their authority. His brother Mago had called Ernesto estúpido. El Jefe Spain would put them all in jail, and have their parents sent away forever. Not so, as it turned out.

Still, it was a close call. Had it not been for el chico negro, Bailey would have choked to death. When they jumped him by the water tower, the boy had fought back violently, and their hanging rope had tangled - they couldn't get it loose. Then the giant black boy came out of nowhere and threw them all aside in a wild rage. Ernesto stole a look back, half-hoping and half-fearing that the gringo had drawn his last breath, but his friend had already cut him down. Bailey was gasping for air, cursing by the side of the tower.

They had no concept of his fury. His compadres had set upon the gringo many times before, to keep him in his proper place. Once, they had beaten him senseless, right across from the hotel. Even El Blanco's father, the mechanic, hadn't stopped them. Ernesto found it strange that a father would watch his son so bloodied and not lift a hand. He had little experience with fathers; he had never known his own, only the constant coming and going of the men who visited his mother. Perhaps the dark-haired mechanic wasn't even the boy's father - perhaps El Blanco was bastardo, like Ernesto and his brother. Whatever his birth, the blonde boy was not so easily defeated.

After the trouble at the water tower, Bailey had tracked them down one-by-one, always when they were alone, tearing his vengeance from them a piece of skin at a time. First Artemio, with a leather belt by the ice house. Then Mago, strung up and beaten until he could hardly stand. Ten days ago, the gringo tied Tomás Castro to a stake and set his heels on fire. Ever since, Tomás had called him by El Blanco. Now, even Ernesto used the name, as a constant reminder to keep a careful eye, especially alone in the dunes.

Ernesto felt well rested and began the short hike back to town. His gaze shifted to the crest of the trail; there was no other way through the mesa here, just a long wash with steep sides that stretched for almost a hundred yards. El Blanco had tried to trap him here before, but Ernesto had left him far behind; his black horse moved fast enough over a distance, but it was no match for Ernesto in a short sprint.

He listened carefully as he made his way along the trail; even the slightest sound carried far on the silent mesa. A low snort and the muffled sound of hoof-beats pricked his ears, and he broke into a dead run, covering the yards in great bounds. In moments, he'd be safe in his own part of town, where even El Blanco would think twice before following. Ernesto grinned into the rushing wind, then howled as a hundred sharp edges tore through the bottom of his feet.

DAVEY WAS BARELY PUSHING the old horse. He made no particular effort to mask his approach. All he really wanted was for Ernie to hear him coming. This would be his final demonstration and he was glad to be done with it.

That last one was far too close for comfort; he'd nearly fried old Tommy Castro. He'd never seen tumbleweed burn so fast. Tommy was easy, even if he was the most fearsome. Castro was big as a tow truck and could've broke him in two for kindling, but once he'd seen Davey come over the rise on old King, he lit out like a jackrabbit.

Just like Dad said.

"Take them on one at time, and never let them forget what happens." Davey pictured his father's face, after the Mexican boys had roughed him up. He thought his dad might've put a stop to it, but he just stood there, half-a-lather from the barbershop, and let Davey fend for himself. "I won't always be around," he said, as he carried him home, "so now's as good a time as any to learn how to handle your own troubles."

He did like his dad said, and the boys who'd made his life such a terror since he'd come to Wellton began to fade away under his ferocity. They were tough enough together, but like most anything else, if you broke it down to find the weak spot, you could work your way through it. Once Tommy heard what Dave had done to Artemio and Mago, he was ripe for the picking. Easy to rope, and even easier to snub tie to a fencepost. *And a damn sight easier to catch fire.* Davey had to cut his new rope just to keep from scorching Tom's cojónes. He'd hated to cut that rope. His old one was stiff from too many repairs and didn't turn over as smooth on his wrist.

But it will do for Ernie Vasquez.

He could see Ernie up ahead, running lickety-split down the wash. He was the fast one, and the meanest of the bunch. Davey figured it was Ernie behind that necktie party - he'd have left him to choke on his own spit if it weren't for Levon Jones. Levon had come flying out of the schoolyard - knocked Ernie and all of his buddies damn near sideways. Levon was a decent sort, and as close a friend as Davey had, outside of his family. Davey sat with him in the lunchroom when the others wouldn't on account of Levon being a colored boy. Davey didn't set much stock by a person's color - snakes came in colors, too - and Davey didn't like any of them. After school, he and Levon would play mumbletypeg and talk about Mexico; Levon's family had lived there for almost a hundred years. His grandparents had jumped a work gang in Arkansas and slipped across the Rio Grande, back when Texas was still a slave state.

Davey had tried to thank him at the tower but Levon wouldn't hear of it. "Damned rednecks!" He spat the words as he cut Davey down. "Ain't gonna' be no more lynchin'. Not now, not never!"

Levon came and went with the pickers that passed through every harvest. But he'd be back, and Davey reckoned that Levon Jones could sit anywhere he felt like, no matter what anyone had to say.

Davey slowed his horse; Ernie'd be close to the trap by now. It didn't take long to figure out you couldn't catch Vasquez like the rest; he was just too damn fast. Davey thought he'd had him once before out here, but Ernie had left him staring at his dust on the other side of the tracks. This time, he figured to use Ernie's speed as the bait, and take a trail where Vasquez could easily outpace him. Only this time, Davey had salted the wash with broken bottles, litle pieces buried and brushed over beneath the sand.

He heard a sharp cry from up ahead. *This time, there'll be an end to it.*

As he reined up beside Ernie, he could see things had gone sideways. No wails of anger, no Spanish curses, no flailing fists, just a figure curled over and silent, a dark red stain spreading out around him. Davey slid down off his horse, grateful for the stiff leather soles on his boots. His man-trap had worked too well; instead of sending Ernie to his knees, he'd kept running for a dozen yards; a long bloody track led to his crumpled body. The flesh was torn from his heels all along the way, until the searing pain took away his legs and he collapsed into the dirt.

Davey cut long strips from his shirt and bound up Ernie's legs at the ankles and the thighs. He threw the bloody boy up on King, mounted and kicked the old horse with all his strength, clasping Ernie to his hips. The startled horse bolted into a gallop, propelling them all out of the wash.

A soft rain began to fall. The white mist felt like hot steam across Davey's eyes; he prayed for mercy, prayed that the tourniquets would stop the bleeding until they reached the other side of town, and that he hadn't crippled up for good the fastest boy he'd ever seen.

BILL GALE liked the Bailey boy. Davey was a scamp, but he wasn't mean or overly prissy like some kids these days. Under Arizona law, the boy hadn't done anything illegal, and nothing that Bill might not have done himself.

Lawrence was in Yuma, so after she patched up Ernie, Mrs. Spain insisted that Gale take Davey over to his father and have Dee him read the Riot Act. Not that it was necessary; even Bill could see that Davey was half-scared out of his wits by the damage he'd done. Under the best of circumstances, Ernie'd be a long time healing - most likely he'd pick up a nasty gimp in his step.

"Probably served him right," was all the comment Gale could muster. He glanced out the window of the storeroom where Mrs. Spain kept her makeshift infirmary. The summer shower was building in intensity, and he for one, would like to get outside and enjoy it. Any rain this time of year was a welcome relief. He felt the same way about the ongoing feud between the young buck Mexicans and the Bailey boy; it was rare entertainment in a town where good fun was scarce.

"This business of an eye for an eye is getting out of hand." Madeline Spain was incensed. She was barely able to stitch up Ernesto's feet, and if Davey hadn't stopped the bleeding, the Vasquez boy might not have survived to see the scars.

"This isn't Tombstone, and these aren't just black eyes and bruises." She held up the bloody rags. "Just look at this, it's the twentieth century, for God's sake, and these boys are still keeping blood feuds."

"Yes, ma'am." Gale exhaled slowly. He resisted listing the various provocations that Ernie's bunch had visited on young Davey. There was only one way to sort it out and that was between the boys themselves. He could just about guess what Dee Bailey would say; he'd seen Dee's jaw clench when his son was beaten black and blue behind the barbershop. Still, Bill knew better than to cross Madeline Spain; she held all the purse strings in Wellton and she wasn't afraid to pinch them when she had a mind to.

"Now then, you take David down to his father and tell him exactly what happened." Madeline turned to go back in the general store, where she'd left Ernesto chewing on some hard candy. She took three steps, then spun and tossed the bloody rags to Gale, catching him by surprise. "And take these with you."

"Yes, ma'am." Gale stuffed the wet rags in his back pocket, wiped his hands on his pants legs, and walked quickly out the side door.

On the steps and out of earshot, he muttered under his breath. "Not for all of your money, Lawrence Spain."

Gale looked up the alley. Davey was under the eaves of the Mercantile, perched on a stack of empty lettuce crates. He was feeding the green remnants to his horse while it nuzzled around his neck in the rain.

"How's Ernie?" Davey looked as if he'd lost his best friend instead of his chief tormentor.

Gale barely raised his voice above a whisper. "Feasting on *la Señora's* peppermint, I 'spect. Now, fetch your three-dollar horse, and we'll go see your dad."

"Mr. Gale, I didn't figure to cut him up so bad."

"No one ever does, Davey."

The boy collected his reins, and they headed down Main Street towards the garage. Despite the growing rain, a small crowd was gathering by the pumps. As they passed the hotel, more people filtered in one by one, some at a dead run. Gale thought the boy had pulled a sly trick, but hardly one worth a congregation. Doubtless, Dee Bailey had heard all the gory details by now, and had plenty of time to contemplate his response.

Bill thought of his own daddy's temper amid the misdeeds of his youth. There was that one episode with Charley Barnam's daughter; his butt still stung on that account. And his little difference of opinion with a town constable - that one cost him dearly, too. He pictured his father, red-faced and drunk, swinging his stiff black strap like a piece of lumber. Gale shuddered as he glanced down and wished the Bailey boy a better reward.

"From the looks of that crowd, you'd think you murdered the little pecker." Gale flashed a thin smile. He tapped Davey on the shoulder. "Don't worry, once they let on it's a greaser boy, all the pressure'll come off."

Davey didn't take much comfort in the border patrolman's words. Gale's disregard for Mexicans was as well known as his taste for their women. Still, he didn't figure on this much of a ruckus; no crowd had gathered when Davey got the tar beat out of him.

The commotion continued to build around the gas pumps. A tall man in a yellow slicker stood up in a truck bed, waving wildly, after which half the crowd went scurrying in opposite directions.

"Y'know, I don't think those folks give a good goddamn what you've been up to."

Gale was right. All of the crowd's attention was focused on the man in the pickup and none on their approach. Sam Kingston hurried by, his mailbag slung over one shoulder like a poor man's Santa Claus. He grabbed Bill Gale by the arm.

"Better head for cover, Bill. There's a real gully-washer coming in." Sam pointed back to the garage. "Ezra Johnson's come all the way from Painted Rocks, says the storm's twice as big up there and headed this way!"

Gale looked to the east. There was good reason for the postman's haste. Dark thunderheads were rising with the wind, filling the horizon and blotting out the mountaintops. The raindrops had begun to sheet, tilting from vertical to horizontal. Back in '31, Coyote Wash had overflowed its banks and the water ran four-feet deep down Arizona Avenue. Davey's dad had chained Gale's pickup to the gas pumps; they waited out the storm in the hayloft of Spain's barn with half the folks in town. Two lives were lost that day, and even the railroad bed washed out at the edge of town.

"Go tell Mrs. Spain to get the word out along the line. Better open up the canals now or they're sure to breach later!" The border patrolman was shouting despite himself, the exploits of two young boys long since vanished in the rain. "I'll see Davey to his daddy and work the ranches to the south!"

Kingston nodded, shuffling quickly down the street, his leather bag growing heavier by the moment with the weight of the downpour.

"They say God looks after the stupid and the young." Gale laughed as he lifted the boy up on his horse.

"What?" Davey thought the rain must have waterlogged his ears.

"Nobody hangs a horse thief in a gully washer!" The borderman slapped the gelding's rump and shouted, "Get your butt home, Davey!" King startled into a trot, and the boy grabbed his mane to keep from slipping off.

Bill Gale tossed the bloody rags from his pocket and headed for his truck. He had a lot of ground to cover in a very short time.

THE RAIN STOPPED after an hour, this time, as quickly as it began. Madeline had watched the rippling sheets come down in waves; there was more than enough to wash away her melancholy. She loved the rain. It was an infrequent friend in Arizona, unlike Baltimore, where you could almost set your clock by the early afternoon showers, the ones that came in off the ocean and made the streets sparkle and painted the lawns a lush shade of emerald green.

After the storm, Ernesto's mother and his younger brother Mago came to take him home. Madeline had assured them that the boy would probably recover, as long as there was no infection. She had given them some cotton and peroxide to wash the wounds and a little sulfa powder to add to the dressing. His mother was relieved, and one more dose of hard candy seemed to reassure both Ernie and

Mago.

Madeline wouldn't take any money, as if they had any to give. Despite her occasional airs, she enjoyed the company of the local population, especially the Mexican families. They had an unvarnished view of their situation, holding tight to their familial bonds, in order to survive the sometimes brutal treatment of their new masters. Though Mexico had claimed this part of the country for the better part of a century, the original settlers were often viewed as little more than livestock. Madeline had felt the cold stares herself.

She knew that some people viewed her old world heritage with suspicion, if not downright bigotry. It made her want to lash out, to put those foolish idiots in their place, until she realized that she had become just like them.

Over time, she began to take it out on Lawrence, denying him his simple pleasures, silently punishing him for keeping her in this backwater town, so far away from the things she loved. She buried herself in her work to no avail, finding only resentment there. Walled off by the lingering sadness, she sank into a weak malaise that took all of the taste out of her meals and her marriage.

She felt herself retreating into isolation, growing bitter and more distant every day, desperate for some shred of warmth outside herself, trapped by the people she loved in a town she had begun to hate. Her resentment began to migrate, falling first on Floy Bailey, for something she had that Madeline didn't.

Dee.

In a weak moment, she went to see him. It was late. The garage was empty, with only a lantern's light to show her standing at the door. Alone with him, she let her guard down; she told him of the spreading emptiness inside her, hoping and fearing at the same time that he might be the one to fill it.

There were long moments of silence. Long, deliberate silence.

"Mrs. Spain... Madeline." Dee took a step closer. His eyes were on hers. He could see her desire, and his head began to bow.

Her eyes watered; she couldn't explain why it was that she trusted him, but she always had, from the moment he walked through that door, so long ago.

"Dee, I just want to feel alive again." He was only a step away from her, so very close.

"And you will." He paused to let her catch her breath. "But not like this."

She stepped back, fearful of his reproach. He stepped forward to fill the gap between them. Her feet felt frozen to the floor.

"I love my wife." His smile spread slowly, broad enough to carry them both.

"And you love your husband."

His gaze was kind, his voice, calm and sure.

"I see it in the way you look at him, even if you don't." There was no judgement, only the dark mirror of his eyes.

Something held her. Something gentle.

"I see it in the way he looks at you, wishing he was more of what you wanted."

She closed her eyes, glistening.

"Waiting for you to want him."

Sweet silence.

Her eyes opened, brimming with tears.

It was if they were together again, on that very first night. Dee, content with his half-a-loaf, steadfast in his quiet resolve. *Lawrence will be here any minute.*

The Lawrence she had known so many years ago. So strong and so endlessly kind, before she let her bitterness coat their marriage in regret.

She could see them both now, standing with that same unbending soul.

Patient, as always.

Lawrence, left standing at her door, night after night. Ready to take her to the picture show, ready to take her to Yuma – to New York or Paris, if only she would let him. She could see him standing there, so familiar and so all at once new.

Lawrence.

Dee caught her eye. "Let it go," he whispered. "And he will run to you."

Dee backed away slowly. Closing his eyes, he showed her the rough palms of his hands.

She left him as quietly as she had come. And the next time she saw him, it was as if nothing had ever happened.

For his birthday that year, Madeline bought Lawrence a two-seater airplane, a Curtis Jenny - one that Dee had found for her in San Diego.

She loved the rain. It washed away everything.

DON'T BELIEVE EVERYTHING you've heard about this old country. There's more to be seen, every time." Doc rolled up his window and lit a cigarette. "Civilization hasn't eat it all up yet. There's still places no man's ever been. It'll break your heart sometimes, it's so pretty." He looked at me and grinned. "Even a hard case like you."

Not that I was much of a hard case. My head still hurt from the night before.

"I wouldn't exactly call this beautiful." Parched grey hills bordered the road for miles ahead.

"Too close to town. Wait till we get to the real desert, you'll see."

I was raised in the city, more of a big small town really, and was still in awe of any real wilderness. Aside from a few campouts in the Cub Scouts and a rock concert or two, I wasn't much of an outdoorsman. I played at it, retreating to the city when the odds weren't in my favor. Doc and I were as different as any two men could be. But we shared a love of horses, and a genuine delight at life on the open road. This time, it was two-lane blacktop, headed south on US 95. We'd left Needles early, after Doc had kicked me out of bed and into a restaurant for some hot coffee.

Like all the others, this trip was filled with stories about old cars and life on the desert. Dave Bailey talked about the desert like you would an old lover; how it could provide everything you'd need, yet turn on you in the very next moment. He lingered on its stark beauty, the cold, clear nights and the oppressive heat of the day. People of every description came in and out of those tales. And almost always, the conversation would come back around to his father.

"My dad used to soup up carburetors in his shop. He got so good at it, even the Highway Patrol used to come around, just to have him tune up their cars." He fingered his cigarette while looking out the window at the distant mountains.

"What'd he do to them?"

"Damn near everything. Once he built this setup on an old Auburn car. Shoot, that's the fastest ride I ever took in my life - from Grass Valley to Yuma with my Uncle Irvon. We left up there that evening, had breakfast in Yuma the next morning. Like I say, that's back in probably '38. I'm telling you, that sucker, goddang it, had great, big old wheels on it and little, narrow tires. It looked like a sports car, like a racer. Hell, it was rough riding across that Mojave Desert - wasn't nothin' but dirt roads all the way. And the faster you went the better it was, the cooler it got. But hey, we'd go across there back then, at a hundred and thirty, hundred and forty miles an hour in that thing."

Dave paused to relight his cigarette. He would roll the tobacco loosely, sometimes one-handed, and the cigarettes would go out like clockwork every couple of minutes. It never seemed to faze him; the dry butt would hang from his lips or dangle on his fingers until he saw fit to light it again, usually to gather his thoughts or punctuate a sentence.

"You know, everybody thinks them old cars wouldn't even get up the road. The only thing about them cars back then - they'd go fast, but it took you a mile and a half to get rolling. But once you got to rollin', you had it made, boy, you could go. Hell, we had this Mercury convertible, 1937. And that sucker, goddang, we could go a hundred n' twenty miles an hour just like nothin'. I mean we still had pedal to give. We did."

His cigarette faded out, and the great god Nicotine tapped me on the shoulder. I lit a store-bought menthol and offered him my Zippo lighter. He took a deep drag and coughed, caught his breath and pushed his old straw hat back above his forehead.

"Yep, that one old cop clocked me at a hundred n' twenty miles an hour. When he turned the light on me, I pulled over. This cop says, 'You were starting to pull away from me'." Doc cleared his throat and smiled. "But he was pretty good. He only wrote it up for seventy miles an hour, I think." Doc's chin went up at an angle. "Anyway, it cost me twenty bucks."

I laughed out loud as we crossed the vast countryside, smoking too many cigarettes and drinking way too much coffee. Doc wandered from one decade to the next, and we watched the mile markers count down all the way to Yuma, Arizona.

A PILLAR OF FLAMES

JULY 1936

Aztec, Arizona

FLOYD STRICKLAND was a good driver, or so he thought. He'd never had an accident, not even a scraped fender, for as long as he'd been behind the wheel. His Great Uncle Herbert had taught him how to drive, first admonishing him on the high price of automobiles, and then on the value of quick reflexes, as Uncle Herbert had always considered the notion of two-way vehicular traffic altogether unwise.

Herbert Strickland was a chief engineer on the Southern Pacific, and there fore appreciated the elegant symmetry of a single locomotive on a straight track. He had written numerous letters to the newspaper editors of the day, even going so far as to petition the Governor in his cause. His proposition was succinctly stated: that automobiles were altogether different in their nature from wagons and men on horseback, and therefore more prone to calamity. He recommended that all main thoroughfares be devised in concert with the railways, using only one lane, and allowing travel in just one direction at a time, with due regard for cross-walks and sidings. Strickland's musings fell on deaf ears, and so, being a bachelor, he took charge of educating each of his brother's children in the proper handling of what he considered to be an unduly dangerous vehicle.

Young Floyd never finished his apprenticeship under Uncle Herbert; the chief engineer was killed in the biggest head-on collision ever suffered on the Southern Pacific Railroad. Nevertheless, and perhaps in dedication to his great uncle, Floyd had continued to hone his driving skills, slipping his father's Ford out of the garage at night when no one would notice, always careful to keep a keen eye out for trains. When the young man left home for good, he put aside every spare coin he could toward the purchase of his own vehicle, and finally, after two long years of bucking hay at the Spain Barns, he scraped together enough money to buy his own rig.

He bought the truck in Yuma, from a widow woman who could no longer afford to keep her late husband's Dodge out of sentiment alone. She told Floyd that she couldn't even shift the gears, but had left it parked in the garage, visiting from time to time for the pleasant memories it engaged. Her husband had been a guard at the Territorial Prison, and his habit after each six-day shift was to stop at the grocer and purchase a picnic lunch, thereafter to take her out along the Colorado, where they'd spend a pleasant afternoon. Floyd had listened patiently to her tale, mindful that those few extra moments might lend the Widow Larsen a kinder regard in her asking price. He was right, and saved ten dollars for his trouble.

All day and into the early evening he had driven the old pickup, first to Wellton, where he was congratulated by all his friends, then out and around along the railroad right of way. He still had a goodly portion of his ten dollars gas money left, and seeing the Swede lingering about by the cafe, Floyd stopped to show him his newfound treasure.

The two of them had worked together for most of a year at the Spain Barns, though Floyd could never hope to move as much hay as the giant Scandinavian. Swede's real name was nearly as big as he was, and totally unpronounceable, except for Mrs. Spain, who made a special effort to use it whenever he was around. Swede could buck twice as many bales as Floyd could in less than half the time. He would swing them up on the stacks with one arm, his hay hooks spinning in great loops, like some kind of giant catapult. Mr. Spain had taken to bragging on him, arranging elaborate wagers to demonstrate his top hand's prowess. With his own eyes, Floyd had seen the Swede lift not only a 50-gallon drum over his head, but also Lawrence Spain, who straddled the drum like a saddle – all for the gaudy benefit of a two dollar bet.

The Swede was suitably impressed by the curved silhouette of Strickland's Dodge, and to celebrate his friend's newfound acquisition, suggested that they take the truck up to Ralph's Mill in Sentinel. This was mostly due to a similar affection that the Swede had for Ralph's daughter, who'd been known to share her charms as freely as her father's beer. Floyd had no great thirst for either, but he did like the notion of the sixty-mile drive to Sentinel. On the way there, just outside of Aztec, they spotted a broken-down Lincoln, steam pouring from its open bonnet.

"We'd better stop."

Three women sprang from the car, waving their arms in signal fashion. Floyd pressed the brakes, sliding the truck onto the rocky shoulder. "Well, I'll be damned," he said, instantly regretting his language. "It's a bunch of nuns."

As their headlights streaked across the dark figures, Swede muttered something in his native tongue, then switched to English mid-sentence. Floyd thought he heard the name Martin Luther, but couldn't recall anyone by that name in Yuma County. He'd never seen the Swede so nervous before, and wondered how three women dressed in black and white could make his large friend seem so suddenly small. Whatever the reason, it mattered little to Floyd Strickland. He wasn't leaving three church ladies by the side of the road, not on this night or any other.

* * *

THE BIG MAHOGANY CABINET held the finest radio Floy had ever seen. She delighted in polishing its wooden veneers, carefully wiping the dust from the burled knobs and latticed grilles. The console was built by the Radio Corporation of America in New York City. Floy pictured the great buildings and the giant ships whenever she listened to its faraway broadcasts. There were orchestras larger than she'd ever dreamed of, and music from Europe, and songs so fresh that she'd never heard the words before, and plays and comedies and news from across the continent that had happened that very same day. She was enchanted by it all, and never alone, even when she was lonely.

Everyone had talked about 'the wireless' for years. She had listened once or twice on a crystal kit that a neighbor had built, but she felt confined by the cables and out of touch with her family underneath the headphones.

But this cabinet radio was different, with a large cloth speaker that filled her little parlor with sound - more like a fine piano in the manor house of some wealthy family.

Dee had brought the remarkable set home one night, saying he'd taken it in trade on a valve job for a Buick Model 27. Like everyone else, the couple was bound for California and had brought the console along, tied to the top of their car, all the way from the East Coast. Dee had said it was a fair trade - that he'd given them a little extra besides, in gas and oil. Floy was quite certain of his charity; her generous nature paled beside that of her husband's. Still, the exchange was clearly in their favor, for ever since, each evening was filled with music and adventure, with all the family huddled around the gleaming cabinet. Even her father found time to wander by, almost always when a baseball game was playing, and especially on Thursday nights for *Fibber McGee & Molly*. Dee couldn't or wouldn't be bothered, and except for the President's fireside chats, would hardly listen at all, preferring to spend what little spare time he had reading.

The magical radio played on as the girls brushed each other's hair by the chaise. Davey was stretched out on the carpet, carefully calculating his numbers, Dee secure in his parlor chair. Floy leaned back on the worn sofa and closed her eyes. Tonight's program featured Gene Autry's lonesome guitar, the night sounds blending in and out with his drifting serenade. She glanced at Dee, seemingly oblivious in his book, his toe tapping silently all the while.

Life had come full circle. The girls were doing well in school, and even Davey was paying some attention to his lessons. Dee had turned the garage completely around for the Spains, each year more profitable than the last. God knows, the country was still in turmoil, with banks failing and bread lines curling around city blocks, but somehow, in their splendid isolation, they had found a small kernel of hope. Grandpa Cox's job at the high school was only part-time, but he'd still found odd jobs enough to get by. And with the rooms they cleaned at the Spain Hotel, there were far more than beans in the pot every day.

Her brother Irvon would return from time to time, fresh from his travels, with word of some wonderland or another, almost always in California, where jobs were plentiful and coins fell from people's pockets like raindrops. Nowadays, it seemed like only Daddy caught his wanderlust. No matter where Irvon had come from or how broke he was when he returned, John Cox would christen that the land of opportunity, a fresh start and a new future for his family.

Perhaps he was right, but Dee would have none of it. Each time, he'd remind him of the tortured retreat from Oklahoma, the barren work camps, the misery and the hunger that their children had endured. And each time, her father would walk away silently, and she'd shudder at the thought of her family torn apart again.

For now, there were no such agonies. Irvon was off and gone again and Papa had settled in quietly. Even though they didn't own the house they lived in, there was plenty of work to be had and food on the table. She was grateful for it.

Most of her strange apprehensions about the town had disappeared, and she had become almost friends with Madeline Spain. Nothing like Dee and Lawrence, of course; she doubted any two peas had ever been taken from a pod more alike. If she had any fears at all, it was mostly that they would kill themselves or somebody else, flying madly about on their motorcycles or looping around in some airplane. On a whim, Madeline had bought Lawrence a two-seater in San Diego, from a man who claimed to have been an ace in the war in France. Now, the two men would fly off together in search of wrecks on the desert, or do cartwheels high above their little town.

She was grateful for their friendship; it was the first time she'd seen Dee so close to anyone since Benny had died. Nothing seemed to faze their camaraderie. The two men's exploits were legend; at County Fair, people would come from as far away as Phoenix to see what their next stunt might be. She glanced at the quiet man reading across the room, and wondered what new spectacle he and Lawrence Spain would dream up come September.

The singing cowboy was on his last song when Penny started barking on the front porch. Their little dog was no bigger than a jackrabbit, but her ferocity could send a full-sized man scrambling for cover. Sam Kingston had sworn never to set foot in their yard again after Penny had massaged his ankles. Nowadays, Floy had to gather the mail at the Post Office, even though Dee had put a box in by the side of the road. Sam had taken to circling the block in opposite directions so he wouldn't have to pass by his tiny nemesis.

"Call off your dog, Davey." Dee Bailey didn't look up from his book.

Davey jumped off the floor and ran to the window at full speed, hoping to see what mayhem Penny might have caused. He liked a good show, and Penny would often deliver if the stranger was frightened or didn't know how to handle a persistent animal.

"She's a good watchdog, Dee." Floy liked Penny and would even play with her when no one else was around.

"She's a menace to society." Dee smiled inwardly, wondering what unlucky stranger cowered at the little dog's attack. A sudden yelp surprised him, and he rose from his chair to head for the door

"Dad!" Davey pulled back from the window, confusion in his face. "They're beating up on Penny."

Dee threw the door open, his fists balled in anticipation. He expected to see some drunken hobo from the nearby train yard; Dee had warned them about coming around the house. He wasn't in the mood to tolerate another nocturnal visit, especially if anyone was abusing the little dog. He stopped short, unclenched his hands and stood hesitant in the doorway.

"I... ah, can I help you?" Dee's face turned a bright red. He hurriedly tucked in his shirt and straightened his stance.

The little nun flicked her cane like a rapier, sending Penny scurrying for the cover of a porch chair. She gave Dee a knowing smile, and motioned toward her companions.

"The sisters and I were told you might be able to assist us."

The pale grey light made it hard to see, and Dee had to squint to adjust his eyes. There they stood, three nuns in a line, all clad in black and white and racked up like bowling pins.

THE OLD TOW TRUCK was a hard starter, especially on cold nights, when the rapid change in temperature sent condensation deep into the coiled wires that gave it life. Dee wiped the moisture away from the distributor cap and motioned to Davey. "Better bring the jumper, son."

Davey tipped the dolly that carried two big truck batteries, careful not to let their considerable weight pass the balance point and topple over on him. His father had wired them in series; the result was a powerful nudge on even the most stubborn ignition.

The boy had often wondered what mechanical whimsy had made his father's principal work vehicle such a poor advertisement for his skills. Davey had lost count of the number of times his dad had torn the old Cadillac down, replacing one part and rebuilding another. There seemed to be an unspoken duel between them, the recycled luxury sedan and the relentless mechanic, each one working their mischief upon the other in an epic struggle for the upper hand.

Perhaps the old limousine resented its reincarnation as a lowly tow truck, exacting its revenge in the form of fouled spark plugs and loose compression. His dad had said it might be a lost cause, with time better spent dismantling the beast for salvage than in nursing the final miles from its steel carcass. Still, the old car was a gift from Lawrence Spain and the only big bore tow in the valley. Bob's Gas in Gila Bend had a ¾ ton, but it could barely tow a bicycle off a sandy shoulder, hardly a match for the big twelve-cylinder's hydraulic winches.

As if on cue, the Cadillac's engine sprang to life, its insides spun on seven hundred amps across the jumper cables. Dee Bailey pulled the cable ends from the starter and slid them inside their wooden keepers. "Hop on up, Davey." Dee brought the long curved hood down tight, muffling the great beast. "Let's see if we can get our little sisters back on the road to heaven."

* * *

THE SWEDE took a long pull off a bottle of Falstaff beer. "Back home, Reverend Larsson called them the Devil's church…" He kept his voice low, not wanting the barmaid to think that anything could shake his blonde confidence.

He and Floyd had gone straight to Ralph's Mill in Sentinel, even after the sheriff had asked them to stop and give Dee Bailey a hand with the tow. Swede had sulked about it for the first 5 miles, finally convincing Floyd that they had at least a half hour's head start on the old tow truck. More than enough time for a quick beer.

Floyd didn't like going against Lawrence Spain, but he felt a need to settle the Swede down. Besides, they might have even more time than that if Bailey's old truck was acting up again.

Loueena Adams palmed Floyd's glass and replaced it with a full bottle of cold beer. Floyd couldn't help but notice her cleavage; the display was as deliberate as her smile. He tried to look away.

"No, thanks, we've got to see about a wreck." He was hoping to keep sharp and make up any lost time by traveling at highway speeds.

"Don't be silly, Floyd. Swede tells me you've got a new truck." Loueena bent over the bar, the edge of which provided a perfect platform for her considerable charms. "Time to celebrate."

Floyd pondered the nature of that celebration as Loueena's father opened the cash till. Ralph Adams was a retired Chicago policeman, and was nearly as big around as his daughter was big above. Ralph had come south in '31; he opened the Mill shortly after repeal in '33, when Sentinel County went wet. Some folks said Ralph was on the take and tied up with gangsters, that his real name wasn't even Adams. Floyd didn't know or much care, but he did know about the big shotgun Ralph kept behind the bar, and decided that any celebration of his wouldn't include the fat man's daughter. Ralph's beer was cold, and that was more than good enough.

"Swede." Ralph tore open a wax paper bag of pretzels. He poured them into a basket on top of the bar. "What say you help me move a few beer barrels?"

"Sure, Ralph." The Swede slipped off his jacket and folded it over the bar. He gave Loueena his best smile, his powerful arms stretched wide behind his head. Swede liked to show off, and moving a few kegs for Ralph Adams might soften his resolve where his daughter was concerned.

"Honey, take Swede in the back and show him where we keep the empties." Ralph sat down on a whiskey crate and lit a King Edward cigar. "That's a good looking truck, Floyd. Dodge?"

"Sure is." Floyd beamed. "'22, and good as gold."

"I had a '22 Dodge, back in the city." The pinewood crate creaked mournfully as Ralph shifted his weight. "Not a lick of trouble."

Loueena slipped her hand into the Swede's, squeezing gently as she led him through the storeroom door. Her father had set loose on two of his favorite subjects: the Great City of Chicago and finely crafted automobiles. He wasn't likely to leave his perch before his long cigar was fully spent. The Chicago portion of his lecture was just beginning as she pressed against the giant farmhand.

"NOT MUCH MOON. Better get the flare box."

Davey did as he was told, one glance confirming his father's words. It was a coal black night, and some of the big trucks on their way down from Phoenix were known to cruise at over eighty miles an hour.

"Busted hose." His dad lifted his lantern from the manifold and closed the hood. "Set out the flares and I'll get her hooked up."

It was surprising how many people would take out across the desert without checking the water level in their cooling system. Davey figured even he could run a wrecker out here, if he carried enough hoses and radiator caps. The boy opened the service galley and gathered five flares and a handful of wooden matches. One by one, he lit the flares at 25-foot intervals, marking a gentle curve that arched around the Lincoln and down the highway. By the time he'd placed the last one, he could hear the hoist straining under the weight of the big sedan.

"Don't dawdle, Davey." His father was setting the safety chains, his smooth motion the legacy of a thousand repetitions. "I promised your mother I'd have you home before midnight."

"Coming, Dad." Davey was watching the flares' reflection in two yellow eyes across the drainage ditch. Old Joe had told him to wait for a blink to define the eye's angle and the shape of the face. He reasoned a flat face from the small brow, maybe a kit fox watching for a passing rat. The grinding of low gears told him that his father was growing impatient. Davey picked up his step, fell into a lope and jumped into the cab.

"What was it?" Nothing escaped his father, not even small eyes by the side of the road.

"Kit fox, I think."

"Probably." Dee Bailey pulled away from the shoulder and worked the gears through second and into third. "They like those old ditches, chock full of brown rats…"

"Yep," Davey agreed.

"… and curious boys." The dashboard lights played off his father's face, betraying a slight smile. As the old Cadillac gathered momentum, the window wind began to brush his father's hair. Davey pulled his coat up around his face and drew in a deep breath of night air.

"Dad, how come nuns are so scary?"

"I wouldn't say they're scary, son," Dee replied. "They're just not what you're used to. Sometimes that's all it takes to spook folks."

"Well, I don't like 'em. Especially the one that took out after Penny."

"I 'spect it was more the other way around, son."

The big sedan lurched as it toppled into a chuckhole, one of dozens that dotted the highway all across the flat plain. Dee pulled hard left to compensate and the Lincoln veered wildly on the hoist, striking the edge of a rut and swinging back into line. The distinctive clang of a bouncing hubcap spun out behind them.

"Damn." Dee's hand slipped to the gears, and the Caddy downshifted.

"We gonna' stop, Dad?"

"Sure we are." Dee Bailey believed in bringing back all of the tow, not just the easy parts. "Wouldn't want the Holy Sisters to look out of place with only three shiners."

With a steady brake and two more downshifts, Dee had the two vehicles stopped by the side of the road. He shifted into reverse and backed down the shoulder on a straight line nearly fifty yards. "That's about as close as I can place you, Davey." Dee reached into the glove box and took out a lantern. "Let's see if you're as good at hubcaps as you are at foxes."

Davey jumped out of the cab and headed into the scrub, figuring that a hubcap would never land where it was easy to find. He rocked the flashlight side to side, hoping to catch a glint of chrome.

"I'll bet he finds it, too," Dee whispered under his breath. His young son had a knack for finding things. He wished it wasn't quite so often trouble. Dee dropped from the cab and moved to the hoist. A bump big enough to spring a hubcap might just as easily breach a chain.

"I found it, Dad!" Davey called out in the darkness, knowing that his father probably couldn't hear him. He had wandered another twenty yards into the desert, following a hunch and the suggestion of a shiny object in the distance. The fancy hubcap had bounded over a wash and ended up wedged in the crotch of a saguaro. Davey knocked it out with a stick, respectful of the mighty cactus' thorns.

As he walked back to the highway, he could hear an engine racing in the distance. The sound unnerved him. He began to move quickly, picking his way through the brush with his lantern. Headlights flashed on the highway behind him. He could make out a small pickup barreling through the darkness. Davey broke into a dead run, forgetting the barbs and the thistles along the way, screaming at the top of his lungs for his father.

Dee Bailey was under the wrecker with the motor running, re-attaching one of the strap hangers for the Cadillac's muffler, jarred loose by the big pothole. "For five dollars, I'd send you to the junkyard, you stubborn old toad." Dee had replaced both hangers not six months before, but this particular tow truck didn't distinguish between new and old, only between broke and about to break. Something pricked his ears in the wind; he thought he heard Davey.

"David?" He stayed still and listened carefully. He could just make out his son's voice, and another long, wailful sound. He rolled out from under the Cadillac and started to stand.

A raw flash of light blinded him as the roar of the oncoming truck resounded in his ears. In the bare instant left to him, Dee Bailey threw himself beneath the hoist, spinning to gather his legs into the cave formed by the overhanging Lincoln.

The speeding pickup struck the back of the big limousine at 88 miles an hour; large portions of its undercarriage remained with the Lincoln. The rest of its shell careened off the ramp, landing some thirty-five yards away. As it touched down, the truck's occupants were thrown through the windshield into a stand of greasewood, whereupon the Widow Larsen's 1922 Dodge burst into a pillar of flames.

LAWRENCE SPAIN couldn't sit still. He'd already walked the perimeter of the building five times and smoked most of a pack of cigarettes, and he hadn't smoked for years. Every time he went in the waiting room, a big Cocopah nurse would shoo him out and tell him that the doctor would speak to him as soon as he had anything to say.

Madeline was already on her way with Floy; he couldn't stop either one of them from coming, though God knows he tried. Near as he could tell, there might not be reason to come at all. The seats in his Chevy were soaked with blood; he'd made a split second decision not to wait for help and loaded Dee's broken body into the back seat, next to what was left of the Swede's left hand. Bloody as he was, the Swede had managed to lift the broken hoist off Dee Bailey with his one good arm before he collapsed. They'd left Floyd Strickland right where they found him.

The Indian hospital wasn't anything fancy, but it was closest - and Lawrence knew he didn't have much time. The Swede was bleeding out fast and Dee wasn't coming around no matter how hard he tried. Probably just as well, with all the damage to his head and shoulders.

Lawrence had made Davey stay in town with his mom. How the boy gotten to Wellton so fast he'd never know; he must have thrown himself in front of every car on the highway.

When the boy wanted to go back with him, he'd kept it simple. "She needs you now more than your dad does…"

A grey pickup swerved into the dirt parking lot. In the dim light, he could make out Bill Gale, Madeline and Floy Bailey. He ran to the truck and took Floy's arm; she was pale and shaking, barely able to walk. He brought her into the waiting room, and the Cocopah nurse swooped her up and took her back through the double doors. Lawrence tried to follow, but she stopped him in his tracks with a hard look.

"Family only."

Lawrence heaved a sigh and went back outside.

Bill Gale stepped into the light. "Miz' Bailey's pretty broken up. Your wife kinda' put her back together on the ride up here." Gale's voice held a new admiration for Madeline Spain.

"Where is she?"

"Said she needed some air. Told me to tell you she took a walk to settle down. She'll be back."

Lawrence looked around for any sign of Madeline. "Which way?"

"She was pretty damn clear about it." Gale never struggled with expressing himself. "That was a wicked ride, Lawrence. Leave her be."

Lawrence nodded. He looked up at the high hospital windows. There wasn't much to see, and he leaned back against the single light pole. The place might not be much more than an infirmary, but it had been here since 1852, and Lawrence knew right where it was and just how fast he could get there.

"You got a cigarette, Bill?"

"I didn't know you smoked."

"I don't. But I could change my mind."

Gale reached in his pocket and offered him a plug of his tobacco. "Chew?"

"It can wait." Lawrence took a deep breath. "Thanks for bringing them up here. I think I'll walk, too."

"So, Lawrence... what the hell's going on?" Gale had to ask. He'd seen the remnants of the old Cadillac and the smoldering inferno off the highway. "

"Strickland's dead. The Swede's near bled out - and Dee? I don't know, Bill." Lawrence shook his head. "I just don't know."

*　*　*

MADELINE stared at the high windows, dim lit in frosted glass. There was nothing to see and nothing to say. She had done all that she could for Florence Bailey. All that she knew how to do for the man that she loved.

She could let go now.

Her tears flowed like rain.

HE WATCHED HER in silence. Lawrence had known for years how she felt about him. It really didn't matter. In a way, the depth of her love for Dee had made it all the more beautiful that she had stayed with him. He didn't care, because he loved him, too. Loved him for the beautiful way he held his children, for the simple joy he took in flying, even when he couldn't see well enough to land.

Dee's eyes had begun to fail him, so Lawrence made all the landings now at Fair time, and let Dee flash the wings and do the barrel rolls. When Dee came to him and asked to borrow the plane for one last flight, there were tears in his eyes.

Lawrence painted large runway numbers on a dirt landing strip so Dee could find the distance. He'd smiled as they took off, Dee in his goggles and long scarf and Floy dressed in her Sunday best. They were gone for hours.

The moonlight held Madeline in silhouette against the frosted windows. He would wait in the shadows for as long as need be.

WANDA COULDN'T BEAR to hear her mother cry. The sound of her tears tore at her insides like a paring knife.

Thankfully, it wasn't a frequent event.

Things were better now that Daddy was home. Still, there were nights when Wanda would catch a glimpse of her mother sitting alone in her father's chair, tears drifting slowly down her cheeks.

When he was in the hospital, Momma had refused to leave his side, taking her meals in trade at the hospital kitchen. She slept upright in a chair next to his traction bed. Grandpa Cox and Aunt Edith took over at home, and everyone worked in shifts to keep the household afloat. Wanda helped too, taking messages and greeting hotel guests alongside Mrs. Spain.

Wanda slipped in behind her mother at the dressing table. She tried to keep silent, but couldn't help letting out a tiny sob. Floy turned to see her youngest standing there. She wiped the tears away with her sleeve and took Wanda up on her knee.

"You're getting to be too big for this."

Wanda shook her head no, and hugged her mother tightly.

"You can go with Grandpa, Mom. I'll stay and take care of Davey." Wanda whispered, "He's the only one who really needs it anyway."

Floy couldn't help but grin and ran her fingers through her bright red hair. "And you would, too. I know that."

"He listens to me."

"Yes, he does." *And sometimes, his father, too.* Though not so much, lately. Ever since Davey had taken a job at the Spain Barns, his independent streak had been widening.

Everyone else was in the street with her father and brothers. Their Chevrolet wagon was all packed up and ready to go; they were only waiting for Floy to come outside to say their last goodbyes. This time, there would be no stopping John Cox. Brother Irvon had showed up with a handful of gold nuggets and a newspaper full of help wanted ads.

Davey had said goodbye already, after a last arm wrestling match with his cousins Alpha and Omega. He left with a wave of his hand - gone off to hunt on the mesa, or to spend another evening singing and dancing with Artemio Cabrera and the Mexican boys.

Dee had given his father-in-law a full embrace and was back at the garage, determined to put in a full day's work despite his hobbling gait.

Things had finally begun to settle down in Wellton.

The accident had scrambled half-a-dozen lives. Floyd Strickland was killed instantly. Sven Jorgensen lost his right arm at the shoulder. Mr. Spain was forced to hire extra help at the barns; he was kind enough to put Davey on and pay him a grown man's wages, even though it was only part-time. Madeline Spain had adopted almost everyone it seemed - the whole Bailey family was either working at the garage, in the hotel or at the café.

When the doctor bills came due, they were tiny. Floy asked about it, but all the Indian hospital would say was something about 'an anonymous benefactor'. Floy felt relieved and yet somehow ashamed. Ashamed that she had misjudged Madeline in all of her imagined jealousies.

Floy sank into the warmth of her daughter's embrace, grateful for the ones who stayed behind.

Family ties had always formed the boundaries of her life. It never really mattered to Florence Cox Bailey where she lived, as long as she had the comfort of her loved ones all around her. Now, they were leaving, taking part of her with them. She could already feel the empty space around her father's absence.

Dee was on the mend at least, and sister Edith had found her heart at the Rosebud Café, determined to marry young Slim Parker. Like Davey, Edith felt at home in this little desert town, so Daddy felt free to make his way to the golden west.

Floy held her little Wanda, not so little anymore, and wiped away both their tears. They walked outside, hand in hand, ready to say goodbye one more time.

THE DAY WAS WARM AND STILL, with barely a breeze. We'd been driving around Wellton for ten minutes, and Doc seemed to be a little disoriented.

"We used to play down by the packing sheds. Not much left now. I'm not sure where the old town went."

When the new highway came in, the old main street through the center of town lost its prominence. Only the railway had kept to its original path. Some new school buildings were here and there, interspersed with empty lots, single-family homes and abandoned houses. We saw a concrete-block strip mall, a freestanding laundromat, and a Quikmart convenience store with a double set of gas pumps. An irrigation canal marked the edge of the mesa. To the east, a large mobile home park masked the scant outline of a parched municipal golf course. The structures were spaced incoherently, on a grid that mixed the old with the very old and the somewhat new.

Doc studied the landscape as we drove along, trying to adjust to the vastly different surroundings. Eventually, we came to a railroad bed with a single set of tracks. He insisted that we turn west and follow them as best we could.

After a minute, we came to an abandoned freight landing attached to a long adobe building. A double railroad siding sat next to it and further down, a number of three-sided sheds with corrugated roofs.

"That's it," he said. "Though it ain't much now. They used to pack boxcars full of produce out of here. Alfalfa, too." Doc let out a deep breath. "Kept a big ice house down at the end of the tracks."

I stopped the car. We both got out and stretched our legs in the empty station yard. Pop leaned across the hood and flicked his cigarette butt into the dirt.

"Damn."

The second half of the 20th Century had come down hard on Wellton. As new structures spread out to replace the old, the original town had simply disappeared, as if gravity had randomly compressed it into nothingness.

"Where was the hotel from here?" I wondered aloud.

Doc straightened up, turned a slow 180 degrees, and pointed. "That-a-way, I think…" He peered back at the packing sheds. "I took a job down here after Dad got hurt."

"What did you do?"

"Packed ice. Peeled produce. Whatever we could." He pulled his papers from a shirt pocket and started to roll another cigarette. "We had to work, wasn't any way around that. If you wasn't in school, then you had to make your own way. Couldn't sit around the house making baskets."

Pop pushed his hat back and wiped his brow. "We all had jobs, either working at the garage filling in for Dad, or out on the mesa with one of the dairy barns. My sisters worked at the hotel, cleaning rooms."

I looked out in the general direction he'd indicated. The long rectangular sides of two old house trailers were stacked together, bordered by low flat rooftops and an empty lot. I tried to picture what had happened to the little desert town that I'd heard so much about. Something caught my eye above the trailers. "How big was that salt cedar you said was out front of the hotel?"

"About 30 feet tall, I'd say, maybe a little more." Pop lit his cigarette. "Course I was quite a bit smaller in them days." He grinned as he exhaled and leaned back against the '56.

It was good to see him relax. Ever since we'd arrived, the years seemed to be pressing down on him, like they'd done with the town. "Let's take a ride. Maybe we can find Bakers Tanks."

Pop straightened up again. "Yes sir, that's a plan." Over the years, he'd told me a dozen times about the hidden water hole where he trapped wild horses with his friends.

"But first I want to take a look at something," I said.

We got back in the car. Betsy rumbled back to life, and we made a wide circle out of the railroad yard. I kept to the route we'd followed along the tracks, turned north on Dome Street, then doubled back on Arizona Avenue. The neighborhood was mostly small homes and trailers. A couple of men were working on a rusty-white pickup truck while barefoot kids played in the street. We passed a little blue building on the corner with an unlit Budweiser sign and a thin gravel parking lot.

I could see the chopped silhouette of a large salt cedar tree on the right, about twenty yards beyond the blue building. The big tree had probably stood there for seventy years, but only its massive trunk remained, with just a few volunteer branches climbing into the sunlight.

"Stop here." Pop said suddenly. We parked beside a deep lot with a chain link fence out front; two old cars on concrete blocks obstructed most of the view. We had passed right by it on our earlier drive through town. The old tree sat about thirty paces behind the fence. It had been cut down and burned back long ago, but its crown root had survived, sending out fresh shoots of green-grey. Those long limbs were what I'd seen waving above the rooftops from the railroad yard.

"Is this the hotel?" I asked.

"I think maybe so." Doc got out of the Ford and stepped between the wrecked cars. He slipped through a gap in the fence. "Least ways, it sure could be."

The remnants of an old adobe structure stood silently at the rear of the vacant lot. It was open to the elements, with all the doors and windows broken or gone, the hardware fallen on its floors. The back end of the building was completely missing, as if torn off by some giant hand. Silently, we walked inside, the crunch of broken glass under our heels, a slight breeze blowing through the battered window frames.

"Yep." Pop seemed to breathe in the years, and see the place for what it once might have been. "This is it." He pointed out front. "You can see where the big porch used to be out here. And this is where you came in and sat." He turned again. "There was rooms all along the back - and a kitchen." His pace quickened. He stood by the rear of the building. "And out here some little cabins they built that you could stay in."

He stepped back through the doorway and was suddenly oriented, as if a bright map had emblazoned itself onto his mind. "Right down there is where the garage was." He pointed southwest to the corner intersection. "And about three doors up we had our little house." We walked toward the street and he stopped by the big tree.

"Dang, this thing must have growed sixty feet tall before they cut it down." Doc peered at the great stump, its slim, green branches reaching for the daylight.

"How big was it when you were here?"

"We used to play in it. Climb up and scare the hotel guests." Doc cocked his chin. "Used to piss off Mrs. Spain something awful. I don't think we could get our arms around that thing now if we tried."

Pop headed for the break in the fence, stopped and turned to face me. His voice held a kind of amused resignation. "Well, that's all that's left of it, now."

"Plenty for me," I said.

It was true. There was something timeless about the great old tree and its desperate branches. The raw smell of the bark, the crust of salt on its leaves, and the big empty lot with all its broken bits of past left behind. Everything there called to me. I looked down the street at the little Mexican kids playing in the sand. For a moment, I could see the town where Pop lived, see it through his eyes, how the desert sun must have felt in the mornings, and what the sound of the birds might have been at night. I looked at the little bar down the road, and I didn't even want a drink.

"Let's stop here for a minute." I motioned to the blue building. "I want to ask about the hotel." Doc gave me a puzzled look and I replied. "C'mon, we can have a soda pop."

We walked along the edge of the road to the pale blue building. The aluminum screen door complained bitterly as I opened it, and my eyes went fuzzy at the sudden adjustment from the bright noonday sun. The inside of the building was dark and unoccupied, with a single wooden bar on the right side, fronted by five or six round bar stools. A few empty tables with dark plastic tablecloths stood against the opposite wall. A dimly lit jukebox was the only light at the edge of a tiny dance floor.

A large man behind the bar turned to see us, somewhat surprised, as if we might not be the people he'd expected, or had come through the door at the wrong time of day.

"Hello there," I said. There was no reply. The man was much older than I thought at first, and more round than large. His dark hair was ragged and thinning, with the look of black dye fading into grey.

"We were just visiting next door," I offered. "That's the old Spain hotel, isn't it?"

For a moment he looked wounded. An opaque haze fell across his eyes. "You want something?"

Doc had moved to the bar. He leaned forward, squinting in the half-light.

"I'll have a Coke with ice." I turned to Doc. "Pop?"

"Same."

The barman turned to a metal ice chest behind, scooped some shaved ice into a pair of short glasses, then opened a blue can of soda. He poured half of the can into each glass, placed them on the bar and turned away.

I put a five-dollar bill on the bar, picked up one glass, and slid the other one to Doc. The cola was bitter and tasted of artificial sweetener. "We went next door and took a look around," I said, playing the role of the curious stranger. "My friend used to live here, a long time ago."

The man turned and glanced at Doc, and for the first time, I got a good look at his face. It was swollen and heavy like he was, flushed with too much blood in bad circulation. He had a dripping discharge from his flat nose, and his breath seemed short and labored.

"How long have you lived here?" I asked, still probing.

"A while," he said. He slipped the five into a cash drawer and put two dollars change on the worn wooden bar. I pushed the remaining bills toward him with a questioning gesture. He took the tip, and in one smooth motion the bills disappeared and a handkerchief wiped the mucous flow beneath his nose.

"You're Huey Spain, aren't you?" Pop's words rang out like a church bell in the empty bar room. They seemed to hang in the air.

I stood and looked, and looked again. He was about the right age; beyond that I wouldn't know.

"No." There was nothing else from him, no recognition, no surprise, not even a convincing denial.

"I'm Dave Bailey," Doc said with a broad smile. "Do you remember me?"

"No." The man turned away and fiddled with his handkerchief, swiping quickly at his broad nose. He coughed a low, hacking cough, wet with congestion.

"Dave Bailey," Pop offered once again. "We used to know each other, way back when..."

The rough cough continued; the soiled cloth gathered spittle from his lips in reflex. The barman shook his head, turned and seemed to disappear into the wall behind him.

I put my glass down and wiped my hands on my jeans. "Maybe you know Huey Spain, then?" I stepped closer to the end of the bar.

The fluorescent buzzing of the jukebox and a muffled cough was the only sound in the room.

"Well, good luck to you, then." Doc never even picked up his glass, never said another word in that room, just looked me in the eye and pointed his head towards the door.

"Thank you, sir." I picked up an open book of matches from an ashtray on the bar. The grey man huddled in the corner, his back three-quarters turned, stone silent.

We stepped out into the light and the air. I inhaled deeply, noticing I'd half-held my breath inside the darkened room.

"Maybe he thought you were the law," Doc grinned. I had forgotten about my smooth white cowboy hat, the kind I saw as a kid on Roy Rogers. I'd taken to wearing one, and a crisp leather jacket, when I traveled with Pop.

"You think so?" I asked, half-imagining.

"Not really."

We laughed at the idea of me being any kind of authority, but the odd tension that we both felt still remained.

Then we got in the car and drove away.

HONEY IN THE HIVE

Idaho-Maryland Mine
Grass Valley, California

EVERYTHING WAS WET, either soaked from the drops that fell incessantly from the ceiling, or moist with the mist that surrounded every breath. Water would collect in the slightest depression, the crease in the top of your shoe, the thin cracks along the nape of your neck, or in any junction of anything that was dry before you came down in the skips.

The descent was always the worst. Even after he knew the bottom was going to drop out every time, Davey's stomach could never reconcile itself to the inevitable. He'd heard that the sudden fifty-foot lurches were a kind of baptism for newly hired muckers, to give them a feel for the shaft and take the edge off their imagined fears with a taste of real terror.

Perhaps it was for his benefit, so he waited patiently until he recognized everyone on the skip as old hands, certain that at last, he could let himself relax. And then, just as he inhaled the rushing air, the steel car would fall headlong into the mine with no resistance on the cable, and his insides would fly up into his throat. After a while, it dawned on him that the man in the shaft house had no idea who was in the skips, only that three bells had sounded, and it was time to lower away.

Once down below, it wasn't so bad. At least the floor wasn't liable to drop out from under you, and the walls of the drift were solid, if unrelenting. Davey Bailey was six weeks in the Idaho-Maryland, six weeks and seven-hundred feet underground, ten hours down and fourteen hours out. He thought it something of a lark, and except for the harrowing drop, more of an adventure than a job. He'd done heavy digging before, and by his standards, a yard an hour was poor purchase for a good man with a shovel, even flat on your back with only six inches breathing room above your head.

Bailey was a mucker, one of the subterranean moles that moved into the drifts after the blasting crews, clearing away the rubble through spaces that would barely accommodate his body. Wedged between the face of the old shaft and the new, he would shovel and rake the cracked rock past his torso and into the chutes for the pusher, who dumped it in the ore cars destined for the main shaft and the stamp mills above.

His small frame always guaranteed Davey the tighter crevices; older and larger men would work the standing faces. He doubted his foreman had ever seen him erect for more than the length of a smoke break. The other men would sit, loading their pipes or swapping lies, but Davey would always stand, as much to restore his circulation as to break the monotony of the horizontal. He'd strip down and pour his water bucket over his head, letting the cool liquid send steam spinning off his shoulders. Stretched out like a cat, he'd rub his body dry with a towel, then wrap the rag like a hood under his helmet. Some of the older miners called him a tidy fool, but it wasn't for dirt's sake that he performed his little ritual.

It was the damn stinking wet that plagued him; walls dripping like cold, muddy sponges, carrying a chill that numbed his bones. He must have been on the desert too long, he craved heat. His showers were meant for the pure pleasure of getting dry, if only for a few moments. Nine hundred feet down, the temperature was about 50 degrees year round, and the moisture would work its way through almost everything. If it weren't for the giant pumps that ran 24 hours a day, the entire mine would be underwater.

His Uncle Irvon had said the coldest place in the world was some mountain in Tibet, where your breath would freeze before it could get past your nose. Davey promised himself never to travel further north than the Canadian border; frozen glory was better left to the newsreels and Admiral Byrd. At least you could climb out of the Idaho-Maryland, and overhead, Grass Valley could get downright hot.

It was two years since the Bailey clan had moved to California. Uncle Irvon had led the way; he'd taken a foreman's job at the Empire Mine down the road. When he returned to Wellton with tales of cheap land and plentiful work, Grandpa Cox had caught the itch, too. If it weren't for his dad's accident, the rest of the Baileys probably would have followed along even sooner.

At first, Davey had hated the move. But as he watched his father build their stick-frame house and his sisters find their brand new beaus, he began to feel better about the whole thing. Their new home was right next to Grandpa Cox's cabin on Union Hill, and anyone could see that his mother was as happy as she'd been in years.

He still missed the desert, missed the distant sunsets and the stony quiet of the surrounding mountains. There was wild land around Grass Valley, not the same as his roughneck wilderness, but wild nonetheless, with plenty of buck deer, bear and even the occasional mountain lion.

His father found steady work at a Roseville auto dealership, making good money. He'd built quite a reputation as the best mechanic within a hundred miles of Sacramento. Even the Highway Patrol heard about him and were sending their cruisers to be supercharged.

Davey was glad for his family - they all seemed happy here. But it wasn't the same as his wild Arizona.

Sometimes, he and Wanda would sit out on the porch and listen to the night birds, just to see if they could hear the same ones that used to call in Wellton. Wanda was the only one who seemed to care as much as he did about leaving their little town. She was still a desert rat inside, yearning for the sand and the cactus and the quiet that was so complete you could hear your own heartbeat.

But like her big sisters, Wanda was learning to like boys. There were plenty of them, too, what with three girls courting age in the Bailey household. Grandpa Cox practically lived by his parlor window at night, watching the porch swing next door to make sure that all was well with the young maidens. Consequently, Davey did all his courting out by the rock quarry, in an old Model A that his father had rebuilt for him, as did any other boy who knew about the close proximity and volcanic temperament of his mother's father.

That Model A was going to be his ticket out of here. That's why he'd signed up to work in the mines. If he stuck it out long enough, he could make his own grubstake and take off for the desert. He'd been back a couple of times already, once last summer on the freights, and once with Uncle Irvon the summer before that.

His mother was beside herself when he told her he'd decided to quit school. For Davey there was no way around it; he could make a man's wages in the mines, and hell, he was all of sixteen now and could make decisions for himself. She laughed when he told her that, and said to try that thought out on his father. Needless to say, she was right.

"Don't be in such a hurry to grow up, son." His father had put his book down and leaned forward in his chair. "It ain't all it's cracked up to be." There was quiet concern in his dad's voice. "Ask yourself - do I have good reason for what I'm about to do?"

"I want to make my own way, Dad." He'd seen how his father had struggled, all the sacrifices he'd made for so many years. It was high time he helped out. There were plenty of good reasons. One of them he didn't mention - the girl he'd met last summer in the packing sheds, the same one he'd like to find again someday.

In the dark of the drift, he savored the sound of her guitar and the smell of almonds in her hair. The Imperial Valley would be his first stop on the way back to Wellton.

Lost in his imagination, he lost the grip on his pickaxe, too, sending it careening off the side of the drift and into his forehead. The resulting howl echoed through the mains, followed by a long stream of curses, more at his own carelessness than the growing lump across his forehead.

"If a cheap tongue could move rock, we'd hire out for sailors, *n'est-ce pas?*"

There was no need to see the dark face at the bottom of the drift. He would recognize that rough French accent anywhere.

"Blackie, you'd never get them past the six-hundred mark." Davey wiped the pooling blood from his brow. "They'd figure they was bound for Hell."

"And they might be at that." Blackie reached for his kerchief and ran it across his broad neck. "Slide down out of there and let's have a look at you."

"No need, I slipped a stroke, that's all."

"I don't recall asking, *Monsieur Bailey.*"

Davey scraped the last few cobbles out from behind him and into the chute. He slid down the slight incline and onto the floor of the main tunnel. No sense arguing. Blackie Verdonne was a powderman, and short of the shift foreman, straw boss. Blackie placed the charges and supervised the drilling, making sure each blast sent down just enough rock for the next mucking crew, but not enough to collapse the drift. He was used to having his way.

As Davey's feet touched solid rock, he felt a strong hand grasp his jaw.

"Stand still and shut up. That's a nasty little gash you've got there."

Davey looked down at the Frenchman's face. The bright yellow fire of burning carbide gas dotted his eyes. Blackie was one of the few old-timers who still used a carbide lamp, preferring its milky glow to the steadier beam of the new battery lights. He was a small man, smaller than Davey, but broad, and hard as the drifts he worked in. Davey felt his chin was set in steel as Blackie worked his head from side to side.

"How many?" Blackie's hand slid in front of the glow, his fingers spread wide apart. Davey's head was throbbing; he struggled to get a focus, counting quickly up to five and then six. He wasn't willing to let the Frenchman know he'd lost sight of his own senses.

"Five," Davey mumbled under his breath. He tried to slip his jaw free and square his head.

"Six." Blackie released his head with a twist. Free of his grasp, Davey fell sideways against an ore car. "This one, she cuts down on the lucky guess." Blackie held a single stick of dynamite between his second and third fingers. He slipped it back in his pack. "Don't make me wait for a mucker, lad."

"Yes, sir."

"That's more like it." Blackie turned and headed for the main shaft. "Stow your gear and come with me."

Davey did as he was told and followed the powderman to the main. He waited as Blackie signaled for a skip. The steel car came to a stop at their station landing, and Davey got in beside him. He wondered if his small show of independence would cost him his job. As the bells sounded for their ascent, he decided not to care, if petty men and cheap tricks were the fashion down below. The steep drop took him by surprise. His head began to spin; he expected the car to rise and not fall. He swayed as the skip came to rest at the thousand-foot level.

"Steady, now." Blackie lifted the boy from the car with one arm. He gathered him by the torso, moving quickly down the main tunnel. "That little slip was worse than you thought."

The powderman was right. His stomach was still uneasy and they were well off the car. The bells for the lift weren't coming from the shaft but inside his head and he started to say something but the words came out like gurgles, because he'd never been to the thousand foot level before and didn't realize it was so much colder down here, since his legs were numb and his battery must be down and then there was just the darkness.

FRESH FROM THE SMITH, the bull steel was sharp and cut with every stroke. He could feel its hot breath on the downswing of the jacks, their hammers striking cadence like heartbeats. Stone chips stung his eyes and salt tears filled his mouth, his tongue dry leather in the sun. He could hear the pistons in the pumps, warm air above for cold water below. There were no lamps in this drift, just the ring of the bits as they crushed black rock into dust, filling his lungs to send him scrambling for the surface. He was crawling now, scratching his way up the side of the shaft towards the beckoning light and clear air.

"Feeling any better?" A distant voice slid in between the pounding at his temples, a blurry silhouette across the pulsing light above. He was out of the drift, but the jacks were still working.

"Nasty cut, that."

His hand moved automatically to his forehead, the feel of skin replaced by the woven texture of gauze. He caught a whiff of sulfa and drifted with the smell.

"Don't try to get up." The silhouette was speaking, words dripped like moisture from the walls. "What's your name, son?"

He knew only one thing: he was in a small room. He'd never been there before.

"Where am I?" The room was cut from stone, full of wooden boxes and pieces of string. He felt light, unencumbered.

"Powder room." The silhouette had a face, dark but friendly. It bent down close to look at him. "Remember your name yet?"

A weight like water descended, carrying his name. He floated to the surface. Blackie was there. "Blackie."

"*C'est moi, c'est la vérité.*" A toothy smile appeared within the fog. "True, that's me. You're Davey Bailey, in case that's slipped you."

"I... guess it did." Davey's hands felt heavy. He pressed his fingers against his eyes. "Got any water? I'm dry."

Blackie moved to one of the powder cases and lifted the lid. "This won't put a fire out, but it might help your headache."

The liquid burnt the back of his throat, did a cartwheel in his gullet and landed like a stone in his belly. Davey fought the urge to retch and sat bolt upright. His eyes sprang open.

"Good French brandy, that." Blackie smiled as he brought the oval-shaped bottle to his lips. "Purely medicinal." The stained cork squeaked like a noisy rat as it slid home. "I keep her with the powder, away from prying eyes."

The lurch in his belly was replaced by a spreading warmth.

Blackie pulled a tin ladle from a hanging bucket; he bent down to bring a dipperful of water to the boy's lips. "Now, drink this. Slow and easy."

"Thanks." The cool water quenched the heat in the back of his throat. Davey swallowed hard, then swilled and spat.

"Not two hours in a man's house and you foul the floor." The powderman tossed the ladle back in the fire bucket. "You'll get no calls from Neal Street with those manners."

Davey pictured the burly Frenchman in a Neal Street parlor. The mine owners and their fancy ladies lived high on the ridge in Nevada City - the miners down below in Grass Valley. He flashed a grin. "We Baileys are working folk from

Union Hill. Don't think we'll ever see the insides of Nevada City." The throbbing in his forehead brought him back to the moment.

"Thanks, Blackie."

"Think nothing of it, *mon ami*." Blackie opened his lunch pail and took out a small round tin. "I let the cave rats nursemaid you most of the time."

Davey glanced around the room in reflex. He saw no rats, and no sign of how long he'd been there. Down below, there's a numbing sameness to the day; no change in the light and no clocks to watch, only the passing of the bells to tell the hour. He'd worked graveyard ever since he signed up, 7pm to 6am - that way he could still finish high school. It was the best deal he could strike with his father. He wondered how the day shift stood the lack of sunlight in their lives. "How long was I out?"

"Like I said, two - three hours." Blackie slipped a key into the wire band around the crimson tin, and with a cock of his wrist, peeled the top. "Hungry?" Blackie peeled out a tiny fish; the oil on the little anchovy glistened, first on the fish, then on a corner of Blackie's beard.

Davey's stomach rebelled at the thought. "No thanks."

"I would have taken you topsides, but I had a big string to set." The shiny fish continued to disappear, one after another. "*Un bang grandé.*"

It was quiet in the stone room. Davey could hear the grinding of small bony scales. He fought down a wave of nausea and pulled himself upright, leaning cautiously against a wooden timber to steady the tilting floor. "I better get back in the drift before I'm missed."

"Missed? *Merde*, you're long past your shift." Blackie dropped the empty tin into his lunch pail. "Besides, that lazy fool never comes below on a Sunday. He's halfway to Sacramento by now."

Blackie was right. The shift boss was a choirmaster for the Methodist Church in Dixon. He always left early on Saturday nights. Davey didn't like him and he didn't like Davey, but there'd be no trouble about it today.

"You think you can walk?"

"Yeah. My head hurts a little, but probably no worse than it should." Davey examined his surroundings for the first time.

He was in a small room, barely ten by ten, reinforced with heavy timbers, and stacked to the ceiling with powder cases and round cans of fuse. He'd never seen so much dynamite in one place, even back when his dad and Benny Gibbs hauled nitroglycerine.

Blackie twisted the top off a waterproof can and spun a line of dark grey cord onto the floor. With a single motion, he looped the fuse and cut it, spinning it onto his shoulder like a lariat. As he moved towards the door, the Frenchman paused, stroking his black beard. He considered the young mucker carefully. "*Allons-y.* I will show you something no man has ever seen."

Davey wondered at the invitation, then stepped gingerly to the door of the chamber. He steadied himself on the large bars that crossed the threshold. They were heavy and smooth; dark brown metal coated green with vergris.

"Copper," Blackie said. "Can't make a spark. No iron, no steel inside of here."

Davey shuddered at the thought of a stray spark, then remembered Benny Gibbs once more. He would tell his dad how he got the bump on his head, but not where he had spent the morning.

"Catch." Blackie tossed him a lump of clay, about the size of a tobacco pouch. It was heavier than it looked and surprised him, slipping from his hands despite a desperate attempt to keep it. The black clay fell to the stone floor with a dull thud, and Blackie scooped it up, grinning. He placed it gently in Davey's hands. "It's only punk, *mon chér*. No worry about that stuff."

Davey let out the breath that was stuck in his throat.

"Here's what you worry about." The bearded man opened his hand and rolled his index finger gently over three shiny caps. They were small, about an inch long, with a tiny spike protruding from each end. "Fulminate of mercury. Just a little heat or a little bump..." his eyes widened, "and boom."

The gleaming caps bounced in Blackie's palm and Davey winced.

Blackie carefully folded the blasting caps into his kerchief and pressed them into his breast pocket. The powderman pulled a thick latch over the bars on the wooden door and padlocked them with a heavy brass Yale. "Now comes the fun part, Davey." The Frenchman nodded his way and turned to go. "Bring your hot potato along, and we'll put it to good use."

The young mucker followed Blackie Verdonne into the shaft, fingering his lump of clay in the gloomy silence.

"SHE'S GOT AN OILY FEEL when she's fresh." Blackie tilted the fuse into his lamplight and slit the rough end of the dynamite with his knife. "Never use a dry stick, all the nitro's been boiled off. She'll blow you straight to hell, *tout de suite.*"

Davey listened closely to the Frenchman. He'd been fascinated by explosives ever since he'd met Benny Gibbs years before; Davey had tried to learn what he could about the magic powder then, but his father would have none of it. "That stuff doesn't care how smart you are, or how tough. It'll kill you all the same." Turned out his dad was right where Benny was concerned. Still, Dave had heard the same speech about fast cars and whiskey - seems like a lot of things that make life more interesting also make it shorter.

"Hand me that punk." Davey gave the clay ball to the powderman and Blackie peeled it into three sections, rolled a brass cap and a fuse into each and pressed them, one at a time, into three separate holes in the rock face. "You don't have to cap every hole, just enough to set off the other ones. If your powder's fresh, everything blows."

The stone face was dotted with deep punctures, each one filled with dynamite. On the way in, Blackie had told him how he'd drilled all of those holes alone, on account of this being some kind of special project for the big bosses. Davey figured he was being greased for another practical joke until he noticed the subtle differences in the shaft. Unlike others in the mine, there were no drifts moving out on the sides, only the one long incline that took them from the thousand-foot level to an isolated dead end. It was unwired and unlit, the only dark main in the Idaho-Maryland.

They had followed a single compressed air line up the shaft, stapled into the rock every twenty feet. Blackie said that a regular crew took the work this far; the Frenchman had been told to clear the last ten feet on his own. It was possible; Davey had seen Blackie hoist one of the heavy pneumatic drills all by himself, with no tripod, and muscle it two-foot deep for a blasting hole. He wondered how long the powderman had been working at the fifty-odd holes in the rock face before them.

"Here's where the young don't get any older." Blackie's tone brought Davey back to the present. "Splicing and timing." The powderman twirled three separate fuses into one, letting them converge for a hands length before he cut off the excess. "Let them run together too long and the heat cuts them apart - too short and they won't stay lit."

"Follow me." Blackie started back down the incline, looping fuse off his shoulder onto the floor as he walked. "That happens, and the next shift comes in on top of twenty sticks, just waiting under a ton of rock." Blackie looked his way and lifted a brow.

"First mucker finds the blasting cap wins a prize."

Davey had heard the story before - an entire crew blown away by the single swing of a pickaxe. Whatever remained was sent to the stamp mills, the blood crushed out with the ore.

The flare strike of a kitchen match lit the walls of the drift, its sudden glow casting long shadows against the stone. Blackie lit the stub of a fat cigar and drew deep until the tip shone red. He touched the ember to the end of the fuse. Like an angry snake, the grey cord hissed and spun, a thin, red line spitting smoke as it ran behind them toward the rock face above.

"Better get moving." Blackie lifted his pack and sauntered down the main, puffing casually on his short cheroot. Davey kept pace beside him, resisting the urge to break into a jog, but mindful that his feet were moving quicker and quicker despite himself.

"Don't get excited." The little Frenchman seemed for all the world to be strolling along the Champs-Élysées. "You'll just fall down, and then where will you be?"

Davey smiled in spite of himself, his gruff companion's expression a reminder of his Grandpa Cox, who never failed to use those same words in the midst of any melee. Davey matched his step to the pace of his guide, embracing the inevitablity of the impending blast.

"That's better." Blackie reached out his arm and held the young man's shoulders as they moved through the shaft. "I knew I'd marked you right. Takes good sense to see your way around down here."

Davey didn't have time to reply before the powderman grabbed his collar and jerked him sharply to the side. He hadn't noticed it on the way in, but there was a deep depression in the shaft, almost a false corner. The powerful Frenchman held him tight within it, his body pressed flat like piece of tin in a steel vise.

"Fire in the hole," Blackie hissed, his eyes less than an inch away from Davey's. The smell of stale smoke, brandy and oiled fish curled at the young mucker's nose as a crashing hurricane wind blew everything away.

DAVEY COULD HEAR THE FRENCHMAN scurrying up ahead.

"Sacré bleu!"

The force of the blast had sent his head reeling again; he struggled to keep his bearings as they returned up the shaft. Great clouds of dust moved past him, fouling his vision and filling his lamplight with billows of grey. The air was choking thick with sulfur, forcing him back against the wall to suck down each chalky breath.

"Get on up here where it's clear!" Blackie's voice echoed in the drift. "You'll drown in that dust if you stay down below!"

Davey heard the sound of tumbling stone above and pushed himself up the corridor, not daring to draw breath. He held his kerchief across his nose and mouth to filter the bitter haze. The dust began to settle as he moved further along, allowing for an occasional desperate gasp. His lamplight garnered scant detail on the murky path. He'd never gone in so soon after a blast; usually the powdermen would set their charges over a shift change, allowing a full ten hours to dissipate the fog of debris. The walls of the drift were still shuddering with the impact; sand poured out of fine cracks amidst the stone, timbers groaning under the shifting mass. Davey thought himself in a fine mess, and wondered what sort of madman he was following into this dark tomb.

Davey could see a dim sliver of light ahead. The sound of a pickaxe against loose rock pricked his ears. He had half a mind to turn around and leave the powderman to fend for himself. Davey's head was clear enough, and by all accounts he was long past quitting time. There was little opportunity to consider the notion. He had to throw himself to one side and then another to dodge the keg-sized stones that were tumbling down the shaft.

"Keep a sharp eye, Davey!" Blackie's carbide lamp lurched out of the darkness and into Davey's face, the powderman's eyes wide with excitement. "I tell you, you'll never see another day like this."

The little Frenchman was covered with dust and bleeding from both hands. As quickly as he appeared, he turned and scrambled back up the shaft, crawling over the hard scrabble like a crab. Davey hitched his step to keep up, bending low to avoid the rubble and stay to the path that Blackie had cleared. Cresting the broken pile, Davey's lantern light revealed a broken chamber hewn from the stone.

"Like the Mother of God!" Blackie wailed. The glow of his lamplight bounced like a mirror on the luminescent wall. "It's the Motherlode, *mon chér!* Sure as I'm standing here!"

Blackie's laughter bounced from wall to wall, spinning inside Davey's head. Their ghostly lantern beams defined the sight before them. Davey had seen gold before, and lots of it. Every man-child in Nevada County had. The foothills were shot with it, in every creek and every river, in the Empire Mine, the Jamestown, the Lost Creek, and the Idaho-Maryland. But this bonanza was twenty-feet high and nearly thirty feet across, and not quartzite, vein or placer, but a great sheet of gold, smooth and yellow as butter, and thick as honey in the hive. Davey marveled at the wealth here, enough to buy anything anywhere.

"What would you do with it, boy?" Blackie grinned as if he'd caught a rainbow in his teeth. "What would you do?"

Davey let his mind wander for a moment - it filled up like a barrel in a waterfall. The hoarse ratchet of a rifle bolt stopped the water cold.

"Secure the area, gentlemen."

The crossing of their lantern beams put their number at five; two carried carbines, one a small surveyor's kit, and the other two nothing but their fat wallets and handkerchiefs. Davey had never seen their like before in the Idaho-Maryland Mine.

He wondered which one was Idaho.

WE WERE APPROACHING Tacna, Arizona on old US-80, about 12 miles east of Wellton. After 20 minutes of driving, we hadn't had much luck locating the road to Bakers Tanks. Doc had always gone there on horseback or in his old Model A, following one of the dry washes that led south into the edge of the Mexican desert. Now, some 50 years later, most of the original access points were blocked, either by broad fields of lettuce ringed with irrigation canals, or by high barbed-wire fences set out to discourage illegal immigration.

"Which way now, Pop?"

"I wouldn't know. Damn if they ain't moved everything, even the desert."

We saw a large painted sign for the MacElhaney Cattle Company, and Pop whistled softly to himself. "I wonder if that's Billie's old clan?"

"Billie?"

"Prettiest girl you ever saw. Least ways, when I saw her, she was." Doc took on a wistful look and I pressed the question.

"Girlfriend?"

"I guess you might say that." Doc hesitated for a moment. "On one of my trips down here… we were out in the desert trapping horses and took a little break, went in to Yuma to see a movie or something. She was right behind me in line. Me and the boys were talking about some horse that none of them could ride, and I said I could ride that sucker, you betcha'. Wasn't any horse that I couldn't ride in them days." He paused. "Or so I thought."

"And she liked that?"

"No, she asked me to put out my cigarette."

Pop laughed and so did I.

"We were standing in line, and she didn't like the smoke. So I did, and we got to talking and ended up watching that whole movie together." Pop tilted his head and looked at the unlit cigarette in his hand. "Hell, I couldn't tell you what that movie was about... not a damn thing."

I glanced his way, imagining the youthful suitor. I'd seen several photographs of him as a young man, one lovingly framed on a table at his sister's house in Lake Tahoe, and a few more treasured ones that she kept neatly folded inside a worn leather album. Doc was a striking young man, lean, eyes keenly focused, his straight blond hair long and swept loosely across his brow. Even at that age, he always kept a creased straw hat cocked halfway back on his head, with a bright smile that defied melancholy. Nowadays, he wore the same kind of hat, but his face was grizzled with stubble, his square jaw wrinkled by time.

"Anyway, she says to me, 'I've got a horse that you can't ride', and so I goes to her place the next day… and well, it wasn't a hard ride at all." His smile broadened, and then he looked straight ahead.

"Yes, sir. There's been three women that I've really loved in my life. Becky. That little gal in the packing sheds." He looked out the passenger window. "And Billie."

Down the road, a small white building sat at the edge of a green highway marker. The sign read: Tacna, AZ, pop. 239. The little cafe looked friendly enough, with folding tables, chairs out front and a red and black 'OPEN' sign placed in the front window. I pulled into the parking lot and shut the motor off.

"So what happened?" I asked.

"She and I spent most of that summer down here, off and on. Rode those horses all across the desert and who knows where."

Without the road sounds, the motor or the wind, the inside of the old station wagon grew stone quiet. Pop pursed his lips and spoke. "Her dad took a liking to me. Offered me and her a big horse ranch up Wyoming way, or a whole spread down here. But I turned 'em down."

"You mean as a wedding gift?"

"I suppose. But I wouldn't go for it. I looked right at him and said I was too young and had too much left to do. There was just too much that I still wanted to see. I thought for a second there he might shoot me." Dave's whole demeanor had changed, his head back, slumped against the seat. "Billie was there. It broke her up pretty bad. She went up north to have the baby."

The quiet in the car was deafening. Pop lit his cigarette and took a deep drag. I turned off the tape recorder and gestured toward the café door.

"Coffee?"

"You bet."

He pulled up on the chrome handle and the passenger door opened a few inches. "That one hurt. Still does sometimes." He stopped to gaze out the window.

"I think she had a little boy. At least that's what I heard."

THE NATURAL WAY OF THINGS

OCTOBER 1941

The Sonoran Desert
Arizona–Mexico border

DOC UNWOUND THE LEATHER STRAP from around his saddle horn
and lifted the water bag to his chest. Prying its cork cap from out of the pressed
metal gullet, he rolled the bag tight and folded the last few drops out of its belly
and into his mouth.

"That's the last of it, there'll be no more till morning." Like most people who
traveled alone, he made his own good company.

Astride the long rim of the mesa, he could see the three burros shuffling
single file into the mouth of a canyon, nearly a quarter-mile distant. He'd been
following loosely behind since he'd caught sight of them some two hours ago. The
canyon held the failing light of day in deep shadow, but he knew the burros would
be easy to track once inside, and not likely to climb unless they found water or
gathered up for the night.

A small brace of doves filtered down out of the reddening sky and slid
noiselessly into the shadow of the canyon walls.

There's water close by.

He didn't like to place his faith in burros alone. They were willing to range
for days, and none too particular about sulphur. But the doves were a sure sign.
Once, and sometimes twice a day, a dove would seek out water. Though prone to
secrecy, if you could spot them at dusk or dawn, you could bet that there was water
nearby.

Dave Bailey slid down off his saddle and loosened the cinch. The big chestnut mare stretched out for a mouthful of scrub grass, and he hefted the Mexican
rig off her withers and onto the ground. He tucked the saddle into the crook of a
mesquite tree that had scratched its way up through the sand. He'd camp here for
the night, and find the water come morning. Rattling down the rim of the mesa
in twilight was a fine way to break your mount's leg. Dave was in no hurry, and
sure of his reward.

It was only a matter of time.

He was three days out of Wellton, on El Camino del Diablo, the Devil's

Highway - the same thirsty track that had claimed so many settlers a hundred years before. Few folks believed in tales of good water and game out this far, but Dave had never come back without something to show for his trouble, and none the worse for wear.

This time, he figured to be gone for a while.

His head was still on fire and his thoughts were a smoky haze. Women were a puzzle he could never hope to solve. They gave so much and wanted so little. But right this minute, it was more than he had to give.

He unwrapped the newspaper from around the last bit of cheese round he'd bought from Mrs. Spain, and considered whether to borrow any life from the mesquite for his fire. He thought better of it; nights were mild this time of year, and his eyes had adjusted to the failing light. Besides, the old tree was fresh company for the night. No sense in chopping up one's companion just for firewood.

Doc didn't say much to the tree, and even less to his horse. He was partial to light conversation with animals, but never made long speech with any of his mounts, as it led to soft thoughts and a soft head where one's welfare and the animal's diverged. He'd water his horse from his canteen, but not at his own expense, and only if the extra distance bought survival for the both of them.

He'd always been amused by the strange affection movie cowboys lavished on their horses. He felt sure it meant they'd never spent much time taking care of the beast. Not since old King had he felt any real kinship with a horse. He pictured the big black gelding and wondered if he was still alive somewhere - maybe up on the mesa where Dave had let him loose, chewing on buffalo grass and farting into the wind. He thought he'd spied him once or twice before, at the edge of a mustang herd, running wild. The thought pleased him, and he glanced at the big chestnut mare, hobbled for the night some 15 feet away.

"Now, if a man could travel fifty miles on the back of a pretty woman... that would be a real chance for companionship." He spoke directly to the mare. "And a fine reason to carry more than one canteen."

For a bare moment, his thoughts turned to Billie. He shook them off with a wince, tucked his hat up under his head, rolled over and went to sleep.

MORNING ON THE DESERT carries a chill, no matter what the mercury. Doc rubbed his hands together for warmth, then bent over his poncho where he'd left it the night before. Stretched out above a depression scooped from the sand, a tiny hole in the poncho's middle formed the shape of a cone. Moving the surrounding pebbles aside, he wrung the canvas into the enameled cup below. He let the last few dewdrops wet his lips.

His horse stood some twenty yards away, a half-hobble twisted around its front legs. Doc had seen horses stray for miles in search of water, even hobbled all the way around. Some would crow hop, walking like a man does the breaststroke. This horse had never been so deep in the desert before, and like most town horses, couldn't smell water in a bucket.

The big mare nickered as Doc approached. He hoisted his saddle and tightened the cinch. Curling the stirrup backwards, he swung up and over in the vaquero manner, never trusting to fate the temperament of an animal known to spook at its own shadow. The best horseman he ever knew cracked his head like an egg on a town horse, all spit and polish and thousand-dollars' worth of thoroughbred. Plain horses, like plain women, made for level companions.

Maybe things would be different if she weren't so damn pretty.

A THIN LINE OF AMBER LIGHT was rising over the rim of the far canyon; morning was coming up quickly. Doc settled on a curling track off the mesa, carved by who knows how many years of one thing or another traveling down before him - perhaps the rocky path of some ancient dinosaur.

He pictured the time he and his dad had pulled some college boys out of a hard wash gone muddy in a sudden thunderstorm. Their professor was knee deep in red mud, sure of some sort of knighthood for a pile of old bones. Dave couldn't place any of the words the professor used; he talked more like a lawyer than a man who knew animals. His dad said they were the names of giant lizards that lived out here thousands of years ago, when the desert was more of a swamp than a sandpit.

He took the dinosaur tale to heart; there wasn't a night when his father wasn't reading about faraway places, or a journal from some university. But the bonehunters, they were just book smart, or they'd have known not to camp in a dry wash with storm clouds about. Doc flashed a grin at the rocky trail; more likely a sign of the three burros he'd been following.

He caught sight of the burros' track again in the soft sand of the canyon wash. It was an easy trail to follow. There'd been no rain for almost two months, and the thin cracks of dried mud were widening and going to dust. Doc didn't bother to keep quiet; he was hoping to flush the doves he'd spotted as he passed, making for a quicker path to water. It could be hidden up in the rocks, where the burros might not find it.

The gunshot took him by surprise. The sharp report rang out like a deep crack through the canyon, bouncing from wall to wall in the morning silence. The doves flushed from the high rocks; his horse bowed up as they banked down across his path, their wings beating with a wailful fluttering sound.

It was too much for the walnut-sized brain of the mare. She bolted sideways, turning in midair to hurtle headlong out of the canyon. Doc stayed in the saddle, more in testament to the high pommel of his vaquero rig than to his riding ability. The big horse made flight her only priority, and when Doc pulled up on the reins, the mare began to buck. Not the measured, rhythmic buck of a horse in the breaking pen, where Doc was master of discerning pattern and intent, but a rump-shuddering, headlong panic, made doubly dangerous by the soft footing and scattered rocks all along the trail. In the fraction of a second left to him, he took his best chance to stay in one piece.

As his horse barreled upward, he dropped his boots from the stirrups. Bracing against the saddle, he jerked the reins out hard to one side, pulling the horse's head nearly into his lap. Releasing the reins, he pushed off the horn, throwing his body out and away from the animal's path.

Her center of gravity pulled out from under her, the big mare fell head over heels into the dirt. Doc rolled his shoulders on impact, trying to make the best of a bad situation; he'd have done okay, had it not been for the prickly pear cactus that filleted his left leg. He raised his head and spat dirt, then felt along the edge of all his favorite bones.

Satisfied that everything was bruised but nothing broken, he looked over at his horse. The mare stood quietly, looking for all the world like she had never left the ground. Doc drew in a stomach-punched breath and stood up gingerly. Inventory: one broken rein, easily tied off, one shredded pair of pants, and one damn fool shooter due for a visit.

He checked his rig for damage. A scrape could work its way up to a breakdown, so he always carried scrap leather, an awl, and latigo lacing. After stitching his rein back together, he worked some oil into the saddle and checked his cinch straps for wear. His saddle was a good bit older than he was, but didn't show its years by the care he gave to it.

The horse was another issue.

Despite her relaxed appearance, the mare had taken quite a spill. Doc ran his hands over each of her legs, gently squeezing and prodding for any sign of a break or a splint. The horse had strong, straight legs; that's the reason he'd picked her out. And a hard head to boot, judging from the size of the gash that ran alongside it. The mare had rolled up and over on its head; the hair was burnt along the top of the neck, and part of one ear was left dangling. Sand in the wound had already dried up what little blood had flowed. Her legs were sound; Doc reckoned that the horse would heal up fine. She would never again be known as 'that chestnut mare', but instead by her one shredded ear. Still, by all rights, she might have been lame, and Doc thought better of the jar-headed town horse than he had before.

"You look as though you could use a drink." Doc settled into the saddle and turned the big horse back into the canyon. "I figure I can arrange that, seeing as how you ain't dead, like you could be." He had a good feeling for where the doves had flushed, and moved quickly up the canyon incline, knowing that the water would be close by.

Doc felt his horse shudder as they approached the spot where she had spooked; the doves were long gone, but the horse knew something bad had happened here. The mare began to snort, pacing in a rapid step, with little forward progress. Doc tried to soothe her with his voice and some firm encouragement from his heels.

Something more was in the air, and he brought her to a stop. Sliding to the ground, he looped his reins around a low jacinto bush. Silently, he pulled his rifle from the scabbard slung beneath his saddle. From around the edge of the rocks he heard a low scraping sound. Doc slid forward on the crest of a large boulder, slipping his hat off on its drawstring and onto his back. As he reached the top of the rock, he heard movement on the trail below and raised his rifle.

It was the burros.

Only two were standing, shuffling about the heaving body of the third. He could see where the bullet had passed through its shoulder, cracking the bone and rendering its left leg useless. From the blood spattered along the trail, he could tell they had climbed up here in a panic, racing from the sound and the piercing terror. His eyes quickly took in the surrounding canyon walls and the wash below. There was no sign of anyone else.

So he waited.

If the shooter meant to track this beast, it'd be short work with such a bloody trail. But Doc had a feeling this was more for sport, a single shot on a whim, and the son-of-a-bitch a poor marksman at that, with no intention of finishing the job he started.

Doc had no great affection for donkeys; they had fouled his traps too many times, and he'd shot them himself when they'd proved too bothersome. But he believed in a clean kill, and none just for sport. A burro on a spit was a decent meal, even off the desert. His Uncle Slim had built many a pit to barbeque burros, and the Mexicans in town had made fairly an art of it for la Fiesta de Guadalupe. He watched the animal's convulsions and decided he had waited long enough.

The other burros ran away as Doc slid down beside their wounded companion. The little jack groaned, gasping for breath, white foam flecked with blood flowing from its nostrils. Doc reached into his sheath and drew out the Barlow knife his father had given him when he was a boy. It was sharp as only an edge honed for forty years could be, and it slit the jugular of the little burro without hesitation. Doc watched as the animal's life bled out on the stone, then dressed the loin from the carcass and walked slowly back to his horse.

FINDING THE WATER was easy. Doc could see the big agave cactus from fifty yards away, its broad leaves glistening in the morning sun. There were dozens of cactus dotting the canyon walls, dull and tightly bound up like great, spiny artichokes, tucked away in any crevice where just a little shade or moisture might be found. But this one was different; it had a much darker hue, and unlike the others, its sharp fronds spread out to greet the light.

Dismounting beside the great cactus, Doc let his reins slip to the ground. After all they'd been through, he figured the mare wouldn't wander; she could sense water nearby. He moved carefully around the edge of the agave and bent low to gather a handful of dirt. It was soft and moist. The big cactus was wedged in close to the canyon wall, grown out of a widening crevice that went from inches to yards apart at the top of the rise.

Doc examined the crevice, drawn by moisture and a sure sense of reward. Three feet up the rock face, his fingers found a small iron pipe, almost rusted shut, but still dripping a tiny bounty. The mare nickered as she caught the scent, and he moved to collect his prize.

"Angelo will never believe this." Clearing away the orange-brown crust, he looped his canteen's drawstring over the pipe. Clear water fell drop after drop into the gullet. "Now, who says there ain't water on this old desert?"

Doc leaned against the dark crevice, pushed his straw hat above his brow and smiled. Almost by reflex, he reached into his shirt pocket for his works. The flat leather pouch opened easily, and his fingers settled smoothly into the memorized motion that produced one of his handmade cigarettes. The coarse tobacco was getting dry; most of its moisture had leached into the leather. He might have to compromise and start using one of those fancy foil pouches.

"But I'll be danged if I'll smoke a store-bought," he muttered at the mare.

His cigarette lit, he considered the battered horse before him. She wasn't half so mule-headed as he once supposed. The mare was glued to the spot where he dropped the reins; she was ground-tied after all. He wondered if dropped reins would've stopped her buck; he'd heard tell of horses that well tied to ground.

Two smokes and a short catnap later, the canteen was full and his horse watered. Further up the canyon, he came upon an old hardrock mine, and just past the entrance, the remains of a small shack. Inside, underneath a camp stove, he found a tattered copy of *The Arizona Weekly Citizen*, dated 1889.

He marvelled at the well-preserved newsprint. Tucked up beneath the entrance, the lean-to's roof had kept its contents secure. Doc thought about all the men who'd come here, too far out from Wellton or even Bakers Tanks, to carry any water by wagon.

Not enough rain out here to wash your face.

Deep down, he knew better. It could rain like hell here, enough to flood purgatory and Wellton, too. Like it did in '31, and that time he almost killed Ernie Vasquez.

He wondered which came first, the trickle of water or the rocky mine? Had they found anything else, or just enough moisture to keep their dig alive? Perhaps some forgotten treasure was here, lost to the sand and the relentless sun. Questions best left where he found them; he scratched his mark on the jack timber above the entrance and mounted his horse. Large, dark clouds were rising to the north; maybe the chance for a cooling rain.

Knowing she was well rested, Doc put the mare into a slow lope. He figured on using that advantage to catch up to whatever idiot fired the shot that spooked his horse and crippled that donkey. He wasn't sure what to do about it, but these things had a way of working themselves out. And no matter what, he'd found good water that even the damn burros couldn't foul.

Twenty minutes later, he found more than that. Riding out of the canyon's end, he pulled the big mare back on its heels in a rolling stop.

"Damn me for a fool!"

He spat the words out through clenched teeth and pivoted his horse, the shouts of a Mexican border patrol echoing in his ears.

LIKE SHAVE SOAP IN THE WIND, white lather worked its way up the chestnut's flanks and across her heaving chest. Her broad neck was stretched forward in a full gallop. Doc's head lay close to her mane, eyes forward on the trail, searching for potholes and logjams. As much as he liked the straightaways, he yearned for another turn in the canyon, as the Federales didn't need to catch him in order to do him damage. Like Grandpa Cox always said, never kick a dog barefoot.

A bullet whistled by, underscoring that conviction.

It's hard enough to hit anything from horseback, especially when you and your target are moving. But the soldiers could dismount. Once down, they made fair marksmen with their surplus Springfields. Every time the terrain began to level out, Doc would count enough seconds to aim, then turn his horse suddenly, slipping in as close as he dared to the boulders and the cactus. But the big mare was tiring; he could hear it in her lungs. The great, rolling breaths were gone, replaced by a pumping gasp for air. He prayed hard for a hairpin turn.

"C'mon, baby, c'mon!" Doc pressed the mare, knowing he had underestimated her before. How could he be so stupid, barreling down into Mexico like a rabbit after a fox? He wasn't sure what he'd stumbled into; he got only a glimpse of a prison stockade and a full troop of Mexican cavalry.

Dang, if they didn't send the whole bunch.

A curl in the track granted some breathing room, and the mare gave up little of her head start. Soon, he'd be safe on the Arizona side, but he didn't put much faith in that, as long as he was still within rifle shot.

He caught a whiff of ozone. Storm clouds were breaking overhead; he could feel the air grow heavy and the wind rise. A fine mist turned to broken drops, then hard rain as he raced on through the canyon.

Maybe that'll slow them down.

A rifle shot ricocheted off the rocks behind him.

Maybe not.

The driving rain had another effect; his overheated horse was cooling down. Doc eased off on the pace, letting the animal choose her gait in the slippery footing. The rain was making it difficult to see, and he figured the Mexicans weren't faring any better. Maybe worse, because he'd passed this way only a short while ago. The loose sand in the wash was rapidly turning to muck, and he was feeling better about seeing the ocean someday, when a sudden rifle shot clipped his canteen, bursting it like a child's balloon.

"Goddamn it!" He couldn't hear himself against the breaking thunderclaps. Lightning lashed the mesa above.

The rain was falling in great sheets now, and his horse, oblivious to the turmoil around her, cemented Doc's admiration by galloping full force as the sky fell all around them. Two antelope broke across their path, scrambling up the canyon walls in a panicked rush for higher ground. Doc pulled in the big chestnut, hauling the reins clear up to his chest. The mare reared back on her hind legs, breakneck gallop broken against her beating blood.

"Hyhaaa mule!"

Doc turned the mare with his spurs laid into her flanks, rolling the sharp dowels against her quivering flesh as she bolted up into the rocks. This was rough country with scant vision to steer by, but there was no time to spare - an upset here would be nothing next to what was on its way. The mare made a fine broadside target, but the only thing that mattered now was gaining altitude and gaining it fast.

The big mare stumbled and went to her knees; he used his spurs again and she leapt higher, straining as she scratched her way up the side of the canyon. Doc pushed her harder, pushed her through the boulders and the mesquite, pushed her muscles past the pain shooting through them. From below, he could hear a low rumble building, the rushing swell amidst the sheeting rain falling from a black sky.

He let his horse settle on the next flat; the mare shuddered at her sudden reprieve. Doc turned and shouted into the boiling flash flood below.

"Let's see you swim, boys!" Laughing, he waved his hat high over his head. "Swim all the way back to Mexico!"

The great wall of water crashed unchecked through the canyon, a thousand rocks and trees stripped away in a juggernaut flow to the Sea of Cortez.

S O, YOU HAVE ANOTHER SON?"
The waitress had just warmed our coffee and taken our empty thermos away for a refill.

"Somewhere." His eyes closed, and he paused for a moment. "I reckon he'd be about your age now."

"Don't look at me. I was born in Florida."

He shook his head and poured a shot of sugar from the glass dispenser.

I thought better of my wisecrack and changed the subject. "You sure that was Huey back there?"

"Sure as I'm standing here. Except I'm on my butt." We were seated at a long counter. The little cafe was empty, except for the middle-aged waitress and what looked to be a local at one of the tables along the sidewall.

"How could you tell? It's been a long time."

"Some things don't change about a person. The way they stand. The way they look you over, the eyes and such." Pop paused. He glanced through the cafe window towards Wellton. "Whoever he is, he ain't long for this ol' world." He lifted his coffee cup and took a sip. "TB."

"You mean like tuberculosis?" I thought back to the darkened bar and his persistent cough. "Maybe that's why he wouldn't talk to us."

"Maybe. Huey was always the stubborn type. And proud." Doc put his cup on the counter and frowned. "But I do know that TB." He motioned out to the highway. "Back when Dad got hurt, we used to bring him up here to the hot springs. He would sit in that hot water for hours, said it made walking easier again. They had a place right next to it for folks with TB."

"How bad was he hurt?"

"Laid up for six weeks or so... even then he couldn't get around much. He never moved quite the same after that, and his eyes seemed to get a lot worse."

The waitress returned with a full thermos and offered us a slice of home-made apple pie.

"Are the hot springs still up here?" Pop asked. He peered across the counter at the thick Dutch apple pie, waiting patiently underneath its glass lid.

"I'm not sure," she said. "We just bought this place about a year ago."

Pop had something of a sweet tooth, so I said yes for both of us, two pieces à la mode; he made no objection and we settled in for a while.

"They closed it down about 20 years ago…" The man sitting at the side table spoke just loud enough for us to hear him. "But they're talking about opening it up again. As some kind of health spa."

The man was thick and graying, somewhere well above 60, dressed in a clean plaid shirt and khaki pants. By his relaxed pace and the well-read newspaper parked in front of him, I placed him as recently retired.

"Are you a local? Lived here for a while?" I asked.

"Since '53," he said. "They kept that place open 'til about 1970. Some folks lived out there all their lives."

I'd heard stories about hospitals that claimed a cure for tuberculosis. In the '30's, at the height of the epidemic, some of those sanitoriums were little more than forced quarantine posing as a medical treatment. Some were converted to polio hospitals, but the stigma of the White Plague still remained. If that was Huey Spain back in Wellton, he'd grown up in age where TB was, if not a death sentence, a sign hung around your neck that said pariah.

The waitress brought our apple pie hot from the microwave, with a scoop of vanilla ice cream strategically placed on top. "I hope they do open up," she said. "We could use something else to bring folks out here."

Pop had made a new friend with his fork, so I took a look around the café. A painted highway map of the southwest hung above the cash register. Pink flowers indicated Tacna and The Desert Rose Café, with yellow dots to the west for Yuma, San Diego and Los Angeles – red dots for Gila Bend, Phoenix, and Flagstaff. Below the map was a printed mileage chart.

"Have you ever heard of Bakers Tanks?" I asked.

"Sure. Some of the kids like to go out there and shoot." She paused for a moment. "And other things."

"You know how we might get there from here?"

She shook her head. "I've never been there. Just heard about it."

"I can tell you how to get there." The man at the table was getting up to leave. "You have to go back west to mile marker 31. Take a left off the highway. You'll come to an irrigation maintenance road. Follow that east a half mile till it crosses a dirt road… then head south. You'll run right into it."

"Thanks. Do you mind repeating that? I'm not from around here." He did so, but I could've sworn that all the distances had changed, and the mile marker, too.

Pop finished his pie and started up a conversation with the man about Bakers Tanks, and who knew who way back when. By the time I finished paying the bill, the man was gone. Doc was outside rolling another cigarette.

"I think I dated his cousin in the '40's." Pop whistled a low tone.

I looked in my jeans pocket for a light, and pulled out the matchbook I had taken from the bar in Wellton. As I reached to tear out a match, I noticed some bold print on the cover:

'Drink, Dance, and Relax'
at the
Arizona Bar & Package
Wellton, AZ

Beneath the slogan in bold letters it read, 'Your Host, H.L. Spain'.

"You were right." I showed the matchbook to Pop.

"Well, I'll be." He took the matches, lit his cigarette, and stared at the writing. "Mind if I keep 'em?"

I smiled at our little souvenir, and so did he. Doc tucked the matches into his shirt pocket and we set off to find Bakers Tanks.

OCTOBER 1941

Bakers Tanks, Arizona

ANGELO MANZANELLI sat at the tail end of a long drunk. Not your plain, ordinary payday drunk, but a Fourth of July special, with a head full of cotton and two burning eyeballs. He gathered a thought and started to express it; instead, it issued forth as a low, lingering belch. Doc had left camp nearly a week ago, and Angelo was beginning to get a little nervous. Not so much for Dave Bailey; that guy could live out on the desert forever. But life in the horse camp wasn't near as clear-cut without him. Things had been pretty much OK till Kenny Kraddock left; everybody working on the trap corrals, cutting greasewood and building rails, but then Kenny up and went to check on his mom in Globe.

And here's ol' Manzanelli, left alone to babysit a bunch of Mexicans. Angelo's thoughts were jumbled, but he knew that much for sure.

He could see both Bonita boys through the campfire blur, laid out around the big mesquite tree. Doc had told him to keep a careful eye on them, as they didn't have much experience. Gary was stretched out under the tree, picking at his guitar between pulls on a half-empty tequila bottle. Danny Bonita was hunched over next to the fire. Staring into the coals, his blood-red eyes were glazed like a waxed apple.

Angelo had been on and off the desert with Dave for almost seven weeks now. Back in high school, the stories he told of easy money and pretty girls had sounded a lark, and Angelo was eager to come along. But tonight, he found himself longing for the comforts of home: his feather-bed mattress, his mother's hot pasta and the slow, easy life in Grass Valley. More likely, he was plain old homesick.

Still, it had been quite an adventure; riding freight trains, chasing horses across the desert, shooting guns at sunset camped out in the middle of nowhere. There were dozens of new faces: sheriffs, bartenders, shopkeepers, uncles, aunts and cousins - all part of the curious collection of farmers, Indians and roustabouts that Doc called friends. Everyone seemed to know Dave Bailey.

Not just in Wellton, either. He and Dave had spent a fair amount of time across the Telegraph Pass in Yuma. Dave kept a room in the Yuma Hotel open all the time. It cost him a dollar a day, but he said it was well worth it for a hot meal, a shower, and a warm bed when they came in off the desert. Dave even let him have the bed once in a while. Angelo liked that hotel; hot water all the time, and you could sleep in a bedroll on the floor without once worrying about some rattlesnake slipping in-between the sheets.

Lately, he'd had that room all to himself. The last couple of times, Dave had taken off with his girl in the Model A and left Angelo to fend for himself in town. Which he did quite nicely, thank you very much. Dave was right – there's some real pretty girls in Arizona.

But none pretty as Billie.

Doc's girl had an easy smile about her. She could make them all laugh, even when things weren't going their way.

Billie asked him why all the boy's called Dave 'Doc', and Angelo told her the cookie box story; about the time when Dave and Kenny and Angelo were sitting in the hotel dining room, eating steaks and drinking beer, and how Angelo figured that Dave must be making good money trapping horses, or else kept a grubstake from the mines, 'cause he paid for everybody that night. And how, right in the middle of dinner, a bellman walks in and starts calling out for "Doctor Bailey - package for Doctor Bailey!" They look up, and sure enough, the box said 'D.R. Bailey' and was filled with sugar cookies from Dave's mom. Angelo told her how everyone had laughed and teased Davey all night long, and how from that day on, they'd all called him 'Doc'.

Billie got tickled by that story and started calling him Doc, too. After that, Angelo saw Dave less and Billie more, and sometimes neither one of them for days at a time.

But something happened, and Angelo never saw her again. He wondered why, and when Doc came back from Yuma the last time, he asked him how come, and why he seemed so much sadder than he used to be. But Dave said no, just leave it be, and then he rode off alone into the desert.

That was six days ago.

"Hey, Danny," Angelo forced himself up to a sitting position. "Toss me over some of that cactus whiskey."

There was no response. The eyes of the Mexican boy never left the fire.

"Well, fuck you then." Angelo staggered to his feet. "Hey Gary, try to get some blood back in your little brother's brain."

Angelo lumbered over and took the bottle from its resting place. He took a short swig, washed the burning liquid around in his mouth and swallowed. As the warm fluid hit his stomach, he felt an urge to vomit, then thought better of it, and slid down the tree trunk alongside Gary.

His big head fell against the Mexican boy and he whispered, "You figure he's gonna' be all right?"

Gary Bonita regarded the silent silhouette of his younger brother. It had been a full day since Dañiel had fallen off the train; Gary wished that he hadn't let these two talk him into going back to Yuma.

"I am sure he will be fine, *Ángel*."

Angelo hated the way Gary mexed his name. It was bad enough being a big Italian kid without being made a Mexican, too. Even so, he never called Gary by his Spanish name Geraldo, or Danny by Dañiel.

"It's Angel-o, Angel-oo." He stretched out the last syllable of his name, letting it lengthen into a howl. "Angel-oooooo!"

Bonita laughed at the big gringo, his head thrown back, crying in the night like some wounded cow. There was a sadness in the sound, one that matched his own mood. Gary took the bottle from Angelo and drank; he threw his head straight back and wailed at the stars. They took turns, howling and drinking and laughing, until they both fell dizzy into the dirt.

By the fire, Dañiel Bonita lifted his head.

Through a thick haze, he could hear the coyotes howl; he heard his mother tell him they were lost souls, come back to earth to mourn their misspent lives. In his warm dream, his fingers counted beads on a silver rosary, ritual birthing ritual, holy water washing away the silt. His mind began to clear. The dancing lights turned to campfire, coyotes to compadres, and the long wails into laughter.

He saw Geraldo and the big American face down, spitting in the dirt.

A sudden color came into his grey world, and he felt light, almost invincible. He would show the others how to mourn for lost souls, for Dañiel Rodrigo Bonita had returned from their stalking grounds and knew all of their voices. He put his chin to his chest, gathered his voice from deep below and moaned like a dog at the moon.

"Jesus Christ!" Angelo spun around, the boy's abrupt cry piercing his fearless demeanor. Angelo grabbed Gary by his shirt and tossed him at his brother. "Best check on your kin. I think he's talking to you."

Gary crawled to his brother's side and grabbed his head with two hands. "*¿Dañiel, que pasa? ¿!Esta bien!?*"

Dañiel touched his hand to his brother's frightened face and spoke. "*Estas tan loco como el gringo.* You will frighten the saints, Geraldo, and we will have no protection."

"*Mi hermano,* you have returned!" Gary pulled his younger brother close and made the sign of the cross. *"Madre de Dios, gracias."*

Angelo welcomed the strange howl. Worry had dogged him ever since the accident. Better than no sound at all; at least the kid made sense to his brother. Tomorrow would be a better day. Kenny should be back, and maybe even Dave. He was just starting to relax when a strange voice cut through the night, setting him on his heels.

"Keep up that caterwauling, and I might have to skin the bunch of you."

Angelo peered into the darkness, trying to source the odd voice. Dave had told him to sit with his back to the fire; now he wished that he had. His eyes had grown accustomed to the firelight, and he couldn't see a thing beyond it.

"Doc, is that you?" He hoped so, and wondered where they'd left the camp pistol.

"Now, who else would it be?" Dave smiled to himself in the shadows. He let his voice resume its natural tone. "Course I could've brought along a brass band. You jugheads still wouldn't a' heard me coming."

Angelo squinted past the fire and tried to focus. "C'mon Dave, we was just having a little fun." Angelo tried to stand up. As he did, his balance left him, and he fell backwards on the sandy ground.

Doc stepped in from the shadows and threw his bedroll down. "I can see that, Ange. You're lucky it's me and not some other damn fool." He glanced at the Bonita boys and wondered at their silent embrace. "Where's Kenny?"

Angelo straightened, searching for a posture that would stop the sudden spinning in his head. "Gone to Globe. He had some skins."

Kenny Kraddock was a crack shot, and made just as much money taking the dollar bounty off coyotes as he did from trapping wild horses with Doc. And he was a steady hand. Doc looked around the camp, noting the whiskey bottles and the general disarray.

"For five dollars, I'd shoot you myself. You even smell like a dog."

Angelo looked down at himself. Despite all his efforts, he had obviously thrown up. It looked as if he'd been lying in it for some time.

"Well, I uh..." Angelo searched his memory for a way to change the subject. "We had some trouble with Danny, and I thought maybe a little whiskey would help."

"I don't care if you pour it on your pancakes. Just don't make a mess out of my camp." Doc knelt beside the fire, pulled the iron grill back over the coals, and resurrected the coffee pot from amongst the embers. "What happened?"

Angelo glanced over at the Mexicans. Whether from relief or pure exhaustion, they had passed out in each other's arms, oblivious to the world around them.

"We went to Yuma. Danny fell off the train and hit his head. I didn't think he was gonna' make it."

Doc stoked the fire, tossed a pan on the grill, and walked over to the mesquite. Two lettuce crates were tied high in the tree to keep their provisions safe; he lowered one, rummaging through it till he found a coffee tin. "How long ago?" Dave poured some coffee grounds in the pot, filled it with water from the camp barrel, and placed it on the grill.

"Two days." Angelo was starting to come around. Things were still hazy, but the echoes were subsiding. He could smell himself now, unpleasant as it was. "We took the Meteor back to Wellton."

"Dammit, Angelo, ain't I taught you nothing?"

"It's not what you think, Dave. We knew it was gonna' stop. I got to talking with one of the passengers..."

"What was her name?" Angelo was a big, good-looking kid. He had a way of making sure the girls knew it.

"Louise, I think." Angelo grinned through the fog. "Anyway, she says the train was gonna' stop and pick up her daddy, and we knew we could just get off without killing ourselves. The slow freight wasn't due for six hours, so we climbed up on top while they was pulling out and let ourselves take the fast way."

He learns fast. This was only Manzanelli's first trip to Wellton, and already the big man was taking off on his own. "That don't explain what happened to Danny." Doc poured some of the boiled coffee into an enameled cup and gave it to Angelo. "Here, drink this."

"Dave, that wasn't my doing, I swear." Angelo let the hot liquid fall into his mouth, and fought the urge to retch.

"I just lay down over the side, and was talking to this gal through the window, and Danny, well, he wants to do the same. So I offers to hold him, but he don't want me to, and anyway, old Gary wants to go down, so I hold him by his legs, and he's a-playing the guitar and singing, and we was getting food from her, and a couple of coins from the old ladies on the train, and having a high old time."

Doc poured some coffee into his own cup and savored the dark brew. It was the one luxury he would carry into the desert. He closed his eyes and imagined the big Italian holding Gary over the side of the train, laughing and singing and probably half drunk. Angelo could do it, too. He'd seen him lift three times his own weight in the breaking pens, wrestling mustangs into the saddle.

"So Danny says he wants to go down, too, but he won't let me hold him, says he don't trust no gringo. So he talks Gary into it." Angelo cocked his head at the two brothers. "And Gary dropped him."

Doc glanced at Angelo, then back at the boys.

Danny was always the stubborn one, more prone to dark spells than his brother. Doc had picked them up by the side of the road in the Imperial Valley, some three months ago. They said they'd been waiting over two days for a ride. Doc didn't have much luck at hitchhiking either. No wonder the young Mexicans hadn't fared any better. But they'd proved trustworthy enough, and Doc loved the sound of Gary's guitar, so he let them come along to his traps, and introduced them to Mrs. Spain. She let Danny wash dishes for his Uncle Slim in the café while Gary did odd jobs and sang in the cantina with Artemio Cabrero. Doc never had a brother. Seeing one fall from a train must have been hard.

"It's a wonder he lived."

"I thought he was dead." Angelo took another sip of coffee and whispered. "Gary wanted to jump off right then and there, but I held him tight. Once we got to Wellton, we ran back and there he was. He seemed OK, all bruised up, nothing broken. But for two days, he didn't speak or nothing, till right before you come in."

"Too bad, maybe he could've talked some sense into you."

Doc reached into the supply crate and tossed a piece of fatback bacon into the pan. The hard grease exploded in a crackling fusillade. He unwrapped the last of the burro's loin from his oilcloth.

"Let's see what chewing on a little mule will do for you."

The whirl of smells hit Angelo's belly like a hard fist, knotting up the coffee and curdling the whiskey in his bile. He jumped up, tripped over himself and ran for the bushes, heaving as he went.

It was early light by the time Angelo stumbled back into camp. He had stripped down to his shorts; he looked to Doc like some hard rock miner before the showers, pale white and shrunken. Doc rolled a crust of hard bread around in the last of the bacon grease, swallowed his coffee, and leaned back on his bedroll.

"Don't make yourself too comfortable, Angelo."

He tossed the last of his coffee into the fire and reached for the water barrel. A cupful of its contents thrown onto the sleeping Bonita boys sat them bolt upright in surprise.

"We're breaking camp and headed back to town." Doc eyed the Bonita brothers and then Angelo.

"I want to buy some dynamite."

THE SPARSE SKELETON of an abandoned mobile home park stood silent on the side of the highway. Right across from it, yet another mile marker. Despite my vague recollection of the cafe man's directions, we were somehow lost again, creeping along the road as if looking for a lost dog.

Out of nowhere, Doc said, "Pull over." About 50 feet in front of the next marker, a small gravel road veered off through the scrub brush towards the south. Pop leaned forward to glance through my open window. "See that little mountain over there?"

In the near distance, I could see what looked like a pointed hump of rock, the blue haze of afternoon sun behind it. "Yeah, I think so."

"Well, behind that, if we can get around and head southeast, we'll run right into Bakers Tanks."

I looked at the little dirt road and then at Doc. "You sure about that?"

"They can move everything else, but I don't think they can move that mountain."

I checked behind us for oncoming traffic and made a sweeping turn across the highway. The '56 bottomed out as we rolled onto the gravel track.

"Just keep heading for that peak, there should be an easy way around it." Doc seemed suddenly energized. "And if I'm wrong, we can always camp out and wait for the Border Patrol to come arrest us." He laughed and pulled the red cup off the top of our silver thermos.

"Yessir, that's where she is… good ol' Bakers Tanks." Doc poured himself a cup of coffee and settled in for the ride as we bumped and swayed along the thin dirt road.

I was hoping he was right and figured that he was, but still glad we had a good spare tire. We'd stopped at a store and bought some extra jugs of water before we left Wellton. Betsy wasn't prone to overheating, but we were on a desert, after all. If the sun set before we got around the mountain, we had a camp stove, a big cooler, and a couple of sleeping bags. I kept the '56 in low gear, and we made slow progress for the better part of fifteen minutes.

"You know, Pop, I have a feeling this might be the right road. Besides, if I'm gonna' get stuck out here, it might as well be with an old desert rat." I meant it, too. Just then, there was no place else I'd rather be, and no one else I'd rather be with. "Want some jerky?"

He nodded yes, and I reached for our brown paper snack bag.

We sampled jerky at almost every pit stop; salmon jerky, buffalo jerky, turkey jerky, even plain old cow. Over the years, we'd tried hickory smoked, teriyaki, peppered, brown sugared – just about every kind known to man, God, and the local convenience store. We'd made it a practice to pick out the different brands and recipes, packaged or custom, even the loose pieces that were casually offered in a simple wax paper bag. I handed Pop a slice of 'Oberto Old-fashioned', our current favorite, and tore a piece off for myself. It was pliable and tasty. Used judiciously, it could blunt my gnawing cigarette reflex and keep me under two packs a day.

"Stop!" Doc spat the word out like a warning shot.

I slammed on the brakes; they were the height of mid 20th century drum-brake technology. The big chassis fishtailed to a standstill.

"What is it?" I looked around for some sign of trouble.

Pop's coffee had spilled in his lap, and onto the glove compartment door that he used as a tiny tray table. He tossed his unlit cigarette out the window and brushed the spill away with his hand. "Remember those ocotillo thorns I told you about?" Doc pointed at the middle of the road ahead of us.

Part of a large spiny bush lay right in our way, probably blown in by a hard wind. Obscured by the drifting sand piled up against it, the long stems likely would've crossed our path.

"Go take a look," Pop said. He opened his door to get out, and I did likewise. I walked over to the bush, knelt down and reached for one of the stalks.

"Watch your fingers," Pop called out. He'd ambled up behind me, rolling a fresh cigarette as he came.

The olive grey stalks were nearly 12 feet long and covered with spiny thorns; I ran the tip of my finger across one of the barbs. "Nasty."

"Don't get stuck, it'll burn like hell. We used to lose all kinds of tires to those bastards. I ran across a big one once, had to put nearly 20 patches in an inner tube.

Little tiny patches," said Doc. He held his fingertips about an inch apart. "Lucky to fish enough rubber out of my kit to keep a' going. Like I say, not likely to pop a modern tire unless they slip past the steel belt, but in them days, they'd play hell with you, especially at night."

He lit his cigarette, took a deep drag and blew the smoke out with a silent whistle. He paused and looked to the south. "God, I love this old desert."

"You used to make fences with these?" I asked. "Damn, they must have cut you up something awful."

"Not so bad when they're green," he said. "We'd cut 'em down and weave the limbs like a basket. Even a burro won't cross them things if they don't have to."

I pried a long thorn off one of the stalks and put it in my shirt pocket. We kicked the rest of the branches out of our path.

"How much further?" I asked. The road had long since become more of a dirt track. We were up close to a low set of hills with rugged peaks, surrounded by jagged rock formations. The hills were ringed by sand, sagebrush and cactus.

"Not far, I think. We just need to come around the other side."

We walked back to the car and continued on around the trail. Based on the number of stray beer bottles, it must have seen some occasional use. I kept a careful eye out for more ocotillo, despite the modern manufacture of my tires.

About ten minutes later, we came to a large flat area. All the vegetation was gone, and the ground had been beaten down into hardpan. Two rusty 50-gallon drums sat together in the center of the flat; someone had used them as burn barrels. Alongside them were a few beer bottles, scraps of wood and assorted bits of trash. Outside the clearing, a couple of large Saguaro cactus were torn dead; scavenged for their long, supporting ribs, either as souvenirs or as deadwood for a fire.

"We're here," Pop said.

"This is Bakers Tanks?"

"Not hardly." Doc looked at me as if I was half-blind, then pointed south. "We'll have to walk in from here."

"How far?" I wondered if we should pack in supplies, and how to leave the station wagon.

"Just put your boots on and let's take a walk." Pop was already headed due south at a fair clip. I jumped out of the car and quickened my step to catch up. There was a sudden dip in elevation and a change in the terrain.

Hardpan gave way to a rocky wash, with shallow flows of sand. Blue rock scrabble was caught in the long crevices that lined the wash. Where moist soil had gathered, bits of green foliage clung to the sandstone; clumps of deer grass and cactus pear, the occasional sage bush, mesquite, or red yucca. Our descent stopped at an enormous flat boulder, spread out like a cliff wall above the surrounding ground. We climbed down on the smooth rock until we hit a broad plateau, and there, caught between the cheeks of two great rock flows, was a clear pool of water.

Doc's smile was as big as I'd ever seen it. He knelt down along the edge of the tank and brushed his hat back and forth across the surface of the water, sending bright ripples out away from the shore. "By golly dang, I told you there was water on this old desert."

"Yes, you did." I think I was as glad as he was to finally stand in the place that I'd heard so much about. There was no one around for miles that I could see, and for an instant, I could imagine him as a young man some 50 years before, building his traps in a time that was his alone.

"How did you catch the horses?"

"Wasn't much to it really." He looked up from the pool where he was soaking his red bandana. "They'd walk right in, as long as you didn't get in their way." He pointed toward the smooth sloping sides of the rock tanks. "Hard to get back out that-a-way, so we'd build a funnel at the end and leave it open at night, then slip back down before dawn and close 'em in." Doc stepped away from the edge of the water. He gestured to the open desert. "That was the tricky part, getting down here without the stallion catching on that we was closing the gate."

"Then what?

Pop brushed the wet bandana across his throat and around his neck, then tucked it into his back pocket. "Well, the good ones we'd keep around for breaking; the burros and the stragglers we'd take on down to Brandy at the See-Boar Ranch." Pop turned his head and looked at me knowingly. "Sold them for tiger food."

"Tiger food?" I was surprised by his revelation and the raw enthusiasm behind it.

He was enjoying the moment, languishing in his old haunts, leaning against the twisted spine of an aged mesquite tree. In one swift motion, he pulled a cigarette from his breast pocket and lit it. "Ol' Brandy had a deal with the San Diego Zoo; he'd take them clear over to California. They used them mustangs to feed the lions and the tigers." Pop flashed a grin in a stream of grey smoke. "And them burros - Brandy had this Indian woman cooking and cleaning for him. She would bar-b-que 'em up, dress 'em and bury 'em in hot coals for most of a day. She was damn pretty too."

He paused. "Ain't nothing like bar-b-que burro. I'd give my eye teeth for a taste of that again." He laughed and ran his tongue across his full set of upper dentures. "If I still had teeth."

"I'll have to keep an eye out for some." I sat down by the mesquite and watched as a tiny lizard jumped out from behind a rock and sprang away.

"You do that."

Doc took a butane lighter out of his shirt pocket and re-lit his cigarette. "Brandy had a bunch of folks working on that place, fixing fence and irrigating. Sometimes, me and my crew, we'd break horses up there. It was one hell of a good time."

I looked over at his face. It had been a difficult trip. There wasn't much left of the old Wellton, and the loss had worn on him. Most of the places he had known were gone, and for some reason, Huey Spain was clinging to his anonymity. But out here in the desert, Pop had found a chunk of granite that held his past as close as it held the infrequent rain.

He gave me a broad smile and let go another puff of smoke. "We did that and a few other things."

HECTOR RAMIREZ was deathly afraid of heights. For most of his village life, this hadn't made much of a difference, but once he joined the army, each night of guard duty was a constant agony. First, the long trip up the ladder; that was the most difficult part, as each rung made his heart climb higher into his throat. Halfway up the tower, he'd pause to catch his breath, careful not to look down or lose his grip on the weathered treads. The worn rungs groaned under his weight, thin splinters piercing his hands with the force of his grasp. Eyes closed tight, he would feel for the top of the platform, sliding his body forward on the floor like a snake. Rising to his knees, he'd thank La Virgen de Guadalupe for safe passage, and pray his return to earth might be equally uneventful.

He had served the monthly tower duty for three straight weeks. If the roster held true, only one week more, followed by sweet relief on solid ground. Perhaps then his dreams would soften, no desperate drop into the abyss, no more screams as the knives of El Diablo pierced him. Each morning, he would make his careful descent, relieve himself, then slip away to his hut, there to lie awake until the numbness of the tower passed away from him. Only then would he take his café de olla with the other guards.

Lying on his mat, he could hear the prisoners pounding rock, the rhythm of their labors laying chorus for his dreams to follow. He saw himself climbing in a dark mission stairwell, the prayers and chants circling about him. His small hands touched the great bell, and he looked out over the village and into the mountains where his grandfather's herds were grazing. The hymns were soft, and he felt a warming peace in the music. But then he would slip and fall again, while all around him the bells cried, tortured faces flying past him as he plummeted into the night. Each time, the Dark One would take him, only to awaken drenched in his own sweat, dreading the night to come.

His mother had begged him not to join the army. She took Hector out, away from the village, to the place where his father was buried. Guillermo Ramirez had died in the Great Revolution, fighting los hacendados beside Zapata and Pancho Villa. His mother had said it was a noble thing, but it had come to mean nothing, like all battles on this earth. Only the struggle for the souls of men would count on the day of reckoning. It was for this thing that her son was born, for the Holy

Church. She cried for him and he wept, but he left for his barracks the next day and had never returned.

Hector looked out along the crest of the mountains, careful to keep his distance from the edge of the tower platform. He stayed seated for as long as he thought no one would notice, rising only to his feet when he felt there might be someone in authority nearby. There was not much to guard against anyway, for only a fool would venture this far out in the desert. "Fools like me," he thought. "Fools who can't escape the Mexican Army." Hector heard a familiar voice come from the barracks and quickly stood to attention.

"Ramirez!"

Hector stepped carefully to the edge and peered down.

"You will be lonesome tonight, eh?" Coarse laughter followed and the sound of other voices.

Hector knew better than to answer the gruff cry. His sergeant was a temperamental man, as brutal to his troop as he was to his prisoners. It was payday, and Sergeant Gómez had been drinking since suppertime; he might not wait for the town cantina to begin his cruel sport. The other guards were filing out of the barracks and into a battered truck parked in the center of the compound.

Gómez took a shovel from the flatbed and walked over to one of the prisoner's huts. Barely able to stand straight, he beat the blade against the flimsy walls. "Perhaps you will miss me tonight?" There was no reply from within the hut. "The girls, they are very pretty, and the tequila is just as wet. Maybe I will bring some back for you?"

The stumbling sergeant cackled and threw the shovel against the side of the guard tower. The ancient truck engine sputtered to life; dim headlights fell against the wire gates. Gómez swayed like a tree in a stiff wind, bending backwards to gaze up at the tower platform. "Be watchful, little Padre."

Hector swallowed his anger. "*Sí Señor.* I will be very diligent."

The sergeant turned from the tower, crossing himself with a sneer. He fell backwards into the truck bed. "That is good, little Padre. And I will do *novenas* on the belly of a whore."

THE GATES OF THE STOCKADE opened on cue. A big green flatbed rumbled out on the dirt track, loaded with Federales. It was over 30 miles to the nearest Mexican town, and by Doc's reckoning, no one would be back before mid-morning.

Won't be another time as good as this.

No telling how much longer he could keep the others interested in this little escapade. Angelo was growing restless, and Gary had his hands full keeping Danny out of the camp whiskey.

They'd worked their way down from the old mine silently, leaving their horses a quarter-mile away in a small draw off the main canyon. Doc had kept this little party in mind ever since they got back from Yuma, introducing it to the others one at a time.

He'd told the boys that the case of dynamite was for the mine he'd discovered, to see if they could work some new nuggets out of the old diggings. But each day, on his regular look-see around the mine's perimeter, he would slip down to the end of the canyon.

Once there, he'd settle in on the rocky rise above the stockade quarry. Bill Gale had warned him about Mexican prisons, labor camps where men were pressed beyond their endurance, broken like the rocks and shale they mined from dusk to dawn. Even forewarned, what he saw went beyond his comprehension.

The prisoners were brought out at first light and worked till the sun fell behind the mountains, cracking rock and carrying ore straight through the blistering heat of the day. Somewhere between the regular beatings and his general dislike of authority, Doc began to memorize the movements of the guards.

He wasn't prone to fuss about a bunch of jailbirds; Doc had spent a little time behind bars himself. He was just bone tired of seeing folks treated like animals. Besides, the Federales that bushwhacked him came right out of this place. He figured to even that slate once and for all.

Doc had gotten Angelo to go along because Angelo always went along. Danny and Gary were more reluctant. Their attitude seemed to shift once they saw the relatively few guards. Doc didn't know that much about the Bonita boys, but one thing he did know for sure: they'd done some jail time, maybe in this very place. Danny had wanted to let loose with the rifles right then and there, but Doc had kept him in tow.

"We don't want to kill nobody," he said. "Just ruffle a few tail feathers."

Once he'd hatched his plan, he sent Danny down alongside the prison work gang to whisper the news. Tonight was their best bet; almost all the guards would be in town, and anyone left behind wouldn't be likely to stick their head up once a case of powder went off.

It's tonight, or pack it up and go home.

"Angelo." Doc spoke softly, even though they were fifty yards away. "Take four sticks and set them next to those corner posts."

Angelo nodded.

"Gary, you take three and spread 'em along the fence. I'll blow the main gate and the horse corrals."

The stockade was about six hundred feet around, surrounded by mesh and barbwire, strung taut on tall wooden posts. Doc took his father's Barlow knife and stripped out three long strings of fuse. He capped the bundled sticks of dynamite and carefully attached seven feet of fuse to each, then passed out the assembled charges.

"Don't linger once they're lit, or we'll have to peel you off the fences."

Danny shifted his weight and gave their leader a sullen look. Doc motioned to the top of the rocks and whispered, "Somebody has to stay up here and cover us. If we're spotted, lay down a pattern - and don't stop firing till we're clean out of Mexico." Danny straightened up, satisfied with his responsibilities.

"Let's go."

The three men collected their gear and moved carefully around the face of the large boulder. Doc put a single finger to his lips. "Take it slow and easy. It's so dang quiet you can hear a sidewinder."

The two men nodded and started down the hill.

"Don't forget these." Doc reached into his rucksack and tossed them each a bundle of kitchen matches. "Wait for my signal, then let her fly."

Danny slid forward onto the crest of the rocks and chambered a round into his rifle. Doc glanced back at him and lowered his voice. "You're supposed to scare 'em, Danny Boy, and that's all."

THE MOONLIGHT CAST an icy glow on the hillside. Dañiel Bonita watched as Bailey made his way down, slipping from boulder to boulder, his profile masked from the guard tower above. From time to time, he could hear the others, kicking up rocks as they descended. Angelo reached the wire fence first and was crawling towards the corner. Geraldo knelt behind a large outcropping, stringing fuse out from his bundle of dynamite. Bailey had worked his way from the main gates to the corral, his silhouette barely visible in the dim light before dawn.

Dañiel shouldered his Winchester and pulled the barrel down, leveling the tip of his gunsight at the center of Dave Bailey's back.

HECTOR RAMIREZ was praying again. In the eyes of his fellow soldiers, he was always praying. Those prayers had changed over the course of his military service; the simple repetitions of his youth were gone now, replaced by more elaborate appeals for redemption. He took comfort in the quiet, far away from the taunts of others and their mocking disregard for faith. He had reconciled himself to their disdain and years more in the Devil's service.

As a boy, he had many dreams. They would alternate between a soldier's glory and the simple service of a village priest. When he chose the soldier's life, all the pleasure went out of that dream; what was left was coarse pride and cruelty. Every day, he was assaulted by the sound of whips, the smell of blood, cheap drink, and women in dark rooms. His dreams had turned to a curse, and only the anthem of his prayers could take him away from the horror in the darkness.

Half awake, he knelt down on the tower floor. Somehow, the sounds were different this night, scrambling around the edges of his prayer. They seemed to move beneath him in shuffling footsteps, the call of a night bird, and the sudden hissing of hot steam.

HUDDLED BENEATH a rock overhang fifteen feet from the stockade fence, Angelo Manzanelli considered the folly of his youth.

Bound to die young, breaking jail for a bunch of Mexican horse thieves.

He cursed the day he met Dave Bailey. *Should have beat him to a bloody pulp.* He wondered if he could have, seeing as how Dave never seemed to give up, no matter how bad he was beat. Instead, they had become best friends.

They met at Nevada Union High. Bailey was always lollygagging about with the girls, fresh from some adventure, spinning tales about riding the rails, the distant desert and the great big country outside the little town of Grass Valley. Angelo would feign disinterest while hanging on every word, thinking he too should be doing wild things and wondering what life was like across the border.

Well, now he knew.

It was dangerous, and liable to get him killed. Still, no one could say he hadn't gone right to the edge, riding freight trains and roaming around the desert, sashaying by every pretty girl that caught his fancy. He caught himself smiling, and thought better of his predicament.

The soft whistle of a mourning dove cleared his head, and he crawled down to the edge of the stockade. Doc had told him to wait 30 seconds after the signal to light his fuse; Angelo spent half the time counting and the other half looking for the quickest way up the hill.

IT WAS THE THIRD TIME the thought had come to Dañiel Bonita.

I should have killed him when I had the chance.

The first time he had Bailey in his sights, he hesitated. A single unmasked shot would point to him as the culprit.

Three times, he had a clean shot, and each time, as if warned by some voice in the wind, Bailey shifted behind a rock or moved from the line of fire. Now, he'd disappeared completely. Dañiel would wait, and catch the gringo as a dozen explosions broke the silence of the dawn.

Dañiel had been planning to kill Bailey for weeks, keenly interested in the changes it would bring. Ever since he'd fallen from the train, his thoughts had become glass, clarifying the deep resentments that so troubled him before. His brother seemed content to travel with these norteamericanos, shifting from place to place at their whim and living off the scraps from their table. But he knew better; they were just like the fools in the prison below.

Only we toil for white masters instead of brown.

Not so long ago, all of this land had belonged to his people, taken by blood on the swords of his Spanish ancestors. The father of his grandfather had been a titled man of great prestige, a Don, with many lands in the province of California - lands that were stolen by gringos in the Treaty of Guadalupe Hidalgo. Now, his grandsons washed dishes for white women and sang for their supper.

Even this rescue of the campesinos was little more than a joke for the gringos, a passing fancy before they returned to their rich houses and motorcars. And this Bailey was the worst of all, for his false friendship and stupid generosity.

For many nights, Dañiel had thought to cut his throat and that of the big man, too. But he'd never seen his chance, never caught the gringo unawares. Bailey would have to die first; there'd be no end to the pursuit if he struck and failed. The Italian would be easy prey, lost in the desert without his friend. Dañiel never spoke of his plan to Geraldo. He knew his brother would have no part of it, content to finger his guitar and play the fool in the town cafe. But a shot in the night - that would solve everything.

A nightbird's cry cleaved his thoughts, and he searched below for his oppressor, sighting his rifle as he scanned the edge of the fencewire. Any second, explosions would rip the barricades, revealing his target in the smoke and haze below.

The ratchet step of a rifle cock behind him turned his stomach. He brought his eyes from the gunsight and turned around, certain of a Federale's bullet.

"You!" Dañiel's face went ashen white. "How did you get up here so fast?"

"I used a longer fuse."

Doc slid down beside Bonita and drew his sights on the tower platform. "Better pay attention now. Things are gonna' get a little crazy."

THE INITIAL BLAST took out the center of the fence line, instantly shooting the razor sharp wire out like a bullwhip, slicing through one of the main tower supports and the roof of the empty guardhouse. The wire whipped back in a snapping arc through a nearby hut, decapitating Juan Ricardo Ramos, a prisoner under life sentence for the rape and murder of the wife of a wealthy Nogales banker. The second and third explosions went off almost in unison, crushing corner posts, leveling corrals, and shattering the main gates.

Most of the prisoners stood in dumb shock, their camp torn apart in a blaze that rose all around them. Many had heard that a wild bandito would free them from captivity – that the walls of their prison would crumble in pieces. But no sane man among them had believed those tales. It was only the tortured imaginings of men without hope.

Still, they ran to gather water and weapons, to capture the few horses that remained and make their way into the hills. In their wild dash for freedom, there was no time to consider their benefactor, no time to worry about the gunfire all around them.

The fires in the stockade sent long flames licking into the sky, lashing at the guard tower above. Swaying on its three good legs, it lurched like a pendulum in the early morning breeze.

HECTOR RAMIREZ WAS LOST in his dream again, but this time, he did not fall. The fire and the dust of Hell was all around him, swirling through his tower sanctuary. Clinging to the edge of the precipice, he wrapped his bloody fingers around the ledge. He could hear demons and the hot breath of the Dark One down below. Once in the pit, he would never rise again. Eyes clinched tight, his fingers gave way and he fell into an empty sky.

"TIME TO GO." Doc laid his hand on Bonita's shoulder and motioned toward the mouth of the canyon. Danny pulled away and took aim at the soldier that fell from the tower.

"Leave him be." Doc leaned over and pulled Danny's rifle out of line. "He ain't gonna' give us no trouble."

Bonita snatched at his rifle and glared. "Who are you to say?"

Dave felt his gut tighten. He decided to ignore it.

"Listen Danny, we probably pissed off most of the Mexican Army already, but we can sure as hell piss off the rest of them. You want 'em to come looking for us, instead of them jailbirds?"

Danny looked down at the stockade. The fallen soldier was rising slowly from the dust. Bonita fingered the trigger on his rifle. "They'll never find us."

"Maybe you're right. But they'll look a lot harder for a bunch of murderers than they will for a few convicts. *"¿Comprende?"*

Gary burst around the side of the boulder at a dead run, out of breath and laughing. "Now we are the sons of Villa! *Vivan de libertadores de los campesinos!"*

Danny saw his brother flush with pride and caught up in his good humor, embraced him wildly. Angelo Manzanelli was right behind him. He slapped Dave on the back.

"*Olé*, buddy, we're on the most wanted list now!"

"Let's get the hell out of Mexico, so's we can keep it that way." Doc picked up his rucksack and headed for the mouth of the canyon. "It's a long way to those horses."

He looked back at his army of liberation, and wondered if they all weren't candidates for the loony bin.

HECTOR RAMIREZ STOOD ALONE in the broken stockade. He was alive. There were no devils here, only smoke, fire and confusion. One of the prisoners took his rifle and spat on him; Hector did not resist. It was likely the very least he deserved, after his complicity in their torture. There was no sign of anyone else. All of the others were gone except for one, the one who had lost his head.

The body of Juan Ricardo Ramos lay in the middle of the camp. It was similar in size to his own. Hector took his time and carefully exchanged clothing with the torso, leaving his bloody uniform gathered about the headless corpse. He looked for the missing head; it had rolled beneath the shadow of an ore wagon.

There was bread and a little sour wine in the cook shack, where he filled a canvas sack with beans and a goatskin pouch with water. It was over a hundred miles to his village, and he might not find food and water again for a long time. After he said his prayers, he began to walk, always keeping the rising sun on his left side.

He buried the head along the way, in a clearing by a small stream, and disappeared into the wilderness.

I T WAS COOL AND DAMP underneath the railroad bridge. Betsy was parked with her back lid open, and we'd pulled out some of our camping gear. I managed to fire up the Coleman stove and was rummaging around for some instant coffee. Doc had clamped together one of our old army cots, the wood and canvas kind that you could fold up like a deck chair. There was ice, milk and a few pieces of fruit in the cooler, along with some canned chili and wheat bread, more than enough for supper.

Two days out of Wellton and we were deep into Utah, headed north and sometimes west, avoiding the interstate when we could, and Nevada altogether, as Pop didn't care much for my behavior in the Silver State. There were times I had to agree with him.

Usually, we would stop at a small town motel. We made better time that way, and could catch a shower and a hot breakfast before we started the next day's drive. But this time, the route didn't map out, and by dusk we were a long way from anywhere. After a few miles of roadside exploration, we spotted an old railroad bridge that looked like a good place to camp. From my hitchhiking days, I knew that most bridges had an access road below for maintenance or recreation, and this one was no exception.

A shallow creek sat beside us, filled with catbrush and willow. Dense foliage was piled up high on the bank, so access to the water was limited, except for a worn deer trail marking the way. I took a closer look while Doc rested, and we waited for our coffee water to boil. There was nothing particularly remarkable about the place, just a slow, muddy stream that had forced the railroad to build the big trestle bridge perched 40 feet above our heads.

I could hear Pop whistling an old tune as I hiked back into to camp. The coffee water was boiling. I pulled two blue enamel cups from the kitchen box that we carried in the back of the station wagon.

"Find any fish?" he asked.

"None we can catch, unless you can shoo them out of the creek with your good looks." By this time, the sun had fallen, and the only illumination we had was the Coleman stove and lantern.

"Not my line of work." Pop had settled into camp, his feet up on the cooler and a fresh cigarette in his hands. "This here is nice country, Bill. I never knew there was so much water hidden away in these parts."

"Like Bakers Tanks, eh?"

"Bakers Tanks was better. Didn't have to listen to the traffic. We could make camp for weeks." He pointed to the jar of instant Folgers. "And we had real coffee."

"Something tells me coffee wasn't all you were sipping." Pop didn't drink anymore, but I knew he'd had a taste for it at one time.

"I guess not. We'd do most of our drinking in town though, leastways I did. Otherwise, it's a good way to get your head kicked off." He looked away to the creek bed. "Or worse."

I'd spent enough time with Doc to know when a darker memory surfaced. "What do you mean by worse?"

He brushed the question aside with a look. After a moment, he answered. "Well, down there, the usual. Girls and fights, the occasional dustup." He seemed to change his mind mid-thought. "But I think maybe it's the whiskey got Danny hung."

"Hung? You mean, like with a rope?" I thought I knew a lot about those days, but every once in a while, Pop would let a detail drop that I'd never heard before.

"Yep. We went into Yuma one night, went to the hotel and then to the show, but Danny didn't want to come along. He just walked away. Next morning, we found out he was locked up in jail. Turned out he stole some guy's car - shot and killed him.

"How'd they catch him?" I gave Pop a cupful of instant coffee. Black, laced with two sugars.

He took a taste and winced.

"He didn't get far. They found him dead drunk in the car. I guess he ran out of gas or something. After the trial, they hung him. Just like in the movies." Pop took another sip and raised his head. "He was Mexican, wasn't never going to come out good for him. I used to go over to Yuma to see him, sometimes. Me and Angelo would take him cigarettes down to the jail."

I could see the memory pained him.

"Where did you meet Angelo, Pop?"

"He went to school with me in Grass Valley, drove a truck at the Idaho-Maryland. A lot of my buddies worked in the mines, Ol' Albert Sker, some of my cousins, Tommy Johnson, too. There was a dozen mines operating around there in them days."

"Is that why you moved to California?"

"Not exactly, but dang near."

He held the metal cup close with both hands, the bright glow of the Coleman lamp milky in his glasses. "One day, Uncle Irvon came to town, sat down and poured a bunch of nuggets out on our kitchen table. Grandpa Cox, Alpha and Omega, all my cousins, they took off for up there. But Dad, he wants to stay in Wellton. It was after his accident, and he was finally starting to get around better."

I mixed myself a cup of instant, added a little milk and sugar, and started to open a can of chili.

"If your chili's as bad as this coffee, I think I'd rather starve."

"You're mighty particular for a man on foot in the middle of nowhere." I was glad to see his good mood return and kept on opening the can. He was right, though. The coffee was miserable, even by my own meager standards. The chili wasn't liable to be much better. It was one reason I liked to stay in town, so I wouldn't have to suffer my own cooking.

"So how did you end up moving?"

"I think Dad would've stayed. But Mom, she was antsy. She was always real antsy without her folks. So we'd go up to Grass Valley and visit. Mom liked all the green, said she was tired of the desert brown and grey. And sometimes, I would go up there myself with Uncle Irvon. He'd take me to see my cousins, and then I'd ride the rails back down. I did that for a couple of years, went back to the desert, even after we moved."

The gas was turned up all the way on the stove so I could see to open the can in the dark, and now the chili was burning. I couldn't stir it fast enough to make up for the extra heat. Pop grinned at my poor kitchen skills and took another sip from his cup.

"Once her dad and her brother and the cousins was gone, Mom wasn't happy. So she just looked at Dad the way she did sometimes and said, 'I miss my family'. And that was all there was to it. We were moving."

He cocked his head and smiled. "So, I guess you could say I followed Mom and Dad, or maybe they followed me."

"I hope you like burnt chili."

"Like I say, I've lived this long…" Pop gave me another grin. "Might as well try the chili."

A PAIR OF GREY DOVES were nesting in the canyon walls. They watched silently as a dark figure with a shuffling gait passed beneath them.

Old Joe had slipped out of his shack the night before, slowly making his way down the dry wash that cut alongside the mesa. He had grown tired of the constant drone of night sounds in the town; muffled conversations behind closed doors, a leaky compressor at the railroad yard, and the slow parade of cars passing by the hotel. Now that he was in the canyon, the night sounds were pure, uncluttered by metal or glass, a song of everything around him painting pictures in his mind.

He was glad to be free of the town. Perhaps the night sounds would teach him to sing a cure.

When the sickness had taken him, he thought at first it was the white man's whiskey. In a single moment, something had robbed him of his tongue and half his movement. The Big Woman found him hours later, lying on the dirt floor of the old shack, an empty bottle beside him. But she couldn't rouse him, and after a while, she sent for her husband the sheriff, who picked him up off the floor and carried him to his cot. The Big Woman had washed his face; he felt warm on one side of his nose and cold on the other. When he tried to speak he bit his tongue. The blood ran down his neck and pooled in the hollow of his collarbone.

For two weeks, the Big Woman had tended to him every morning, feeding him cold soup and beans. She made him drink water, even when it poured out of his mouth and onto his belly. After a few days, he pulled himself upright with his left arm, and lashed his shoulder to the wall with a length of latigo.

Every day, he would thank her with a nod, and she would reappear in the evening to empty his piss jar and bedpan, until one night she came and there was nothing in them, because he had pulled himself upright, and made a splint for his weak leg from the remnants of a chair, and hobbled outside to do his business.

She still came in the mornings and brought him beans, but he had taken to boiling herbs on a potbelly stove and drinking the jimson tea all day long. He told the Big Woman it was powerful medicine and would cure him, and after a time, she had even begun to believe him.

Joe peered at the doves resting in the deep shadow. He could sense them in the silence, necks ruffled and cocked, aware of his awkward movement. They had decided he was little danger. Safe and warm in their nests, they watched as the old man shuffled by, content in the darkness, before the light set them free to forage in the canyon.

They didn't hear the snake. But Joe could.

It was sliding along the base of the rocks below their darkened alcove, its flickering tongue hunting for the warm body heat above.

Joe moved quickly, more quickly than the dozing doves could have imagined. As he grabbed the snake, they leapt into the air, wings flapping in thunderous applause. Joe swung the snake round his shoulders, its rattle cackling violently in angry protest. The long snake struck again and again at Joe's head and hands, chattering as he beat it bloody and senseless against the canyon wall.

Joe swooned with laughter and teetered on his splinted leg. Using his leg as a tent pole, he leaned against the sandstone and tried to catch his breath. His pierced shoulders tingled. Blood ran down his arms and into his hands.

He heard the lesson of his Squaw Mother; her cool water words, medicine to rest the spirit and keep his heart hidden from the snake. He felt glad that he gave the words to the yellow-haired boy so long ago, that her words might still live.

Blood painted his fingers. Twice Joe smeared his hand across his cheeks in a slash of red. He took his knife from his belt and cut the splint from his leg, then straightened to his full height. He spoke his name out loud to greet the morning.

A red sun burst upon the canyon walls, and Old Joe disappeared.

Naki'zas began to dance and sing.

HE WAS UP before first light.

Time to freshen the devil's pot he'd been boiling for the better part of a week. Doc conjured some coffee from the bottom of his kit bag, adding new to the old like he did every morning. It was a well-worn tradition passed down from Grandpa Cox, the magic beans a luxury brought out by wagon to the Oklahoma territories. They gave color to the pastel brew and sharpened his senses for the day to come.

A pair of grey doves bolted into the morning sky, their sudden abandon pressed by some hidden rumble in the east. Doc looked up to the heavens and felt a passing chill.

Something had begun to scratch at him. He couldn't put a name to it - just a slippery place in the back of his mind, where his thoughts would stumble and steal his comfort.

It might have started when they hung the Mexican boy, or maybe when Kenny ran off to join the Army. Or maybe it was just because he missed his Mom and Dad. Still, he'd seen good people come and go before, and plenty of folks up and dying. It was the natural way of things.

Or maybe it was Billie.

His eyes closed in reflex. He put the thought away and all the ones that waited after. There was pleasure in the pure silence of early morning and the hot black liquid in its warm metal cup. Time enough to suffer his thoughts when he was old and crippled.

In the distance, he thought he heard singing, or maybe it was the pitch of the wind as it passed through the ancient Saguaro behind him. The wind song spoke of old times, old friends, and his sister's clear blue eyes.

David Russell Bailey took a last swallow of coffee and pitched the rest into the fire. It was only a few days into December. If he broke camp now, he'd be home in time for Christmas.

DOC TURNED THE MAP up and down and then sideways, but like a fitted sheet it wouldn't fold up the same way twice. "Gol' durn it."

I took the crumpled papers and put them next to me on the long bench seat. "That's how come they sell so many maps."

Pop growled and spun the top off the thermos. "Forget the map," he said, singing out the directions. "We'll take the long way. Highway 50 right after Garrison, and pray for a gas station!"

"Praise the Lord and pass the thermos." Pop had taught me coffee was the best way to cool down on a hot day, better than a cold drink. Something about getting your insides warmer than your outsides. Like most things, he was right about that, too. I held out my cup, and he poured halfway to the rim.

We'd just left Beaver City, Utah, bound for home from New Mexico. It was our first big trip in a couple of years; all the way down to the Coronado National Forest and back up to Albuquerque. Along the way, we found where they filmed *Red River*, sampled lots of jerky, and passed some time watching a roundup outside the Navajo Nation.

There wasn't much to Beaver City, sort of a crossroads between Salt Lake and Denver. It did have a good coffee shop and a couple of gas stations. And one curious distinction; it was the birthplace of the outlaw Butch Cassidy and Philo T. Farnsworth, the man who invented television.

Oddly enough, my office in San Francisco was right next to Philo's old laboratory, something I knew about only because I'd stop to read almost any historical marker, especially if I wanted an excuse for a cigarette. By this time, I'd gone back to work in the city. I had a wife and a daughter now, and more bills to pay.

"I really do like this out here," Pop said.

We'd just crossed the Beaver River, and the landscape was spreading out into long valleys, ringed by low ridges crisscrossed by fast-running creeks. The surrounding mountain ranges were covered in Pinyon Pine, Juniper, and Aspen.

"She's mighty pretty, yes sir." Another good thing about two-lane blacktop; you had the chance to look around without the constant distraction of passing cars. I had to remind myself to keep my eyes on the road, the countryside was so beautiful.

"I almost moved to Utah once, right after the war."

"You never told me that." I took a sip of coffee; it was just hot enough to discourage a full swallow.

"I never told you a lot of things." Doc pulled out his tobacco pouch. "Especially with that tape recorder running." He glanced at the pocket dictation machine that I bought at Radio Shack before we left California.

"Statute of limitations?"

He laughed and shook his head no. "I believe they'd have a hard time proving anything without a signed confession."

The road began to curl towards the north. I pulled a chrome handle out below the dash and engaged the electric overdrive. "How'd you feel about the war?"

"I didn't really care to go at all, once my friends were gone. I was driving a cab for ol' Howard Statz, and fighting with the draft board about my hernia." Doc finished rolling his cigarette and reached for his Bic lighter. "I had a good thing going in Grass Valley." He lit the tip, inhaled, and coughed spasmodically. After a moment, he caught his breath and exhaled. "Gonna' have to quit these things someday."

"Me too." Pop's persistent cough was beginning to worsen.

I knew I should quit, but like most things that weren't good for me, I enjoyed them far too much to let go. I truly wished Pop would, even if it cost me the guilty pleasure of our shared addiction.

Doc took a deep breath and continued. "Between the whorehouse and the taxicab and the whiskey, I was making a pretty good living."

"Whorehouse?" I handed him my empty cup and wondered what came next. "What whorehouse?"

"Oh, during the war, we had a couple of places outside of town. The lady that ran the one would give me a dollar for every soldier that came out there in my cab, and sometimes I'd have 6 or 8 of them in there." He flicked his fingers in a waving motion. "She'd line 'em up like bowling pins and knock 'em down."

"Just her?"

"Nah, she had another girl working there, but she didn't get them in and out like that old gal could. I don't think some of those boys lasted over 30 seconds." We laughed, and he coughed again. "Yes sir, I had me a good thing going, but like things do, everything changed."

"How so?"

"Well, I got tired of waiting around for them to fix me up, so I went down to Roseville and got the operation myself. I guess I was having too good a time, and all of a sudden, the next thing you know, I was 1A." Doc fingered his cigarette and scowled. "They didn't want to fix my hernia, but they'd sure as hell let me pay for it. So I says, to hell with you, and joined the Merchant Marine. I always wanted to see the ocean."

"Why the Merchant Marine and not the Navy?" I could see this was important to him, in a way that wasn't obvious to me.

"The pay was a whole lot better, and I could stay stateside in between shipping out." He looked at me with a grin. "With my little gal."

BEGINNER'S LUCK

IT WAS MUCH HARDER to leave her this time. He hadn't expected the knot in his throat.

The ride down to San Francisco seemed to last for hours. He longed to get off the bus at every stop, to turn around and head back to Grass Valley. But he wasn't going to. He would keep his seat. Like his dad said, a man's name is only as good as his word. And the United States Merchant Marine had his on the dotted line.

The big Trailways bus careened through the long valley, past the tasseled rows of corn, the roadside fruit stands and the flooded rice fields ready for seed. Dave watched a farmer set the perimeter of his plot ablaze; the burning stubble formed a billowing grey cloud that rose low along the horizon.

Becky had made him a cheese sandwich and some cookies. He took a cautious bite.

He thought about his mother's apple dumplings and wondered what it would be like to eat out most of his life. He'd made a game of it with Becky, never letting her know the truth, always picking out something new on the take-out menu, driving up to Truckee or down to Roseville just to try out a new diner. All the while, wishing he could think of some way to get her and his mom in the same kitchen on the same day.

Dave's smile softened. Laughter and good loving would have to do.

The soldier next to him had a hungry look. Dave gave him the cookies and tucked the dry sandwich back inside its wax paper bag.

At least he could eat his own cooking aboard ship.

"I DON'T BELIEVE you've got anything at all." The man across the table fiddled with his cards. He eyeballed Dave suspiciously.

Dave liked the feel of the pocket pair of threes beneath his fingers, a lucky deal on an unlucky ship bound for the Pacific islands. They'd hit bad weather at the Farallons, and the next 5 days had reminded him of that little horse in Nevada, the one that never turned the same way twice. Despite his hard won sea legs, even he had sought the comfort of the rail, and this was his third ticket.

They'd been at sea for 8 days. Once their cargo was secure and the motion sickness abated, monotony had settled in. Dave had become something of an old hand, such as they were, since riding ammunition ships was not the occupation one would choose hoping to collect a pension. Still, there was no such thing to be had during the war, so when it came time to choose his billet, he opted for the dangerous duty and not the milk runs to Pearl. Of course, it didn't hurt that every hour aboard was hazard pay and worth a hefty bonus if he ever made it back to shore.

Dave Bailey joined the Maritime Service, not for love of country, nor even for the sea, but out of spite for G. Arlen Pepper and the Grass Valley Draft Board.

The war had broken out all of a sudden, and like most of his friends, he had marched right down to enlist; Tommy Castro, Johnny Lanyon, him and Verle McLaughlin all went down together in one bunch, signed the papers and got promises to be in the same outfit; all US Army, all headed for Camp Beale. But Dave's physical came up crooked - he'd had a stiff nut for a couple of years. It didn't bother him much, he'd compensate with his upper back and legs, but they called it a hernia and said he'd have to have the surgery before he could go to basic.

"Just take this ticket, go down to the draft board. They'll get you fixed up, then you can report." The doctor stamped his papers and sent him on his way. He watched as his friends boarded the long grey bus; he didn't know it'd be the last time he ever saw Johnny and Verle. One took a grenade in basic, the other one died on Omaha Beach.

The man across the table was still looking at his cards.

"It's on you, are you going to call or just sit there 'til breakfast?" Dave considered his opponent. The other man was fish bait, first ticket, barely 20 days out of the academy. He was older than the usual raw recruit, about 45 or 50. It wasn't the first greybeard Dave had seen; The Merchant Marine would take almost any man fit for sea duty. This fellow seemed to have a good feel for the cards though, and was taking more than his share of the pots.

The older man didn't respond, just continued shuffling his cards to and fro. Dave didn't mind. It wasn't as if he had anywhere else to go. Once on board and battened down, it was 10 days to the Marshall Islands, then on to who knows where, and the bullets could start to fly at any moment.

Dave reckoned that he might have liked the Army better. Camping out agreed with him, even on a hard rock bedroll, and surely a better chance to shoot at something than he'd get slinging hash on some overloaded rust bucket. But G. Arlen Pepper wasn't having any of it - said he'd have to wait in line for his operation behind everyone else.

If I had a nickel for every time I pestered that damn draft board, I could raise this pot to the moon.

The grey-haired seaman put his cards down and palmed a handful of twenty-dollar bills from his stack. "Call your raise," he said. "And up a hundred."

The next three players called both raises. They had a good seat for a race they knew could start at any moment.

Dave didn't hesitate. He made his call, then peeled off three one hundred-dollar bills. "Plus three." A standard ration cigarette appeared from the crumpled package inside his denim shirt.

"Too rich for my blood." The ship's Negro cook frowned in mock disappointment.

"Johnny, a nickel's too steep if you ain't got a pat hand." Dave lit his cigarette and blew a long, smoky trail at the ceiling. "I never seen such a snake in the grass."

Johnny Washington tossed his hand into the growing pile of discards. "Davey, you just don't like powerful competition, that's all. Besides, we're on duty in half-an-hour." The chief touched Dave's shoulder and stood to go. "If'n you ever finish this hand."

One by one, the three remaining players faded, leaving only Dave and the new man heads up.

"Call, plus another three." The older man snap-counted out another raise.

Dave figured the new man wasn't bluffing; he hadn't yet caught the all-or-nothing compulsion that kicked in after the first real firefight. One good look at a squadron of Zeros and some guys would start making big bets on every hand. Most would learn better. The weak-willed ones would lose their whole stake in the very next poker game.

The Captain knew this, and even though there was a regular payroll on-board, the purser wouldn't let any man take all his pay. It was a well-worn custom on ammunition ships – a big cash box that all the men could draw from, for poker and the occasional well-oiled shore leave. But fully half of the men's wages would be held on shore for their return, or more likely for their families, since the ammunition ships of the Merchant Marine were the most vulnerable in the fleet. A single spark in a cargo hold could explode an entire vessel. They were an all-volunteer crew on an all-volunteer mission, in an all-volunteer service.

Years before, when the US Congress passed The Merchant Marine Act, the goal had been simple; build the ships faster than the enemy could sink them. So far, the shipyards were barely keeping up.

"Don't go all hasty on me now," said Dave. Perhaps there was more to this man. A thousand dollars was a considerable bet, even on this old tub.

Like so many others on the outbound leg, Dave kept a pasteboard box full of cash right below his bunk. There was nowhere to spend it and no reason to steal it, since no one was willing to take on the risk that such a theft would entail. There was little patience for a thief or a laggard on the Western Victory. The distance from the boat deck to the boiling sea below was only a matter of an accidental trip or a sudden poke.

"You don't suppose I could get a peek at those cards?" Dave asked. "It would make my next decision a whole lot easier."

The older man laughed in spite of himself. He glanced at his two hole cards. "Ace queen," he said, nodding quietly. Dave considered the five face-up cards across from him: two 10s, a deuce, a jack and a king. If true, the man had an ace-high straight. A solid hand, even in seven card stud.

Dave's exposed cards: two nines, a five, a three and a jack. With the pair beneath his palm, he could easily raise again and take the pot; his opponent was primed for it. But he sensed the fellow had made a decent gesture - the opportunity to save himself six big bills, which he in turn, was happy to acknowledge.

"Pocket threes," he replied without hesitation.

The older man quickly calculated Dave's hand. "Ouch. I had you on a busted flush - or maybe two pair."

"Honesty is its own reward." Dave rolled his hole cards over: a full house. It was a long way to the islands, and every man for himself was a damn sure way to end up alone. He noted the mild surprise in the older man's eyes.

He would take the greybeard's money, all 900 dollars of it, but no more.
The pot was plenty big already. Besides, it was time to go. The captain had little
patience for a late breakfast.

SKYLER DICKS was a crack shot with a rifle; his father had given him a single
shot .22 Remington when he was only eight years old - he could knock the red
off a woodpecker at fifty yards. He was just as good with a shotgun, skeets or fowl;
Skyler knew how to follow a lead and let the bird come to the birdshot. But he'd
barely gotten by at gunnery school. For some damn reason, he couldn't make good
with the big .50 caliber on a moving target. Skyler thought his rifle skills would
transfer with him, but even after hours of practice, his accuracy hadn't improved.
Sometimes, he wondered if he was there just to fill a quota; he'd heard the shelf
life of a cargo ship's gun crew was short at best. The Naval Armed Guard was no
place to work your way up through the ranks.

Back in New Orleans, he'd had a good job at the port, working nights on a
pilot boat. He was offshore when the tanker Virginia went down, the whole sky lit
up for miles around. 180,000 gallons of gasoline torched by three torpedoes from
a German submarine. They pulled some floaters from the water, but the burns
were so bad only one man had survived. Skyler enlisted the next day. Navy basic in
Shreveport, then on to Gunnery School in Gulfport, Mississippi.

He'd requested an Atlantic berth to get a shot at some Nazi U-boats, but was
mustered out to San Francisco instead, assigned to one of the new Victory ships,
fresh from the Richmond boatyards. How he'd ended up in the Pacific he couldn't
say – the Navy probably know what they were doing.

Not like the damn Merchant Marine.

They had no common sense at all. Colored boys served everywhere in the
Maritime, as oilmen, able seamen, engineers. Skyler had heard tell there was even
a Negro merchant captain. Sure, there was a need for warm bodies, what with the
war and all, but at least the Navy had the common decency to keep folks separated,
not all crammed up right next to each other.

Luckily, the Armed Guard had their own crew quarters, up close to the forward gun mounts. It took him less than 20 seconds to get from his bunk to his gun
tub. On the way there, Skyler paused to gaze at the rolling sea and wondered if the
Japanese had many submarines. He turned for the ship's mess with a shrug. Not
due for another 10 minutes, time enough for some coffee before the next watch.

Maybe then he could get down to the real job at hand – killing Japs.

"YOU'VE GOT A NICE WAY with the cards - or are you just plain lucky?" Robert Fisher moved through the aft companionway, right behind Dave Bailey. They were on their way to the Western Victory's mess hall.

"Don't want to get too lucky," Dave replied. "They say you get real lucky right before you die." Dave was tucking in his shirttail as he walked. He hitched up his khakis with a black leather belt. "I'd just as soon lose a poker hand than lose my head."

"Come to think of it, so would I." Bob followed close behind. "But I wouldn't want to make a habit of it."

"Something tells me that's not your weakness."

"Not for me. A good card game is just about the closest thing to heaven on earth."

"Damn, we got to get you to a better whorehouse." Dave pulled a new package of Pall Malls from his shirt pocket. He offered one to the older man.

"No thanks, I don't have a taste for them."

"Smokes or girls?" Dave pulled out a cigarette. He lit it with the brass Zippo he'd purchased on his last shore leave.

The older man chuckled, then leaned back against the bulkhead to let one of the Naval Guards by in the narrow passageway. "A good poker game is better than either one, actually." Fisher spoke quietly. "Truth be told, that's how I came to be here. I heard the best poker games on the planet were aboard these ships."

Fisher was telling him straight. High stakes games on ammunition ships were something of an open secret, and rightly famous around the union hall. Dave didn't realize their novelty had passed out into the world beyond. On his last ticket, it was no rarity to see thousands of dollars wagered on a single hand. "You mean you come here, and you didn't have to?"

"I did, although my family didn't think too highly of it at the time."

Dave recognized the elegant tone in the older man's voice. He noted the pace and clarity of Fisher's words, like a fine racehorse on a smooth track. "Old money," he thought, and wondered if there was much left of it. Could be the fellow was as careless with his inheritance as he was with his ace-high straight.

"You are a gambler. Well, your dollar's good as anybody's, I suppose." Dave motioned the older man into the mess hall. "And the coffee's free, that's for sure."

Johnny Washington was scowling at him from across the hall. Dave pulled a fresh apron from the hanging rack and headed for the main galley.

"I SAID I'LL HAVE MINE BLACK. Black as you." Gunner's Mate Skyler Dicks was running late; he'd stopped to listen to the ball scores, and the young colored boy pouring coffee in the chow line was slow. He raised his voice again. "And hurry up."

"Say what?" Johnny Washington stopped carving strips from the wide bacon slab on his butcher block. The Chief Cook moved through the galley with a speed that belied his sixty-four years.

"Yessir, I... I will, sir." The mess boy stuttered his reply.

"You'll do no such thing." Washington pulled the bewildered boy away from the chow line. He motioned the Naval Guard to the door. "And you, you get out of my mess if you can't keep a civil tongue." Johnny's jaw clenched as he fingered the hilt on his big carving knife.

Dave's eyes lifted from his kneading table. He was beating out enough dough for a hundred biscuits, but he knew for sure that more than bread was rising. He dropped the dough ball and slid a rolling pin into his hand.

"Go on, Skyler." Dave was next to the mess table before anyone had seen him coming. "Get on out of here."

The burly six-foot guard was ready to pounce, his freckled face red and puffy. He recognized Dave from their frequent gunnery drills and hesitated. Bailey was in charge of the merchant loader crew that stood alongside his station's gun mount.

"Go on." Dave moved quickly between Dicks and the fuming cook. "Get on up before somebody puts you on report. I'll bring you some coffee after a while." Coffee on deck was a regular part of kitchen duty, but mostly the mess boys took it up. Dave Bailey was a Baker. He didn't have to carry food, wash dishes or prep meat and vegetables - union rules.

Skyler softened. This wasn't the time to let his temper get the best of him. Bailey was the one man on this ship that had taken any time or trouble with him. The merchant sailor seemed to have a knack for the .50 caliber; he'd spent hours teaching him about the big gun. Yesterday, he'd shown Skyler how to slide an empty shell casing beneath the butterfly trigger, to keep the weapon from firing accidentally. The Naval Guard loosened his fists and stepped backwards. He kept a wary eye on the angry black man and his long, curved knife.

"Go on. I'll see you later." Dave turned from the retreating man and placed a hand on Johnny Washington's trembling wrist. "Let him go, Chief," he whispered under his breath. "He's just a big dumb soldier boy, don't know any better."

It wasn't the first time he'd seen Johnny Washington pull an angry knife. The last time it happened, the offending party had to be transferred to an escort ship for medical treatment. Only the Captain's personal intervention had kept Johnny in the Merchant Marine, and not in some stateside brig.

Dave made a promise to himself not to get between that blade and its intended victim again.

THE FIRST PART OF THE VOYAGE was fairly uneventful. Long fraternal card games and short naps, lots of biscuits and white gravy. They were part of a large resupply convoy, bound for the Marianas Islands and parts unknown.

There were nights when the poker got as stale as the cigarette fog that floated above their table; Bob Fisher and Dave Bailey would climb all the way aft, above the rope lockers and the ammunition holds, far from anyone except the late watch. Below them, the turning sea washed out in great spirals from the giant 18' propeller. Above them, a pitch trail billowed from the boilers to stain a sky lit with stars.

Sometimes, the sea would glow green from horizon to horizon, a firefly mist on an infinite lake. They would sit for hours, telling stories. Journeys on a western desert and tales of old San Francisco.

They talked about women, about racehorses and old horses, tall sailing ships and fine hotels. There were fire dances and hard rock mines, and the number of steps in a waltz.

Right below them, beneath the rope locker in the Number Five hold, there were 2000 tons of high explosives. Beyond that in Number Four: 10,000 impact fuses for high altitude bombs. Number Three held 4000 tons of mortar shells. Number One and Two: anti-personnel mines and small arms munitions, topped off with general cargo. And if that weren't enough, there was also the matter of 20,000 gallons of bunker fuel.

They talked about a lot of things on the aft deck.

But they never talked about that.

TO THE NORTH, furnace flats straddled two jagged mountain ranges, one bordering the west and the other to the east. "According to the map, this place is called Snake Valley." I pointed west outside my window. "There's a lake out there somewhere. Want to stop?"

"Nope. I'd just as soon skip anything named after snakes." Pop looked past me and wrinkled up his brow. "I ever tell you about the time I come across a mountain full of rattlers?

"Not that I recall." I knew Doc didn't like snakes, but not exactly why.

"This here was down in Wellton. Heck, they was stacked up like bedsprings. Nighttime, black as Hades. I caught a whiff of dirty socks, that's how come I knew they was out there."

Pop was right about the smell - the same as old laundry. A diamondback got in my basement once. I thought it was a mouse behind the washer-dryer, until it started rattling and scared me half to death.

"Must've been a hundred of 'em. Sidewinders like them hot boulders. That desert gets cold at night, and they all come down to the same spot, right next to Copper Mountain. Found that bunch on my last trip, right before the war."

"So what happened?"

"I walked backwards till I got to the Pacific Ocean." He gave me a wry smile and pulled out his tobacco.

"How'd your buddies like playing poker with a man named Doc?"

Pop shrugged. "They didn't. People knew me by Dave aboard ship. I think just you and ol' Angelo call me that now." Pop shook some tobacco into his roll. "We had nicknames for some folks. There was this one kid, skinny little guy. We used to call him 'bonecrusher'."

Funny how nicknames could travel with you for a long time and then just disappear. I used to be known as PJ, all because of a pair of baggy seersucker pants.

"How long were you out at sea?" A flash of red caught my eye. The batteries in my little tape recorder were wearing out.

"Sometimes for months at a time. All depends on the cargo, what they need-ed and where." He took a deep breath. "If you got shot at, or your ship sank."

"Jeez."

"We was easy targets. Merchant Marine took the highest casualty rate of anybody in that war. Seven hundred ships." Pop lit the cigarette he'd been rolling. "Worst thing about taking a hit was you stopped collecting pay the minute you hit the water." He tilted his head to blow out a smoke ring.

"You're kidding?"

"Nope. Union shop. If you weren't aboard ship, you didn't get paid. Surprised the hell out of some guys when they made it back to the states."

Doc didn't talk much about the war, unless I pressed him. I could under-stand. There were some things I didn't like to talk about either. The red light was still flashing, so I clicked the tape recorder off.

The hidden lake beckoned in the distance, oasis-like, shimmering in the sunlight. I would have called it a mirage, if it weren't for the map and the road signs.

IT WAS ONE WEEK after D-Day, but no one on the Western Victory knew anything about it. They were sailing under radio silence, first to the Solomon Islands, then across the central Pacific to rendezvous with a convoy off the Marianas.

By the time the Western arrived, 3200 Americans, 27,000 Imperial soldiers and over 10,000 Japanese civilians had lost their lives on Saipan. Most of the civilian casualties were suicides.

The Victory ship stayed anchored one mile off the island for months, carefully unloading the impact fuses she carried in cargo hold #4. An Army Air Corps officer came aboard to oversee the delicate job of offloading the high explosives. Each carton had to be hand carried, packed into the landing crafts one at a time.

Every night, Dave would watch on deck as wave after wave of B-29s took off from the high plateau above the beach. The Army officer told him that the giant bomber planes were headed straight for Japan, for Tokyo itself. The roar of their engines was continuous, like the roll of tides on the beach.

Each B-29 Superfortress carried 20,000 pounds of incendiary bombs. They were like bees swarming, so many taking off and landing that Dave lost count. Their marker lights trailed lazily into the night sky, impervious to the empire that had lost its desperate foothold on the island of Saipan.

Deep down, he knew it was the beginning of the end of the war.

* * *

Chabua Airfield, US Army Air Corps
India–Burma Theatre of War

LAWRENCE SPAIN ADJUSTED HIS SEAT in the anteroom outside the adjutant's office. He stared at a worn copy of Stars & Stripes on the table beside him. Like most Army newspapers, it was out of date. Anything more recent would have found its way to the duty room. He noticed the months-old progress in Europe and the fall of Saipan.

His coffee had grown cold waiting for the CO. He didn't know why he'd been summoned - maybe another search & rescue mission. Maybe another Gene

Autry USO show.

He'd been flying "the Hump" for over a year. The route itself wasn't complicated, once you got past the temptation just to look out the window. The Gandaki River Gorge was as wide and as deep as the Grand Canyon, maybe deeper, if anyone could see to the bottom. Most days you couldn't, for the thick fog and low clouds that obscured the view. To ride the Hump, you had to thread the needle through the gorge, cross the Santsung Ridge at 15,000 feet, and land at Kunming Airfield in the mountains of eastern China. It was 500 miles across the snow-capped peaks, if you could beat the thunderstorms and the gale force winds. Or the hail, which came out of the sky like angry golf balls, sending your airplane hurtling up and down a thousand feet at a time, like a yo-yo on a giant string.

Thousands of those re-supply missions were being flown to the struggling Chinese army. It didn't help that the greenest pilots in the Air Corps were assigned to the task. Freddy Spain was fresh out of flight school when he got here; no wonder his son was lost.

Hundreds of aircraft had gone missing, their flight crews buried in the snowy deep. It was a high price to pay, but the powers-at-be thought it better to keep the Japanese busy fighting Chiang Kai-Shek, than to set them free against the American forces in the Pacific. His oldest son was part of that price.

When Freddy went missing, Lawrence had bucked for a transfer to India. It was a long shot, but he had to take it. A pilot could bail out, escape the Japanese, and maybe find his way into China. He'd promised Madeline to search for any sign of their son. He couldn't bear to tell her the truth; the icy mountains rarely gave up their victims. Not after 6 months, not even after 6 hours.

Why Lawrence had been spared, he would never know. The war seemed to pick numbers out of a hat, like some mad bingo game. One family spared and another one decimated beyond recognition.

Madeline's letters were like a funeral dirge; his cousin John at Normandy, Kenny Kraddock, Sam Kingston, and the Vasquez boys at Pearl.

Even old Bill Gale.

He wondered how Davey Bailey was doing. He'd left Wellton barely a boy, but kept coming back as a young man, as if he'd left something important behind. Davey's dad would never have to go to war again. The last time he saw him, Dee could barely see far enough to read the paper, much less fly a plane or shoot a gun. He was glad for his old friend's reprieve. Maybe Dee Bailey's son would make it out of this war alive.

The duty officer returned, carrying a stack of folders, some small manila envelopes and a snap salute. Lawrence returned it with a slight nod.

"With the Colonel's compliments, sir." He handed Lawrence an envelope and exited the way he came. Lawrence unfolded the crisp paper inside. He read it three times. The first time, he glanced over his shoulder to see if it might be some kind of cruel joke, then again to make certain of his senses. He could barely read it the third time through his tears.

> TRANSFER ORDERS: effective 18 February 1945
> Spain, Lawrence A., Major #47768399
> Re-assigned to Cadet Training School, Flight Operations
> BILLET: Yuma Proving Grounds; Yuma, Arizona

He was going home.

DAVE LIFTED THE AMMUNITION BELT onto his bunk. It was cumbersome and heavy. Each cartridge was over six inches in length and weighed almost a pound. The first time Dave handled one was at the Maritime Academy on Santa Catalina Island, where some plank-faced gunnery sergeant tried to make an example out of him.

"Do you know what this is, Bailey?"

"Well sir, offhand, I'd say it's a damn big bullet."

"No, sir. This is your ass." The grizzled sergeant pushed the pointy end of the .50 caliber cartridge into Dave's chest, reinforcing each word with another steely jab. "And unless you learn to love it, load it and fire it, you can damn well kiss that ass goodbye, because some squinty-eyed Jap is going to blow it clear into the Pacific Ocean."

The gunnery master had hideously bad breath, like a swollen deer left to bloat in the sun. He had a full plate of dentures on his upper palate, and didn't clean them for days at a time.

"Make friends with this thing, know it like your girlfriend's tits. Keep it clean, well secured and ready, and it will save your life someday."

Dave winced at the thought of Becky's smooth breasts violated by the sergeant's fragrant words. He replied loudly. "Yessir, Sergeant sir!" For some reason, sergeants liked to be shouted at, even at arm's length.

"Very good, Mister Bailey." The sergeant looked up and down the line of merchant recruits, scowling. "Now, let's see you hit something with it! Report to the firing range at 1500 hours. Squad dismissed!"

It took him a little while to learn how, but Dave hit all of his targets, with more accuracy than any of the other cadets. At first, the sergeant was angry when he'd seen how he pulled it off. Later, the master sergeant had offered the young recruit a position as gunnery instructor, with a permanent berth on Catalina Island.

He'd spent long nights in his bunk, lights out, fingering the bolt, barrel and chamber on his M1 Garand, memorizing every edge of every surface, tearing it down and putting it back together, again and again. Eventually, whenever an officer came by for inspection, the sergeant would bring him forward.

"Bailey, show the Captain how we break down a weapon in this squad." Dave would disassemble the rifle in a blur, then reassemble it with a series of seamless strokes. He liked showing off a bit. It kept him from the drearier duties on the island. But he didn't want to end up a specimen in this sergeant's trophy case.

"You're a slippery son of a bitch, but you're no fool, and you handle a weapon as well as any man I've seen," the sergeant had said. "We could use you here."

"Thank you sir, but I'd rather take my tricks to sea." Dave wielded his carefully crafted reply. "More Japs out there, Sergeant, sir!"

"More money, too," he thought to himself. He really didn't care about killing anyone. Unless they shot at him first.

Dave had given his berth in the Merchant Marine some serious thought and had already decided on his ticket – ammunition ships. If he was going to get his ass shot off, he wanted to make damn sure it was gold-plated. He had plans for him and Becky after the war.

Sitting on his bunk in the Western Victory, he slid a .50 caliber armor-piercing round into the prongs of an ammo belt, then slid a tracer round into the next open clip. Dave repeated the pattern over and over - one tracer, one AP round, one explosive round.

It wasn't the way the sergeant had taught him; Dave had reasoned it out for himself. The standard method was 3 AP rounds, one explosive round, and then one tracer. But that had made it too damn hard to lead the big gun onto the moving targets, so Dave had slipped into the ammo dumps and custom built his own cartridge belts, one tracer for every other round. When the tracer shells barked out of his belt, it was like a flashlight in the dark, a long trail of light pointed right at the towing targets offshore. He'd even gone so far as to shoot the turnbuckle off of one of the towing chains; that had really pissed off the ground crew. The sergeant just laughed and told them to tow the damn thing faster.

Now that he was out to sea, he still cut his own belts, and kept one full ammunition box beneath his bunk, in case they ever got into a real dogfight. Dave was battle-stationed on deck, right next to the Naval Guards, first relief. If they ever got hit, he was next man on the totem pole; it was his job to keep the big gun firing.

If he had to do it, he figured to do it his way.

Dave drilled with the .50 caliber crew every week; he'd seen Skyler Dicks taking extra target practice with little improvement. He decided it was time to pass on a little of his special confidence, and maybe save himself the trouble of replacing Dicks in a firefight.

He put the 40-round belt onto his shoulder and carried it up on deck, along with a fresh tray of coffee. A full ammo can could weigh over 100 pounds - he carried only enough belt to make his point. The ship lurched as he moved out of the passageway, and he almost slipped on deck.

"Skyler," Dave cried, "give me a hand with this thing!"

The Naval Guard jumped to meet Dave at the forecastle. Carrying the mess tray with heavy ammo belt was an obvious balancing act.

"Take the belt." Dave leaned to his left. The heavy string slid into Skyler's hands. "Set up just like I told you. Hook that one in line before your next live-fire drill."

The gunner's mate looked at the custom ammo belt and scowled. "Tracers don't do enough damage…"

"And a miss don't do none at all."

Dave opened the Stanley vacuum bottle. He poured the steaming coffee into thick white mugs for the gunnery crew. "Just remember - tracers work both ways." Dave clapped Skyler on the shoulder. "So don't miss."

"Thanks Dave." The big man inhaled the strong aroma rising from his mug. One good thing about that bastard with the big knife; he made the best coffee Skyler had tasted since Gulfport. Plenty of extra chicory, ground in with good, dark beans. And the closer they got to Okinawa, the more he would need it. The naval gun crews were four hours on and four hours off, round the clock, until they reached Nakagusuku Bay.

"You know, you never told me. What ever got into that old man?"

"You did, Skyler. So don't go calling somebody boy again, or nigger, or any of that other fool talk you brung from home." Bailey slid a fourth mug off his belt loop and filled it. "He works on this boat just the same as you and me, and his blood's just as red. And if we go down, he'll die the same way, too." Dave let the thought sink in. He took a taste from his cup. "And keep in mind, that big knife of his ain't no virgin, neither."

Skyler frowned. He fingered the new ammo belt. "You swear by this thing, huh?"

"That little pattern could have kept me stateside, if I'd wanted it to." Dave tipped his chin with a broad wink. "But I didn't want to miss the chance to see you splash one."

Bailey's confidence made Skyler feel as if he might actually hit what he was aiming for. Dicks pulled a brass shell out of its connecting clip and spliced the custom ammo belt into the breech of his Browning M2.

Dave smiled. "2000 yards is about all she'll go straight. Don't get in a hurry, 'cause you'll just waste them tracers."

Skyler Dicks spun the big Browning into a flight of imaginary Zeros.

Dave sat his mess tray on the deck and stepped away from the gun turret. He removed the crumpled letter tucked away behind his Pall Malls, holding it loosely over the rail. After a long look out to sea, he sat down against the bulkhead and opened the envelope.

February 4, 1945

Dear Dave,
I know you weren't expecting this, and neither was I. Stuart came back.
It was a big surprise to everyone. Harold said that happens sometimes,
that the missing turn into wounded behind the lines.

He's not in very good shape. His father wrote me and told me he was
coming home. "Pretty banged up" is all he said. I got money and called.
Stu lost the use of his right arm, and he's badly burned.

So I have to go back. I know this isn't what we talked about, but it's the
only thing I know how to do.
I love you.
Becky

He'd been carrying the letter for the better part of a week, ever since they'd left the Philippines. Dave had only gotten one letter before, from his mom. His dad's eyesight had failed such that he seldom wrote anything at all, preferring to speak it out loud and let her write it for him.

They'd said how proud of him they were, and what all his cousins were up to, about who married who, and the ball scores, and about Verle McLaughlin dying on Omaha Beach. There were other things too, things he suspected were about Tommy Johnson at Camp Beale or some such thing, because someone had taken a black marker to the letter and scratched those lines out.

I wish they'd done the same to this one.

When he met Becky for the first time, he thought she was real pretty and pretty wild, too. She was in the back of one of Harold Statz's cabs, with her cousin from Marysville. Harold was her uncle; his brother in Kansas had sent Becky out to California to forget about losing her husband somewhere in North Africa.

Dave had driven cabs for Harold for the better part of a year, while he waited on the draft board to schedule his operation. He'd even gone down to the hospital to pester them about the deal, but it seemed like the government was rationing hernia stitches, too.

Becky was a bright light, and every man she'd see would buzz around her, hungry moths drawn to her flame. Harold had asked Dave to be her escort for the spring dance at Lake Olympia, and to keep his eyes peeled for soldier boys who'd had a little too much to drink. "They tend to misbehave," he said.

Harold would know. He'd turned a blind eye to Dave's principal sideline - selling whiskey to the soldiers who were up on leave from Camp Beale. Dave kept a case of pint bottles stashed off the side of McCourtney Road. Yuba County had gone dry around the training camps, so the Army boys would come up the road plenty thirsty and usually plenty horny, too. Most of the girls in town wouldn't have anything to do with them, and they'd end up in Dave's cab, for a little liquid courage and a trip to the whorehouse.

So Dave went along to the lake with Becky and his cousin Alpha, and Becky's cousin Louise, to the big dance floor that was built right out on the water. That's where they had their first kiss. Alpha bet him a dollar that he couldn't make any hay, and Becky overheard the bet, and then she up and kissed him without even asking. She just laughed and said, "Take his money and buy me a lemonade." And he never stopped loving her, from that day on.

Harold was none too pleased about it, said that she was still married, but he could see that she was happy again and that was all right with him. Dave didn't go down to the draft board anymore and began to think more kindly of G. Arlen Pepper.

They'd go for rides in Dave's '39 Plymouth, out along Highway 20, and camp in the moonlight and swim naked in the reservoir, warming themselves on a Pendleton blanket that Dave kept in the rumble seat. Becky would talk about the hills around them, so different from her home in Kansas. Dave would show her where the deer bed down for the night, and the owls nesting up in the digger pines.

He knew they were living on borrowed time, either for the draft board, or her husband being MIA, or just the plain fact that they were living in a world at war, where everything was upside down and no one knew who was going to make it past their next birthday. And then they would make love on the blanket or up against a tree, or in the cold clear water of the Yuba River. Sometimes, it was so sweet that he would catch her crying, and when he asked why she would say, "It's for this moment, because it's all mine. But I can't keep it, and I'll never have it again."

He would just laugh, and sing her one of the camp songs he'd learned in the packing sheds, and she would hold him close and sing along, and they would fall asleep on the old Pendleton.

There was a moment when he thought about the grey sea, about how deep it was, and wondered if he could swim all the way back to San Francisco. Below the rail, the water pitched and turned. It seemed almost inviting, cold like the waters of the Yuba.

Barmaids are better than mermaids.

The stray thought drifted into his mind and he spoke it aloud, softly, to the sky and the sea. He pitched the letter over the side and walked back down into the galley.

"SIX HANDS IN A ROW! Believe it or not, I even hit an inside straight." Bob Fisher laughed as he split his biscuit, then ran it through the bowl of steaming white gravy perched on his mess tray.

Dave had come out from the galley to say hello. Lately, he'd been spending a lot of time alone, and hadn't seen Fisher for days. Since he'd gotten Becky's letter, he just didn't feel much like playing cards.

"You should have seen it, Dave. Biggest pot I ever saw, even on shore."

Bob was sitting with the second shift from the boiler room: two engineers, an oiler and a watertender. The Western Victory's big oil-fired steam engines were built in Scandinavia and shipped to Richmond, California, where the ship was built around them in enormous dry docks. The Kaiser Steel Company launched three Victory ships per week, all built on a massive assembly line. It took seven men to man the engines. Bob was a second loader; his job was to keep the bunker fuel pipes hot enough to let the thick molasses flow 24 hours a day.

Dave clapped the older man on the back and leaned in. "Next time I sit down at a table with you - remind me to change the deck." He was glad for Fisher's good fortune. It lightened his mood.

"You know, Dave, before that, I hadn't won a good pot in a week." Bob gave his friend a wide grin as he broke open another hard roll. "And I'm even beginning to like your biscuits." Fisher took an enormous bite of the crusty bread. "Luck is a funny thing," he mumbled.

Dave took a long look at his aristocratic friend, at his oily hands and tattered grey coveralls, his mouth full of gravy and his table full of boiler room companions.

"That's for damn sure."

* * *

THE NAKAJIMA HAYABUSA was a formidable airplane. This particular aircraft had been a tactical fighter, a survivor, piloted with enough skill to best any opponent. Light and easily maneuverable, such a plane had destroyed many of the Emperor's enemies, serving Showa Hirohito with distinction.

The sturdy Hayabusa was nothing like the disposable wood-framed Tsurugi that made up most of the squadron; Tsurugi had a single torpedo underneath their belly, quickly built for one flight only, with landing gear that fell away after take-off.

On this day, the two planes were perfectly matched.

With just enough fuel to reach its destination, this would be the Hayabusa's last mission. Any aircraft that couldn't find its target would be lost, its final moments spent in aimless flight, only to fall lifeless below. For a Kamikaze pilot, returning to base was a journey without honor, a source of shame, or even a bullet to the brain if cowardice were suspect.

Taya Yoshida wasn't concerned about a lack of prey – he was following a long line of Zero escorts down to his guardian destiny. A flotilla of easy targets ranged below him; troop transports and freighters strung out lazily two by two, their destroyer escorts frothing at the sea alongside them. He felt a sudden thrill at the chance to serve his God-Emperor and his homeland. The killing song of the Special Attack Corps floated through his mind:

> *The Divine Wind brushes my eyes*
> *Eirei, Guardian Spirit of all honor.*

He wasn't surprised when they took him out of flight school early. Taya knew the call to graduation was the next wave of assembled planes from the Mitsubishi factory. That, and a fresh report on the position of the American fleet.

As he left his airfield, young girls waved cherry blossoms by the taxiway. The other pilots smiled and gave salute. He kept his hands wrapped around the yoke, the killing song sounding in his heart. Women tossing flowers were a show for the weak; he had better things to do with his hands. The 500-pound bomb beneath the fuselage would be his only weapon; there was no ammunition in the aircraft's twin machine guns.

Moisture from the clouds condensed on the cowl of his windshield, the tiny rivulets racing beside him as his aircraft buffeted downward. Taya turned to the west, bowing his head to the sacred mountain just below the horizon.

With a last glance, he closed his wing flaps a quarter turn and raised his throttle to 7000 rpm. Taya pushed the yoke steadily forward, shifting his body weight as the shuddering aircraft descended into a screaming dive.

THERE WERE EIGHT GUN TUBS on the Western Victory: one .38 caliber on the stern, six twin 20mm cannons around the bridge deck, and one single Browning M2 .50 caliber, above the forecastle on the bow. This particular Browning was manned by a big Louisiana boy with a nagging lack of self-confidence.

The lightweight .50 caliber rounds were of limited use against most surface targets, and getting a clean shot from a rolling deck against a moving target in an open sky was just as unlikely as it was difficult – it was all eyes and hands and instinct. Skyler Dicks didn't feel like he had any of the required skills.

He didn't mind being stuck out in front of the ship in a thin tub, the armor barely stiff enough to stop a spear. He didn't even mind the ribbing he got from the other gun crews, when he missed most of the targets at gunnery practice. He just didn't want to miss when it came time for the real thing. He wondered if that crazy story Dave had told him about the tracers was true.

Skyler closed his eyes and took another taste of the black man's brew. Bailey was right about one thing. Damn, if that bastard didn't make the best coffee in this man's Navy.

TAYA HAD BEEN TO OKINAWA once before as a child. He remembered the sound and the smell of it, all ocean and soft breezes, the great harbor stretching out across the length of the sunset. There were sea turtles hidden in the dunes, and blankets of tall grass and big black pots of fish soup and noodles. His grandfather had taken Taya with him on one of his official inspection trips for the Diet;

members of the Yoshida family had served in the government for generations.

On the beach, they had flown a bright box kite with a yellow tail. It was the only time he could remember his grandfather laughing out loud. It was an empty beach, where no one but Taya could hear him. Up until that day, there was only honor and duty and the Shinto Way.

The killing song faded as his aircraft descended, and Taya heard the song of the Ryukyo Kingdom. The three strings of the sanshin echoed in his head, plucked in the tight snakeskin tub that made the ancient instrument's hollow twang. He and his aircraft fell out of the sky like raindrops in a banjo wind.

THE KLAXON HORN sounded with a piercing blast, reverberating off the close confines of the passageway. Dave didn't hesitate. He turned into the mess hall, and pulled a duty helmet and vest from the muster station just inside the galley door. He glanced at the clock above the long row of tables; it was exactly 1500 hours.

Dave stepped into the companionway, passing quickly through the web of moving bodies. He had only one thought: first the ammo, then the gun.

Ammunition was stored and handled below the forecastle, forward of the cargo holds. Already, his merchant gun crew would be pulling extra boxes of shells and heading for their stations; Dave kept one custom load beneath his bunk and another in the main stores. His quarters were only a few steps away. He slid inside, lifted the heavy ammo box from beneath his bunk and hurried up on deck. He wondered if Skyler Dicks had taken his advice, and loaded all those extra tracers.

"JESUS!" Skyler screamed as he saw the wave of airplanes descending out of the clouds. His coffee cup bounced off the edge of the gun tub and crashed onto the deck below. Hot black liquid spattered in a peacock pattern of dark beads.

"Ready turrets!" The ship's gunnery officer barked out his commands while furtively pulling up his pants. He had dropped them only moments before, to piss into a galvanized bucket stashed behind a nearby fire station. A spreading stain darkened his khakis when his pants closed too quickly for his sphincter.

Sirens wailed. The harsh metallic cry of "All hands, man your battle stations!" echoed off the walls of the Western Victory. Just off the starboard side, their destroyer escort opened fire, its sixteen anti-aircraft batteries howling into the sky. As if on cue, the sea stiffened, and the bow of the Western crashed into the waves, white foam and green brine showering along her gunwales.

All across the convoy, hundreds of men streamed across the decks at break-neck speed, each to their respective duty stations; some to gunnery, some to fire teams, medical or damage control. Others found radio shacks or boiler rooms, a thousand footsteps practiced a thousand times, drill after drill on ship after ship.

Aboard the destroyer USS Twiggs, Commander George Philip ordered full flank speed, calling out defensive positions for his fleet. Instinctively, he had his forward torpedoes armed against the possibility of a hidden submarine. As he spoke, he fingered a worn Bible, kept in the rear confines of his chart table.

The convoy lurched ahead as one, transports and freighters jockeying for position behind destroyers and tenders, their broadsides turned into the wind.

"Oscar 10 o'clock!"

"Oscar 6 o'clock!"

Radar signatures lit up on green glass screens. Spotters cried, "Bogies at eleven!" and "Zero! Zero! Zero!" Orders flashed on the bridge deck of every ship. Some were half-heard or half-answered, but all executed in mechanical patterns, born of constant practice and bridled adrenaline.

SKYLER DICKS pitched his torso forward into his gun mount, steering the long barrel with the trunk of his body, his chin down, eyes aligned along the length of the steel tube. The open slot between his twin armor shields made a runway that led up into the bright clouds. A loud hum began to fill his ears, like the roar of the big diesel in his daddy's pump house. He shook his head, and bristled at the beating of the blood inside his own brain.

"Keep your distance, Skyler, you can bet they'll come right to you!" Dave Bailey stepped up beside the gunner's mate and threw down his ammunition box.

Almost on cue, the sky exploded in white sulphur smoke and shrapnel, the big guns of the nearby destroyer drowning out every sound except the blood rushing in a man's ears.

TAYA HEARD BANJO STRINGS, the twirling notes rising in his mind. Below him danced a line of ships, steadily compressing as he fell: nine, three, two, and then all at once, just one.

It was a cargo ship, long and ugly, covered with masts and spiny booms, making good speed. There were small arms and anti-aircraft guns aboard her, like almost every other vessel at sea.

The ships were bound for Okinawa, for the next great battle to come. They were sure to be filled with soldiers and munitions..

Already the Americans had bombed Tokyo and Kobe, striking at the factories, harbors and fishing villages along the coast. There were nights when the sky was bright with the flames of phosphorous bombs, incendiaries exploding blindly, racing in the Fujin wind from house to house, consuming everything. Miles of Tokyo were turned to white ash. Taya lost his mother and sister to one of those raids.

He hated the Americans, hated them for not understanding the treachery of the Chinese, for not seeing the destiny of his people, for not remaining in their tall buildings on their giant continent.

Taya didn't mind this was only a cargo ship. It held everything that he wanted to destroy.

THE POUNDING OF HIS BLOOD was all around him.

"Wait for it."

Planes fell like leaflets from the sky, great streaks of smoke and flame and bursting fuel as the relentless battery of guns tore at them in a merciless barrage.

"Wait for it..."

Skyler could see the silver plane clearly now; it was familiar, intimate, bearing down on him as if it was here for him alone.

"Now." Bailey pressed the point of his knuckles hard into the gunner's lower back.

Skyler grimaced. His fingers squeezed the butterfly back, shoulders braced against the staccato punch of the erupting shells. A bright, white line rose from his weapon, long pencil streaks smearing against the chalky sky.

TAYA WAS CAUGHT in a flock of blackbirds once, rising suddenly to his aircraft, moving and slicing as one, flashing around his plane like a great school of fish escaping the jaws of a predator.

This time, the gleaming fish were not dodging and weaving, but bursting forward at incredible speed, flashes of white phosphorous punctuating their path. They tore through his wing edge and then his windshield, and then his cowl and then his shoulder blade, glass shattering across his eyes and peppering his face with hot sand.

Taya struggled to see the edge of the ship, the gun tubs and the hulking shapes below. He felt the yoke tear away from his hands, as a sleek white bird exploded in his skull, silencing the banjo.

THE HAYABUSA HIT BEHIND THE PORT BOW at 270 miles per hour, 5200 pounds of wood, aluminum, and tempered steel. The fighter's remaining fuel blossomed in a wash of flames, climbing the bridge deck to catch the fire command officer and two seamen in a wave of melting heat. The fire spread immediately onto the bridge itself, pouring through the shattered windows and rushing at the men inside.

Its single bomb cratered on the main deck, descending into the powder magazines where it exploded, igniting 300 tons of ammunition and ordinance, and blowing out the three decks below. 56 crewmen were incinerated in the initial blast. 36 more died while trying to save the ship. A lucky few managed to drop into the falling lifeboats. Many would leap into the sea 120 feet below, desperate to escape the inferno. 83 men drowned, fighting for breath in the choppy sea. There were 188 survivors.

An enormous column of smoke and fire rose 400 feet into the sky, rolling black clouds of burning bunker fuel, peppered by explosion after explosion. The USS Twiggs burned for over three hours, slowly dying, until it sank broken into a grey sea.

Commander George Philip's Bible evaporated in the first few seconds. He was last seen grasping the bridge rail in a desperate effort to stand.

THE RAIN FELL RED in thick crimson drops mixed with flakes of paint, metal, and bits of bone. Amidst the howl of sirens, steam and dying men, Dave saw a man's arm fall to the deck, then a severed trunk, the shredded remains propelled by the howling blasts. As the destroyer foundered, great chunks of rail, pieces of gunnery metal and wood planks flew down onto the Western in whistling clumps from the sky.

The air battle above continued for another 45 minutes. Under the withering fire of 300 guns, nineteen Kamikazes and their escorts splashed into the sea. Diving Zeros made looping strafing runs across the ships and through the wounded in the water below. There were three more direct hits, and as many near misses.

Torpedo bombers pierced one transport hull; fires broke out sporadically until the damage control crews could prevail. No more ships were sunk, but 18 more crewmen lost their lives, two onboard the Western Victory.

When the all-clear finally sounded, an odd silence fell over the ship. Dazed and tattered men wandered the deck, wondering whether to rescue a severed hand or a bit of flesh. A blood-red mist hung over the Western for an entire day. The

Captain had each watch take a turn at washing down the decks.

On the foredeck, Skyler Dicks cleaned, oiled and reassembled his Browning M2 over and over again, until his hands stopped shaking. He'd watched the tracers rise up to meet the silver plane with the red sun, seen them tear pieces from its cowl. He saw the sudden shift in its trajectory, spinning wildly away to pierce their destroyer escort.

It was his first kill in his first battle, and he had saved his ship, but only at the cost of another. It was a price that would haunt him for the rest of his life.

* * *

East China Sea
7 Nautical Miles off Okinawa Island

THERE WERE ONLY TWO CASUALTIES on the Western Victory. One seaman fell on the stern deck during a Zero's strafing run. His name was Cal Perkins, an ammunition loader on the five-inch .38 caliber. Perkins was from Boise, Idaho, where he farmed potatoes with his big Scandinavian wife and their two sons.

The other casualty was a loader in the boiler room; the Western was making flank speed when a 4-inch steam pipe burst under 6,000 pounds of pressure. The resulting blast sent a piece of steel clean through the body and a Red Diamond deck of Bicycle playing cards.

They were his favorite brand.

Dave found two more Red Diamond decks, still tightly wrapped in cellophane, on top of a chest next to Bob Fisher's bunk.

He gathered up the cards and put them in a pasteboard box with Bob's other personal effects. When he opened Fisher's locker, he lingered for a moment on a small photograph; Bob standing with a handsome older woman – his sister probably, by the easy way Bob held his hand around her shoulder and the simple fact that he'd volunteered to leave her so far behind.

She had the kind of silent mothering gaze that big sisters often had. Back in Wellton, he'd seen Velda Jean look him over in the same way: concerned but a little distant, and more than willing to let him go his own way.

At breakfast that day, the purser had asked Dave to collect Fisher's gear. The Captain would hold Bob's belongings for the next mail shipment, then send them home with his wages due and a letter from the Navy Department. It was an unpleasant duty that usually fell to a shipmate or a friend. Scavengers weren't tolerated. If suspect, they were likely next in line.

Bob's wallet contained over six hundred dollars. $12,000 more was tucked into five film cans in a leather case with his toiletries. Dave found a heavy silver wristwatch there, with an inscription laid around the backplate:

To my beloved son, on his 18th birthday
- R. W. Fisher II
April 24, 1912

Dave shook the watch and listened for a telltale tick. He heard nothing. The leather band was stained by decades of sweat, now dry with years of careful storage.

Bob must have been number three. That's a pretty lucky number, most days.

Dave unbuttoned his top pocket and pulled out ten carefully folded bills. A thousand dollars - his poker winnings from the day they first met. He rolled the hundred-dollar bills up tight, then slid them inside one of the cans in Bob's shaving kit.

He hadn't figured on getting to spend the money anyway, and didn't want to put those bills in another man's pot.

The grey-haired woman would know what to do with it.

"Luck is a funny thing," he said out loud.

He stuffed the shaving kit into Bob's duffel bag and lifted the canvas sack onto his shoulder. It felt lighter than he'd expected. On the way to the purser's office, he wondered how heavy his might be.

Y OU SAW A LOT OF TROUBLE out there, didn't you?"

"Too much of it, maybe." Pop spoke with some finality.

"Were you going to marry her?" I looked over at him. "Becky, I mean."

I watched him as carefully as I could without putting the old Ford in a ditch. There were times, especially where a woman was concerned, that Doc's posture hinted at something else, a sense of what might have been instead of what was.

"No, it was a lot more complicated than that. We were just lovers." He let out a deep breath, almost a sigh. "But we had a little house up on Union Hill."

"And you kept it?"

"No, I let that house go." His mood shifted, almost as if a door had closed that nothing could get past. Doc lightened up noticeably. "After I got back from Okinawa, I moved in with my buddy Johnny Lanyon. We talked it over and all at once, we decided we was gonna' throw us a party."

I marveled at his sudden whimsy in the face of all that sadness. "What kind of a party?"

Pop smiled and lit a freshly rolled cigarette. "I said, 'Johnny, I got three thousand dollars in my pocket. Let's throw a party.' And he said, 'Only if I can match it.' And from there, it kind of took off on its own. We took all the food out of the cupboards, went and got six or eight old washtubs and called the ice company and said 'fill 'em full of ice'. Then we went to the brewery in Nevada City and had a beer truck come down and deliver."

Pop leaned over towards me; he spoke with a touch of pride in his voice. "We stacked those shelves with every kind of booze you could name, I don't care what it was. I called the taxi company and said I wanted a taxi sitting out front at all times. I'd pay 'em just for sitting there. All the drivers knew I was back from the war, so we had a cab out front 24 hours a day. We kept that house open 'round the clock for 30 days."

"How do you know it was thirty days?" I imagined myself in the same situation, and wondered if I could survive that long without going to jail or getting beat up.

"That's all I could be around for. When you were in the Maritime, you only had 30 days on shore before the draft would kick in. Tommy Johnson let it go one day past, on account of it was a Sunday, and the FBI came by to pick him up."

"They arrested him?"

"No, but they let him know they knew where he was, and told him to report the next day. So Tommy, he went down and enlisted in the Army of the United States." Dave drew a deep breath and started to cough, catching his breath as he spoke.

"Was he at the party?"

"He might have dropped by with Wanda, that was before they got hitched. 'Cause he enlisted, he ended up training soldiers down at Camp Beale. He spent the rest of the war down there."

"I don't know how you can keep a party going for thirty days."

"Well, you have to stay drunk, that's part of it." Pop gave me a big grin. "And have lots of ice. It was hot as blazes, as I recall. Sometimes, there were 30 - 40 people in that little house. It was right behind the cemetery. So when you got sleepy, you could go outside and lay down on the headstones and cool off."

"Nice." I pictured the graveyard scene unfolding. Doc took another drag from his cigarette.

"And we had a tab down at the Colfax Market, so anyone could go get food if they were hungry. We had a chandelier hung down right over the stairs. Everybody threw money in it when they left the house, and when we ran out of food or beer, we would climb up and go get some more." Pop circled his arms to show the size of the hanging lamp. "It was a big old thing. But we let it go too long, and it pulled clear out of the ceiling."

He laughed and coughed, and laughed again. "That house belonged to Johnny. I think his mother gave it to him. He sold that house for thirty-five hundred dollars. Said that was the only way he'd have that party - 50/50. He went down to the real estate company and sold that son-of-a-bitch." Pop leaned forward to emphasize his point. "When he sold it, he sold it with the deal that we could live in it till the party was over, and that's just what we did." Pop shook his head. "I don't know how we got to be as good a' buddies as we was, because he was as different from me and my way of being as you could be. I was kind of a roughneck, and he was sort of… a little sister, y'know."

"Little sister?" I wondered if that meant what I thought it did. Pop nodded and smiled at me.

"He was, he was that way, but he was just about as good a buddy as I had in them days."

"What did the neighbors think of all that?"

"Not much. It was the war, things were different then." Pop picked up the thermos to pour himself another cup. "And we invited everyone on the block. Anybody who wanted to come could come on. But they couldn't drive away from there drunk – that was the one rule. Like I say, we had a cab out front, day in and day out."

Pop paused to take a sip. "We only ever got one real complaint. Old Simpson the cop came by and made out like we were making too much noise, said some of the neighbors was complaining."

Doc leaned back in his seat and painted the air with his cigarette. "But see, I knew all the neighbors had been in that house already, so they weren't complaining. We had young and old and everybody. So I told one of the Gallina girls to take Simpson in the back room and give him a little." Pop's grin grew as wide as I'd ever seen it. "And boy, she did. Never got another complaint. I think they got married right after that."

I pictured the cop and the girl and the cabs and the chandelier. "Must have been pretty wild…"

"Well, it was and it wasn't. There were lots of times when it was just real quiet. People played the guitar, singing and talking, and sometimes the gals would cook, or we'd play poker."

He held his cup in two hands, and raised it to his lips. "I met Marian at that party." Pop grew still and gazed out the window.

I kept my eyes on the road; a change in the landscape was taking us steadily downhill. As we left the low hills, the blacktop straightened out and opened up onto a vast, flat plain. The gray-green of the hills faded to a dull brown, long blades of grass giving way to sand and rock as we descended. A faded metal sign peppered with bullet holes read:

'Welcome to Nevada'

The Silver State

"Old Highway 50, Pop."

"The loneliest road in America, or so they say."

Doc relit his cigarette and blew a trail of smoke into the wind. Grey asphalt turned to ancient concrete; low dunes rose along the edge of the highway.

"This part right here is probably why."

SS Western Victory
Nakagusuku Bay, Sea of Japan

THE WESTERN VICTORY lay at anchor off Okinawa, beyond the reach of shore batteries and nestled in amongst the destroyers and Navy escorts. Radar pickets surrounded the merchant ships to guard against aerial attacks and the occasional lone submarine. The big cruiser St. Louis was nearby; the constant barrage from her six-inch guns made a steady drumbeat in the background. Despite the pickets, there were waves of Kamikaze attacks to reckon with; one long day saw over a thousand Japanese planes downed by the American fleet.

After the convoy settled in, a regular shift of amphibious landing craft sped out to the cargo ships, braving the Japanese guns on the overlooking cliffs. Once loaded, they'd return at breakneck speed, resupplying the Marines that were fighting their way inland. The men on shore called it the Yangtze Express. The Western's crew and the Navy stevedores settled into a steady rhythm, slowly and methodically emptying the Victory ship's enormous cargo holds. Occasionally, the Captain would let some of the crew go ashore with the landing craft, 'so the men could steady their legs'.

The Higgins boats were unloaded on shore by a battalion of Negro Marines, who had to resupply the combat forces even when they fell under heavy fire. Johnny Washington made friends with their crew and was a regular on deck whenever the marines were aboard.

The Captain gave the stevedores his standard safety speech: respect the rail, police your butts, and never forget the cost of a single mistake. Drop a fuse or a stray cigarette down the wrong hatch and there's little chance of escaping the consequences.

"It's bad enough the whole Japanese Empire wants us dead, without some yahoo doing it for them. God favors the feeble-minded," the Captain had said. "But not at sea."

Most of the work was uneventful, with all the good-natured ribbing that goes on between the various services. There was gratitude for coffee and meals taken in the mess, and some of the visitors took notice of the hot water piped up from the boilers and requisitioned a quick shower.

Three weeks into the cargo operation, a tall Marine master sergeant came out to the Western on one of the landing craft. He and two other marines carefully rigged a boom line around a heavy burden wrapped in canvas. Once aboard, they summoned Johnny Washington, who called for Dave Bailey and one of the mess hands.

"Dang, Chief, if that ain't the biggest pig I ever saw." Dave had seen desert javelina and wild boar in Grass Valley, but this beast was beyond anything he'd ever imagined. Stretched out, it was seven-feet long and weighed in at over 400 pounds. Armed with jagged 6-inch tusks, the great beast was an Inoshishi boar from the island's jungle forest.

"That thing damn near killed us all last night," the sergeant drawled. "Until we took a Thompson to it. And I weren't so sure that was gonna' stop it."

The machine gun had made a kind of Swiss cheese out of the boar's head.

"We heard it coming out on patrol. I thought it was a bear, 'til the damn thing charged us." The sergeant poked its hairy flanks with his boot. "Stay dead."

"Sarge here thinks we can bar-b-que it," said one of the men. "But we could sure use some help." He looked longingly at the chief cook. "Nothin' but c-rations in our camp."

"Yeah, we figured maybe you could cook it for us, and we'd trade you for some of the native hooch." The sergeant shot a glance at Johnny and then Dave.

Dave had heard about shochu; distilled by the locals from sweet potatoes, it was said to pack a considerable punch. He exchanged a smile with Johnny Washington.

"That's a big pig. Take some time to do him." Johnny gave his baker a knowing wink.

"Just how much of that tater whiskey have you got?" asked Dave.

The sergeant laughed. "We got a cart full. But I wouldn't call it whiskey, more like turpentine mixed with brown sugar. But it'll sure spin your motor."

Johnny looked the carcass over, calculating the time to butcher, season and cook. "Give me two days, and we'll have you some ham. Good and plenty, done up right."

Dave spoke under his breath. "Can you cover for me, Chief? I'd like to go ashore, help collect the hooch." Dave had been looking for an excuse to get off ship, ever since they'd lost Bob Fisher.

Washington nodded quietly. "Best be careful, Davey."

Dave turned to the marine. "Mind if I come along - to protect our investment?"

"If I were you, I'd stay put. At least out here, you can see them coming." The sergeant scowled. "But it's your butt, if you want to tag along."

Dave figured he'd crossed the whole Pacific Ocean without losing his ass. He might as well get it blown off on land.

"Take your big knife to that thing, Mr. Washington. I'm gonna' get us some sippin' whiskey."

*   *   *

Kakazu Ridge, Okinawa Island
Fox Company, First Marines

THE MARINE SUPPLY LINES snaked through rice paddies and deep ravines for two miles, ending at the base of a fortified ridge. A full battalion had been hunkered down in the valley below it for weeks. Dave kept close to the master sergeant's ammo squad, slogging through the intermittent rain. They were making for a small outpost behind the main lines, where weather-beaten men took a brief rest from the long battle for the island.

Dave was uncomfortable in a way he hadn't been for the entire war. He'd seen plenty of blood before, and more than a few men killed at sea, but the certain nearness of the conflict was constant here.

On their way to the camp, Dave had seen a young girl approach some soldiers by the side of the road. The girl seemed to be begging for food, until one of the soldiers went to her - and she released the grenade she was hiding. The explosion blew the girl to pieces, along with the hands of the man who had offered her his meal.

There were screams and the howls of angry men, and tourniquets and morphine and red mud and vomit. One soldier wept as he kicked the leftover body parts into a ditch. The pieces washed downstream like crimson leaves in the muddy water.

His party had kept on walking, dodging the foxholes that cut across the old gun emplacements. There was very little conversation, just the sound of boots and the labored breath of marching men. A corpsman ran by on the path, followed by a rush of other men.

After about an hour, they reached a small clearing with a few tents and a makeshift camp. The marines tossed down their heavy packs. Some broke out letters or simply closed their eyes, disappearing in place.

The sergeant told him to take a seat while he fetched a local villager. An old man in a tattered grey robe returned with him. Bent over by age and arthritis, he moved with sticky deliberation. The sergeant asked him to retrieve the shochu. The old man replied in broken English that he couldn't manage it by himself.

"Boston, go with Shen-jen here, and fetch the juice wagon." The marines had found the earthen jugs in an abandoned village and hidden them in the bush.

A young private shuffled to his feet. The afternoon sun was close to the western ridge as they wandered out of camp.

By the time they returned, it was nearly dark.

"We'll take you out come morning, Mr. Bailey. Meanwhile, make yourself at home." The sergeant gestured to a broken stump that had found new life as a camp chair. Some of the other men had built a small fire and were heating round tins on a wire grill.

"Far enough off the line for a small fire, but we still have to post pickets, so don't sleep too deep. We may have to move out anytime."

Dave sat down and glanced around the camp. It was rough-hewn, the kind of camp that men cobbled together when they might have to leave at a moment's notice. Packs were broken down and stowed carefully, rifles perched alongside. Some of the soldiers were already asleep, some just dozing, waiting for the next patrol. Dave felt distinctly out of place.

One marine sat off to the side of the fire, cleaning his weapon. The freshly burnished pieces were tossed into his open helmet. He eyed the sergeant. "Old Shen-jen says the Japs are telling everybody on the island we're murderers, that we'll rape their little children, their daughters and their wives. Tear their limbs off one by one."

Another man fingered his combat knife. "I might too, if I get the chance."

The sergeant spat into the fire; spittle crackled into mist on the hot grill. "You're black and they're brown," replied the sergeant. His voice was low and harsh. "Now you tell me, what's the difference?"

He looked right at Dave. "We don't kill civilians, not if we can tell that's what they are. And hell, that ain't so easy all the time."

Dave felt grateful to be stationed out to sea, where the ships had flags and even the airplanes had pictures painted on their sides. "At Saipan, we heard a thousand Japs jumped off a cliff into the ocean." He tossed some small sticks into the fire, one at a time. "Took their babies and their children, too. I guess Old Tojo told 'em they'd get a better seat in heaven if they all died that-a-way."

No one spoke for a few minutes. The flames ate the sticks away to hot, red stalks. Dave lit a cigarette and closed his eyes.

As a boy, his dad had told him about returning from the first big war in Europe. How he'd gone to Tulsa to celebrate Memorial Day with a few of his war buddies, and a riot had broken out; somebody said a black boy touched a white woman in an elevator - and a mob tried to lynch the kid. Two or three hundred black folk were murdered and a whole section of colored town burned to the ground. His father said it made him ashamed to be a white man.

Surrounded by colored men, some no older than he was, they were all trespassers in a land where none of them were welcome.

Dave opened his eyes. The camp was quiet, broken only by the crackling of burning coals. In the firelight, everyone looked the same.

"Here. You didn't come all this way for nothing." The sergeant pulled a canvas-covered canteen out of his pack. He poured some amber liquid into a tin cup. "Take a pull on that."

Dave sniffed the cup. The odor bore a slight resemblance to kerosene. He took a careful swig.

"Whoa…" Dave cleared his throat. "That does have a kick to it." The liquor burned warm down his throat, then crawled up to his voice box, growling hot. Dave gave the sergeant a broad smile.

"Sweet potatoes, just like Thanksgiving." The sergeant poured another dollop into Dave's cup. "I think old Shen-jen himself might be the brewmaster. He's downright protective of the stuff."

Dave nodded. This time he took a smaller sip. Once accustomed to the taste, it was really quite pleasant.

"We can't keep them jugs out here on the line, or we'd all end up drunk and disorderly. I'm glad to be rid of the stuff." The sergeant put the canteen back in his pack. "Well, most of it, anyway."

SITTING NEAR THE EDGE of camp at dawn, Dave watched the soldiers go through the everyday motions of war and peace. One man cleaned his rifle, another took a cold-water shave. One broke the crusty slag off his boots, another made the ritual reading of a letter from home. The master sergeant sat upright against his pack, holding a fixed stare on a worn photograph.

Dave mentioned he was hungry. Someone offered him a dusty tin of k-rations. He tried to be polite, but couldn't get past a couple of half-hearted mouthfuls. He put the can away quietly.

Two young marines were out in the middle of the road, batting a weathered ball around with a fat bamboo stick. The old villager was there, with a two-wheeled cart full of palm fronds and clay pots. Shen-jen was pleading with the sergeant and motioned to the earthen jugs. They argued for a moment and the sergeant walked away.

"Boston, grab that hooch, and get it out of here."

The sergeant pulled Dave aside. Dave started to ask a question, but was cut off with a look. "Time to go." He motioned for Boston to help with the cart.

Dave could see the old man, down on his knees by the side of the road. Maybe he mourned for his island, or maybe for the life he once knew.

"This is how it is." The master sergeant quickened his step. "It might be a Jap, or an old man or a little kid. But it's all the same fucking war." The sergeant turned to go. "Get back to your ship as quick as you can."

BOSTON PRODDED DAVE in the ribs and gestured toward the road below. A rifle platoon had gathered with a staff sergeant and a 1st lieutenant. Dave could barely make out the sound of the lieutenant's voice.

"There will be no more fraternizing with the local natives, no exchange of trade goods, and especially no consumption of island beverages, including fresh water, unless treated or boiled." The lieutenant seemed upset.

Boston gestured again. Dave picked up his rucksack and followed him into the bush.

"Sarge says to get you down to the landing lickety-split." The private spoke rapidly under his breath. "On account of we got new orders this morning." The young man took hold of the cart and started pulling.

Dave followed as silently as he could.

"Big doings on the island, some kind of crazy Jap offensive or something."

The long howl of an accelerating SBD Banshee drowned out the rifleman's voice; the scout plane was streaking low over the treetops. Dave hurried to keep up with the young marine.

"There's a boat waiting, when you get back, just toss the meat in there along with some fresh ammo - those guys'll get it to us."

Dave wondered how anything could make its way through the growing chaos he saw along the road. A dusty row of truck transports suddenly appeared, behind them long columns of men marching as if out of nowhere.

Both men attacked the bush trail, pulling and pushing the cart in turns through the thick muck. After a short trek, they reached a small landing, built alongside a muddy-brown creek that emptied into the sea. One of the canvas-covered motor launches that ferried ammunition was tied up at the dock.

"Stow that aft, and make it fast." The motorman spoke with urgency. He wrapped a woven pull cord around the outboard motor. "We shove off in one minute." The pilot jerked sharply and the motor sputtered back to life. Dave could hear the low boom of a distant battery, persistent shellfire rising above the motor's rumble. Dave jumped into the stern and started packing jugs as quickly as Boston could hand them off.

The young marine passed across the last jug and offered his hand. "Good luck out there."

"Thanks, Boston," Dave clasped his hand firmly, then untied the spring line and pushed away from the dock. "But best keep your luck. You need it worse than I do. You and everyone else on this damn island."

The motorman rocked the throttle hard and the launch pulled away, throwing a rooster-tail wake behind it. Dave fell back into the rail, but his stomach remained where it was.

Zig-zagging downriver, the cargo launch made a poor target for the Japanese guns above. The motorman kept her full-throttled all the way across the breakers and out to the Western Victory. For a spare jug of sweet potato wine, the stevedores made short work of the cargo exchange: a score of clay jars for two dozen tightly wrapped bundles of spice-baked ham and barbecued spare ribs.

COME NIGHTFALL, the shochu flowed freely in the larder, in the ships mess, and some said on the bridge deck itself. The poker pots were the largest that Dave had ever seen, and he swore that he could hear women singing in the companionways. Dave won double his month's wages that night, and Johnny Washington filled an inside straight worth well over a thousand dollars. Even Skyler Dicks was there, laughing alongside his old nemesis.

Dave thought it was a night to remember and started to look for Bob Fisher, until he remembered that Bob was no longer aboard.

ALONE ON HER BACK PORCH, Madeline Spain watched the sun go down in silence, waiting for the sound of a car on the driveway, or for any sound at all. It was well past the time Lawrence usually came home, and long past time when he'd call to see if she needed anything from the store, or to tell her that he had extra duty at the airfield.

It was so lonely in town now; Huey was at Radium Springs taking the consumption cure, and her daughters were away in San Diego, working for the War Department. She'd left the hotel in the charge of employees, none of them family, and she couldn't bring herself to check on them as frequently as she once had.

It was as if time itself was slowing down; she longed for the company of her old friends. Anyone, even Sam Kingston, with his scurrilous gossip and incessant whistling. A training accident took Sam, right after Pearl Harbor. Wellton had sacrificed so many of her own: Bill Gale, Artemio Cabrero, Mago and Ernie Vasquez. And Freddy. Of all the young men, only Sven Jorgensen was left in town - still bucking hay with his one good arm. Madeline considered the Swede's lost limb a small price to pay for escaping that hideous conflict.

In the quiet of the evening, she thought about Ernie, about the time the Bailey boy had nearly crippled him in that stupid feud of theirs. Davey had continued to visit now and then, roaming about the town and the desert with his ragtag friends - handsome, lighthearted, and entirely unreliable. The boy had inherited his father's charms, but none of his steady purpose.

I wonder if this godforsaken war has claimed him, too.

Like everyone else, the Baileys had left for the promised land of California. How she hated that state, with all its highways and bright colors and slick promises. It had robbed her of so much she loved: her children, her friends, and now, her modest sensibilities.

Dozens of soldiers passed through Wellton every day, but they were nameless and faceless. She refused to get to know them, so aware that with all their vitality, they were still fragile, like glass, destined to be broken on the hard rock of war. They descended on the hotel like locusts, ordering drinks and steaks and anything else they could get their hands on that wasn't Army ration, laughing out loud in their immortality.

Just like Freddy.

She turned away from the sunset, hot red in the sky above the mountains. A squadron of B-28 bombers crested in the failing light, bound for the proving grounds that were all around Yuma County. Seven satellite airfields were scattered within miles of Wellton: bombing ranges, civilian training fields, pilot schools and artillery airports. To the west, Camp Horn was a desert training center, headquarters for General Patton before he took North Africa from the Germans.

So much pride and so much purpose.

His father had taught him to fly when he was just a boy, long before Lawrence enlisted and was sent away to Europe. Freddy joined the Army Air Corps on his eighteenth birthday, keen to show his skills. Six weeks later, he disappeared in the Himalayas.

Madeline walked back inside the house. *Thank God, at least his father came home.* Lawrence was newly stationed at Smiley Field and the war would soon be over. Perhaps some semblance of normal life would return to her little town.

She heard tires kick up gravel on the driveway and hurried through the narrow hallway that led to her front door. Madeline swung the door open, anxious to hold him close and break the spell of faded evening.

The headlights of a dark sedan were raked across the open porch. Two uniformed figures stood silent, grey silhouettes frozen at the front steps.

A low moan rose into a wail. Madeline Spain sank in the doorway, bare knees on the wooden threshold.

POP HADN'T BEEN feeling so good lately. I stayed extra quiet to let him sleep in. By the time he got up, it was nearly mid-morning, which was pretty unusual for him.

We'd pulled into Tonopah the day before, in late afternoon, with unsettled weather up ahead. After we gassed up, we stopped to look at a pawn shop and had a meal in the town diner. A few long haul truckers gave us the weather report, and we decided it was best to stay in town overnight.

There was a casino across from the motel. I played a few rounds of cards and Pop played his Keno numbers - then we headed for bed. We were both pretty well spent from a long day on the road. Doc seemed distracted; maybe something was on his mind or maybe it was just the weight of a particularly bad meal. We'd seen a sign out front of the diner for liver and onions, Pop's favorite, but the kitchen had already run out, so we settled for sea bass. Probably not the best call in Tonapah, Nevada.

The truckers said the freak storm was likely to last the whole day. By the time we got out of bed, it was clear we weren't going much further; fluffy white snowflakes were everywhere, and I didn't want to chance taking Betsy out in it. I'd always had trouble navigating snowfall; my lack of depth perception sometimes gave me vertigo. I went outside and pulled open our kitchen box, grabbing the thermos, some instant coffee and a box of saltines. At this rate, we might be stuck in Tonopah for a while.

I poured our leftover coffee in the pitcher on the hotplate and tried to warm it up. The power went out before it had a chance to boil. One glance outside told me the whole town was dark, even the stoplights. The coffee was lukewarm at best, but if all else failed, I could pull the Coleman stove and lantern out of Betsy.

Outside the wind was howling; blowing snow was starting to pile up against the windows. It made me think of Pop's early days in Oklahoma. I asked him about the Dust Bowl, but he didn't seem to remember much about it - mainly just dirt everywhere and the constant wind. And the mounting sense of trouble he could feel at home. His mom and dad had struggled, along with everyone else.

"That was a tough go for short dough." Doc pulled two pairs of socks out of his little blue suitcase. "We got stuck in some kind of labor camp, livin' in tents. Dad was as tied up as I'd ever seen him, not since Benny died."

"Benny?" I winced at the cold coffee and lit a cigarette. "Who's Benny?"

"I never told you about Benny?" Pop pulled another pair of socks on over his first and smiled.

"Nope. You never did."

"Well, I guess now's as good a time as any. We might be here for a while." The windows rattled and the wind howled as if to underscore his assessment.

I made a break for it and got the Coleman gear and my tape recorder. We sat on the edge of the motel beds, drinking hot instant coffee, and waited out the storm.

Maybe another day in Tonopah wouldn't be so bad after all.

BUFFALO GALS

"SOME DAYS, I'd just as soon work on a wagon as an automobile. There's not the puzzle about them. 'Course there's not the excitement, either." Dee Bailey leaned over his forge and added a leaf of coke to the fire. "That king pin broke 'cause she wasn't hardened up right. You got to quench at least a half-dozen times or she's brittle, not strong." Dee drew the pin from the furnace and passed it through the basting trough. The red-hot metal sizzled and belched steam. He held it close to his face; the amber glow lit his dark eyes. "This one should outlast the both of us."

"I didn't know you were such a good smith, Dee." Benny Gibbs had worked up a quite a sweat waiting for this repair, even for a man of his considerable girth. "I'm grateful you could put it first on your agenda." Long drops of perspiration slid down Benny's brow; a growing pool formed at the edge of his starched collar.

"Hard money comes first, Mr. Gibbs. Can't feed a family on credit." It was Dee's first cash-money job since the new baby was born. He was glad for something to do with his hands besides wringing them. Dee checked the king pin for fit on the wagon's singletree, then walked it over to his grinder. "And any mechanic worth his salt had better know his forge, if he expects to keep a car or carriage on the road. Can't help but wonder though, as much money as you make ferrying that nitro, why you'd do so in such an old albatross as this?"

"Superstition I suppose, Dee. I made my first trip in this old wagon. I suspect I'll make my last in it as well." Gibbs brushed the brocade on his vest and his fingers settled on a gold watch chain. "As for the money, well, in my business you don't try to save it for a rainy day."

The worn-out canvas belt on the grinder motor squealed as it worked its way up to speed. Dee's eyes dropped to the whirling stone, ready to polish the last stubborn burr from the surface of the pin he'd just forged. Gibbs was right. A man in Benny's line of work wouldn't give much thought to the future. Dee had seen the craters pockmarking the roads leading out to the oil fields. Still, why any man in his right mind would use an old butt-breaker to haul nitroglycerin was beyond him. Even with the fancy gimbal-mount that Gibbs used to carry the nitro, the odds didn't seem to favor the portly teamster. Dee lifted the metal pin away from his grinding stone.

"Mr. Gibbs, you know, I could rig up some inflatable rubber tires to replace these wagon wheels of yours. I'd have to make them from scrap, and they wouldn't be vulcanized, but I'm sure I could make it work." Dee gave Benny an earnest look. "And they'd be a lot more forgiving in a hard bump."

Gibbs laughed and opened up his pocket watch. Dee could barely hear the tiny chimes over the turn of his grinding wheel, and reached down to cut off the motor. As his hand touched the switch, a weak joint in the grinder's belt gave way and snapped, spinning the canvas strap straight up into Dee's forehead.

In the darkness he heard music play; a thin refrain of *Buffalo Gals* accompanied his last conscious thought.

"I THINK HE'LL BE FINE, Mrs. Bailey. There's a good deal of swelling, and that makes things look a lot worse than they really are."

"But his eyes?" She looked at the linen bandages as if they were a hangman's noose. Dee had finally fallen asleep, or deep into a narcotic haze, she didn't know which.

"Well, yes, and that may cause him some trouble later on, but the important thing right now is that he's going to recover."

Jonathan Colby believed in accentuating the positive. No sense in setting off too much worry to go along with whatever else might be. In his thirty years of ministering to the aches, boils and bones of Chandler County, he'd never yet regretted that philosophy. There'd been some disappointments along the way, sure, but all in all, a little hope always put the right light on things. Even so, he was sure Dee Bailey would never see out of that right eye again, and he'd be damned lucky to keep his left one. "You just keep those cold compresses on, and see to it that he's not up and around too much. I'll stop back by in the morning."

Florence Bailey sensed that was all she would hear from Colby tonight. She turned to look at her unconscious husband in the dim light. He looked so small and fragile. Her voice choked as she spoke. "Thank you, Doctor, I'll see you to the door."

"Mrs. Bailey, I know my way out, and I'll need no escort. You tend to your husband and your children, and let me do the worrying."

Floy reached to the night table and gathered up her purse. "At least let me get your fee." She looked furtively through the folds and pockets of the old lace bag.

Colby's face reddened, and his voice dropped to a whisper. "Now listen here, Florence Cox Bailey. I delivered you and your brother and your daughters and your little boy, and I know there's not a man in this county that doesn't owe your husband money and more. So just put me down as one who's paid a little bit back."

Colby reached out and grasped her shoulders, pressing her lightly into the chair beside the bed. His voice rose as he stepped out through the doorway and onto the landing at the top of the stairs. "Goodnight, Floy," he said, and softly closed the door behind him.

Halfway down the stairs, he turned to look back up; he could see the light dancing off the boy's golden hair, the clear blue eyes, and the tiny hands clasped tightly around the balusters. "Go to bed, Davey," he said, as he moved on down the stairs. "Your Dad's going to be just fine." There was no reply, only the rustling sound of small feet on the carpet as Colby reached the front door.

Outside, in the pale gaslight, he looked up to the sky and said a prayer for this family, and for his country, that these dark times would pass.

"HERE'S YOUR JUICE, DEE. Roll over and let me put it to your lips."

"Hell, Floy, I may be blind, but I still know where my mouth is." Dee felt the room lurch as he pushed himself upright in the bed. He resisted the temptation to fall back into the warm space beneath the blankets.

"Hush now, and don't curse, or the children will hear. Doc Colby's coming and I don't want you soaked to the bone with cider. Take this."

Dee moved the small glass to his lips. As the warm cider touched his throat, he felt the room swim and gulped to finish it before he swayed.

Floy took the glass away. She wiped a stray drop from her husband's chin. "That's better. Now, lay back. The doctor's going to take those bandages off today, and I want you well rested."

"You make it sound as though he's going to chase me around the bed." He reached out to run his hand down her backside and gave her a good squeeze.

"Dee Bailey! You settle down, and don't play the fool." Her hand found his and pushed it back into his lap.

Dee laughed at the mental image of his young wife. Ever the perfect lady for public consumption, but a wonder that he didn't have ten children instead of four. "How long before he's due?" he added with a twisted grin.

"Hush now, Dee!" He could almost hear her cheeks turn rosy. "There'll be time enough for that when you're up and around." She bent down and quickly brushed his cheek with her lips. "I'll be back after I've checked on the children."

"I thought your Dad was here..."

"He is. That's why I'm checking."

Dee nodded as she closed the door. He smiled at the thought of Grandpa Cox and the kids. If he didn't make it out of this mess, then at least John Cox would be there. He was a doting grandfather for the girls, and not nearly the danger to little Davey that his wife imagined. Although at times, he wondered which of the two rascals had a bigger knack for getting into mischief. "Fathers and sons," he said to himself. Dee thought for a moment how things might have been different, if his father had been a little more like John Breckinridge Cox.

"Am I disturbing you?" Dee heard the door creak and caught the scent of hair tonic and toilet water. "Your wife said I might find you open to a little company."

"Well hello, Mr. Gibbs." Dee felt some pride at recognizing the unfamiliar voice and gathered some dignity with his posture. "I'm sorry that I'm not more presentable."

"Not at all, Dee. And it's high time you dropped the Mister from my name. After all, it's in my service that you were injured." Benny settled in at the foot of the bed. He leaned in closer to Dee. "If Benny will suffice down on Canal Street, it will certainly do here."

For a moment, Dee let the image of Gibb's Canal Street adventures free him from the confines of his bed. Before he met Floy, he'd visited that notorious neighborhood a few times himself.

"Fair enough, Benny. And how are you, this fine Oklahoma morning?"

"Just dandy, sir. But never mind me, Dee. It's you I'm worried about. You gave us quite a scare."

Dee pictured the portly teamster in his catalogue suit as he carried Dee's unconscious body the full length of Main Street, and up the rickety stairs to Doc Colby's office. From the feel of his brow and the number of stitches, he knew there had to have been a lot of blood. "I never got a chance to thank you, Benny..."

"Your little overhaul is thanks enough, Dee. I've carried two full payloads since your accident, with nary a wiggle or a bump. But tell me, how are you feeling?"

Dee measured his response carefully. He'd known the outcome long ago. Alone in his room, he'd pried the soft gauze from around his eyes, peering through the blurry light. His left eye would be fine, but he would never see much of anything with the right one again. He answered with a toss of his head.

"I'll be better'n new, Mr. Gibbs."

"Good to hear it, Mr. Bailey." Gibbs rose from the edge of the bed, and pulled his gold watch from a vest pocket. As the watch opened, *Buffalo Gals* played again. This time, Dee could hear 'dance by the light of the moon' chime in full.

"Time for me to be moving on, Dee. Now, be sure to let me know if there's anything I can do for you, my friend." Benny closed the fancy timepiece, and the watch chimes ended as suddenly as they began.

Dee considered the precarious future of a one-eyed mechanic with four children and a trunk full of IOUs that no one could afford to pay.

"I will, Benny. I will."

THE SKY WAS AN ANGRY GREY, but the air was clear, at least what passed for clear in those days. Last week's big dust storm was finally gone, now on its way east to trouble Arkansas, Missouri, and points beyond. Dee was grateful for the chance to clear his head, and despite the time and expense, he had driven all the way to Oklahoma City. The old Essex ragtop he'd salvaged was a real workhorse, and the 50-mile trip had taken less than an hour.

No one seemed to know exactly where Benny Gibbs was, only that he was around somewhere, and had been for the last few days. Finding him was something of an adventure in itself, for Benny's regular haunts were a little more spirited than the ones that Dee was used to. Oklahoma City wasn't exactly Tulsa, but it did have its diversions, mostly there to service the oil field roustabouts and engineers. Dee made his way along Canal Street from one storefront speakeasy to another, until at last he met a woman who seemed to be able to pinpoint Benny's last known location.

"Oh, that one. Why, he's the most generous sort. Not like your everyday tumble." The buxom young lady moved closer, and gestured in a manner that would have sent Floy scrambling for her father's scattergun. "More of a gentleman, like you."

"Why, thank you, that's very kind." Dee smiled, and moved the young lady's hand away from his abdomen. "And a most interesting proposition, I must say. But it's very important that I speak to Mr. Gibbs, and I was hoping you'd be able to tell me where to find him."

"He was just at Number Fourteen, 'round the corner, not twenty minutes ago." The woman leaned into Dee's chest, her warm breath moist on his collar. "I could take you there, myself."

"Ordinarily, I would leap at the chance." She was an attractive sort, with a quick smile, and very persistent. He decided a small lie would do no harm to either of them. "But since the war, well, I just can't do that sort of thing anymore."

"Oh, darlin', we can find something for you to do, I'm sure of that." Her fingers began to roam again.

"I have something to do, Miss. But I'm afraid it involves Mr. Gibbs, and not you." She was a determined girl, regardless of what some might think of her profession. Dee pulled her hands away and offered his most proper nod. "But thank you, all the same." He turned and took a few steps, smiling.

"Don't give up, honey," the young redhead called after him. "I've been known to work miracles."

Dee laughed in spite of himself. "Madam, of that, I am quite certain." He headed for the corner at a brisk pace, his imagination conjuring a wide assortment of miracles.

Fourteen Canal Street was one of many establishments that had sprung up since the passage of Prohibition; it had a small private bar for thirsty patrons, a back room for gambling, and a tiny set of rooms upstairs for yet another variety of sport. It existed, like all the others did, with a wink and a nod from the local constabulary. Dee had never seen much sense in making a criminal case out of people's vices; Lord knows, everybody had some, and the only thing that legislating them accomplished was to make a mockery out of the law. A man's conscience was the only measure of morality that Dee stood by, and he figured that the Good Lord could make any judgments necessary beyond those. He scanned the room for any sign of Benny Gibbs and seeing none, approached the bar.

"Pardon me, sir."

The bartender was cleaning glasses with a white towel. He turned and his face reddened in recognition. "Why, Mr. Bailey, it's nice to see you."

"Hello, Burt." Dee had repaired Burt Wagner's old Dodge a half-dozen times. He'd always understood that Burt was a printer by trade. "Good to see you, too."

Burt's face softened at Bailey's lack of reproach. "Got to make a living, Dee."

"How well I know, Burt." He leaned forward to make his point. "John Cox had to close the Carriage House. No one's buying cars anymore, either." Dee glanced at the near empty bar room. "Listen, you haven't seen Benny Gibbs around here, have you? He's a teamster, about five-seven, kind of stout."

"Oh, Benny. Sure." Wagner's voice dropped to a whisper. "He went upstairs about twenty minutes ago. I expect him any time now, if he hasn't slipped out the back."

"Thanks, Burt." Dee pulled up a bar stool and sat down. "I think I'll wait if you don't mind."

"Not at all. Can I get you something?"

"How about a cup of coffee?"

Burt stepped to the back of the bar. He filled a thick white mug from a glass pot on a hot plate and brought it back to the counter. "It's on me."

"Thanks, Burt." Dee took his time with the coffee, casually glancing about the room. He was careful not to recognize anyone. News traveled fast in small towns; he'd set a few tongues wagging just by being in this neighborhood. Ten minutes slipped by before he heard Benny's baritone on the landing above.

"The pleasure was all mine, I assure you." Footsteps sounded on the stairs. "And here's a little something for your friends." There was light female laughter, followed by the firm click of a latched door.

Dee chuckled at the sound of Benny's voice. He'd taken an instant liking to the teamster. Gibbs was buttoning his vest as he saddled down the stairs. He looked as merry as a groom on his wedding night, glancing at his keepsake watch as it played its cheerful tune.

"Hello, Benny." Dee raised his voice just enough to capture the teamster's attention.

"Why my stars, if it's not the best mechanic in all of Oklahoma." Benny's voice filled the room. "Dee Bailey, how are you, where have you been and let me buy you a drink." He gestured towards the bar. "Burt, set 'em up, we've got reason to celebrate."

If there was ever any chance of keeping his anonymity in this place, it had long since evaporated. Dee wondered what Floy's response would be, if the news ever trickled back to Chandler.

"That's really not necessary, you know." Dee hoped to avoid enlisting in Benny's army of celebration.

"Nonsense, my boy." Benny slid his large frame onto the adjoining stool. He gave Dee a slap on the back that nearly took his breath away. "And there'll be no teetotalers on this occasion." He waved away the bottle that the bartender brought them. "Give us the real thing, Burt. I want a label I've seen before, and not one you've printed yourself."

Burt Wagner might still be a printer, after all. Dee hadn't planned on this kind of encounter, though he knew it was a possibility. Benny's good humor was infectious.

"Come now, Dee, let's get ourselves a table."

"Thanks, Benny." He gave Gibbs his most serious look and took a chair. "But just one."

"Ah, the anthem of the infidel." Benny was clearly in his element. "One drink is like one kiss, good for courting, but small comfort on a cold night."

Burt brought a bottle to their table, with a label even Dee recognized. Benny proposed a toast. "To the good times, may they last as long as we do."

Dee raised his glass and swallowed. It'd been quite a while since Dee had taken spirits, much less good sipping whiskey. It took him by surprise. His voice slipped an octave like the hoarse croak of a frog.

"Well said." Benny laughed and so did Dee, between a cough and a sputter.

"Now, Dee. Having seen your young wife and knowing your general constitution, I'd say you're not here for the usual reasons." Benny's baritone steadied and his eyes met Dee's. "What can I do for you, my friend?"

Dee's eyes lowered. Benny had confirmed his judgment; he was not simply a boisterous man, but a genuine one. Dee pushed himself to say the words he had so carefully prepared. "Benny, you said once that if I needed anything, I should come see you. Were you serious?"

"My word's as good as this whiskey, Dee." Benny smiled.

"That's pretty good." Dee was grateful for the simple ease that Benny gave him.

"Well, then, what can I do for you?" Gibbs moved closer and put his hand on Dee's shoulder. "Make it something easy, like money or a bump on the head."

"I need a job, Benny." Dee watched as Gibbs was taken aback. "I hear they need more teamsters to drive those explosives into the oilfields. You can get me in."

"Dammit, Dee, you don't want that kind of work." Benny was visibly upset. "You've got a wife and family and a decent trade."

"Don't kid yourself, Benny. There's no trade left in Chandler. All the farms are blown away in the wind, and anyone who has anything is holding on to it for dear life. Even John Cox is talking about leaving town - Floy's got half a mind to take the kids and go with him. I'll lose my family if I can't find work." Dee put his glass down and set his jaw. "I've still got life insurance, and I've got five mouths to feed."

Benny stiffened. "Oh, no, Dee. I'll have no part in that."

He knew what Gibbs was thinking and rolled his eyes to the ceiling. "Benny, you've seen my wife." Dee gave him a knowing smile. "You don't think I'm anxious to leave this old world, now do you?"

Benny relaxed and leaned back in his chair. "No, I guess not. But that's not the kind of talk we're used to in my business."

"That's because no one in your business can get life insurance." Benny laughed and Dee gave him a nod. "But I've got it, and I might need it too, if things don't go the way I've planned." Dee took another sip from his glass. "Listen, Benny, I've thought this out. I've got a steady hand, and you've got to admit I can outfit a wagon. Once I'm finished rigging one my way, it'll take a landslide to set off that nitro."

"Sure, you're good with the hardware, but it's usually your team that kills you." Benny topped off Dee's glass and poured himself another drink. "All it takes is one good spook or a runaway, and it's Katie-bar-the-door."

Dee drained his glass. "You've got good mules."

"Well, sure I have, or I wouldn't be here." Benny saw where Dee was headed. "I wasn't thinking of taking in a partner, Dee."

"Not a partner, Benny." Dee sensed an opening. "Just an extra hand. You could teach me the ropes, and I could take up some of the slack for you. We could carry twice the freight you're pulling now."

"I'm carrying just enough to keep up with my bar bill." Benny filled their glasses one more time. "That's all I need." He watched the mechanic's face fall. "But I'd be more than happy to provide some funds to tide you over."

"If that's what I wanted, I'd go see my old man." The mention of his father stuck in Dee's throat. "I won't take charity, Benny." He reached down and tossed the liquor into his mouth. It felt warm and his head began to swim. "I'd best be going. Thanks for the drink." He lifted himself off the chair, fighting against the weight of the whiskey.

Benny shook his head, knowing there was no way past the hard point on Dee Bailey's pride. He pictured the young mechanic's family: the three girls, the plucky little boy and the handsome wife. He didn't care for the sure trouble and small comfort that his dangerous profession would offer them.

There was no easy money to be had in his line of work, for the due bill was one's life and limb, with no clemency or reprieve. He could see Bailey was no coward; he was sure his hand was as steady as his temperament. But Gibbs had always worked alone, and it was hard sledding for him to lay another man in harm's way. Still, he felt a debt to this quiet mechanic; he measured it against his better instincts and the stubborn visage before him. Benny poured another round of whiskey and motioned Dee back into his chair.

"Of course, if we keep on drinking like this, I'll need to reconsider."

Dee slid down into the chair. He'd found work. It was dangerous work, and there would be hell to pay when Floy found out, but it was real work nonetheless. He figured to do a good job of it.

"Benny, you won't regret this."

"The hell I won't," Gibbs snarled. "Burt, bring us another bottle."

Benny put both hands flat on the table and leaned forward. "Now, Dee, tell me all about this fancy wagon of yours."

> *'Buffalo Gals won't you come out tonight,*
> *come out tonight, come out tonight?'*
> *'Buffalo Gals won't you come out tonight,*
> *and dance by the light of the moon?'*

DIXIE MAY WAS A BIG MULE, even by Oklahoma standards, standing more than 16 hands at the shoulder. She was born in Mobile, Alabama, on June 11th, 1915, under a shade tree, during a summer thunderstorm.

Her mother was a racing thoroughbred, brought all the way to New Orleans from London, England, to race in the stakes held each year before Mardi Gras. On the first turn of her first race in the new world, Dixie's dam fractured the cannon bone in her right front foot and broke down, never to race again. Her owner left instructions to have the mare destroyed, but a stable hand figured there might be some value left in the horse and managed to spirit her off the track. The big thoroughbred spent the next ten months laid up in spare paddocks, but managed to heal well enough to get around on her own. The stable hand traded the mare for three jars of corn whiskey and a knife with a broken blade, to a peddler from Mobile. It was there that she met the tall jack donkey that would sire her Dixie May.

As mules went, Dixie had a pretty soft life. She spent most of her time in the stable, with good rations and plenty of clean bedding. Her claim to fame was her steady humor and good temperament. Barking dogs and clanging bells didn't faze her, and she was hard pressed to break out of a walk, even if you fired a rifle shot over her head. But she could pull a wagon straight uphill fully loaded and not miss a step, and had a mule's good sense of the straight and narrow on a steep trail. She'd drawn the same wagon for almost six years now, and never felt the whip once, or the strain of too much cargo. She was happy as mules go, and had plenty of time off between long hauls.

One wagon is pretty much the same as another when you're pulling it, and unless you're drawing as a team, dull work, even for a mule. Dixie May hadn't had a partner in those same six years, and missed the occasional nip or cross pull in the harness. But her owner kept a steady hand, and didn't press her hard uphill, or fidget with the bit like some, so the loss of good company didn't affect her way of going. He was always careful to oil her stays, and kept her collar soft as glove leather. When he was with her, every once in a while she could hear music, tiny chimes singing out behind her. Aside from a nip in the air, or the feel of the ground beneath her, that was her closest contact with the world, for Dixie May was nearly stone blind, and had been so for a number of years. It had never affected her life much, as her handler took her where she needed to go, in or out of her stall, and she him, along the twisting roads that led into the hills.

She could tell this was a beautiful spring morning; all the world was alive with smell, pollen heavy from the swollen oaks, and red clover coming up everywhere. That was the one thing she missed from her early days, the sweet taste of young clover, still wet with dew. Dixie May didn't miss her sight much; in her later years there was so little to see, just the wooden walls of her stall and the same red clay roads. But when she was young and running free, all the world was new, and the taste and the sights and the sounds were rich enough to fill her to overflowing, sending her heels kicking and her legs racing through the grasslands. This was a green pasture morning. She could smell it. She could hear it in the lilt of the birdsong, in the dizzy refrain of the bees gathering around the blossoms.

Dixie May warmed in the sunlight, listening to the roadside, to her master's soft whistle on his perch behind her. She felt his easy hands on the reins, the light wind on her whiskers, and the dull clod of the clay beneath her hooves.

It might have been a faint memory, or a gay salute to an earlier time, but when she let it go, it was a fearsome kick, with all the enthusiasm that the old jenny could muster. She sent her heels high, bounding forward at the apex of her thrust, grabbing the weight of the wagon full in her collar, pulling it to her in a sudden, carefree jerk.

Her feet never touched the ground.

When the shipment was late, a search party was sent out from the oil fields, on the slim chance that the nitro wagon might have broken down. Mechanical problems were few and far between, so the men who went out looking were prepared to gather a few personal effects and little more. The crater was four feet deep and sixteen feet across. They found part of one wheel, some burnt harness, and a crumpled gold watch.

FLOY FOUND HER HUSBAND sitting in the center of the kitchen. His eyes were red, a blank stare reflected in the windowpanes. Her words drifted in the silence.

"Benny's dead."

"I know."

She reached out to touch his shoulder. "Davey heard it from one of his school friends." When the boy told her, she had shuddered, cold fear turned to strange relief.

"It's my fault." Dee Bailey's head hung in his hands, slumped across the kitchen table.

"Don't be silly, Dee. He knew what he was doing." She turned away from the thought that followed.

"I should have made him wait." Dee pounded the table and the sugar jar toppled with the force of his blow. He knew it wasn't true as he said it; Benny was plain determined to have things his way, determined to save the fancy pneumatic wagon for Dee's first trip to the oilfields. And that was that.

"We'll christen that one together, Dee." Benny had laughed. "And I've got just the bottle to do it with. One that ol' Burt hasn't watered down."

Now, there would be no more laughter, no more big plans.

"Don't blame yourself, honey." Floy sat down beside him. "It's not going to change anything."

"No, it's not." Dee gazed at the cresting moon outside the kitchen window. He had known Benny Gibbs for less than three months, but he felt as though he'd lost a brother instead. It was a curious feeling, one that he wasn't used to. Family ties were frayed in his father's house, and he wasn't accustomed to grieving.

"Did he have any family?"

"No." Dee smiled in spite of himself; the only family he could conjure up was a spritely redhead named Carlene. He promised himself an honest visit to console her. "Not like you or me."

"I'm sorry, Dee." Floy meant it, despite the many times she had cursed the day that Benny Gibbs was born.

"Me too, sweetheart." Dee raised his head to look at his wife. "Now, pack your things. It's time we were headed for California."

"No, honey. No." Floy rebelled at her own sense of victory. "Not like this." For weeks, she had begged him to leave, begged him to follow her father west and escape the choking dust cloud that was Oklahoma.

"Oh, yes." Dee pushed himself up from the table. "Now. Just like this." He turned and brought her close to him. "I should never have argued with you."

"It wouldn't have saved him, Dee." Floy pictured the shock-mounted wagon that Dee had worked so hard to build.

"No, it wouldn't have." Dee pressed her shoulders gently, sending her out of the kitchen. "Now, go and get started. Plenty to do before we can leave this place."

He watched her as she left the room and closed his eyes for a moment.

Dee opened a cabinet and took down the bottle Benny had given him for the wagon's christening. He cocked it in mock salute.

"But it might have saved me."

He imagined distant laughter, and a watch chime ringing *Buffalo Gals*.

I WENT TO SLEEP with Benny's story playing in my head. With no elec-tricity, there was no heat in the room, so we bundled up under our sleeping bags and let the storm play out beyond the door. The windows rattled off and on, but not enough to keep me from dreaming about nitroglycerin.

In the morning, Pop was feeling better and up well before me. He brought me a fresh cup of coffee from the motel office and one of those colored plastic spatulas that passed for an ice scraper. This one was promoting 'The Bunny Ranch - a can't miss Historic Landmark'. That claim wasn't strictly accurate, but its sharp edge easily chipped the icy crust off Betsy's windshield. My breath blew white, the sun was out, and any residual snowfall was starting to melt away.

We had better luck at the diner this time; the unappreciated beauty of bacon and eggs is how easy it is to cook them, even in Tonopah, Nevada.

Two cups of coffee and a thermos refill put us on our way out of town. Inches of snow were still on the highway, but the work crews were out in force. I tucked in behind a snowplow and considered myself pretty lucky under the circumstances. The radio said the storm was well south of us and headed east. We were headed west, so it looked like clear sailing ahead.

"That there's a New Holland." Pop was particularly attentive. "Dual rotor diesel. He'll slice up that drift like a hot knife through butter." He proceeded to tell me just how far to stay behind the plow to have a clear field of view and not get blasted by the overflow.

"How come you know so much about snowplows?"

"You can't spend any time up in Tahoe without 'em. Or else your ass is always falling off the mountain." He grinned and lit a cigarette. Pop must have pre-rolled at least a dozen of them as Benny's tale blew in with the blizzard.

"That's where I learned how to toss them boulders down off the highway."

He exhaled a puff of grey smoke. "Building roads for ol' John Keller, a case of dynamite at a time."

"Hand me that jerky, would you?" We'd picked up some smoked elk at the casino in Tonapah.

"Keller must have owned half that damn mountain." Pop passed over our goody bag. "Damn near half, anyway."

The snow plow's blinking amber lights made the icy drive more than manageable. I pulled out a piece of elk jerky and turned my little tape recorder on.

The Maker of All Things waited until nightfall
to sow the seeds of the Wa She Shu.
The East Wind blew the seeds over the waters,
and The People were born.
The Maker let the rain wash away their tracks,
so The People could stay beside the waters forever.
The Maker gave them words
for the Lake and the forest,
for the fish and the lion and the buck.
Only the Wa She Shu can speak those words,
and only The Maker can hear them.

- Washoe creation story

PEOPLE OF THE LAKE

HE WAS ON HIS WAY UP to a rich man's house. From where he stood, Dave could see the massive oaken threshold looming above him. The wide granite steps rose like stone guardians, a dozen feet from the manicured driveway.

Tommy and Wanda told him it was a damn fool idea, but Dave had figured what the hell, he had nothing to lose and plenty to gain. For the last three seasons, Bailey's A-1 Tree Service had harvested hundreds of acres of tall fir and white pine on leased state land. Most of the remaining tracts were pretty well logged over, with every good piece of timber already claimed by the big commercial outfits. He was getting squeezed out, and he knew it.

It had taken a while, but he'd built a good business wildcatting big trees and taking in firewood for the locals and the new casinos. Between that and some private tree-topping, he'd been able to keep his crew busy for most of the season. Or at least he had so far.

Managing that growing business and taking care of his young son had become more and more of a juggling act. Especially now that he wasn't living and working at home. He thought about the old place down in California, grateful that his folks had moved in to keep an eye on things. Even more grateful when Wanda and Tommy had stepped up to keep an eye on little Rusty.

At first, the fledgling ranch was a godsend. After he got back from the war, old man Beedle had told him he could have the whole 10 acres on credit, and that was mighty welcome news for a new father with a new bride. The property was right beside State Highway 49, halfway between Auburn and Grass Valley. It had a year-round spring and flat land that led up to a hillside corner, perfect for him and Marian. By the time Rusty was born, he and his dad had built a simple concrete-block house, and started work on a breezeway pole barn. Less than a year later, there was another baby on the way, three full-size chicken sheds, and even a few pigs. When he got the contract to supply all the eggs for the Auburn Market, they were on their way. He and Marian scrimped and saved for another year, finally putting together enough money to buy some feeder calves. With the post-war price of beef, he figured to make a pretty good life for his little family.

But not, as it turned out, for all of them.

Dave had traded an old army Jeep straight across for a truckload of clover hay. Somehow, a canister of rat poison had leached into the load, and that spelled the end of their good fortunes. He buried the swollen calves in a deep pit, barely deep enough for his regret. Fifty fat calves would have been their ticket out of debt. Instead, it was the wedge that drove him and Marian apart.

He'd known all along that Marian had soft hands, that she didn't much care for the rough country life. But she had done it, by God. She didn't like sorting and cleaning eggs till midnight, but she had done it. And she tried hard to pull him out of his bitter disappointment.

They'd moved to Tahoe, hoping to make a fresh start. He took a job at the sawmill and then another part-time. Anything to get out of debt. He began driving overnight to the ranch to tend the livestock, maybe a chance to make another go of it. Marian accused him of leaving her to fend for the babies all by herself. Maybe to get some breathing room, he wasn't sure.

He thought about the way that they parted. *Gone too long.* Or so she said.

Eyes closed, he took a deep breath and tried to clear his head. Time to put his thoughts to better use, or he'd be tongue-tied at the rich man's door.

Marian was gone now, and so was Della Jean.

That's the way it was, and the way it had to be. He'd never got to know his little girl, but at least Rusty had wanted to stay with him. Yet, here he was again, looking to keep his hands busy and the devil's workshop unoccupied.

Turning those hands over slowly, he stretched his fingers out as far as they would go. It was a tiny ritual he allowed himself when his thoughts were scattered. Looking up to the sky, he remembered that the sun warmed everyone just the same, even the rich folks. He'd practiced all his words; it was time to use them.

Dave stared at the big wooden door. It looked to be carved from one enormous slab of oak; wrought iron bars lay across its leaded glass window. An ornate knocker was mounted in the arched entryway. Dave rocked it back and forth, barking out an echoed clang.

After a few moments, the great door opened grudgingly. Dave peered at the figure before him: a small, brown man with dark, shiny hair, immaculately dressed in black formal attire.

"May I help you?" The man seemed to come to some sort of conclusion and gestured with two fingers. "If you are here as a tradesman, the servant's entrance is around the other side of the house."

Dave smiled amiably. "Well, I do have a trade, but that don't make me a servant." Dave thought he heard movement in the shadows and raised his voice slightly. "I'm here to see Mr. Whitman about some timber."

"Mr. Whitman isn't receiving any visitors." The Filipino butler scowled and started to close the door.

Dave spoke more forcefully, past the startled butler. "Yep, I heard he don't see anybody. Doesn't want to do much of anything anymore, they say." Dave craned his neck to look for any sign of movement. "But me, I don't believe that."

"Good day, sir." said the butler. The big door was almost fully closed when it suddenly stopped moving. Dave heard muffled voices, and the door opened briskly.

"What's that I hear? You have something to say? Well, then say it, young man. Speak up." Before him stood a tall, thin man, in what Dave reckoned to be his early seventies. His form was slightly shrunken, but from the looks of him, he'd been formidable in his day. He was lean, hard muscle given way to age, his straight, silver hair grown somewhat unkempt. The man was dressed in a long coat, loose trousers, and a pressed white shirt with a stiff collar.

"Yes sir, I'd be glad to." Dave nodded in reply. "Shall I stand out here and shout, or would you like me to come inside?"

The older man chuckled and swung the door wide open. "Indeed, come in and be welcome. It's nice to meet a man with some gumption again."

Dave stepped forward into the vestibule, past the scowling butler. His hand shot forward, and he smiled. "Dave Bailey."

"George J. Whitman." The older man took his hand, and Dave could feel the strength of his grip, only slightly diminished by time. "Come in, Dave Bailey, and sit a spell. He turned to the butler and gestured with his chin. "Efren, bring some coffee round to the study, if you would."

Whitman reached around Dave's shoulder and gently propelled them both down the long hallway. He turned to enter a paneled room circled by bookshelves and hung with large oil landscapes. Dave made an effort to keep his attention on the man before him, careful not to lose his focus in the rich complexity of the furnishings around him. They made small talk for a moment or two, exchanging pleasantries, until the older man inquired brusquely.

"You mentioned timber, Mr. Bailey. Yes, I do have quite a lot of it, although every mature parcel is spoken for. You strike me as a bright young man, consequently, I reason that you already know this." The old man peered at Dave intensely. "So, what exactly do you have in mind?"

Dave was grateful for Whitman's direct manner and went right to the heart of it. "Well sir, my proposal is this. You've got three sections of timber up on Harmony Ridge that won't be ripe for logging for another 10 years. They're just sitting there, making you not a penny, nor me neither." He paused for some effect. "I propose to make you a fair offer and see us both profit by it."

"Well, you're right about the timing, I'll say that, but then, that's exactly why they sit there. I logged those sections myself, some years ago." The older man looked somewhat saddened. "And those new trees won't be ready to mill for many years yet, so I'm afraid I'll have to disappoint you, Mr. Bailey."

"That's just my point, sir." With a nod, Dave let the butler fill the coffee cup before him. The little man turned away with a frown. "They seeded back nice, but now they're overgrown with suckers. Crowded in by young trees, too thick for a decent timber harvest." He took a sip of his coffee. "But I'm not after timber."

"Don't tell me you're one of those damn fools that sees a gold mine on every hillside."

"No sir, but I confess, I do like to get out and pan some, when I get the chance."

The older man lowered his cup and saucer and smiled. "Tried that a few times, myself. Mountain streams are good for the soul. Well then, what exactly are you after?"

"Christmas trees."

Whitman grew silent, arched an eyebrow and spoke. "There any money in that, son?"

"Only come December, sir."

The old man laughed out loud. Dave began to outline the profits and the cost; how he'd clear around the healthy timber, culling Christmas trees, careful to clean up his slash. That would give the larger trees better daylight to grow in, making Whitman's eventual harvest that much easier and more substantial.

One cup of coffee later, the silver-haired man signaled his agreement. "Well, sir, I am convinced."

Dave gave Whitman his best smile. "Then all that's left to do is set a price per acre. We can draw up an agreement, and I'll write you out a check in good faith."

The old man shook his head. "No agreement necessary. I've got more than enough paper in my life. And there'll be no money up front, besides. You just do your work, and come Christmas, I'll expect an extra present under the tree." The old man stretched out his hand. "In an envelope."

"Yes, sir." Dave felt a kind of kinship in the old man's hand. "And I'll bring you the tree as well."

Whitman leaned into his handshake and whispered confidentially. "Christmas trees. Now, who would have thought of that?"

THE STATELY MOUNTAIN HEMLOCK was taller than the ones that Tommy usually cut down; as a rule they would take only the smaller trees, those that wouldn't be part of the next timber harvest, or the ones that might get in the way of the commercial loggers when they arrived. It was tricky work, mostly because Dave Bailey insisted that they clean up their slash as they went; they always left the parcel in better shape than they found it.

Tommy Johnson pulled the heavy Pioneer chainsaw to life, rotated its steel carriage, and put the 36" bar against the conical tree. Bailey's A-1 Tree Service had invested in the Canadian chainsaw in an effort to speed up some of the heavy cutting. Tommy was no fan of the mechanical beasts. Only in the last couple of years had anyone manufactured a workable one-man chainsaw. Even so, they were only marginally less likely to take your arm or your leg off.

Last year, Tommy had seen a grown man sawn in two at the mill. A sight he hoped never to see again, especially if any of the two parts were his own.

Rendo and he could make short work of almost any tree with a two-man pull saw, and Rendo could take down some of the smaller trees with just one or two strokes of his axe. The big Indian was a marvel with a double-sided axe, almost as handy with it as he was with a shovel and a pick. Ever since they'd met, he and Rendo seemed to have an almost pendulum-like balance in the way they worked together, each one anticipating the other one's movements and compensating automatically, whether with a saw, an axe, or a shovel.

Dave had hesitated when Tommy had recommended his friend for a job, mostly because of Rendo Bear's well-known affection for alcohol. But Wanda had vouched for him, too, and Dave relented once he saw the way the big man could move through brush like a wildfire. Nowadays, Dave would even postpone the start of a new job just to wait for the giant Washoe to sober up.

Tommy cried "Timber!" and the tall conifer fell in one swift motion, her blue-green needles landing gently in the low swale he had intended for it. A burst of piney fragrance lifted off the severed stump, clearing his nostrils and centering his mind. Moving quickly, he tapped the suckers off the lower trunk, careful to watch for any kickback. Satisfied it was clean and ready to be transported, he started work on the thick branches of a black oak snag that Dave had wanted cleared for the slash pile.

Rendo was piling Christmas trees off to one side of the trail, breaking them down by size and getting them ready to pull down off the mountain. Tommy could see his own breath in the dim light; the weather was turning. They'd have to hurry before the first snows put an end to their efforts.

Dave had already taken a load down the mountain, spinning the smaller trees into a tight pile and carrying them by hand to the logging road below. Dave could carry about 20 trees that way; Tommy could manage about 25, but Rendo could haul two loads at the same time, one tightly wrapped under each arm, at least 40 trees on every trip.

They'd been at it for the better part of a month, supplying two large wholesalers in Roseville, and one retail Christmas tree lot run by Dave's cousin Alpha in Grass Valley. Just for fun, they'd set up a small tree stand out in front of Tommy and Wanda's house, and little Rusty had already made almost fifty dollars.

Rusty was spending more and more time at their house, so much so that nearly all of his clothes and toys were there. Dave would take his meals with the three of them, then run off to his next job, or back down to Grass Valley to check on his folks at the ranch. Taking care of his boy, his business, and the ranch was maybe more than Dave had bargained for.

Still, he thought it wise to mind his own business, and let the man do what he thought was best. Dave was going to do that anyway, regardless of what Tommy Johnson or anybody else had to say.

It had been a hard couple of years for his brother-in-law; driving up and down the mountain, holding down two jobs, trying to keep from losing the place he'd built with Marian. You could see the fierce love he had for Rusty, but it was almost as if the pain of his lost marriage had not only pushed him to work harder, but to distance himself from his only son.

Tommy loved the boy as if he were his own. He loved the boy's father, too. Instinctively, he understood that this was how it had to be, at least for now. And when they found out he and Wanda couldn't have any kids, well, that just made things even easier. Wanda wanted Rusty with her, and Tommy was no more successful than Dave when it came to refusing his little sister.

Tommy finished culling the firewood; Rendo stepped to his side and helped him stack the pieces in a tiered pile. Together, they slid the giant hemlock out of the swale and into the clearing. The sun was waning as a buck mule deer burst from the brush behind the trail, bounding down the mountainside.

"Hello the camp!" came a voice from below. "Quitting time."

Tommy could see Dave Bailey headed up the trail, a cigarette clenched between his teeth and three bottles of beer clutched in his right hand. Tommy and Rendo picked up the big hemlock and carried it to the trailhead.

"Gently now," Dave cried out. "I've got plans for that baby."

THE SUN WAS RISING over the Jarbridge Wilderness, about 60 miles outside of Elko, Nevada. We'd managed to slip away for another road trip and were on our way back to Grass Valley. Doc was gazing out the window; the blue-green hills sparkled in his glasses.

"Look out there, just look out there."

"A thousand acres would be mighty sweet," I said.

Pop shrugged and shook his head. "Where can you go anymore that you don't look out and not see nothing but city after city? I'd say this valley is hundreds of miles across. There's no doubt there's a few little towns out there we can't see, but I'm talking about cities, you know, big towns like we have in California. Ain't that beautiful?"

"It sure is." A long valley of yellow wildflowers led out towards a small crescent lake, ringed by stands of evergreen. Across the low hills, I could see a jagged mountain range, shadowed by the mist of distance.

"That's what I say." Pop leaned forward into his seat and gestured across the horizon. "I tell you what, just a lone rider, years ago, you could take off and ride these mountains all across this country. Man, what a thrill your old heart would get. Like laying out in the desert, looking at the stars. You know, we're such a little smidgen in this thing. God, we think we're so great, you know. The good Lord sure did make it beautiful to start out with, I'll tell you that. Wow."

He was filled with delight, like a five year old at story time.

"Yep, the first guy that looked out on this here, he said, 'That's my friend. Tell everybody to keep off that mountain range, everything out there is mine. If you get on it and try to take it, I'm gonna' shoot your ass'." Pop laughed and coughed. "Right?"

I nodded in silent agreement, remembering how often I'd heard him wish he'd been born a hundred years before.

"Yep, that's the way they did it. By that time, they'd shot everybody that tried to take it, they had the big spread, they had the big pull in Congress, and hey, they'd just pass all the laws they wanted to get it deeded over to 'em. All nice and legal."

"Unless you were an Indian."

"They got the raw deal. No way around that one."

Pop pointed out along the edge of the hills. "See that building out there - other than that, I can't see nothing." He shook his head in mock dismay. "Give it time though, it'll all be built. Too many people, Bill. Too damn many people. They can't keep stacking them up like cordwood."

A stiff gust came up and the old Ford swooned, buffeting across the road. I swung the wheel back against the wind, and we straightened out in our lane. "There's a good little breeze coming through here."

"Yep, that's what you have on these high mountain plains. Them suckers, that wind comes across at you hellbent in the wintertime. Just like Montana." He laughed at himself and rolled his window up. "Well, in fact, I have yet to go to Montana that I didn't freeze my tail off. And I've been there about eight times over my life and every time, I damn near froze."

"Except for Paradise."

"Except for Paradise." He slapped the dashboard and grinned. "You figure it out, how many days we been gone, five, seven?"

"I don't know. We'll figure it out when we get to Winnemucca."

"Well, why are you going up there, god-damn it! We're going the wrong way. I don't ever want to go through that town again." Doc's blood was up. I could see it. His jaw was set and he went suddenly silent.

The last time we went to Winnemuca, it wasn't pretty. Too much whiskey and not enough good sense. More things I could never tell my wife and kids about. My thoughts turned to wives and ex-wives, and the common thread that ran between them: husbands. Pop had been on the same merry-go-round a few times himself.

"Tell me about the first time you met Marian..." I wanted to change the subject before his good mood was completely gone. Mine, too.

"Oh, Marian?" Doc looked my way and relented. "The first time I seen Marian she was a skinny, little sixteen-year old gal. She came up to that big party we threw, the one that went on for so long. I don't know who she came with, but everybody was kinda' ribbing her, I guess, because all the other girls there were eighteen or nineteen years old. And me, well I don't know, I always go for the underdog, I don't care what it is really, whether they're right or wrong. But anyway, they didn't want to socialize with her, so I just took her under my wing. For two or three days, she came around."

"Who else was there?" He'd never told me the whole story.

"Oh, I don't know, a bunch of people we knew. You know, county friends."

"How long after that did you marry her?"

"It was quite a few months after that. Some policeman, he comes up. She was over spending the night with me, and he more or less arrested me." He paused for a moment, then reached into the glove compartment and began rolling a cigarette.

"He took me up to Marian's dad's house. This cop tried to get old Jack to press charges on me - sleeping with a minor. And actually then, I hadn't even slept with her. Hey, she was just a good kid. So this cop says, 'Hey, you got to stop seeing her.' And I said, 'No way, man, if she wants to see me, I don't care what you say. It's up to her, not you. If she wants to see me, we'll see each other'." He finished rolling his cigarette and reached for his lighter.

"This here cop kept trying to get Jack to press charges, but Jack wouldn't do it, because he was a good person." Pop's lighter flashed and smoke filtered into the headliner. "After she and I got married, Jack said he liked me just from what I said that night - that it was her decision, not anybody else's."

"So what happened with the police?"

"I told this cop he had to take me back up to the house, and he didn't want to. I told him, 'Bullshit, you better'. Cause if you don't there's gonna' be hell to pay. I'll talk to - Ben Jenkins, he was chief of police then. I said I'm gonna' talk to Ben, and we'll see. He says 'Well, alright.' And when we were going up there he says, 'I'm kinda' thinking of pressing those charges myself'."

Pop's eyes flashed and his cadence quickened, as if some ghostly shot of adrenaline had filled his lungs with cold air. His cigarette, pinched between his thumb and forefinger, was long extinguished. In rolling gestures, he punctured the air in front of him.

"I said, 'Well then, you better press charges while you got me in this car, because if you come back here tomorrow or any other day, I'll just shoot you dead.' Ain't no going around it, that's just the way I am. And of course he knew it, and old Wayne Brown, he was the sheriff then, they all knew that's the way I was.

Anyway, he didn't come up, because I had my rifle sitting there right beside me, and I'd have shot him if he'd come up and said I was under arrest. Because I'm a real person - I'd rather be dead than have somebody shit on me."

Doc paused for a moment to catch his breath, his words having outpaced his lungs. He closed his eyes for bit, swallowed hard and continued.

"I honestly feel that way. I've been that way my whole life. It's a wonder that I'm still alive, I know that. But that's honest to God the way I feel. You know, I can stand maybe a guy shitting around a little, but when you go to spitting on me, when you think you're better than I am, or you got more power than I do, then we're gonna' have to find it out the hard way."

I felt like I'd caught a glimpse of him 50 years before, long ago in some sandy desert schoolyard. "I'll try to remember that."

"You do that." He grinned and shook his head, his good humor returning. "What the hell, maybe Winnemucca has a good coffee shop to go along with all the whorehouses. Let's get a move on."

I stepped on the gas and Betsy growled, her steel fortress hard pressed against a swirling wind.

NOVEMBER 1951

Genoa Peak
Douglas County, Nevada

DAVE COULD FEEL the lion's presence behind him, maybe 40 feet away, in the low brush that was scattered around the hillside. There was a time when he might have been worried, but not anymore. Not after so many encounters. The first time he saw the big cat, it had sent the hair up on the back of his neck, and he'd made certain to pack his rifle with him the next day. Sure enough, he saw the tawny lion the very next evening, right after he'd made his traditional trek around the hillside. Every night after work, Dave would walk the next morning's acreage. Lately, he kept an eye out for the big cat, as well. This time, he just turned and stood his ground, careful not to exhibit any prey behavior, then went about his business.

Dave didn't know what made this cat so willing to be seen. The mountain lion wasn't making any effort to be stealthy. At first, it had given him a case of the willies, but he figured he wasn't in much danger; this time of year, there was plenty of mule deer about, and the cougar looked to be well fed. He'd seen that much at first glance.

The cat had taken to following him all the way down to the logging road. Two days ago, the whole crew had seen it walking behind him. Tommy had said it looked like a police escort, but Rendo told him that the cougar had made him a brother, and he should bring it a gift. When Dave had asked what that might be, Rendo said he'd ask his father, who still knew the old ways and could talk the big cat's language.

He was never quick to discard what the giant Washoe said, even if it sounded like nonsense. Years ago, Old Joe had taught him far too much about the desert to ever doubt the tribes completely; he knew a simple truth would often hide just below the surface. Until they finished this acreage, he wasn't going to ignore any-one's advice about mountain lions.

"What do you think I ought'a do about it in the meantime?"

"Make friends." Rendo spoke with some authority. "And maybe you could bring some whiskey." There was a brief pause. "For my mom and dad."

Dave liked Rendo's parents. Both in their nineties, they were good people. But prone to argue; Rendo's dad was fond of younger women - his mother had told Rendo that she'd have to kill the old man if they ever shared a bed again. They would only stay together when Rendo was about and could referee. And they all had a taste for liquor.

Dave considered how much trouble might be lurking in his curiosity about the cat. "Where's your dad now?"

"Up at Cold Creek." Rendo smiled. "Bring some whiskey tomorrow, and I'll ask him what to do about the lion."

"Not going to happen." Dave figured to take his chances.

"I've had my fill of mountain lions," Tommy exclaimed. "Can't trust 'em. Last year, me and Ralph Clinton found one dead in the middle of the road, and put it in the back of the pickup. We stopped at Ralph's Resort to spend the night, and tossed that lion in one of the cabins. Next morning we went to skin him, and the damn thing had gone up the chimney. Just knocked out, I guess." Tommy spun his hands around wildly, as if climbing a tree. "But not before it totally wrecked the place, all the curtains, the bed, the couch, everything was just shredded!"

Dave spit a laugh at his brother-in-law's lion act. "I bet you were kinda shredded, too."

"Well, maybe a little bit." Tommy gave Rendo a shrug, and they all turned to go.

A piercing scream echoed from the stand of trees above them. Dave looked at the shadowy hill and wondered what had prompted the cougar's mournful howl.

"Whiskey," Rendo repeated. "Two bottles."

"I'll give it some thought," said Dave.

Cold Creek
Clark County, Nevada

THE BIRCHBARK CABIN was at least a hundred years old, maybe more. Dave could easily tell its age by the chinked log walls and the weathered stone chimney. Rendo's dad had lived there for the better part of the century, ever since he'd left the Carson Indian School to set out on his own.

Dave pulled a paper bag containing two bottles of whiskey out of his truck. He thought it better to bring the whiskey to Patrick Bear directly, not knowing if Rendo would return to work on Monday if he'd left the job site with both bottles in hand.

"I'll meet you up at Cold Creek," Dave had said. Then he drove out to Globin's and bought two bottles. It wasn't the best or the worst whiskey, but it was likely to be well received.

"*Na ga hay*, Dave Bailey." Patrick gave him a nod. The old man was sitting on a thick plank bench in front of a crackling fire; a black pot on an iron tripod hung above the flames. Dave could smell meat boiling; likely rabbit or squirrel, peppered with wild onions and bitterroot.

"Na ga hay, Patrick Bear." Dave always called Rendo's father by his Christian name. He couldn't pronounce the Washoe moniker.

"The Maker greets you," Rendo's mother smiled. Her missing teeth formed a dark cave beneath her wide grin.

"Na ga hay, Ruth." Dave knew Rendo's mother from Globin's Market, where she cooked venison jerky and cleaned vacation cabins. If she wasn't bedded down with Rendo or trying to kill her old man.

"A gift for the house, Patrick." Dave lifted the paper bag with both hands.

"The Maker thanks you, Dave Bailey." Patrick gestured to the three-legged stool beside him. "Come, sit down." The old man spoke a few words to his wife, unintelligible to anyone not familiar with the ancient language. The Washoe dialect, Wasiw, was the oldest on the continent, spoken only in the mountains of the northern Sierra.

The old woman brought out a small, tightly woven bowl, shaped with an oval opening and filled with fresh pine nuts. She placed it on the ground beneath her husband. Dave put his paper bag beside it. The Washoe woman went inside and returned with four metal drinking glasses, each one a different color. Rendo eyed his mother with a smile and chose the blue tumbler, holding it tightly between his knees, as if he were a small boy waiting for a glass of milk.

"I hear you made friends with a lion," said Patrick.

"Maybe. At least the cat thinks so. But I'm thinking things might be getting a little too cozy." Dave hoped he wasn't fooling himself. If anything, that was why he was here; he didn't want to have to kill the lion, or bring in Fish and Game. There were only a few of the big cats left around Tahoe; there was even talk about putting them under some kind of protection.

Tommy had told Dave he was too sentimental, but he figured no harm done in talking to Patrick, especially since it was Saturday night, and there was no work the next day. Besides, Tommy had no business talking; Wanda and him had raised almost every kind of critter known to man or God: bird dogs and racing pigeons, pigs and horses, even skunks as pets. He'd seen his brother-in-law carry a wounded fawn out of the forest and doctor it till it could run away under its own power.

Dave told Patrick the story of how he had come upon the cougar, and how it had stayed so close to him at the end of every workday.

"*O'osh te*, it's the winter moon, her time." The old man smiled. "She's a mother cat, she has cubs, or you wouldn't have seen her twice." Patrick took one of the bottles out of the bag and tore open the seal on the top. "She takes you down the hill, so you won't return to steal her children."

Patrick poured a strong shot from the bottle into each tumbler, and the old woman passed them out around: red for Patrick, green for Dave, and the yellow one for herself. Rendo waited for his father to finish and poured his own, double the size of the others.

"Bring her a carcass, and she'll take you to her children." The old man took a deep draft from the aluminum tumbler. "Bind the meat in colored yarn and sage bark. Leave it behind where you last saw her."

Dave wondered where he'd get such a thing, until Rendo's mother returned with a matted ball of yarn and a handful of rough wood wrapped in soft deerskin. The old woman placed them by his side. She took a seat behind Patrick and began to sing softly.

"Thank you, Ruth." Dave noticed that she took the extra bottle and placed it by her stool. Her song was wordless, pitching up and down in open tones and vowels, with meanings Dave could only try to imagine.

Rendo began to sing with her, and then Patrick. Dave closed his eyes and let their voices blend together in the fading light. After a time the song ended, and Patrick thanked The Maker, and they ate rabbit stew and dried whitefish, and Ruth brought out Hershey Bars that they cooked on flat sticks smeared with sweet potato.

After they ate, Patrick told the story of Wa She Shu, the people of the lake, about The Maker and the Paiute and the Shoshone. He spoke about seeds drifting in the wind, and the day that Rendo took his first buck. Their tumblers were filled and filled again, and they sang and they laughed until both bottles were empty.

The rising moon lit the path back to his truck. Dave brought out the bottle that he'd kept aside for himself and filled all of their metal glasses. For the first time in a long time, he spoke about the desert and his old friend Joe.

HE WOKE TO THE SMELL of hot coffee and burnt acorns. Dave's eyes opened slowly. His neck was askew. At some point, he must have fallen asleep in the truck. Rendo's father was still asleep on the long bench, his blanketed torso tilted against the wall. Ruth was bent down low over the fire, boiling coffee. She stirred a thick brown mush in a flat iron skillet.

Dave pulled himself out of his truck and walked to the fire pit. Ruth poured him a cupful of the hot, black liquid.

Dave took a careful sip. "That'll stand your hair up," he whispered.

Ruth turned and slapped Patrick's knee with the long wooden spoon. "Get up, old man!" she cried. "No one wants to hear you snoring."

Patrick sprang forward with a snort and pulled the wool blankets up around his head. Satisfied his wife was the sole source of his discomfort, he spat a Wokan curse at her, curled his legs up tight and turned back on the slab.

"Good for nothing," Ruth murmured and returned to her skillet.

"Where's Rendo?" Dave asked.

"Down the mountain to get the old fool his medicine." She crooked her head in Patrick's direction. "When he returns, I will go away and his whores can come back out of the forest."

Dave looked over at the stand of trees behind the cabin. Three dark figures stood in the shadows. He could tell by their demeanor they were female, cautiously watching and none too anxious to return.

"Want me to take you down below, Ruth? I don't mind." He figured he might save a little trouble for everyone.

"No, I like it here." Ruth gestured to the old man on the bench and gave Dave a toothless grin. "I get a chance to let my demon play." The dark woman stirred the boiling mush. "And it keeps him alive a little longer."

Ruth turned to go inside the cabin. "Wait here."

Dave took another sip of coffee, and wondered at the unpredictable union that had bound Rendo's parents together. Not at all like his folks, but identical in one important aspect.

Till death do us part.

Ruth returned from the dark doorway with a fresh cut haunch of deer meat, carefully wrapped in buckskin. The thickly muscled leg lay on a bed of rough bark, long strands of colored yarn tied around the deer's fetlock.

"Road kill," she said quietly, sneering at her sleeping husband. "He never hunts anything but young girls."

THE HILLSIDE HARVEST was almost complete; the slash piled up in enormous mounds and the bundled trees hauled down to the logging road. All that remained was to transport the last few loads of Christmas trees to market and a final survey of the job site, making sure nothing was left behind.

Two days before, Dave had placed the buckskin bundle at the foot of a large brush pile, high up on the hillside. He'd felt a little silly when he did so, prey to superstition and whimsy. But satisfied that the bloody gift was far enough away not to invite any trouble.

He hiked up the hill the next day to take a look, and the haunch of deer was gone. He thought nothing of it; either the lion had taken the meat, or another scavenger had made a lucky find. He saw no sign of buzzards, but he was careful to keep an eye out for bear, as they were known to steal a carcass and jealous of any intruders.

Despite his cautious approach, the low, throaty growl took him by surprise. The big cat was almost directly above him, on a high granite ledge. It looked in no way threatening; instead of a low crouch, it was laid out like a sunbather on some foreign beach or a tabby cat in the warm light of a cool day. The lion stretched out to its maximum length. Jaws wide open, it released a lingering yawn.

The sudden leap surprised him. Before he could fully comprehend the moment, the big cat was crouched on the ground only feet away. Dave knew the cougar could rend him instantly, but somehow, just as surely, he knew the cat had no desire to do so. Instead, the lion turned leisurely around in a semi-circle, and padded softly off behind the rocks.

Realizing his good fortune, Dave elected not to push his luck any further. Backing away slowly, he kept his eyes fixed on the large stone boulders above. Once more, the big cat appeared at the top of the ledge, a small cub dangling from her jaws. A second cub lumbered out from beneath her legs, pawing at its sibling in an effort to capture its undulating tail. The mother lion released the smaller cub from her clutches and plopped down decisively behind them.

The two small cubs rolled about on the ledge like kittens on a living room carpet, pawing and growling in pitched battle. As the fierce contest raged, the mother lion lapped her tongue across their matted fur, first one cub and then the other.

A familiar glimpse of color gave pause to Dave's retreat. From his vantage point below, he watched as the tiny lions fought valiantly for their single treasure: a tattered stretch of purple yarn, torn from a velvet heel.

IN THE DISTANCE, Winnemucca was its usual self, a single red bulb on the string of infrequent lights that stretched through rural Nevada. Perched alongside the railroad and the interstate, it was a welcome oasis for long distance truckers and bleary-eyed travelers.

Pop and I had been there before, on our way out of California. We stayed overnight, something I was determined not to do this trip. My resolve had a tendency to weaken after a few whiskey sodas.

Someone had decided to build the little town a hundred years before, next to the only river that crossed the Great Basin, probably a tired settler headed west across the dry sea that was northwestern Nevada. The town was named after a Paiute chieftain, Winnemucca, who decided not to slaughter the white devils that flowed like water through his territory. Later, he paid the same price as the Shoshone and the Ute - starvation on a federal reservation.

By 1868, the transcontinental railroad had reached across the mountains, marking its arrival with an influx of people and commerce. Many of the Chinese railroad workers settled in town and built a thriving community, complete with a Joss House. Like the Paiute, the Chinese were driven out eventually, their temples torn down by the town's civic leaders. None of the Chinese had thought to ask Chief Winnemucca about the quality of the white devil's promises.

Unlike the Chinatown, its red light district had endured; the bars and the brothels were a last vestige of a freewheeling western expansion. Like the small gambling halls downtown, they'd survived and prospered.

"There's a coffee shop up ahead, Pop." I started looking for a parking place. "I'd like to rest my eyes and get a little caffeine in me."

"Sounds like a plan." Doc took a short plastic comb out of his pocket and ran it through his thin grey-blonde hair. He'd always been a dapper man, even now, in his checkered shirt and jeans. Pop had a certain way of rolling up his long sleeve shirts to make them short and tight above his elbows, and he liked to keep his hard straw hat carefully creased.

The last time we were in Winnemucca, I'd left Pop alone in our motel room. It was after dinner, and I said I was going out for a quick drink. He didn't tell me not to go, but his look said everything.

Doc genuinely loved my wife, maybe in a better way than I did. They had grown close in the years since we'd met. She brought him buttermilk and corn-bread; once in a while, she would give him her asthma inhalers to help with his labored breathing. She'd listen to his stories with playful attention, and whenever they were together the tale would always end in raucous laughter.

"I won't be long, can't sleep. Too much coffee," I'd said.

"I like whores." Pop replied. "That's why I don't sleep with them." He took his boots off and laid down on the bed.

As I closed the door behind me, I told myself that my intentions were good. I had a beautiful daughter, a wife, and another child on the way. But I didn't return until nearly dawn.

A parking spot appeared in front of us. I swung the wheel over and we slid gently to a stop. Those angled spaces were a favorite of mine, as Betsy's size and turning radius didn't lend itself to parallel parking. We were three doors down from the coffee shop and across the street from the Pioneer Motel.

Pop grew strangely silent.

"Just coffee, Doc," I said. "And maybe a piece of pie."

THE YOUNG HORSE SWAYED from side to side in the grey pickup, its short mustang legs and low center of gravity offering sparse relief against the winding road. Rendo was up front in the cab, drunk as he had ever been, in celebration of a good day's hunt. Today, he was free. After six weeks on the mountain, Rendo's wages were paid in full, and a full case of dark brown whiskey was perched on the bench seat beside him. Dave Bailey had held back most of his pay all season, to keep him from the condition he found himself in now.

His lodge brother Tommy had brought him to Bailey; he'd worked for the desert man almost six seasons now. In the late spring and fall, they would cut firewood for the tourists and gather Christmas trees. In the summer, they would top tall trees for the white homeowners, who feared the big winds that came off the lake like frozen ghosts.

Rendo was Waší·šiw, and like some of his people, he found precious relief in drink. It blotted out the houses and the roads, the streetlights and the garbage cans that surrounded his spirit lake.

He glanced in the side view mirror. His little Dodge pickup was rumbling down the logging road off a rough sawn ridge, its equine cargo shifting the truck's center of gravity like a pendulum. Rendo had gone up to check the traps he'd laid out after they'd finished logging. Bailey worked in places no one else could go; the desert man had made some sort of treaty with the white chiefs that claimed all the highlands above the lake.

Rendo could go undetected wherever he liked to set his traps; most white men couldn't see beyond a blackberry bush. But to check them frequently, before scavengers could claim the meat and ruin his pelts, this was another thing altogether. For this, he needed permission, a word the white men used to keep the sheriff happy and their high fences where they wanted them.

Rendo had good relations with the sheriff, and no desire to soil the desert man's treaty. The sheriff let him sleep in the jail when it was cold, or when he was too drunk to get back to his moutain cabin. Keeping his traps in Bailey's forest was a good thing, as the many skins bundled in his truck would tell. Once they were stretched and tanned, he and Tommy would spend long nights in his lodge, warm in their fine fur robes, drinking whiskey and telling tales about their childhood.

The ridge was pierced with winding logging tracks that gave grudging access to the mountain. Rendo would park his truck at the edge of the tract, unload his horse, then swing up across the ridge, clearing traps and butchering pelts until the mustang's back was packed full. Now, loaded with skins and whiskey, he was headed back to Cold Creek to see his folks.

Rendo reached into the cardboard case beside him and replaced his empty bottle. As he glanced down, the truck caught the edge of a pothole gouged out by heavy rains. The grey Dodge lurched to the edge of the switchback, then veered again as Rendo spun the wheel. Whiskey erupted into the cab. The truck righted itself and bounced on its old coil springs, launching the yellow mustang across the lip of the pickup bed and onto the slope.

The little buckskin rolled and tumbled down the hill sideways, propelled by its momentum and the steep angle. The mustang burst out of the slope and rolled across the shoulder, landing half-upright in the middle of the road below, collapsed in a moment of outright confusion.

"Ain't that Rendo's old nag?" On the road below, Tommy Johnson and Dave Bailey watched as the horse appeared before them, some 40 yards away.

Tommy slowed his pickup to a crawl.

"I believe it is." Dave peered through the windshield. A light rain had begun to fall.

The mustang spun on its belly, its head and neck straight up, as if looking for a barn with its lost stall. With some effort, the dazed mustang spread its front legs and pushed upward, pulling its hindquarters underneath it. The horse pressed forward to stand fully upright.

"I wonder what the hell it's doing out here."

"I bet old Rendo's on the mountain checking his traps." Tommy set the Chevy's handbrake and turned on his lights. The mustang stood bolt still in the headlights, except for the constant trembling in its legs.

Dave pulled the door handle and stepped down onto the running board. Pushing the door wide open, he leaned across it like a neighbor over a wooden fence. "Dang, Tommy, that horse is flat discombobulated."

"And here comes Rendo." Tommy cut the engine and stepped out of the truck. "I expect ol' Rendo is just as drunk as his horse."

The Washoe's '37 Dodge pulled to a stop and ground its gears in reverse, spinning its wet tires as it curled backwards, forwards, and then back again, until the open bed of the pickup sat next to the shaken animal. Rendo stepped sideways from the truck, teetered, then pulled his pants up to make himself more present-able. Three more steps took him alongside the buckskin, and he swung his arm in a high arc, eyeball to eyeball with his horse.

"Get up in there!" he cried.

The horse looked startled, awakened from its deep confusion, then backed up a step or two and floundered.

"I said get up in there," Rendo barked. He waved his hand again, gesturing towards the truck bed. "Can't you see it's raining?"

The horse shook its head and nickered, then leapt up into the pickup, like a cat on a dining room table. Rendo closed the tailgate, turned and gave a nod to Tommy, then to Dave. "Better get off the mountain. Big snow coming."

Dave watched the Dodge pivot and head downhill, the mustang perched inside, its four legs pressed tightly against the two sides of the pickup box. "We better get down. He might be right, even if he is drunk."

Tommy Johnson had hunted and fished with Rendo Bear ever since he was a young boy. They grew up together, and together they had learned the Washoe ways. When Wanda and he had come back to the lake in '47, the two men had renewed their friendship, building cofferdams on the high streams for Pacific Gas & Electric.

Tommy started the Chevy's engine and turned back to his brother-in-law.

"Nope. When he's drunk, he's always right."

GEORGE WHITMAN was tired, more tired than he'd felt in quite some time. He'd been up late the night before, listening to his son's latest proposition: new roads, new stores, new houses, more people stacked up to the ceiling.

The old man had been polite, even somewhat supportive. But the elaborate subdivision had begun to gnaw at him, first in his study, then just below the sur-face in his sleep.

When Whitman came to the lake forty years ago, it was still a hidden jewel in the mountains, too far by rough roads for travel from the city, but close enough to the railroad to be accessible, if you had purpose and a good vehicle.

The first time he saw her was on a bright spring morning; the snows had thawed enough for his father's Packard to travel the mountain passes standing guard over her pristine waters. His Dad had taken him out in a birch bark canoe; they'd paddled for miles along the shoreline and out into the bay. He saw dozens of rainbow trout and kokanee salmon swimming a hundred feet below.

Lake Tahoe was enormous, a vast blue-mirrored horizon; he'd felt small, in a way that perhaps only the tribes who lived around the lake could know. The Washoe were a singularly lazy people, or so he had thought at the time, content to move from one family camp to another, harvesting fish or hunting deer, pulling camas root and pine nuts from the soft forest floor that surrounded the crystal lake.

He knew better now; they lived in perfect harmony with the lake, in a balance that preserved its glassy waters. The Washoe way was an act of defiance. It galled the men that came after them - men who were ready to strip the trees and the minerals, or anything else of value from the lands around the lake.

"Men like me," he thought.

The hair on his neck bristled as he pictured his son's plans; a ring of tract houses and cross streets circling the lake on properties that he and his family had held for half a century. The old man was no bleeding heart; he had a genuine contempt for the government's constant encroachment on his liberties, but as the years wore on, he had come to a grudging realization - an unrestrained harvest makes for a barren field.

When the Forest Service approached him about changing his use permits, he'd stubbornly resisted. The people from the Preservation Society came next; some of them his neighbors. After they left, his thoughts didn't go to the logging roads and highways he had built, but to the very first moment he saw the lake.

He stepped outside his bedroom door, into the long hallway that led to the main staircase. The great house was unusually silent, even for an early winter morning. Usually by this time, he would have heard the maids whispering as they dusted, or the sound of gardeners digging in the rose bushes. He was accustomed to taking his morning coffee in the study, and wondered if Efren had already put it there, or if his late night had caused some slight alarm to the household staff.

He called out from the hallway. "Efren. Where are you? Is anyone there?" He caught a whiff of hemlock; it made him smile, like his first day up on the ridge.

As he rounded the great mahogany staircase, he stopped, surprised by the stately new arrival rising from the entrance hall below.

The old man laughed as he descended the stairs, careful to keep his balance on the curving banister. He stopped after five steps. A few feet below him hung a single white envelope, tied to the biggest Christmas tree he had ever seen.

JANUARY 1952

South Lake Tahoe, California

TOMMY HADN'T BEEN OUTSIDE the cabin in three days. His last trip required a lurching crawl out of a second story window, followed by the excavation of a fourteen-foot snowdrift. He wouldn't have to burrow again for a while; during the last break in the weather, he'd put away enough firewood to last a week. Wanda's sewing room was filled to the brim with dry madrone.

This time, he could see where he was going. White mist shot from his nostrils like an icy fog, but the sky itself was clear blue, with no storm clouds to be seen anywhere.

What he could see was snow. Lots of it. The accumulated snowpack had climbed clear up to the top of the telephone poles. Tommy called for both of his dogs and tied them to the last gasp of a digger pine. The determined evergreen had somehow managed to angle its way through the snowfall out into what would have been thin air, some three weeks before. He didn't much like leashing the dogs, since they were just as cabin sour as he was, but if they happened too close to the highlines, they'd electrocute themselves for sure. His neighbor had lost a couple of milk goats just that way last week.

He wondered how far Dave had gotten down the mountain. If anyone had half-a-chance to get through in this weather, it'd be his brother-in-law. Twelve days ago, Dave had declared he was tired of beans and no biscuits and got into his pickup truck to set off for lower ground. Wanda had begged him not to go, saying he might get stuck and freeze to death, but Dave had insisted, saying he had a hankering for one of Wanda's fresh-baked ginger snaps. Wanda swore she'd make him some, as soon as the weather cleared and she could get a bottle of blackstrap molasses. But Dave would have none of it. Tommy figured he was going cabin crazy like everyone else, and maybe more so, because Dave Bailey got itchy feet whenever he was stuck in any one place for long. So off he went, with Wanda holding back her tears.

Tommy reckoned that he'd probably find his way down in one piece. But it'd be damn near springtime before anyone got back up the hill with fresh supplies. He was grateful for the venison and fresh fish they had put up in the fall, and for Wanda's pantry full of preserves. Still, they were mostly modern folk now, with an electric chest freezer, store-bought groceries, and all sorts of canned goods with labels on them.

Nowadays, they were living on rice and a 50lb sack of beans, plus the meat they'd put away in the freezer. After the power got unreliable, they dragged the big Westinghouse outdoors and opened it up to let in the cold. They were careful to seal it tight again; bears continued to root around the cabins, despite the worst storm Lake Tahoe had seen in over 40 years.

It had started slowly enough, with a light snow on December 15th, right after they trimmed the Christmas tree. Little Rusty was thrilled, happy to try out his new sled. But once the snow started to fall, it never stopped. Now, here they were, six weeks later and well into the New Year. Tommy felt as if it was the first time he'd ever seen the sun.

His snowshoes glided effortlessly across the packed snow as he moved around the lake. Down the road, he could hear the faint sound of neighbors stirring in the eerie quiet. There were no vehicles out; the snowplows had given up weeks before, helpless against the sky's relentless onslaught. A week ago, the state had airdropped big supply crates into the clearings around the lake; Tommy was grateful for a sack of rice, as the taste of beans had long since grown monotonous. He didn't pursue the broken boxes much beyond that. Wanda and he had gotten by on much less, for much longer. Folks were grateful for the supplies, especially the tourists, who thought they'd come up for just a few days, then found themselves trapped on Christmas Eve, when the state couldn't keep the mountain roads open any longer.

During the last break in the weather, Rendo had come by and offered them some strip jerky and a fresh bottle of Irish whiskey. Tommy had declined the jerky, knowing Rendo would give away his last bit of food without a second thought. Wanda had rustled up some pressed vegetables and trout fillets, and they all feasted late into the night. Tommy accepted the whiskey; he figured Rendo kept enough of that about to see himself through any storm. After they finished off the jug, Wanda bed the big man down in the parlor.

He and Rendo had known each other for almost twenty-five years, ever since Tommy's family had moved up to the lake. They'd became fast friends, hunting and fishing together, and Tommy had damn near become a member of the Washoe tribe, even though he was white and couldn't speak a lick of Washokan.

Tommy turned his snowshoes and made his way back up the hill. In the distance, he could see the A-frame cabin he had built two years before. He and Wanda were happy here, their little plot of three acres more than enough, nestled in the tall ponderosa pines.

"Not so tall now," Tommy said, as he passed by the upper limbs of a giant evergreen. If the weather held, he'd bring out little Rusty and let him touch the top of the silver tips. A rare treat for any boy, or any man, for that matter. Very few would get the chance to walk amongst the treetops.

The icy quiet was sliced by the mournful roar of an overloaded diesel. An enormous white plume billowed above the snow bank some 50 yards away.

"Dang." Tommy shook his head. "I didn't think they'd get one of those things up here for at least a week."

The flashing lights of a rotary snowplow were visible beneath the cascading snow. The two-ton rig was laboring up the far side of the hill. Tommy wondered what the big CalTrans truck was doing so far off the main road.

The giant yellow Snow-Gos were something to see in full operation, their triple augurs mounted out in front of a massive plowblade. Rotating screws funneled tons of snow into a huge fan-driven chute, blowing chopped snow some 40 feet into the air and out along the side of the roadway. The lone truck buffeted against the icy tide, struggling to reach the end of the lane.

Tommy could barely make out the single figure behind the wheel. The harsh reflection of the noonday sun forced a squint. He looked and looked again, certain that his eyes had deceived him.

"You damn fool, what are you doing up here?" shouted Tommy.

The operator flipped a switch and the generator cut power to the whirling blades; the big Oshkosh Snow-Go idled to a stop as the blowers shut down.

A familiar head appeared outside the open cab window.

"Only way to get back up the mountain was to take a job with CalTrans." Dave Bailey stepped out of the raised cab with a wide smile. He stood upright on the truck's big front fender. "So, I joined up." He pulled a cigarette from his shirt pocket and lit it. Grey smoke mixed with his white breath. "Part time, of course."

"Of course." Tommy shook his head in disbelief.

Dave reached inside the cab and pulled out a large canvas bag. "There's Christmas in here for Rusty, and a little something for you, too." He wrapped one hand around the roof rail and tossed the bag across the snow bank to a grinning Tommy Johnson.

"Plus some blackstrap molasses. Tell my baby sister I got a hankering for some ginger snaps!"

THE LITTLE COFFEE SHOP was nearly empty, just a couple of long haul truckers talking quietly at one table. Pop and I took a corner booth; in no time, we were on our second cup of coffee and our first slice of pecan pie. The conversation worked its way around to the end of the war.

"How come you left the Maritime?"

"My time ran out to catch a ship. Before long, I knew they'd come and draft me. I couldn't get the ship I wanted, going where I wanted to go, and I had Marian in mind, too." Doc held the last bite of pie on his fork like a marshmallow on a stick. He paused in admiration, then placed it in his mouth, chewed and swallowed. "So I said the to hell with it, let 'em call me."

"Want another piece?"

Pop shook his head no and took out his tobacco pouch.

"I went back up and asks Marian if she'll marry me, she says, 'Yep'. So I went to tell her dad, and said 'Hey, I want your permission to marry her. Because she was only sixteen, see? I knew what I was doing - he asked her if she knew what she was doing. She says, 'Nope, but that's what we want to do.' So we got married. Then, like I say, we'd only been married a week or two and here comes that damn army. All at once, 'Report To Camp Beale!' When I got outta' that deal, the war was ending, and well, that's when old Beedle had that place up for sale on 49, so that's right where we wound up. We had them two kids down at the ranch, right bang bang. First three years, Rusty and Della Jean."

"So what happened between you and Marian?"

Doc grew silent. I wasn't sure if he'd continue; he was rolling a cigarette with unusual concentration. When the waitress refilled our coffee, my odds improved. Pop finished rolling his cigarette, then poured a waterfall of sugar from the metal-topped dispenser into his cup.

"Well, we worked the ranch for a bit, selling eggs and raising calves. Right at that time, they were something you could raise and make a few bucks off, if you raised enough of them. And the price started going up right when I got that bunch. Like I say, that was probably the highest I ever seen, about fifty cents a pound. You figure you go in, 450 - 500 pounds." Pop paused to light his cigarette. He drew deeply on it. His hands were almost shaking.

"Once we got up above 50 head, I traded my jeep for a barn load of hay." He blew a long trail of smoke, lifted his cup with both hands and looked across the table. "Some really bad hay, as it turned out."

There was a sadness in his voice, but it didn't seem to be about the cows.

"We lost 50 calves out there, and that hurt. Made her feel bad, too. She said, 'Let's just go somewhere else, take five, do something else for a little bit, save some money, and then we'll buy some more and start up again.'"

I watched his eyes for any sign of bitterness, but all I could see was a sort of wistful reflection.

"It wasn't like she gave up on it. It was just one of those things that made you sick to your stomach - to see how you saved every nickel and dime like we did to get those cows. Like I say, we was shining them eggs till the wee hours of the morning. I mean we lived off a garden."

He took another moment. "But anyway, so I told her, I said 'Ok, let's get rid of them things, and we'll just go." Pop stopped cold. It might have been some certain memory, or maybe that he'd just run out of breath. He looked tired, as tired as I had seen him in quite a while.

"Maybe we should get going, too? I told you we wouldn't bed down in Winnemucca, and it's miles to the next town."

"Aw, hell." Pop's mood lightened and he gave me a little wink. "You sleep where your head falls, Bill."

"Well then, finish the damn story." I pointed at my plate. "I still have some pie left."

Pop bared his teeth in mock anger.

"So I just chained the gate. I had the natural spring there, so the three cows we still had, I just left them. And Dad would stop by and take a look, maybe throw the cows out some hay. I got rid of most everything that you have to worry about much."

"Where did you go?"

"Up to the lake. I went to work at the sawmill, up there with Tommy."

"Tommy and Wanda?"

"Yep. And then, when I was at the sawmill, I couldn't get away from being a farmer, I guess, so that's when me and Tommy decided we'd raise some pigs up there. I decided, well, why not raise some pigs down at the ranch, too? So, I got to talking to my dad about why don't him and mom move down to the ranch. And so they closed up the house on Union Hill. And anyway, I put a few pigs down there. I'd go down to the sale and buy a hundred little bitty pigs. A dollar-fifty a piece…"

"When the sawmill was working, I'd work every day, Saturdays and Sundays, too. 'Cause the loggers - they got paid by the load, and they was trying to make all they could in a season. So, hey, I was drawing down good checks. Anyway, Marian got to wanting to go down and see her mother there in Grass Valley, and there was this guy that went to Nevada City every weekend, so she'd ride down with him, and hey, next thing you know, well, I guess they were having a little throw-down with each other, you know?"

One look and I could see the iron plate he'd laid around the wound.

"That's the only thing I can pair. I come home after the mill burned down, well, I come home one night and she says, 'I'm leaving you, I'm going to Grass Valley.' And I says, 'Okey-dokey.' I thought she meant to see her mother. And she says, 'No, I'm through.' Never would tell me why. But I just figured it all out, with old Ray Holland, this guy she rode down with, see?"

"Did he work at the mill too?"

"Yeah, he worked at the sawmill, but he lived in Nevada City." He leaned across the tabletop. "And I say, hey, never did bag one and never will bag one. They say 'that's it' and that's their privilege. That's the way I believe, can't make nobody want to do something that they don't want to do. At least not me — so, why not them?"

"But anyway, I comes down one weekend, and that's when I found out she was with Ray Holland. That's the only time in my life I ever really raised my hand, or touched a woman with my hand. And that was like that, you know, through the window." He flicked his hand in the air, and his eyes flashed.

There was a kind of pain in Doc's eyes that I had never seen before. I stayed silent, rapt with attention.

"She was setting in the car, and I walked up and I said, 'Well, hey, I told you that the kids have got to make their choice.' Who they wanted to go with. There was no yaw-yawing or nothing, but all at once, I says something about 'Hey, you know Rusty is going to be with me 'cause that's what he wanted.' So anyway, she says something to me about, 'Well, you don't care about your kids.' And when she said that, well my hand just went like that through the window, and I just ticked her with the back of my hand, you know. And old Ray he jumps right out, and I says, 'Hey, you get back in that car or I'll kick the shit outta you.'"

"What happened then?"

"He got back in the car."

Doc stared into his empty coffee cup, his jaw set. He looked back up again. "Anyway I told her, 'Hey I don't want no arguing - I told you this all along. I don't want no hard feelings because Della Jean and Rusty, if they ever want to see each other, that they don't have that between us. But don't give me no hassle about wanting to take Rusty.' I said, 'He wants to be with me.'"

The waitress stopped by the table with the check, and asked if we wanted anything else. Pop held his hand over the top of his cup, and I shook my head no.

"So I go down to the ranch that night, and next morning, God damn it, the phone rings, I answer it, and its old Brown, the sheriff. He tells me that he's got a complaint that I pulled a gun on Ray - told him to stay away from my old lady. So he tells me, 'I'll be down to pick you up in a little bit, after he comes in and signs the final papers.' I says, 'Well, I'll be here - but better yet, I gotta' go to town anyway. I'll just drive on over and wait for that sucker to get there.' So I tear ass over to Nevada City, go to the sheriff's office, and I'm sitting in there talking to Brown and the deputy. Brown asks me about the whole deal and I say, 'You know me better. If I pulled a gun on him, he wouldn't have been the one to come in here and say it. I'd be the one to come in here and tell you I shot the fucker.'"

A weary gambler who looked to be on the tail end of a losing streak staggered past our booth and fell into a seat at the counter. Pop didn't even look up. He just kept talking. I felt as if I was the county sheriff.

" 'I tell you what, I bet you a hundred dollars right here across the table that he don't show up here at eleven o'clock to sign the papers.' Ol' Brown says, 'I won't bet you.' I says, 'You've known me now for many a year, before you became sheriff. You know how the hell I am. You know God-dang well I didn't pull a gun on him.'"

Doc looked over at the counter and back to me. "He never did come in to sign the papers. I waited in there till noon. Finally I said, 'Hey, I got work to do. If that son of a gun even walks in here, acts like he wants to, you give me a buzz.' Never heard no more about it. But that's what old Brown said, that it was probably some kind of made-up deal. Ol' Brown knew that I'd never pull a gun on somebody just to threaten them."

"You had no idea that Marian was fooling around?" I was in uncharted territory, but once there, I saw no point in turning back.

He took a breath and bit his lip. I thought I saw a hint of remorse.

"No, because the way I look at it, what I don't know won't hurt me, and I never was a jealous sort of guy. I always thought if somebody was gonna' do it, they was gonna' do it anyway. So what the hell? Ain't no use to sit around… I could have sat around and said, 'I wonder what they're doing?' I'd make myself wrinkle. I'm not that kind of guy. Hey, maybe if I'd have said, 'No, you can't ride down there, maybe things would have been different. But I don't think so. See, I don't believe that. I believe that if things are wearing out, the caring about each other, or the feelings you had for each other, and boy, don't say it can't happen with the best, because it can. You can think the world of somebody right now and in a year, a month, a week or a day, some things can happen that don't make you - maybe not love them, but maybe you just can't be with them."

He was talking about more than Marian, and I knew it. Dave was my friend and more than a friend. He knew more about my life than just about anybody. I thought about my wife and family, so far away for so long at a time.

I struggled for what to say, but all I could manage was, "So Rusty stayed with you?"

"And Della Jean went with the mother." Doc slid across the bench seat and stood up from the table. He put a 50-cent tip on his plate and smiled at the waitress as he turned to head for the door.

"Thanks for the pie."

I sat frozen in my seat, my own life wrapped tight around my insides.

THE DUTCHMAN

A QUICK DRINK and a couple of hands of blackjack seemed a well-deserved reward, after a long week of forestry, freight hauling, and animal husbandry. The kids were down at the ranch; his mom and dad would see to them well enough till morning.

The marquee outside read: *Coming Soon! Judy Garland*, posted in shiny red letters as tall as his youngest son. Harrah's had become quite the high-class joint, not the same hardscrabble clientele as Bill's old bingo parlor in Reno. Bill Harrah was a mover and a shaker now, one of the few old-timers able to resist the Chicago muscle that was crowding out all the original clubs at the lake.

Inside the glass double doors, Dave took in the glossy glamour photo on the showroom sandwich board.

Little Judy has grown up.

Despite the fading hour, five or six tables were still working. He chose the one with just two players, an Oriental woman with a tall stack of dollar chips, and a portly gentleman in a shiny blue suit. The large man was rapidly shuffling a multi-colored stack of chips through his thick fingers. By the look of his stack, he'd been up and down quite a bit, more likely down than up. Dave didn't mind if the man in the wheelhouse was losing, just as long as he wasn't. His preference was a small open table, with a chance to see a few face cards while he calculated his hand.

"Chips please." He pulled some folding cash from his jeans pocket and peeled a single hundred-dollar bill onto the green felt table. His betting habits had changed considerably since the halcyon days on the Western Victory. With a house full of kids and a weekly payroll, he could be quite judicious with his hard-earned money.

"Welcome, sir," the portly gentleman offered. "Here's hoping you change our luck." The large man took a sip from his half-empty highball glass. "My name's A.A. Anderson, mining and milling, with a capital 'M' on the mining." He smiled broadly. "But everybody calls me 'Dutch'."

"Dave Bailey, working stiff. And no one calls me near enough."

Anderson saluted with a wave of his wrist. The Asian woman gave a slight nod and remained silent.

An auburn-haired waitress in a sparkling black outfit appeared on the carpeted runway behind them. She stopped by the table's newest player. "Cocktails, sir?"

Dave tipped his straw hat and ordered a boilermaker. "Old Hickory, with a beer back."

"A man's drink, Mr. Bailey."

Dave wondered what was so familiar about this fellow. He'd never spent much time with men in business suits. He barely owned a tie himself, except for the necessary black one, set aside for weddings and funerals. On really special occasions, he'd make an exception for a handmade leather bolo - a gift from a Mexican friend who happened to be the best horse trainer in Nevada County. He reached inside his canvas jacket and pulled out a half-package of Pall Mall cigarettes.

"I'll have another myself." Anderson volunteered. He drained his highball glass with authority. "Gordon's Gin and tonic, easy on the ice."

The blackjack dealer measured out a hundred-dollar stack of chips and started a new shuffle. Dave placed a bet on two positions, ten dollars behind each hand. He pulled out a cigarette and laid the package beside his chips.

"In a hurry, I see." The big man placed one five-dollar bet and waited for the dealer.

"No hurry, where blackjack is concerned. Sometimes, I like to bet against myself, just to keep the house company."

"A sound philosophy, when well played."

"And that..." Dave paused to light his cigarette, "would be the tricky part."

"Indeed." Anderson grinned, then peered at his hole card. The cocktail waitress returned with their drinks on a tray.

The dealer's hand showed a six on top; all three players stood pat, and the house busted on a face card. The next four hands followed the same rewarding pattern, and the three players were bound together by their turn of good fortune.

All night long, the hands rolled out like sheets on a printing press, in repeating patterns of red and black on green. Lost in conversation, the two men ventured far into the early morning, sometimes winning and sometimes losing, across multiple drinks, decks and dealers, with the ever silent Oriental woman by their side.

THE BAHAMA BLUE CADILLAC coasted at over 70 miles per hour; not much of an effort for the 4-barrel V8, but more than a little ambitious for the quality of road on which it was traveling. Dave couldn't reason why anyone would want to push a vehicle so hard on such a pockmarked road, even a car as well-built as the big Eldorado.

They'd been driving for hours; that put the two men somewhere south of Amargosa Valley. Dave was accustomed to parched scenery from his time in Wellton, but this landscape seemed even more barren than the Sonoran Desert.

Jagged stacks of orange rock stood against a white-hot sky, crushed stone and bleached sand dotted only by thin, sparse brush. Dave pulled his straw hat low across his face to make a little shade.

"How much further?" he inquired. By now, they had crossed into California.

"About 3 more miles, I'd say." Dutch was wearing his best linen suit, capped with a bright yellow tie. Taken alongside the Caddy convertible, he looked as though he might be headed for a wedding instead of an abandoned railroad spur. Dutch flashed a grin and drew a silver flask from his inside pocket. He offered it to his passenger.

Dave shook his head no. He took a closer look at Dutch and felt the stirring of a distant memory. "You know, you remind me of someone I knew when I was a kid."

"Was he a miner, too?" Anderson took a pull on his flask.

"Nope. He used to ferry dynamite."

"Sounds like a risky job."

"It was for him," Dave replied.

The next road sign read Death Valley Junction. It didn't mark much besides a turnoff next to a flat spot in the road, criss-crossed by the sunken rails of a spur line. Dave inspected a crumpled county map. It was full of welcoming names: Devils Hole, Furnace Creek, and the Funeral Mountains.

Death Valley is damn right.

How he'd got out here, so far and so fast, he didn't know. He'd met the man next to him barely 24 hours ago, yet here he was, barreling into country that could boil a lizard as quick as it could fry an egg. He longed for his old '31 Ford: slow-footed, easy to fix, and packed with a good-sized jug of water.

Anderson braked suddenly. He gave the steering wheel a spin and the long car turned onto a gravel road next to the railroad tracks. The blacktop faded as a trail of white dust exploded behind them.

"Up there." Dutch pointed ahead. The railroad track they were following disappeared into the sand. Dutch let off on the accelerator; the stiff whitewall tires crackled as the heavy vehicle slowed.

A broken row of wooden shacks stood behind a long, black iron fence. A couple of abandoned trucks and a rusty crane formed barricades behind a chained and locked gate. Dave wondered what benefit the chain could offer that the desert didn't already provide.

"Just as I promised," said Dutch. "Not a spot liable to attract much attention. I don't think this place has had another visitor besides me in almost 30 years."

Anderson stopped the car in front of the gate, then pulled up on a chrome lever below the dash. A hydraulic motor raised the convertible's top to its upright position. Even after a decade's service, the Cadillac Eldorado showed its pedigree and didn't hesitate for a moment. "I hate to lose the breeze, but these seats will bake our butts off, if we don't put the top up." Dutch shut off the engine and pulled his considerable weight out of the big sedan.

Dave hoped he might get lucky and see the canvas top remain closed for their return. He didn't realize that the car's air conditioning had long since given up. Anderson's preference for the open air was more about a broken compressor than his love of the desert breeze.

With the car silent, Dave was struck by the absolute lack of sound. Instinctively, he knew better. He concentrated and caught the subtle scratch of a passing roadrunner, some 30 feet away.

There's always life on this old desert.

The grey bird glanced at the two men and sped into the brush. There was no other sign of movement for as far they could see.

A jangle of brass keys broke the quiet, followed by the hoarse rasp of a reluctant padlock. Dutch pulled the long chain from around the gate and dropped it quickly to the ground. "Give me a hand, will you?" The big man put his shoulder up against the iron gate.

Dave wrapped his jacket around his hands and lifted the gate's leading edge out of the sand. He knew better than to bare hand black iron sitting in the desert sun. The gate shifted under the Dutchman's weight, swinging in towards the battered vehicles and the open courtyard behind them. A line of crusty, black dunes sat beyond the buildings, tailings from some unknown endeavor years past.

Dave followed behind as Dutch made his way through the rusty vehicles. Once past, they faced an army of steel barrels, lined up like soldiers for nearly 25 yards. There were at least a dozen rows, fifteen deep.

"Pick one," Dutch said. "Pick any one you like."

Dave stood by one of the long columns and wondered what the hell he'd gotten himself into. There were plenty of them, sure, but even a casual glance revealed the word 'POISON', and what looked like a pale skull and crossbones.

Dutch wiped the crusty surface off the top of one barrel, revealing a faded stencil: *Apex Mining and Minerals Company*. He brushed off a few more, all with the same distinctive name and poisonous warning.

Dave took a step backwards. "What's all this supposed to be?"

"Apex was a big player around here. They had over a hundred claims south of Tonopah in the early 20's. But it all played out; they got caught up in The Crash and hit bottom with everyone else in '29."

Dutch rapped on the barrel top with his knuckles; it made a kettle drum sound in the desert silence. "You could buy their shares for a penny - listed on the NY Curb exchange. I had thousands of them; got the rest in a little deal I wouldn't want to tell my mother about."

"What's that got to do with this place?" He could tell at a glance that the site hadn't been worked for decades.

"Started out as a borax mine. Everybody thinks about gold and silver, but it was borax turned this snake oven into pay dirt." Dutch took the flask out of his hip pocket and gestured to the north. "But somebody got greedy. Over there's a flat diggings. They cut into that hill looking for gold, found a little." He paused to take a sip. "Went so far as to put in a clamshell muckraking machine. Dropped down over 1500 feet in less than a year. Found a little silver, some lead, copper, zinc. Lots of heavy metals, but nothing they could process at a profit back in those days."

"How about right now?"

"See, you are a thinking man." Dutch took a deep draft on his flask. He offered it to Dave.

"No thanks. Not while I'm working." Dutch was right. Dave was a thinking man. He was thinking how nice it'd be to find a gas station, a telephone booth, and a big water cooler. He'd just about decided this trip was a bust. The long ride in the desert was nice enough, reminiscent of his days in Wellton. But right about now, he wanted to check on the kids before the rest of his Sunday got worn away.

"So, what do you think we've got here?"

"Well, it's not gold." Dave glanced at the barrels and thought for a moment. "Oil?"

"No. That's not it."

Dutch opened a rectangular wooden case. He took out a black box with a long cable attached. One end of the cable had a small wand that looked like a microphone. He turned a rotary switch on the box and a series of clicks came from a small speaker. As the wand approached the barrel stack, the speaker's volume increased and the clicks turned into a rapid, clacking howl.

"Uranium." Dutch moved the wand in and out, the machine-gun howl growing louder and louder each time. "Enough to fill a goddamn freight train."

DOC WAS TURNING the ashes over before we got back on the road. "This here reminds me of Death Valley."

I could see why. Eastern Arizona was bone dry.

"You spend much time there?" I asked.

"Back in the sixties. I used to get down there almost every week." Doc gestured to the horizon beyond. "Y'know, if you catch that desert at the right time of year, it's covered with flowers for as far as you can see."

"No way." I stopped packing gear into Betsy and tried to imagine the infinite flower garden. It made me think of Oz, right outside of Emerald City.

"Yes sir." Pop scratched at the dirt with his shovel. "Sometimes, in the early spring, right after a couple of steady rains. They get flowers down there that only live for a week or so. Then they go to seed and die - sleep for another 10 years. But when it happens, boy, it's the dang prettiest thing you ever seen."

Doc handed me his shovel and sat down on the tailgate.

"Once, we came down through Jubilee Pass - there were these great big patches of purple and green, blue and yellow, big ol' streaks of red. It was like some crazy painter went wild out there on the desert. I ain't never seen nothing like it."

"What were you doing down there?"

"I fell in with a miner by the name of Dutch. He had this claim down there, right near Amargosa. We worked that deal for a year or two, before it all went south."

I poured myself a cup from the thermos and offered it to Pop. He shook his head no and took a puff from one of the asthma inhalers my wife had given him. These days, he always kept one in his shirt pocket, right next to his tobacco. It was even money which one he'd reach for, the smokes or the inhaler.

Pop held his breath for a moment, then released it. "That was back when I was buying and selling gold. I knew this Chinaman in San Francisco that'd buy all the gold you could sell. Back in them days, it was against the law - you couldn't own it, buy it or sell it. The government had it all locked up at $35 an ounce. But you could get a hell of a lot for it overseas."

"Nixon did away with all that, didn't he?" I surprised myself with that remark. If you'd asked me a moment before, all I would have remembered about Richard Nixon was Watergate.

"Yep, that's when the country started putting war on a credit card. Pay cash, I always say, keeps the mischief to a minimum."

"What was the deal with Dutch?"

"He was a bit of an operator." Pop opened his tobacco pouch and began to roll a cigarette. "I ran with quite a few shady characters in them days, couldn't avoid it up at the lake."

"Was it bad up there?"

"Sometimes. Buying and selling gold was an outlaw business - even when it was legal. High grading is just a fancy name for stealing. I did some myself when I was a kid, in the Idaho-Maryland." He smiled and lit his cigarette. "And a few other places."

"Most of the miners you knew were high graders?"

"Not most, but enough to where Security might stick their fingers up your butt to make sure you weren't slipping out with a nugget." Pop laughed, coughed, and drew another drag. "I used to play a little game with them. Said hello to the same guard night after night, stuck my lunch pail right under his nose for him to search. After a while, he got tired of it, and I'd say, 'Aren't you going to search me?' And he'd wave me right through, so I started packing my tobacco cans with nuggets. When that one guard left, I had to stash them cans behind the gob pile. Still down there, maybe 10 or 20 cans, right at the 700 foot level."

"We should go get that."

"Love to." Pop tossed his cigarette into the fire pit. "But they'd have to turn the pumps on first. Under a million gallons of water."

"Dang." I shook my head. "So what about Dutch?"

"Too much trouble, that one." Pop took his shovel and turned the ashes one more time. "Let's get moving. I want to get over the pass before that sun catches up to us."

"URANIUM?" Dave laughed and gave his new friend a sympathetic pat on the back. "Dutch, I'm afraid you're a couple of years too late."

After the war, Dave caught the uranium bug like everyone else. Despite knowing better, he was tempted to go chase a big strike. The federal government was the only legal buyer for uranium - and the US was paying top dollar. People called it the new gold rush; any fool with a Geiger counter could find uranium. That pretty much guaranteed every fool would try. Thousands of amateurs got lost in the desert, hoping to stake a claim. Once the tall tales hit *Popular Science* magazine, there was no stopping them. Except for one thing.

"The government stopped buying this stuff years ago," said Dave. He tapped on one of the black barrels. "You'd be better off trying to sell the sand under our feet."

"Don't I know it," Dutch said. "That's what killed the deal with my old business partners." He shook his head. "The bottom fell out and so did they. And that's where you come in."

"No, Dutch. This is where I get out." Dave's patience was all used up. He turned to head for the car.

"Wait, wait, give me a chance to explain." Dutch had the look of a desperate man. "I had all the stock certificates - this whole operation, such as it is. But I didn't know what to do with it, especially after the Feds dropped out. So I went to visit Charlie Steen."

Dave stopped walking. He knew that name, as anyone did who had an interest in mining. Steen was a former U.S. Senator, a geologist who made millions in the big uranium boom. His was one of the rags-to-riches stories that started the whole thing. Curious, Dave turned back to listen.

"I met him in some crazy dance hall, he was doing the rumba. He lives right outside of Reno." Dutch was red-faced, pulling out all the stops. "So I told him about how I found the old Apex mine, and everything that had happened. Charlie said, 'Bring me some tailings'. He tested it, told me there was more there than I realized. Not only that, he gave me the name of a good chemist."

"Nice man."

"Good dancer, too." Dutch gave Dave his best smile. "I came out here looking for uranium. But there's more here, lots more. This stuff will pay, I tell you."

Dave was listening. Like most crazy stories, it was probably true, or at least enough of it to catch his interest. "Get to it, Dutch. Just what do you want from me?"

"For me, it's always been boom or bust." Dutch struggled to keep his smile. "After that uranium deal, my credibility is shot. I need someone who can vouch for me, maybe help me mend some fences." He began to flounder. "And money maybe too, but we can get money." Dutch had a voice that might have passed for absolute sincerity. "What I really need is a partner, Dave."

Dave took a long look at Dutch and wondered what the chances were that any of this would hold water. Maybe 50-50 at best. He liked Dutch; he got drunk with him, laughed with him, traveled with him for a long way in a fast car on a hot day.

But there was something else. Part of a memory he knew was important, maybe more important than the money or the trouble, or the mine itself. He remembered how hard his father had worked to build Benny's wagon. How hard his dad took it, when his new friend died in the Oklahoma oil fields. There was a debt here, one that he could pay.

And the name on the IOU was Dutch Anderson.

"Ok." He said it quietly, without hesitation.

No more words were required. Once said, it was done. Dutch put his hand out. Dave took it with a nod of his head. The big man let out a deep breath.

"Thank you."

"Thank me when we make this deal pay." Dave pointed across the yard. "What's in the shed?"

"Some equipment, not much that's worth anything."

"Let's take a look." Once inside, Dave had to agree, but he found what he was looking for - two glass jars with workable lids. He gathered some new samples: One from a random black barrel, and one from the giant pile of loose tailings.

"This stuff's been sitting out here like sand dunes, for 40 years. Dutch waved his arm across the dark mounds. "Acres of it. A ton of black sand fits into one 40-gallon barrel. How many tons do you think are out here?"

"Plenty." Dave tapped on the jars in his pockets. "But I only care about what's in these." It was always the sample you had to look out for; many a worthless claim was salted with just enough precious metal to make it look like a sure thing. Dave would get his own assay, and a careful one at that.

"Take it easy with those," Dutch said. "They processed a lot of this stuff with 2% cyanide."

Dave acknowledged the warning and headed for the Cadillac. The chrome door handles were hot to the touch; he was careful to wrap his jacket around his hand, and then again around the ore samples. Better safe than sorry; a teaspoon of 2% could kill you in less than an hour.

Through the windshield, he could see a swirling mist of heat rising off the steel hood, like vapor off a hot frying pan. Dutch pulled the Caddy away from the gate. Dave was grateful that the canvas top remained closed. He hoped that it would stay that way for the long ride home.

"I THINK IT MIGHT be the real thing, Dad."

"I know what you're thinking, son, but that don't mean you're thinking straight." Dee used his free hand to find the edge of the kitchen table, then rose to take the thirteen steps it took to reach the coffee pot. He curled his index finger into the rim of his cup and poured the coffee deliberately, stopping just as it touched the tip of his finger. "Here's a man says he has a mountain of money staring at him, and all he needs is 5000 dollars."

"He seems real convinced." Dave valued his dad's advice. He'd come straight away from the mine to seek it out.

"Of course he does. Gold fever will do that to a man." Dee Bailey had seen a dozen men chase their dreams deep into a black hole, never to come out. "If it's worth so much, why is it still out there?"

"It's ancient, Dad."

"So am I." Dee smiled. "And I ain't worth so much."

Dave ignored him. "There's black sand there, tons of it, all perched up nice and tight for a hundred yards. And barrels full of processed ore. Somebody had to think it was worth something, once upon a time."

"Yes, but what are you going to do with it?"

"I'm going to take some down to Wong. He'll give me the straight dope on this stuff." As soon as the words left his lips, he regretted it.

"You need to steer clear of that bunch, Davey."

"Pop, it's ok. I know what I'm doing." Dave had fallen in with the Wong clan back in the 50's, when he was moving high grade gold for Jack Santo. That was before Santo, Emmett Perkins and Barbara Graham all got the gas chamber, for killing some little old lady and for God knows what else.

"Just be careful, son."

"I will be." His father had warned him against Santo. And kept the children well out of sight, when Santo and his partner came anywhere near the ranch. "And just so you know, Dad. Wong didn't like Santo any better than you did."

Dave still got the willies when he thought about that bunch; robbery, murder, dead bodies everywhere, little kids stuffed into the trunk of a car. The State of California put them down for good at San Quentin in '55. He was glad to see them go.

When Dave met him, Santo was pouring beer at the roadhouse a mile up the way. Santo had lots of high grade; said he was getting it from some of the miners up in Nevada City. Plenty of gold used to get out of the country with the Merchant Marine, so when Santo asked Dave to move some for him, all he had to do was make a phone call. Turned out, most of that gold came from a much different place than Santo said it did.

"Fool me once, shame on you..." Dee took a sip from his cup. He looked up at his son with cloudy grey eyes. "You know the rest, Davey."

Dave walked his coffee cup over to the sink. On the way back, he touched his father on the shoulder and turned to go. "Like I said, I'll be careful. Give Mom a hug for me."

As he reached the doorway, Dave realized he hadn't told his dad how much Dutch reminded him of Benny Gibbs.

Maybe next time.

Dave was a pretty good judge of a man's character. He'd missed the read on Santo. Greed, pride and whiskey can do that to a man.

He made a mental note not to forget exactly what he was doing on the night he met A.A. Anderson.

* * *

WANDA JOHNSON sat alone in her sewing room, quietly looking through her photo albums. She would do it when no one else was in the house; she didn't like it when Tommy teased her about living in the past. He didn't understand how irreplaceable those moments were; to see her husband in all his innocence, before he went off to war, to see Davey's bright smile before love's loss hardened him like leather.

Dave was away down south somewhere, in San Francisco, or maybe down at the ranch with Mom and Dad. Rusty had gone hunting with friends. It was his last year in high school; soon he would have to decide whether to take a job with PG&E or go off to junior college. Tommy had arranged the job for him. He thought it was a great start. Wanda wanted their boy to continue his schooling, to break the stiff blue-collar pattern that had so defined their family. Just below the surface, she feared the growing war in Asia and the rowdy enlistment talk from Rusty's high school buddies. She'd seen so many go off to war and so few return.

I'll never let go of these pictures.

There was little Rusty, so tiny and strong, before Marian ran off with that Ray Holland. And young Vicki, who'd grown up to look so much like her mother. Tommy's little sister Joyce – she wasn't much older than eighteen the first time Dave met her. Tommy had tried to warn them away from each other, for all the good it had done.

Joyce was drawn to Dave like a bug to a bulb. After her sister-in-law married her big brother, it seemed like all the world was right for a change. To this day, she couldn't figure out what went wrong. One day they were so happy, with Vicki growing up and a new baby on the way, and the next thing you know, Tommy's little sister took off across the country with another man. That was a hard one for Dave to swallow.

For Tommy, too.

She wondered what it was about her big brother that pulled a woman in so effortlessly, then drove them away again in such short order. It was all a mystery to her, so much hidden, so little revealed. What made one marriage last for half a century and another fall apart a month later? Wanda thought about her parents, how she'd never seen them waver. She was as certain of their union as she was about the sunrise.

The pounding of a hammer broke her concentration. Blood warmed her cheeks and her eyes fluttered. She felt an overwhelming wave of gratitude for her sweet Tommy, for his quiet strength and unbreakable good humor.

The noise was part of an ongoing expansion of a large pigeon coop. Tommy had taken up racing pigeons, and like everything else he did, he did so with a single-edged devotion. Already, he was racing breeders with decades of experience and besting them regularly. Just yesterday, one of his training birds had returned all the way from Death Valley, where Dave had released him only the night before.

She turned the page to a glossy photograph taken on her wedding day. They were at a little chapel in Reno, eight hours into Tommy's three-day pass from

Camp Beale. Dave was best man, and Rendo sang a Washoe wedding song, cold sober. Tommy wore a new suit with a bow tie and shiny shoes.

His voice rang out from the kitchen, and she closed the well-worn album. She placed it on a redwood shelf that he had built for her, in the house that they had built together.

She rose to meet him in the doorway, content as any soul could ever hope to be.

IT WAS CHINATOWN, not the part with the colorful granite dragons that all the tourists saw, but deep in the narrow streets and thin alleyways. Rising up on fire escapes, it was filled with three room flats, small, grey dens housing multiple generations.

Dave had been to San Francisco a dozen times before, mostly down on the docks along the Embarcadero, where he'd shipped out with the Merchant Marine. And there was that one time he climbed Nob Hill to see Bob Fisher's sister. With a grimace, he put that episode out of his mind. His eyes were set on finding a certain landmark.

Unlike the natural world he'd grown up in, San Francisco was dense and unfamiliar, with no guideposts of sun or stars. A clever architect might lay order on the urban chaos with a checkerboard pattern or with carefully numbered streets, but in the end, it was always the tallest building or the widest boulevard that prevailed. Steel, brick and mortar made for a certain sameness that Dave found uncomfortable. It was disorienting, especially in the canyons beneath tall buildings and the thin alleyways of Chinatown.

Two blocks off Grant Avenue, beneath a red pagoda roof, he recognized the Eastern Bakery, where he used to meet his contact. A faded green doorway caught his attention, still familiar in his memory. He stopped and examined the door, concentrating on a copper plaque hung beneath an ornate grill.

Dull olive paint masked the heavy grain of the door; the writing below the small trap window was even harder to discern. Chinese characters were beyond his comprehension, but the name J.Y. Wong was written below them, next to an etched set of measuring scales.

This is the place.

He felt fortunate to recognize it, even though he'd been there 3 or 4 times before. The first time was at night; every time thereafter was in the company of men who didn't care to be followed. After those initial meetings, all of his encounters were in public places with faceless messengers, a quick exchange of cash money for gold. Dave had learned to like the old man in charge, even trust him; he felt there might be a grudging respect from the other side.

The old man's proper name was Wong Jing Yue. Mr. Wong had revealed it to him out of politeness, even tried to teach him its proper pronunciation. Dave had struggled to form it properly. He tried to familiarize it as 'Jim', but only once. Sternly corrected, he was always careful to address the gentleman as 'Mr. Wong'. Dave knocked on the door in the customary fashion; his escort took him upstairs on a narrow stairwell.

"Sit down, Mr. Bailey."

Wong motioned to a chair directly across from his high jeweler's table. Wong Jing Yue wore a green accountant's eyeshade and a worn leather apron. A brass reading lamp lit the small room, casting a bright halo that reflected into Wong's brown eyes.

"Thank you for seeing me, sir."

"You look well, Mr. Bailey. And curious, no doubt."

"I am, sir. What's the verdict, Mr. Wong?"

Dave was grateful for the audience. He'd brought fresh samples five days before, eager to hear Wong's appraisal. He knew that any gold and silver content could vary widely from sample to sample, even on assays taken from the same gravels. This was an important second opinion; he wanted to make sure that he wasn't seeing what he wanted to see, or for that matter, what someone else wanted him to.

Wong paused and took a shallow breath. "As you know, not all black sands contain precious metals, but those taken from areas containing placer gold - they almost always do." Wong's English was very good, precise, though thick with accent. "Where did these come from, Mr. Bailey?"

Dave wondered at the old man's curiosity. Wong was usually very close-mouthed.

"An old borax diggings." Dave leaned forward in his chair. He would give away some detail, but not too much. "Folks came after it looking for uranium."

"Uranium is a fool's errand, Mr. Bailey. 40 times more common than silver, 500 times more common than gold."

Wong held up one of the sample bottles to the light. "These samples are very different. That's to be expected, if only from their consistency."

"Different how?"

Wong pushed the green eyeshade up on his forehead and changed one set of eyeglasses for another. He held up a sheet of paper with various calculations, pointing to each one in turn.

"One ore sample has been heavily processed, stripped of most of its value." Wong looked up from the report. "Some radioactive elements; varying from a low of 16 grams per ton to a high of 74 grams. And very little else, besides a few trace elements."

Dave had expected as much. The black barrels were another dry hole. A disappointment to Dutch, but then again, it was probably something he already knew.

"For the other sample, the same. Except for one thing," Wong paused, drawing his finger across the paper. "Silver, nearly 4000 grams per ton. 3926 grams to be exact."

4000 grams. Dave made a rough calculation, and whistled softly under his breath.

"And possibly, platinum." Wong looked over his glasses at the man sitting across from him. "Almost 100 grams per ton. That is just under 140 ounces of silver, and 3.5 ounces of platinum for each ton of material."

"Platinum?"

"Yes, platinum." Wong passed the assay sheet over to Bailey. "These sands are a very valuable commodity."

Two years before, the U.S. government started pulling silver certificates out of circulation, and the price of silver had skyrocketed to $1.29 an ounce. Dave's head spun as he multiplied to find the dollar value: $180 a ton, maybe more, not counting the platinum.

"How much of this material is available, Mr. Bailey?"

Dave made another rough calculation. "Maybe ten or twelve thousand tons."

"Well then, Mr. Bailey, I'd say you are a very rich man."

A WIRY LITTLE MAN had just finished pounding on the hood of our car. I watched him swagger through the crosswalk as he screamed something about the end of the world. He was in the right town for it.

"That was weird."

"Maybe he sees something we don't." Pop fingered the coffee-to-go I had bought for him at the hotel. We were leaving the casino district, headed for the edge of town to pick up US 95 going north towards Tahoe.

"How about a roller coaster on top of a casino?"

On our way out of Arizona, we'd crossed over the Hoover Dam. Just past the intake towers, we saw a billboard for a rooftop roller coaster. Pop had a soft spot for roller coasters, so it gave me an excuse to stop in Vegas. The ride wasn't open yet, but we stayed in town for the night anyway.

"Anything to get you in here." Doc had on a pressed shirt and his fanciest hat, the one with the thin gold band. The hat was carefully creased, and the hard straw was coated with a smooth shine that made it almost waterproof. "Once you're here, they don't care what you do, as long as you leave without your money."

"Your keno numbers paid." While I took a turn at the blackjack tables, Doc kept an open game going, betting on the same numbers he had used for almost fifty years.

"Always do," he said. "But they made it up on you, I betcha'."

He was right. I liked to think I was a good gambler, and maybe I was, until about two drinks in. After that, I could chase my chips like a set of lost car keys. If I wasn't chasing something else.

"That little gal liked you, though." I tried to change the subject.

"The keno runner? She thought I looked like her dad." He chuckled to himself. "Or maybe her granddad."

I thought about my daughter. In twenty years, would she care if anyone looked like me? I'd spent another late night out. Came back to the room long after Pop had gone to bed. He woke up anyway, like he always did.

"Don't come sneaking in. I can hear you, even if your wife can't." He didn't roll over to look at me.

Nowadays, Doc didn't pull his punches. "Either get in or get out," he'd say. But I couldn't seem to reconcile the love for my family with my own bad behavior. Or the nagging sensation that something wasn't right in my marriage and probably never had been. I was aware enough to know that the something was probably me.

What was it, I wondered? The crazy stepfather that mangled me? Or my real dad, the one who'd left me for good in a bus station when I was five? Was it a drunken slap in the face or maybe some wicked scoutmaster?

Not likely.

Those were just the stories I told myself, when I wanted some relief from my guilty conscience. When what I really wanted was a drink - or a good excuse to start a fight, so I could take off and see what the mountains were like around Flagstaff. That's what had happened this time. I made her wrong enough for me to stalk out and do exactly what I wanted to do anyway.

At Lake Mead, Pop told me about the time he took Joyce across the dam on their honeymoon, how they toured the caverns beneath the concrete and the giant generators down below. He told me how happy they were, and after a while, how she wasn't and then he wasn't, and how it had been the same way with all of his wives.

I was on my third one now. I looked over at Doc. "You and Joyce not staying together, do you ever regret that?"

"Like I say, you think you know where you are, and how it'll all turn out. But nobody really does. My folks were as happy as any two people I've ever seen. Maybe it was 'cause there was nothing fancy about it. It was survival back in them days. You had to stick together to make things work. Not just take off and go gallivanting. And there wasn't no such thing as alimony. You either made it on your own, or you starved. Too easy to give up on things now."

"Maybe not so easy as you think." I was still holding on to my sad story.

"Maybe not." Doc looked directly at me. "But like I say, Bill, either get in or get out."

FEBRUARY 1962
Stateline, Nevada

DAVE WAS SEATED at the dollar slots, watching the big board for his keno numbers. Another long day and a well deserved drink on the way home.

An attractive brunette took the empty seat beside him. She was small, slight of frame, and covered in a long overcoat. The silk scarf drawn tightly around her chin made a shawl over her dark hair. She was strangely familiar, as if he'd seen her before, somewhere long ago. She put three silver dollars in the coin slot and pulled the chrome handle defiantly.

That certain mechanical sound, half-adding machine and half-roulette wheel, whirled away. Three bells chimed in succession, catching his attention.

"You know, they're worth more if you melt them down."

"I beg your pardon." The woman had a formal eastern accent, slightly slurred by the icy contents of her tall highball glass.

"The silver dollars." Dave pointed to the oval tray beneath her slot machine as a dozen coins fell in one after the other.

"Oh," the brunette smiled. "You're lucky."

"Well, yes ma'am," nodded Dave. "As a matter of fact, I am."

"I'm sure you are," she replied, with a touch of sarcasm. She took some coins from the tray, reloaded the machine and pulled the chrome handle again, watching as the colored wheels danced before her. Her hands trembled as she slid a crumpled cellophane package from her overcoat and reached for a cigarette.

Dave took a wooden kitchen match from his shirt pocket and flicked it with his fingernail. The white phosphorus tip exploded into a bright flame.

"Oh, you are quite the cowboy, aren't you?" She smiled and leaned forward to touch her cigarette to the open flame. Dave felt sure he must have seen her somewhere before.

"No, ma'am." Her overcoat parted slightly. He could see the edges of a sequined gown beneath it. As her face lifted, Dave looked beneath her brow. He thought he saw the telltale sign of tears wiped away in makeup. "More of a lumberjack these days."

The tumblers stopped spinning with a determined clunk, and three cherries lined up all across the middle row. Bells peeled, and a cascade of Eisenhower silver dollars poured into her tray.

"Well, then." She laughed heartily. "What am I supposed to do with all that?

Melt it down?"

"I suppose you could. I've got a smelter."

She looked at him quizzically, eyebrows arched, her long cigarette perched lightly in her cocked hand.

Tilting his head forward, he whispered. "Hot enough to melt gold. It'll make light work of those things."

"Of this, I have no doubt." She took a deep drag on her cigarette, held her breath, then blew the smoke straight up into the ceiling. Rising from her stool, she rebounded with a throaty laugh. "Well, Mr. Lumberjack, used to be a cowboy... how about buying an old dance hall girl a little drink?"

"My pleasure ma'am." He wasn't at all sure how he knew her, just sure that he wanted to know her better.

In the corner of his eye, he saw a tall Negro man in a tailored grey suit approach them from the rear of the casino.

"Miss Garland, may I help you with anything?"

"No. Thank you, Ronald. I have all the help I need."

HE'D BEEN IN THIS TUNNEL BEFORE, ferrying loads of firewood to the luxury cabins surrounding the Cal-Neva Lodge. The guests thought the tunnel only led to the lodge, but there was also a service entrance that allowed for utility work. In Dave's case, delivery of seasoned oak and pine to the high rollers' stone fireplaces.

They had hit it off almost immediately, the elegant chanteuse and the western stranger. Once Dave realized who she was, he was mesmerized, not for her celebrity, but more for the intensity of feeling that she seemed to pour into every moment.

They left Harrah's in Dave's rusty-red flatbed, cleverly escaping the necklace of guardians that kept her away from such vehicles. They flew high around the lake and down onto the shoreline that held the Cal-Neva Club, where Frank Sinatra kept a waterfront bungalow open for her while she sang at Harrah's showroom.

Her third marriage was on the rocks. She was separated again, and decided to come back to where it all began - to the Cal-Neva, where a talent scout picked a skinny kid out of a sister act, and sent her to Hollywood to ride the frail roller coaster of fame.

They watched the February moon fall over the glass lake, stars everywhere. The night was still, crisp cold and silent in the early hours before dawn.

He built her a roaring fire, with the same wood that he had carried through the tunnel. He showed her how to split kindling, and told her where the old madrone had grown, how to season oak, and when to bank the fire to let the coals settle in for the night.

She told him about singing for the President, about Carnegie Hall, and how she'd become a prisoner of Oz.

He told her about the desert and the sound of coyotes on an open plain.

When she asked him about his life, he spoke about his boys, about his little girl, about Billie, and the life he left behind.

She talked about husbands, about torch songs and love songs, and the divorce papers served on her daughter's birthday. She told him about everything, it seemed.

He made a promise to himself that he would never tell everything about her.

HIS WINDOW WAS ROLLED DOWN for a taste of morning air. The twisting road ran alongside the cabins behind the Cal-Neva lodge. He gave them an easy smile. The sun was rising over the mountains behind the lake, and he was getting hungry. The last few days had been almost unreal, and when he finally got back to work, he started to feel like his old self again.

He stopped into the Mountain Café and ordered breakfast: the usual - eggs over easy, biscuits and gravy, a slice of ham, and a big glass of buttermilk.

A leftover copy of *The Reno-Gazette Journal* was on the bench seat. He picked up the paper and scanned the front page; a hijacked freighter spotted east of Puerto Rico, Congress wanted more troops in Europe, and President Kennedy was going to start something called the Peace Corps.

Man, we could use a little more of that.

He breezed through the classifieds with his coffee, then glanced at the headline on the entertainment page:

JUDY SICK, ROONEY SUBSTITUTING

Judy Garland had fallen ill. She was in the hospital in Carson City. Mickey Rooney was filling in for her at Harrah's. He re-read it slowly, trying to tell what was real and what was Bill Harrah trying to sell more tickets. At the very bottom of the story, it mentioned that she and her husband had reconciled.

He thought about sending flowers, until he realized it was more for his own mood than for hers.

THE DRIVEWAY WAS THE SAME, the oaken door was the same, but something felt different, as if the passing of winter had taken a piece of the old place with it. This last year was the driest he could remember; the season had started out all right, with good rain in October, but then everything had stopped, as if the ocean tides had ceased and there was no water to be had anywhere.

It made for light work on the mountain, easy cutting with very little mud or snow to deal with, but the lack of a real winter seemed to put a damper on everyone's spirits. The bottom fell out of the Christmas tree market; the worst he'd seen in years.

As usual, Dave had brought up a nice tree for Mr. Whitman, with a hefty envelope attached; he was careful to increase the payments each year, regardless of his profit. But they had skipped their traditional coffee in the study, as the old man wasn't feeling well. Normally, they would pin down the next season's parcel together, but this time, Dave decided to wait a few weeks and let the old man get to feeling better.

He knocked on the oaken door. It opened slowly, as it had for the last few seasons. Efren was getting up in years, and the giant door was almost too much for him.

"Hello, Efren." Dave smiled at the greying butler; they'd come close to friendship in the intervening decade. Dave would always bring an extra tree for Efren's grandkids, and they'd share biscuits and honey in the kitchen pantry when Whitman was busy with other duties.

"Hello Mr. Bailey." Dave had never convinced the little Filipino to use his given name, although he'd tried religiously for years.

"Is Mr. Whitman in?"

The butler stiffened, seemingly surprised by his question.

"Efren, who is it?" A sharp voice rang out from the long hallway. "Not some salesman, I hope."

"No sir, Mr. Whitman," Efren spoke quickly. "It's a business associate of Mr. George."

"I'm not expecting anyone." A thick man in a blue striped sweater came to the door. He had bright red hair and a thin moustache, the kind that needed careful trimming each day to keep from overflowing its boundaries. The tall man bore a strong resemblance to his father, but he lacked the same powerful frame, his torso inflated by years of rich diet and infrequent exercise.

"Dave Bailey, sir. Pleased meet you." Dave reckoned to give the man his due.

"I came to see your father and work out the acreage for this next year."

"I don't know you."

"No, sir." Dave felt his blood rise. He let it fall. "I don't expect you do. I've been working directly with Mr. Whitman for some years now."

A head shift showed the sudden recognition. "Oh, you're the Christmas tree man."

"Yes, sir." Dave felt some relief he wasn't seen as a total stranger.

"Well, we're not doing that any longer."

Whitman raised his chin. He glared down at Dave on the top step. "My father always gave that Christmas tree money away. As it turns out, to causes I am not so much in favor of."

"Do you think I might get to see him and talk about it?"

"He's dead," Whitman sneered. "Good day, Mr. Bailey."

The man turned on his heels in the hallway. "And close the door, there's a draft."

The little butler looked as beaten as any man that Dave had ever seen.

"I'm sorry, Efren."

"So am I, Dave."

"JUST HOW MANY of these things have you sold?" Dave was in a hurry to get some answers. He had things to do today, and no desire to spend any more time babysitting Dutch Anderson.

"Not that many. Just enough to make expenses." Dutch was grey, disheveled, and more than a little bit groggy, after Dave had unceremoniously pulled him out of bed.

"What expenses?" Dave thumbed through the stack of stock options he'd found on the motel table. "What did you do with the last five hundred I gave you?"

"I can't just sit in my room, Dave. You can't expect me to do that." The shirt-less man was looking around the room for something: a drink, a shirt, maybe the chance to get away.

"I can damn well expect you to tell me the truth." His temper was growing short. Slow to rise, it was an unruly beast when set free. "How many, Dutch?"

"Dutch counted on his fingers. "Maybe 3 or 4, tops."

"You've got to be kidding me." Dave was still reeling from a morning phone call. The man on the telephone had informed him that he was a principal share-holder in the Apex Mine. He wanted a progress report from the mine's foreman, a dubious title that Dave had somehow inherited without notice.

"That's all of them, Dave, I swear."

"You must be out of your mind. These things make any one who signs them an equal partner - with all the other equal partners. Every one of these fool things cuts my share to pieces. Yours, too. And God knows who else."

"There's plenty to go around Dave. You said so yourself."

He had said so, once he'd gotten the go ahead from Wong. But since then, Anderson had gone on a tear, drinking and playing the big shot all over town, spending lots of money they didn't have.

"If we're raising seed money, sure. But not for whiskey and whores." Dave tossed the papers to the floor. "You gambled with my stake, Dutch."

"I'm sorry, Dave. Really, I am." Dutch was desperate; he could see his fragile dreams slipping away one more time. "What are you going to do? What's going to happen now?"

Dave balanced his seething anger against the year's effort he'd already put in. Site surveys, mineral assays, title searches, heavy equipment - almost all of it on his own dime. He held it up against a big payday that grew more unlikely by the moment. Against a childhood debt to another man he only vaguely remembered.

"Benny blew himself to pieces. I guess you'll probably do the same."

"What?" The Dutchman struggled to understand. "What are you talking about?"

"I'm out, Dutch." Dave turned to head for the door. "Find yourself another sucker."

* * *

Washoe Tribal Lands
Mt. Rose Wilderness, Nevada

THE EMPTY GRAVEYARD was old and nondescript. Built at the top of a small rise, it was 15 yards off a deeply rutted clay road. Most of the markers were simple white stones or metal plates, some with numbers instead of names. There were a few granite headstones and one stone obelisk, broken in two to reveal its iron spine.

Tommy Johnson had been here a couple of times before, once when he and Rendo had dropped off a load of Christmas trees in Carson City. They had taken

Rendo's pickup and on the way back, Rendo had decided to stop off and see his dad. Tommy was grateful that Rendo was driving; the road up to the old cabin was nothing more than a dirt track through broken boulders and tall trees. Once they were there, the old man had shared a bottle with them, and after a half-day of stories, Patrick had taken them up to visit his brother's grave on a snowy hillside.

This time around, it was Spring. On one side of the graveyard, a small garden had been planted. There were dozens of native wildflowers, and by their looks, the tiny plot was carefully tended. Tommy stopped short at the sight of so many different flowers in bloom. He noted they were all neatly trimmed, with a number of cuttings placed on several of the small headstones.

At the far edge of the graveyard stood a long, low mound, covered in moist red dirt. Various items were scattered on top of it: a bone knife, two snow rabbit pelts, some honey jerky, and a soft red shirt with bone buttons. Fresh tracks led away from the grave, evidenced by deep footprints in the surrounding soil. On top of the mound were shards of glass in many colors: blue, green, crimson, and gold. The afternoon sun danced across the bits of glass, casting bright reflections in the leaves of an overhanging oak tree. Tommy thought they looked like fairies flying above the grave.

Patrick would like that.

Tommy took notice of some bright yellow flowers in the garden. He pulled a long stalk away from its leafy fronds. Mule Ear plants grew best in the high meadows, and the radiant flowers could last for a whole summer. Patrick Bear had shown him those wildflowers, and a hundred other things, when he and Rendo were just kids. He wondered how the golden flowers had come to be here and how they had prospered so far from home.

The old man had taught him everything about the deep woods around the lake, about the plants and the water and the fish, about the forest animals, and how to hunt them without anger or greed. In those days, the lake and the trees and the sky had all blended into one, along with every other living thing. Tommy and Rendo had ventured deep into that mysterious world. In some ways, they never came out.

The Maker of All Things took Rendo Bear in the Winter Moon; he was only 45 years old. Cirrhosis of the liver, folks said.

Tommy watched the dancing fairies disappear with a passing cloud.

The loss of his son hit the old man hard. Patrick fell into the bottle, and the old Washoe drowned at the bottom. He was buried next to his only son and the brother he had lost so many years before.

A soft breeze filtered through the oak leaves, and colored lights danced again above the graves of the Bear.

"Thank you, Patrick." Tommy placed the yellow flower on the littered grave. "Say hello to Rendo for me."

DAVE HAD GONE to the liquor store looking for a capper to a long day and nothing more, but the man behind the counter had shown him a new kind of bourbon, saying it was something special. He took one look at the bottle and decided it was time to go see Ruth Bear.

The old cabin was empty. No surprise. Dave half-expected not to see her there. Ruth was still cooking for the Dresslers down the mountain, and he knew she kept a room behind the store. Still, he'd felt the tug on his heart and made the long trip up through the sugar pines.

When they held Patrick's service, Elwood Johnson had come, and John Keller, and even old man Globin. It was a sight to see at the funeral home. There were white folks and Indians of every tribe, townsfolk and mountain men, young and old, rich and poor; a parade of people that the old Washoe had come to know over most of a century.

Tommy and Wanda were there, but Dave couldn't make it. He was away in San Francisco, or maybe he'd been down south checking on the mine. He wasn't sure. That thing with Dutch had taken him away in more ways than he cared to admit.

"The Maker greets you, Dave Bailey."

The sound of her voice surprised him.

"Na ga hay, Ruth." He spoke the words to the empty air.

The old woman stepped out from behind the cabin, bearing a spade and a gunnysack full of black earth. Rendo's little red dog was right behind her.

"I brought something for you." Dave held the brown paper bag up in two hands and smiled.

Ruth put the gunnysack down. She sank slowly onto the wooden bench, using her shovel as a long staff. Her head nodded in response, and she took a slow, deep breath.

He could see that she was cold, her fingers red and drawn. Dark coals were smoldering in the cook pit in front of the cabin. "Your fire's gone out, Ruth."

"So it has, Dave Bailey." Ruth whispered. "So it has."

Dave knelt down and prodded the coals, waving his straw hat across the smoldering pile until the embers stirred to life. He scratched around the cabin for some kindling sticks, and tossed them on the tiny flames. Dave took notice of the scant woodpile. He made a mental note to have one of his men keep it filled from now on.

Ruth was breathing heavily, her eyes closed, the shovel bent forward under the weight of her shoulders.

He stoked the fire with some larger pieces, and took a wool blanket from the cabin's iron bed, wrapping it around Ruth's shoulders. The little dog was curled up next to her feet.

"Have you eaten anything?" he asked.

"Mule deer porridge, and one of those awful sandwiches the Dresslers sell. I think I probably made it, too."

Dave laughed. He imagined the kind of fare that only a tourist would eat. "Well, at least you won't starve."

"No, but I might be poisoned." The fire began to dance, and a warm haze fell across her face. "What I need is a drink. What's in the bag, Dave Bailey?"

"You'll see. Wait here."

Inside the cabin, next to some bright yellow flowers, he found the metal tumblers. He brought two of them out by the fire.

Ruth was stretched out like a cat on the bench, the orange glow of the flames bouncing all around her blankets. Dave handed her a red metal mug.

"That's Patrick's," she said.

I don't think he'll mind." Dave pulled the bottle out of the paper bag and placed it in her hand.

Ruth fingered the strangely shaped bottle, its long neck dipped in red wax. She peered at the label. After a moment, she read out loud. "Maker's Mark."

"Maker's Mark, Ruth." Dave gave her a big grin, and she laughed.

"The Maker thanks you, Dave Bailey."

Ruth held the tumbler high. "And so do I." She gave Dave a toothless smile.

The warming fire crackled as it rose, hot air swirling all around.

Dave wondered if perhaps, it was a sign of things to come. Ruth might drink herself to death, too. Though at a hundred-years old, it'd be a long shot for anyone to call it that.

He was good with whatever came to be, if The Maker made it so.

"YOU'VE GOT TO HELP ME, DAVE. I'm in a lot of trouble."

"What are you talking about? What kind of trouble?"

Dave figured it must be important or Dutch wouldn't be pounding on his door at this time of night. The Dutchman looked drained, white as cake flour. His pale hands trembled, clinched tightly around an ornate wooden box.

"I met this guy at one of the tables, we got to talking. He had a way to get us some money."

"You know better than that, Dutch. There's only fools like me at them tables." It'd been eight weeks since Dave had called it quits. He had no regrets.

"This fellow had a big shot willing to put up some real dough, he was going to come in as our new partner." Dutch shot a look back over his shoulder, as if he were being followed.

Dave pulled the Dutchman into the room, peered out at the empty street and closed the door. "Slow down, there's no one else around. And we're not part-ners anymore, remember?"

"Sure we are, Dave. You know that." Dutch sat down on the easy chair. He clutched the fancy box to his belly. "You just needed some time. But I still gotta' eat." Dutch looked around the room nervously. "You don't have anything to drink, do you, Dave?"

"No, I don't."

Dave was getting riled. He'd heard enough of Dutch's stories to know there might be some truth to this one. How much, he wasn't sure. But another drink wasn't going to make things any clearer.

"Just keep talking. And don't leave anything out."

"Sure, Dave." His fingers began to drum on the box. "So I told this guy the tale, and he went upstairs and when he came back down, he said I'd get a chance to meet the boss..." Dutch started searching his pockets.

"Keep going, Dutch. You're doing fine." Dave reached for his cigarettes, lit one and handed it to the Dutchman.

The big man took a deep drag on the cigarette. He blew the smoke out in a heaving sigh. "They showed me into this boardroom, fancy as anything you ever saw." Dutch took another drag and spoke right through the exhale. "I thought I was doing the right thing. I'd been drinking some, and I was all alone in this big room with all these fancy bottles and shaved ice, and well, I waited for a long time for someone to come get me. And nobody ever came. And so, I took a little drink, and there were some cigars in a tray, and so I smoked a few."

"Get to the point, Dutch."

"There was this on the table." Dutch held the lacquered box like a lifejacket in a stormy sea. "I thought they were just cigars, Dave, I swear."

"Give it to me."

Dave slid the key back on the bronze latch and opened the box. Beneath the engraved lid were sheets of coins, perfect coins, mounted under crystal clear plastic on blocks of blue velvet. Dave counted silver dollars, fifty-cent pieces, dimes and quarters, over a hundred in all. Each one was a perfect proof, marked with a tiny CC. By the inscription, Dave knew all the coins were from the Carson City Mint.

"I just sort of took 'em. I didn't know, really, I didn't look, I didn't know!"

"Where Dutch? Where did you get these?"

"At the Double Diamond."

"Jesus." Dave stared at the contents of the box. All perfect, all expertly mounted. And they all belonged to the biggest asshole in Northern Nevada.

"I thought they were just cigars." Dutch looked as if he would burst into tears at any moment.

Dave considered his friendship with the Dutchman, such as it was, and the certain danger that lay before him. It didn't matter what Dutch said, or even what had really happened. There was only one thing for sure: they were running out of time. He clapped the box shut and tucked it under his arm.

"What are you going to do?" Dutch's whole body was shaking, his fingers clenched tight on the arms of the easy chair.

"You stay here. Don't leave. Don't open the door. Don't tell anybody where you are, don't even make a phone call until I get back."

"Where are you going?"

"I'm gonna' try to get the god-damn genie back in the bottle."

DAVE'S GUT TWISTED in protest as he drove up the steep grade. Though he'd never formally met the man he was seeking, he'd seen him in the casino, even delivered firewood to his big house on the hill. He doubted the man would remember him, or care if he did. This was a slim chance at best.

Maybe the only chance Dutch has.

Halfway to the house, he began to think better of his noble offer. No one knew he had anything to do with the stolen box, or with Dutch either, for that matter. Unless you thought he was more important than all the other rubes that Dutch had swindled. But he still couldn't shake some sense of obligation. He figured the best course of action was to return it as quickly as possible, something Dutch was in no condition to do without getting beat to a pulp, or maybe worse.

Just in case, he left his truck down on the highway and walked the quarter-mile up to the chalet in the dark. He was trying to work out a way to return the case without making any more trouble. Most of all, he wanted to avoid the same fate that might be awaiting Dutch.

The entry road to the chalet home was simple, almost unassuming, but the detail in the landscaping told him there was money here, and lots of it. Dave slipped inside the winding drive and approached the house. It was perched like a crown on a ridge top, high above the lake.

The grounds were subtly lit and laced with deep shadows. Dave chose a path that led him to the front door unannounced. He rang the ornate doorbell, and two men emerged from the large garage, propelled by his sudden appearance.

"What are you doing here?" one barked. His pocket barely concealed the handgun hidden inside.

"I'm here to return this item to its rightful owner." Dave lifted the ornate box into the light.

"I'll take that." The man reached for the box.

"No, you won't." Dave looked the man down. He was thick, dark, and in need of a good shave. "Your boss won't like your fingers on it. And he'll want to know how I come to have it."

The man hesitated. A metallic voice sounded from a brass grill above the doorbell. "What is it, Anthony?"

The dark man pressed a black button below the grill and spoke. "Some guy's out here with a fancy box. Picture of some kinda' building on it. Is that the one we're looking for?"

"Never mind that." There was a pause, and then static. "Bring him in. On the overlook."

The two men walked Dave through a long sculptured vestibule. They turned to enter an open living area. Floor-to-ceiling glass faced outward to the south shore, glittering lights reflecting off the lake below. Beyond the vaulted windows, a tall man in his mid-fifties stood on a wide deck, holding a crystal cocktail glass. He was elegantly dressed, in a dark blue blazer and pressed white shirt. A large diamond sat in a thick gold ring on his right hand.

Dave walked out on the deck and faced the older man.

"Have a seat."

"Thanks, I'll stand, if you don't mind."

"I see you have my coins." The man eyed the rosewood case. "We've been looking for them. Did Mr. Anderson sell them to you? Are you expecting some kind of reward?"

"No reward. Just came to see the box gets back where it belongs." Dave lifted the case gently. "Seeing as how it ain't his, I figured to return it." He looked the taller man square in the eye. "Dutch is a good man. Just a little down on his luck, and not too bright sometimes." Dave touched the ornate lid. "No excuse, but he thought the damn thing was cigars."

"I don't know you." The man looked askance at Dave. He reached into a long silver case and drew out a cigarette. "Care for one?"

Dave could use a smoke, but he didn't care to put the box down just yet. "No, but thank you, all the same."

"Suit yourself." The older man lit his cigarette with a black enameled lighter. The flame shot straight up in a hot pencil tip. "Have you looked inside the case?" The man examined Dave like a curiosity in a museum.

"I took a peek," Dave replied. "Once I found out where they came from, I shut the box up tight." The man seemed to be barely listening. "Old Dutch didn't know what he was doing, he was just dumb drunk."

"Those coins are from the Carson City Mint. A gift from a business associate. Rare, uncirculated, a complete set. Not to be touched, turned, or otherwise examined." The man considered Dave with mild derision. "And certainly not by you, or your drunken friend."

"They're all here." Dave tapped on the box lightly. "I made sure."

"Of course they are." The man exhaled, blue smoke floating above the hardwood deck.

"He would have brought 'em back himself, but he was too shaky." Dave paused. He let the words come out slowly. "And he's mighty sorry."

"Someone comes into my house and takes my things and then expects to return them with just, 'I'm sorry'?" The tall man's voice rose steadily in volume, uncorked and boiling hot. "A man who sought my money as an investment. A man to whom I might have given opportunity."

Dave could see the whole thing was about to go sideways.

"I don't care about his little silver mine, or his government contacts, or anything else." The tall man was beginning to pace. "My time is valuable, and I require a reasonable return."

Dave wondered what kind of promises Dutch had made. Most likely, ones he couldn't keep. *Maybe there is a way out of this.* He took a half-step forward and spoke in a calm voice. "I've seen some of the assay reports. They're solid."

"You don't understand, do you? You think you know something, or somebody, and that makes you cocky." The man crushed his cigarette in a thick glass ashtray. "Everyone in this town thinks they have an angle." He glared at Dave. "Well, don't count on it."

Dave took another step closer to the edge of the deck.

"Men like your friend don't matter." The older man turned to the men by the door and cocked his head slightly. One of them gave a nod in return. The older man smiled and turned back to Dave. "People think they have an advantage, but they don't, really. And so they find themselves on the fringe, trying to get in. Thinking they have something we want." The man dropped his voice deliberately. "But like you, they are all vendors. We buy and sell them."

Dave wasn't listening. He had no time for a rich man's spite. The man droned on as one of his henchmen circled the deck towards Dave. Dutch was probably dead, or soon would be. Dave felt the small of his back touch the railing behind him. He fingered the inlaid box and considered his very limited options.

The problem with jumping off a balcony is twofold: how far down is it to the ground, and just how good are you at landing? Dave could make a pretty fair estimate of the distance, but it wasn't the same thing as actually knowing.

The problem with staying put was even more evident: the shape of a pistol in the approaching goon's pocket.

If he gave them the box, maybe they would let him go, or maybe they wouldn't. No matter what happened, they still might come after him. He figured he'd only been in the house for a couple of minutes. If he were lucky enough to get away, no one would know his name or where to find him.

Dave considered the unknown distance below, his attention half-taken by the stalking gangsters above. He thought about all the horses he'd fallen from, how to tuck and roll safely, and how much he didn't like the shadowy void beneath him. One thought came to the surface unbroken. *If I don't want to jump, these guys will want to even less.*

He eyed the goon blocking his exit.

And they don't have near my motivation.

The big guy named Anthony took another step his way.

Oh, hell. It ain't like you never been throwed.

In an instant, Dave flipped his legs over the balcony and fell into the darkness. He relished the angry shouts above him.

It was a welcome sign that he was still alive.

DUTCH WAS PARCHED, and that made him nervous. He had the shakes, making him even more uncomfortable.

All he wanted was a drink, and for some reason there was no liquor in Dave's apartment. He'd been here many times before, even slept off a few in the spare bedroom, when the kids weren't around. There was always a bottle or two above the Frigidaire, either right on top or tucked away in a cabinet.

Dutch opened the olive green refrigerator. He was willing to settle for a beer, even the pale carbonated water that posed as that noble brew in America.

His father had loved beer; deep dark lagers, rich bocks and spicy dry ales, the ones that lay like silk sheets on your taste buds. When he was a boy, he apprenticed in their family taproom, until the bastard Heineken crushed all the smaller brewers in Amsterdam. Brewmaster Gundar Anderson went bankrupt and took his craft overseas to Milwaukee, there to take revenge on Heineken with the bitter brew that flowed from Wisconsin like piss out of a racehorse.

A short stint in the Army and a geology degree had spared Dutch the family occupation. Now, he wished he'd stayed closer to home.

For a long time, he sat silently in the overstuffed armchair. He thought about his past, the recent and the far away. He caught himself staring at the locked front door, wondering how long it would take Dave to return, or if he would return at all. The jitters were getting worse. No beer in the fridge, and his small flask was long since empty.

He decided to make a quick trip to the Camp Richardson liquor store, open till 11 o'clock and only a mile down the road. He'd be back safe inside with a decent bottle of gin in less than 15 minutes, and no one would be the wiser.

A CASUAL OBSERVER might have missed the big blue Eldorado; it was well off the main road and neatly tucked beneath a ponderosa pine. But Johnny Patronis was not a casual observer. He was a devotee of old cars, especially Cadillacs, and even though he'd never laid eyes on this particular vehicle or its owner, he knew exactly what he was looking for: a 1956 Cadillac Eldorado Biarritz, Bahama Blue, with Nevada plates.

For almost 12 hours, Johnny had been driving around the populated shores of the lake, searching for any sign of the flashy convertible. By chance, he had seen a flicker of moonlight bounce off one of its chrome fins. Patronis doused his lights and pulled over slowly. He parked his black Buick discretely, about 15 yards away from the turtle-waxed Caddy.

He kept his door closed and his profile low in the vehicle, making a note of each house within walking distance of the Eldorado. All were typical of the neighborhood: three older homes and one small duplex, each well off the main road. He observed the house lights were either dimmed or turned off completely. After watching for any sign of movement, he glanced at his watch and tucked his revolver into the map pocket at the bottom of the driver's door. Johnny settled back on the bench seat, hoping to catch a few hours sleep before morning.

The Cadillac's door slammed shut, and its engine turned over. Patronis woke with a start. Without hesitation, he slid the .38 snubnose from its hiding place and walked briskly up to the driver's side window from behind. Johnny noted the crisp blue and white upholstery with genuine admiration. He hoped that any telltale stains would be promptly and professionally cleaned.

The big convertible's engine was still idling when the postman discovered it the next morning.

P OP TOOK A SIP of coffee and looked out his window at the passing dunes. We were on the edge of the Toiyabe National Forest. Miles of alkali flats and sagebrush lay before us, a perfect landscape for the sad tale of A. A. Anderson.

"So, you didn't see what happened to him?"

"No, but I had a pretty good idea. There were cops all over the place." Pop put his cup down on the open glove compartment door. "I drove by real slow, didn't even stop to go in the house. Dutch's Cadillac was parked on the other side of the street. Ambulance, cop cars, lots of 'lookee-loos'." Doc held his hands steady on an imaginary steering wheel and looked straight ahead. "I just kept right on going."

"What happened next?"

"I went down to the Caltrans yard to get my gear. I was still working part-time that season. Wanted to clear out my locker. Ol' Albert Simpson told me a couple of guys had come looking for me, and I knew there was gonna' be trouble."

"What do you mean?"

"Albert was all nervous like." Pop pulled a tobacco pouch from his jeans jacket. "Said they were a couple of tough guys. I asked if they knew my name or anything, and he said no, just that they were looking for some guy named Dave, owed them some money." Pop paused, opened his tobacco pouch, then closed it up again. "Albert told 'em to go look down in Sacramento - there was nobody here by that name. He was a good friend, Albert was."

"Then what?"

"Like I said, I got my stuff, gave my notice and cleared out. I didn't go back to work for Caltrans until..." Doc put the tobacco back in his pocket. "Hell, I didn't go back to the lake for years. Pissed my sister off something awful."

"Sounds like you had good reason."

Pop was silent. I sensed a growing discomfort in him. He was unsettled, as if he no longer fit on the old Ford's bench seat.

"Lookee there, Bill." Doc pointed out the windshield. He read directly off a tattered billboard. "*Sacred Mountain Trading Post.* Let's stop and stretch our legs."

A hundred yards ahead, the trading post was little more than an A-frame shack with a gas pump and a dumpster.

"Not much here." I slowed down and turned off the highway into a graveled yard. "Well, at least we can stretch our legs."

"Yes, sir. At one time, this was probably a growing concern." Doc looked out beyond the padlocked pump. "Must be a lot of government land."

"This could be a reservation, don't you think?" I could make out a few wooden structures in the distance: a water tower and a windmill next to a big flatbed truck.

"That may be, we may be on a reservation." Doc got out of Betsy and put his hands on his hips. He leaned back and stretched, then looked out across the horizon. "That may be why you don't see much around anywhere. I never noticed a sign saying we was in one, but it just might be. So that's a good thing."

He pulled his hat down low over his eyes and headed for the store. "Nobody bothers you on Indian land."

AT ITS BEST, Highway 49 could be a leisurely road, enjoyed by tourists and townspeople alike. The road did have some difficult sections, steep grades with poor embankments, thin shoulders and blind curves that challenged the impatient and the unprepared. But no section of it was quite so unyielding as the stretch from Placerville to Auburn, above the southern bank of the middle fork of the American River. In less than the space of one mile, it dropped in elevation over 1000 feet in a dizzying pattern of repeating switchbacks, some no more than 150 feet long, barely wide enough for two cars to pass each other safely.

In the early fifties, Dave had traveled that stretch over a hundred times, carrying restaurant garbage down from the lake on Highway 50 and then across 49 to his place, midway between Auburn and Grass Valley.

He made the trip late at night once a week, after he'd finished his Saturday shift at the sawmill. The Tahoe diners and coffee shops would keep their table scraps for him; scraps that he fed to the pigs down below on the ranch. He'd tend to the animals, say hello to his Mom and Dad, then turn and head right back up the mountain on Sunday night, just in time for the morning shift on Monday.

He and Tommy Johnson had kept 30 or 40 pigs; he'd take them down to market at the stockyard or sell firewood and Christmas trees to the brokers in Roseville. "A full load up and a full load down," he'd say. Like a long distance teamster, he knew there was no profit in hauling a truck full of air. This time, he was driving the same dark route, with nothing but memories in the bed of his Chevy.

The years had been good to him, despite all his female troubles. He had loved Marion and Joyce in the only way he knew how. Maybe someday, he might know how to do it better, but then again, maybe not. For now, he had his kids and his folks, and Tommy and Wanda and Velda and Beno, and all of his cousins and nephews. All the Baileys lined up against the world, just like they were in Wellton.

His folks were getting up in years though, and soon things would have to change. Dad was pretty much blind now. Mom was spending more time in bed, and even the little chores around the ranch were getting to be too much for them.

When he'd bought the place, it seemed like such a good idea, what with a new bride and all. He didn't know his first marriage would end so soon, or his second one even quicker than the first. He wondered where Joyce was now, and if she ever missed the children.

Dave followed his headlights into the next curve, thinking about the ever-changing distance between people. Just what was it about his life that sent the womenfolk scurrying, yet kept his children so close to home? He loved his wild boys and his beautiful girl, though sometimes it was hard knocks raising them alone.

Not by a long shot.

He corrected himself as he angled the pickup out of a sharp turn. He was never in it alone - he never really had to be. His mom and dad given up just about everything to be with the grandkids, and Tommy and Wanda had taken Rusty in like he was their own. After a while, everything had just sort of worked itself out.

Almost everything, that is.

Dave pressed his brakes into the next turn and accelerated the Chevy out of the sweeping curve. The road was about to straighten out on the long flat stretch that led into Cool, the last big straightaway before the switchbacks above Murderer's Bar. He pushed the accelerator pedal to the floor and glanced up at his windshield. The big black Buick was still in his rear view mirror, about 300 yards behind him, and gaining fast.

IT WAS FUNNY how he got to thinking about women at the strangest times. Even at 90 miles an hour. He'd driven this road so many times that he figured his thoughts could outrun most anything. Even the car that had tailed him ever since he left the Caltrans yard.

Tonight, his mind kept drifting back to Billie, how she'd loved him so sweet for the very first time. How they took the day and rode down to the Colorado, and how she listened to him like no one else ever had.

He told her how some folks couldn't get past the memory of him as a boy, and how he wanted to be treated like who he was, and not who he used to be. And that sometimes, people wanted him to be something that he wasn't ever gonna' be.

Maybe that's why he left her, to get back on the desert, so he could be himself again. He liked to think about Billie. And sometimes, he would think about the son he left behind.

A SUDDEN LURCH pushed him back into the present. The Buick smashed into his rear bumper, forcing the Chevy sideways towards a spin. Dave counter-steered into the turn and punched the gas pedal. One wheel lurched off the roadway, slamming forward as it gained fresh traction on the pavement. A sharp explosion made him think he might have burst a tire, but he knew better and kept his head low in the shadow of the truck's cab.

Dave could feel the growing intensity of the high beams right behind him. He had only moments before the Buick would overtake him. Long violent shadows fell across the roadway as their headlights crossed each other, two engines screaming against the canyon walls.

One by one, he counted the curves. In another quarter-mile, the road would straighten out into a long, slow descent, making him an easy target for the Buick's bigger engine. He veered wildly side to side, holding his pursuer back for the sharp curve that was just ahead - a sloping crescent turn that bordered on a steep drop into the canyon. Dave eased up on the accelerator, slammed the clutch pedal, and downshifted into second gear. The Chevrolet shuddered violently, drifting to the inside of the curve as the Buick pulled up on the outside.

A pistol roared from deep inside the black sedan, its muzzle flash exposing the driver's profile. Through the Buick's headlights, Dave caught a glimpse of the gaping drop ahead and threw his steering wheel hard to the right. The truck's running boards shrieked against the black sedan while its tires screamed to hold the pavement.

The big Buick flew off the road at full speed in a long arc, gathering momentum as it fell. It tumbled down the hillside through jagged shards of manzanita and lodgepole pine. Seconds later, the black sedan cratered on a granite ledge, its spine broken and oozing life. A steel cage, crushed like a beer can under a hobnail boot.

Dave watched the headlights as they left the roadway. The drop was more than 600 feet, and the violent sounds pierced him like the bloody deck on the Western Victory.

He slowed to a stop and peered into the canyon. He'd seen men die before, some in the war, some on the job, and some just because they plain got tired and didn't want to be around anymore. But he hadn't been the one to send them to their maker. It was a different feeling, one he didn't care for much, even in his angry jeopardy. He made a decision, and now they were dead and he wasn't.

"I guess that'll have to do," he said out loud.

He put the truck in gear, pressed the gas pedal and headed for home. It would be a long time before he passed this way again.

POP WAS ENGAGED with the man behind the counter. This fellow looked to be a native, dark-skinned with aboriginal features. The man had asked where we came from, and Pop was regaling him on the brand new sights of Las Vegas, Nevada.

"Like I say, a roller coaster on top of a hotel, the dang thing ran up and down for three city blocks."

"Bring me a picture next time." The Indian seemed amused in a stoic sort of way.

"I'll do that." Pop said.

I asked the man about the weather report and how far it was to the next town. It turned out we were just north of Indian land, between two mountain ranges. He was Shoshone, part of the Yomba reservation.

"How far to get there?" I asked. We'd spent some pleasant time in the Navajo Nation a while back. Maybe a little side trip was in order.

"Not far, maybe 10 or 15 miles." He pointed to the black clouds that were gathering in the west. "No blacktop, you got 4-wheel drive? It might snow tonight."

"Nope," I said. "Just an old station wagon." Icy roads didn't agree with Betsy. She had a tendency to fishtail.

"It's a good road, gravel, takes you all the way down to Ione." He leaned forward and whispered. "It's a ghost town."

I found that an odd remark from a man in the middle of nowhere.

Doc was rummaging around the store, looking for jerky, or perhaps some black licorice. There was a stack of colored booklets on a counter. He picked up one and read the headline aloud. "*Seven little known facts about the Yomba Shoshone.*"

"One dollar," said the Shoshone. Pop held the cover at arm's length, eyes squint behind his thick glasses.

"Sounds fair," I said, and gave the man a dollar. We were likely to be the day's big spenders.

Doc continued reading. "The Yomba Reservation was one of the last above ground nuclear test sites. Between 1951 and 1968..."

A side trip to the Yomba Reservation was sounding even less desirable. We took their land and their children. If that wasn't enough, we had to drop an atom bomb on them, too.

"Bring it with us, Pop." I figured the man behind the counter had heard it all before. "I want to beat the snow, if we can."

We took a minute to look at some Indian blankets, and Doc got one of those single-serving ice cream cups with the flat wooden spoon. I bought two packs of Marlboros and some corn chips. Ten dollars and 15 minutes later, we left the little trading post behind, seventy-five miles from Fallon and a warm place to bed down.

JUNE 1962

Grass Valley, California

IT WAS AN UNFORGIVING DRUNK, the kind that withers away into sharp-edged suffering. A dull hum populated the inside of his head. It rose with each breath to the dry roof of his mouth, falling bitterly onto his swollen, aching tongue.

He wasn't at all sure how he got where he was and even less where that might be. His eyelids were crusted shut; he strained to peel them open against the sticky mucous web that bound them together. The ground beneath him felt hard and prickly. He tried to rise and realized that his left arm was asleep, its circulation cut off by the weight of his own body.

From what he could tell behind half-closed eyes, it was night, deep night and cold, lights out all around. No telltale sound, no night birds and no traffic noise. There was nothing, nothing except the tingling in his arm and the constantly expanding pressure inside his skull.

He pressed his legs, trying to lift the dead weight. He staggered and fell backwards against a hard surface, a wall perhaps - tall, flat and solid. It spun him sideways and he lost his balance, lurching forward into the dirt. When he tried to rise, his torso twirled and he fell again, this time with a mournful groan.

Time passed in tingling snowdrifts, conscious thought struggling to replace the haphazard fire of his nervous system. A ragged kind of self-awareness emerged. He knew that he was cold and wet. He knew that he was angry, crazy angry, and maybe a little bit afraid. Angry at himself, for burning up his grubstake on a wild bet, for letting Dutch die and for putting his children in harm's way. He was angry at himself, for jumping off that balcony instead of crushing that bastard's head in with his fancy box. Now, he'd killed two men he didn't even know, left to wonder when the next man might come.

"Who's there?" The voice sounded urgent, close. He could sense a grey shape moving through the muddy darkness. Footsteps, and the grey shape solidified into a man. A sudden memory of violence heaved adrenaline into his brain and he jerked wildly, pitching himself headlong into the wall. Red-eyed and angry, pain streaked across his forehead, blood pounding in his eyes.

The old knife leapt from his belt into his hands. It had lived by his side almost every day of its life, for rope snarls, for whittling and the occasional game of mumbletypeg. He swung the blade wide and screamed, "Get back!"

"Davey, is that you?"

The voice was close and familiar. The name curdled in his belly.

"Son?"

He felt the knife in his hand and flung it to the ground. He longed to see his father, but couldn't bear the sight. Fearful that he might have struck him, he was hamstrung, unable to clear his mind or his senses. Resistance gave way to revulsion and in agony he retched. Vomit flew from his mouth in hot chunks.

For a moment, he teetered against the red cedar barn they had built together, tears straining to escape his swollen eyes. Like a tree cut clean at its roots, he toppled headlong into the dirt, right beside the Barlow knife his father had given him so many years before.

ROAD SOUND was the only noise to be heard. I'd listened, dumbfounded, for the last 20 miles.

"And that was my last drink." He sat dead still, eyes straight ahead. "There's nothing good comes of it. You take the drink, and the drink takes you."

I knew there was more to the story, but I was hesitant to ask. When the silence seemed a little too loud, I spoke.

"And then what?"

He answered without hesitation. For 5 or 10 minutes, he told me how he'd left Lake Tahoe for good, closed his business and slipped quietly out of town. All the while, I watched for any sign of regret, but I could see none.

"Tommy tied up all the loose ends for me. He was always a good friend, more than just a brother-in-law." Doc took out his fixin's and began a roll. "I never told Wanda what all happened. Some things you're better off not knowing."

Pop pinched some tobacco into a rolling paper and twisted the ends shut. He talked about his life after he left the lake, about his family, his children and his mom and dad. I noticed a growing ease in his reflections. When he left Nevada, he had left more than just the trouble with Dutch behind. He lit the cigarette and his chin came up again.

"First time since I was married, I stayed home and raised my kids. About high time, too. Got to see 'em grow up. Hell, I still had to work for a living, but I was on the ranch pretty much every day. I always managed to make ends meet, what with side jobs and such. And after 5 or 6 years, I got back with Caltrans, part-time."

"Did you ever have any more trouble?"

"Never saw 'em again. I stayed up nights for a lot of years with a Winchester by the door, but I never heard hide nor hair of that bunch again."

"What do you think happened?"

"Maybe they got tired of looking for me, or maybe they didn't know where to look. Don't matter much, really." Doc paused for a moment. "But I'll tell you what, I haven't been back to that lake once, except for Rusty's graduation."

"And you gave up the gold mining?"

"Nope, just the drink." Pop laughed and began to cough. After he caught his breath, he crushed his cigarette into the ashtray. "I gotta give these things up, too."

He took a deep breath and let it out slowly. I could hear his lungs rattling, even over the sound of the old Ford.

Over the years, I'd seen Doc quit smoking a few times, but he'd never made it stick. I considered my own bad habits, the smoking, the drinking. And the other things.

"Pop, I know you don't like my drinking."

"No, I don't."

I pictured how he'd almost killed his father and wondered if I hadn't done worse, or might someday. The people I'd lied to, stolen from, the cheating and the broken promises. The times I should have been home and wasn't, because I was off playing the big shot, hiding from myself by pretending to be somebody else.

I thought about Doc's dad, half-blind, pulling his son out of his own vomit.

Now, I had a son, too. "Hell, even I don't like my drinking."

"You say so, but then you're right back where you started." Our last night in Vegas was fresh in Pop's mind. "It's not my business how you live your life, but I hate to see you hurt yourself. Or your wife and kids."

I knew he was right, that I was pushing the limits I could come back from. There were things I still couldn't remember from the night before. Whiskey had become my medicine, the only thing that let me escape the nagging guilt and remorse. The same medicine that gave me permission to do whatever I wanted to anyway. But lately, my medicine had stopped working.

Pop looked across at me and spoke. "I had a chance a long time ago - to have a son, to have a life that was different from anything I've ever known. I've got no regrets. But I do know it would have been different if I'd thought it through."

We stayed quiet after that, for a long time. On the outskirts of Fallon, the snow began to fall, and we took a room for the night.

AUGUST 1962
Medicine Bow, Wyoming

SHE STILL THOUGHT ABOUT HIM. Not so much these days, but in the beginning, almost every waking moment. At first, she'd wanted to hurt him, to take a piece of lumber and swing it across his face and wipe that damn smile off it.

Not anymore though.

As Russell grew, she began to see it all as a gift, like Zeus had come down to Wellton and left some perfect treasure on her doorstep. She still couldn't sit a horse without thinking about his father. About how he rode, like some kind of wild Indian, attached at the hip, knees down in the wind.

The Colorado River had the same effect on her; the steady flow of it, the feel of the sand on the shore and the sun's warm light down in the canyons. Those were the memories she kept now, not the pain and the betrayal. When she came here from Arizona, that was all she could think about, how he'd left her, how he was there one moment and gone the next.

Billie laughed at herself and kicked a stray stone down off the steps. That was what she loved about him; he was like the wind, blowing in all at once, sometimes hot and sometimes cold, here one day and gone the day after. Gone for good, it turned out.

She was grateful for it.

Had he stayed, the memories would be different, and so would she. She had come to like who she was. It was enough.

Across the barnyard, Russell was buckling suitcases to the back of his car. God, he looked just him; lean, sharp-eyed, with that same easy smile and confident stride. She wondered what Paris would make of her western son. Most likely, he'd remake the town in his own image.

When he got the Fulbright scholarship, she was thrilled. He'd escaped the hamster wheel. The land would not define him. He had choices now, no longer hostage to the weather and the price of beef cattle.

But it'd been a long 20 years.

After Daddy got sick, they sold the cattle company to Chicago beef packers and moved north. His medical bills had taken most of the money, and the passage of time had eaten away the rest. Her father had been her rock, always loving, always kind. He gave Russell strong hands and taught her patience and forgiveness. It had taken her years to embrace it, to feel the peace that came with understanding.

When her father died, they had managed to keep the headquarters, 80 acres and the main house. It was more than one man could take care of, but doable for a woman and a young boy. Billie hired her father's old foreman, and together they had made it bloom. Now, they raised the best harness horses in all of Wyoming territory.

Russell closed the car door. He called out for Isaias.

The old Mexican came out of the barn and embraced him fully. She could see Maria in the shadows, weeping. The four of them had made a home here, her son and the little Mexican family she had come to think of as her own.

Her perfect son wiped his hands on a cloth towel and folded it neatly. He took a last look around the place, saw his mother and walked over to the steps where she was standing.

"Watch out for pretty girls," she said. She had used her beauty as a weapon more than once, hot to the touch, cold fire meant to burn.

"I'm going there to study, not to fool around."

"And wear a raincoat." It was a code they'd both agreed on back in high school, when he got his first car.

Russell shook his head with a grin. "I will."

For the first and only time in his life, she would give him his father's advice.

"The only free cheese is in the trap."

He laughed out loud, beaming. He had the same broad smile.

"I love you, Ma." He hugged her, held her close and wiped away her tears. Then he drove off, just like his father.

The tears were different this time. They were tears of joy.

TALKING TO THE MOON

SEPTEMBER 1972

Union Hill

Grass Valley, California

TWO YEARS since Dee went completely blind.

Sometimes, Floy would just sit in the dark, letting her world become his world for a while. After a time, she never turned the house lights on past sunset, welcoming the cool grey as it settled in all around them. It was especially pleasant in deep summer, when the long hours of sun baked the foothills like a forgotten casserole. The July droughts would crisp the pine needles and make every step a crackling hum.

Most days were light and easy. She would make lunch in the morning before it got hot. Occasionally, one of the girls would visit and bring food, and she wouldn't have to cook. She didn't mind cooking; she had the new electric stove that Davey brought, and a washing machine, and a brand new Amana Radar Range. It seemed like every time someone invented something new, Davey would go buy it and bring it round the house.

Wanda and Tommy came to visit often, and sometimes Davey would come along with them. Wanda would complain that the only way she'd get to see her big brother was to visit her Mom and Dad. For some reason, nobody could get Davey back to the lake once he'd left it behind. "That part of my life is over," he'd always say.

In the afternoon, she would play with the grandkids, dispensing sugar cookies and lemonade. Vicki would help, and little Ricky always sat up on her lap, waiting patiently. Lenny was just like his dad, impetuous, always in a hurry, unwilling to wait an extra moment, out the door to terrorize the ground squirrels or play with the dog.

The boys would curl up around Dee's feet and listen to the stories of long ago Oklahoma, in the days when Indians were as common as taxicabs. The boys devoured their family history; Dee would tell them all about his visits to the Kiowa reservation, and how he flew his airplane over the open prairie like some character in an old movie. Last time, the boys told Vicki they were going to cook her dog and eat it, just like the Indians did.

When Dee lost his last bit of sight, he was beat down, but only for a little while. "I'd really just like to play ball with the kids," he said. "There was never enough time when ours were little. It'd be nice to catch up some." That was the only complaint she ever heard.

After the grandkids were gone, they would listen to the news together, and sometimes, an old radio show that they might have heard down in Wellton. Floy wondered what had become of the grand old wireless. She'd given it to Madeline Spain when they left. Madeline said she couldn't accept it, but Floy wouldn't take no for an answer, saying they could never repay the Spains for all their kindness. The two families had lost track of one another over the years, but there would always be a place in her heart for Madeline Spain. After all, they were both in love with the same man.

The crickets began their evening serenade. Floy took Dee's hand and led him to their bedroom. They lay quiet in the bed, deep in the dark, and held each other like they had for fifty years. The aches and the disappointments, even the wrinkles disappeared for a time, warm in the night's embrace. She would stroke his hair, and he would touch her cheek, and there was music in the silence.

Last week, she had slipped away with Velda Jean to see the doctor. The lumps in her breast had gone hard and painful. He told her in as many words to settle her things, and stay close to home. She had sworn Velda to secrecy, and the doctor had given her a bottle of pills. She took them only when things got really difficult, grateful that Dee couldn't see her wince as she lifted an arm or rolled over onto her side.

She would have to tell him soon. It frightened her like nothing before, in all her years. Not for what would happen, but for what came after – for the girls and for her Davey. She and Dee had settled on their plan long ago. They would never be apart in this world or any other.

She smiled and stroked his hair, and he began to hum her favorite tune in the darkness.

THE OLD WOODEN TRAILER sat on top of a sparse hillside. It had four wheels with rubber tires, but was built more like a gypsy wagon than an Airstream. Sheathed in boards and battens, it had a pitched roof and wooden hitch poles, made to be drawn by a single horse. The wind was whipping against the loose canvas shutters, lashing the water barrels that hung from its battered walls. Off to one side of the wagon was a cast iron pot, hung low over a fire pit.

"Take a look at that, Pop."

"That's a sheepherder's rig," replied Doc. "He'll be out here somewhere. Find the sheep, and we'll find him."

"Looks like a lonesome business."

"Yep. This here country won't support cows, leastwise not how you or me would graze 'em."

We were back on Highway 50 again, somewhere west of Utah and east of Ely, Nevada. It had been six months since our last adventure; my wife and kids had gone to visit her mother, and I decided to steal a few days traveling with Pop. On the way back, we'd seen a sign for the Great Basin National Park, but we chose to keep on westward until the sun went down, or we reached a good place to stop for the night.

"Here's your sheep, Doc." The sloping hillsides began to fill with grey silhouettes, some trailed by little white balls of fluff.

"And there's your sheepherder…"

A quarter mile ahead, I could see a single figure on horseback, about 30 feet off the road. I slowed to take a closer look and moved into the opposite lane, out of respect for the horse's unknown sensibilities. The rider barely turned his head to note our passing. He was dark, almost almond-colored, either from his ancestry, the sun, or both. The man wore a hat with a round top and a short brim; a green bandana was wrapped around his neck. His shirt sleeves were long and buttoned up tight, hands draped lightly across the saddle.

"I'm gonna' stop," I said, and pulled over to the side of the road. Pop frowned at me, as if I were violating some sort of unspoken etiquette.

"I just want to say hello." I cut the motor and got out on the shoulder. It felt good to stretch my legs. After a long spell behind the wheel, even Betsy's wide bench seat could get to be tiresome. I walked toward the horseman and noticed Pop hadn't left his seat.

"How are you, sir?" With no traffic and 50 miles from anywhere, it was quiet as a stone. The dark man appraised me with mild indifference. I pointed. "Is that your wagon down the road?"

He glanced over his shoulder and nodded quietly. I sensed it might be a short conversation. A closer look told me he was much older than I'd thought, probably in his late 70's.

How long have you been out here?" I fumbled for a change of subject. "We're on our way to California, back from Utah."

He nodded again and smiled. There were wide spaces between his few remaining teeth. "*Ona,*" he said.

I couldn't place the word or the accent, but he seemed friendly enough. "Is there a town, or a good place to camp around here?"

"*Mendian zehar.*" A grin spread across his weathered face, and he spoke again. "In the hills."

His English shocked me. It was brittle, as if it'd been spoken only once or twice before, in a town somewhere, long ago.

"*Auto onak.*" The shepherd pointed at Betsy. I could see Pop through the big glass windows, watching. "Ford. Good car." He offered his translation slowly, then whistled for his dog. It came barreling down through the startled sheep and settled next to the horse's hindquarters.

"Thanks. I think so, too." Betsy had that effect on almost everyone. She conveyed a kind of instant familiarity that transcended language, age or culture. I heard his compliment as a gentle goodbye.

The old man tipped his chin. "*Seguru bidaia.*" He turned his coal-colored horse into the hillside and squeezed it up the slope, sheep spreading like a wave's wake around him. His insistent herd dog encouraged any stragglers to follow close behind.

The walk back to the car was silent, bathed in miles of empty landscape. I paused to watch the rider's silhouette in the failing light. The old man was right to head for camp; night would soon be upon us all. As I opened the driver's side door, Pop's butane lighter lit up the cab. He blew a curling trail of smoke into the headliner.

"Well, did you get to say hello?"

"I think so, he didn't have much to say." I closed the door and fished around in my pockets for the car keys. "Indian, I think. I couldn't understand much."

"Basque." Pop said. "You can tell by the dog and the wagon. They been out here for a hundred years."

"Basque?" I'd heard the word before, but I didn't recognize the meaning. "Is that one of the tribes?"

"Nope. They come over in the Gold Rush with everybody else. Up from South America, across the sea from Spain. When the gold didn't pan out, they went back to doing what they know best - sheeping." Pop looked back behind us. "Might be the last of his kind."

"I thought that was a odd accent. Didn't sound like anything I've ever heard." I found Betsy's keys, and she started on the first spin, like she always did. "How come you know them?"

"Ran across 'em on one of our trips out here. We was on our way to Reno, a bunch of us, coming back from Wellton. Back in them days, we'd take off as soon as we got enough gas money together and set off for who knows where. That time, it was Verle, cousin Alpha, and I think ol' Kenny Kraddock was with us - we swung by Globe and picked him up on the way. We were off to see the Baileys, what was left of them, the ones that stayed behind in Oklahoma."

"Did you have a lot of family there?" The sky was darkening. Betsy's headlights made long white cones on the asphalt.

"Some, we Baileys have always stuck together." Pop grinned. "Even the ones that don't like each other."

I thought about some of the arguments I'd overheard on the ranch, and the hot, white heat of Doc's temper. It would only last for a moment, but that moment could be bruising.

"Ol' Kenny, he damn near got himself shot that time. We went to a dance in town with my cousin Tom. Well, Kenny goes to dance with some girl, and her boyfriend went after the both of 'em. This guy calls her a whore, and so Kenny bopped him good. He and Kenny went right off a balcony on top of a car." Pop re-lit his cigarette and shook his head. "That was one hell of a fight."

"What happened?"

"Not much. The guy takes off, then he comes back around outside. Threatened to kill us all with a .38." Pop's grin widened and he set his jaw. "Old Tom, he was as big as an ice house, he calls out, 'Tell him to come on, I'll shove it up his ass'."

I couldn't help but laugh. Bar fights were always funnier the further you got away from them. Even mine.

"Damn thing is, Kenny didn't make it past his first mission. He was a tail gunner." Pop exhaled slowly and stared at the passing hills. "You never know what's gonna' to take you out in this ol' world. But that was one hell of a fight, I'll tell you."

Things grew quiet. I pressed the gas pedal, and the big Ford accelerated into the darkness. Doc cleared his throat a few times and took a deep breath. His exhale ended with a hoarse cough.

He ran his fingers along the dashboard's edge, turned to me and spoke softly.

"You know what? Let's stop in Tahoe on the way back. I want to see my sister."

MARCH 1979
Placer County, California

PERCHED ON THE FORESTHILL BRIDGE, Dave Bailey studied the
enormous canyon underneath him. He pictured the kind of havoc that a sudden
release of two million acre-feet of water might unleash on the Sacramento Valley.
The north and middle forks of the American River came together here, and down
below, gigantic earthmovers were carving up the canyon to prepare it for a 700
foot-high dam.

Dave had been to the Hoover Dam before; the federal government built it
when he was still a boy, but he'd never gotten a chance to see it, until he and Joyce
took a joyride to Vegas on their honeymoon. They'd stopped on the two-lane
highway that ran right on top of it, watching as the mighty Colorado foamed out
in arcing waves below.

Every once in a while, on his way down to the job site, he'd sit up on the
bridge and consider the changes that machines had wrought on the life he once
knew. Back in Arizona, his dad had worked on the All American Canal, servicing
the big diesel haulers that stretched like freight cars all the way back to Boulder
Canyon. He could still remember when the Colorado ran free, when he and Billie
used to take their horses and go skinny-dipping, making love beneath the shade
of its high canyon walls.

He treasured those distant days and the mysterious life that surrounded him
there, when he could get a sense of himself and the world around him, without all
the trappings that progress had slapped on top of everything, like a cheap, shiny
dress on a beautiful girl.

Where he sat now, the river below looked like a winding silver thread, slashed
by a dozen angry claws. Witness to one more slab of concrete poured on top of
the natural world. 40 years ago, Old Joe had warned him not to be so proud of
the white man's monuments, that they too would pass into dust. Sometimes, he
wished they would just hurry up and go.

He treasured those distant days and the mysterious life that surrounded him
there, where he could get a sense of himself and the world around him, without all
the trappings that progress had slapped on top of everything, like a cheap, shiny
dress on a beautiful girl.

He let out a deep breath. It was quiet on the bridge. No traffic, no people, not
a single sign of a human being. He lit a cigarette and wondered how long it would

take this particular monument to sink back into the sand. He figured it might be quite a while.

The Foresthill Bridge was a steel marvel. Built 730 feet above the canyon, it was balanced on three arched trusses and two enormous concrete columns - so high, that folks said you could parachute from it and not crash below. The third highest bridge in the country, and a favorite attraction for suicides, right behind the Golden Gate Bridge.

Dave didn't plan on jumping, even when his occasional melancholy set in. Not while there was work to do.

The sun was setting low across the rim of the canyon. Soon, it would be dark, time to start his shift in the pump room above the cofferdam. He tossed his cigarette over the edge and watched as the tiny red tip shrank into nothingness. Time enough for melancholy when the job was done.

He walked to his pickup and began the long, winding journey down.

JUST ONE DEUTZ diesel-electric pump could move over 3000 gallons a minute; there were five of them in the Auburn Dam pump house. Their primary job was to keep the water level in the cofferdam from overflowing, inundating the main dam site downstream. It was still cold in the mountains, and the upstream flow was relatively light; two of the five pumps were idle, and one was bypassed for maintenance. Its other siblings were running at full speed to take up the slack.

Dave opened the trap door at the bottom of the idle pump. He scraped his Barlow knife across the caked mud in the giant catch pan below. Keeping his blade at a flat angle, he held it in the light of an overhead bulb.

"See all those little reflections?"

Albert Simpson nodded. He peered quizzically at the blade. "More?"

"Sure as we're standing here." Dave knelt down and pushed his hands into the muck. "But we won't be standing around for long. Grab that wheelbarrow, will you?"

Dave ran his fingers along the bottom of the tray, feeling for the telltale grit below. He smiled as his hands felt polished river rock and gravel. The coarse particulates and silt would fall by their own weight into the catch pans, congealing into a thick, gooey muck. Dave's job was to clear the pans each night, to prevent the slurry from clogging the intake screens and damaging the pumps. Albert Simpson performed the primary maintenance, keeping the big diesel's filters changed and adjusting their mechanical valves.

Ordinarily, both jobs would be done by just one man, but six months ago, three of the diesel-electrics had shut down unexpectedly. When the pumps malfunctioned, Albert convinced his supervisor that the primary water intakes needed more regular maintenance. With Albert's recommendation, his old friend from Caltrans had taken on the job. He and Dave had worked the split shift together ever since, maintaining the massive 3-ton pumps and the long network of pipes that fed them.

"This is such a sweet deal." Simpson looked like a five-year-old at a candy store window.

"Yes, it is." Dave gave his friend a knowing wink. "Just as long as they keep these pumps running."

"They have to, even if the state doesn't finish the dam." Albert pushed the wheelbarrow alongside the catch pan. He handed Dave one of two flat-bladed shovels. "If the river gets to running fast enough, that cofferdam won't hold. Those pumps are the only thing keeps it in one piece."

"Albert, those fool engineers got no idea." Dave glanced at the swirling waters outside. "That old girl can get mighty angry. If they ain't smart enough to catch a pump full of black sand, they dang sure ain't smart enough to stop this big river." Dave laid a canvas drop cloth in the gap between the access door and the wheelbarrow. "And, like I say, won't none of this matter much if we get another big shaker." Dave started shoveling the gritty muck out of the pan. He smiled at Simpson. "Reminds me of my days in the Idaho-Maryland."

"You know, I never believed half the tales you told up in Tahoe." Albert took his shovel and pitched in, alternating strokes with his friend. "I guess I know better, now."

Dave leered. "Maybe someday, I'll know better too."

Working in tandem, the two men filled the barrow pan quickly. Dave tilted the heavy wheelbarrow out the door to the equipment yard. He lifted the tarp off his truck bed and stashed it behind the miner's sluice box that was hidden below. Albert routed one of the emergency fire hoses to the upper end of the box and tightened it carefully. Dave opened the bronze fire valve; a smooth sheet of water rippled across the screens that laddered down the length of the long wooden box.

Dave hoisted a full scoop of dark muck and threw it into the sluice box. "Let's get to shoveling. We got maybe three more loads before morning."

DAVE TIED THE HEAVY TARP over his pickup bed and returned the water hoses to their hanging racks. He and Albert had spent the better part of the night cleaning out the pump; they would rotate to another one on their next shift.

They'd been doing the same job for two months, careful to hide their tracks each night, and even more careful to see that the pumps ran flawlessly, for without that due diligence, their goose would choke on its golden egg.

The evening's labor was fruitful. Albert left with a wide-mouth mason jar full of pea nuggets, tiny pieces of placer gold washed down the river channel into the pumps. Dave carried a twin mason jar and a small jug of black sand. Later, he would process the sand through mercury and pan it out for any hidden flakes of gold.

On some nights, they might catch only a little black sand, or a few coarse nuggets buried in quartz. But occasionally, when the river shifted its course, or a big storm rolled through the mountains, they would take out a harvest undisturbed for a thousand years.

As Dave left the pump house, the morning crew pulled in on the access road. The truck slowed and the shift foreman nodded hello. Dave glanced at the barrel full of tailings that still remained. The foreman noted the location, smiled and nodded again, an unspoken agreement each time the sluice box was in operation. Later that day, a trusted co-worker would quietly gather the tailings for a second pass. Down below, on the dam site itself, heavy equipment operators had discovered several promising quartz veins; that material would be removed just as discreetly.

This was the silent contract between working men in the gold country, the same unspoken agreement that had been around for a hundred years. These men had no banker's notes, no letters of credit and no mineral rights. They held no deeds, built no company stores and broke no picket lines. They were sweat labor, and at the end of each shift, whether a thousand feet below or on the edge of a drainage ditch, they looked out for one another, always with a careful eye reserved for management.

Albert Simpson left that morning carrying the only nest egg he was likely to receive from the Auburn Dam. When the mill closed or a mine shut down, management would always get their due. But for labor it was, "Sorry, can't pay your retirement. Fill out this form, and we'll get back to you in 90 days."

Dave had heard it all before. After the war, the Navy Department had promised the Merchant Marine full veteran's benefits, a GI bill and decent health care. That was 34 years ago.

He was still waiting.

He tapped the thick glass jar on the seat beside him. "I reckon we'll have to make do with our own little pension fund."

THE SUN FELL down below the hills, and U.S. Highway 50 looked as lonely as its nickname. Pop and I decided to turn off on a gravel road to see if we could find a good camping spot.

All we found was an abandoned dirt track crossed by a broken chain link gate. Beyond the gate, a rutted switchback road opened up onto a vertical rock face. The sign on the broken gatepost read:

Schindler Mining and Development Company
NO TRESPASSING
UNDER PENALTY OF LAW

We ignored the sign and drove past the fallen gate. The place was as barren as the road that led into it. A large, flat patch of beaten ground was just inside, where once platoons of mining trucks stood ready to haul rock and sand. Now, only the scattered bones of a few flatbeds remained, along with a dusty pink-and-white Ford station wagon.

"You never finished that Basque story." We were parked against the stony embankment, surrounded by a low barbwire fence. "How'd you meet them?"

"Like I say, we were on our way back from Oklahoma. Didn't have no money, so we were looking for work all along the way. We'd stop every time we saw a likely outfit, see if they might want to sign us on."

Pop was perched on a camp stool, sipping coffee from a red thermos cup. "We worked some at the ice house and the packing sheds, wherever there was a railroad line." He glanced at the surrounding hills, now lit by a rising moon. "Out here, we'd stop if we seen anybody at all."

I lifted a cold Coke from the cooler and put a match to our Coleman lantern.

The hissing gas exploded in a burst of white light, drowning out the night silence.

"Put that thing out," Pop said, "I can't see my own shadow."

He was right. In the pitch-black Nevada desert, even a quarter moon gave off enough light, and the whole sky was covered in a blanket of stars. The night was still warm from the heat of the day, and if we needed anything special from our kit, just the dome light in the '56 would do. I closed the gas cock and the silence returned. The night bugs scattered about in search of another bright moment.

"We ran into one of them sheepers, just like that fellow back there. He was Basque, first born son. His wife had passed on. Had no kin." Pop peered into his empty cup. "He was the last one. Just wasting away out here."

I saw the sheepherder reflected in Pop's eyes, and understood why he hadn't left the car to greet the oldtimer. Doc was a willing companion, always eager to say hello, to trade a story or ask for a bit of information, but this time, he must have seen more than he cared to, or perhaps a reminder of something he didn't want to see again.

I looked up into the night sky. I'd seen enough sand that day. "God, look at those stars."

"They say there's a million stars and a million planets." Doc picked up the thermos, unwound the cork top and poured. Steam rose from his cup and curled around his fingers. "I bet you there's a million, million moons."

"Don't forget the comets and the asteroids." Pop's easy change of humor raised my spirits.

"We used to lay out here and count shooting stars. We was working on a big horse ranch for this German couple, breaking two-year olds." Doc tucked his cigarette inside his palm, out of the slight breeze. "God, that woman, she could cook. German lady. She'd make us a big breakfast, a big lunch and supper, too." He smacked his lips in mock approval. "Mhm, hmm. Ham and eggs, fried chicken, mashed potatoes and gravy, big flat noodles. Pork chops as big as your hand. And those sweet biscuits you could make love to."

I gazed out beyond the hills and wondered at the random turn that led us there. A mist of stars hung overhead, tomorrow's road a long line of alkali flats beyond us. After all that talk of biscuits, I was hungry. Reluctant to let the dome light mask the shimmering Milky Way, my silver Zippo flashed instead.

Pop retraced his steps, from the ice houses to the horse ranches and the labor camps along the way. Right before they reached California, he and his friends had stopped in Reno, where they slept in an empty cave at the base of a limestone mountain.

"It was summertime and during the day, me and my buddies would set pins by hand at the bowling alley in town, then bed down for the night in the cave. Yes, sir." Pop blew a circle of smoke rings into the sky. "Come to think of it, it was a lot like this place."

After that, we were quiet for a long time.

"You know, we think we're so much in this old world. And we aren't just but a tiny, little itty-bitty part." He spoke just above a whisper. "I do believe there's a hereafter of some kind. I do believe it with all my heart. What it is, I just don't know. I only hope we get to see the ones we love one more time."

The moon was up, and the stars above us shone like faraway diamonds. Time joined hands in two places, and the desert bugs and I settled in for the night.

APRIL 1979
Auburn Ravine
Placer County, California

TWIN HEADLIGHTS streaked across the pump house as a blue sedan pulled in on the access road. Dave was standing in the doorway. He noted the clean whitewall tires.

"Albert, we've got company."

Albert stepped deeper into the pump house. He took a cursory look at the tools and gear. There was nothing to draw any special attention; he and Dave were only doing scheduled maintenance. Albert wiped his oily hands on a cotton rag and stepped to the doorway beside Dave.

"Little late in the evening for a social call," Dave drawled. He arched an eyebrow and tapped a Pall Mall on his chrome lighter.

"Good evening," the man called out, glancing at a clipboard as he exited the car. He was clean shaven and wore a dark suit. "I'm looking for David R. Bailey and Albert L. Simpson."

"Well, there's no other fools out here this time of night." Dave lit his cigarette. The yellow flame illuminated his face. "You found 'em."

The man gave them both a friendly smile. "Got a letter for each of you." He pulled two sealed envelopes from his clipboard and held one out. "Mr. Bailey?"

"Right the first time." Dave leaned forward to take the envelope. He tucked it into his shirt pocket without a pause.

"And Mr. Simpson?"

Albert gave Dave a questioning glance. He took the second envelope and held it gingerly in both hands. "What's this all about?"

"Can't say as I know, sir." The tall man shook his head. "I just deliver them. But unless you've got a rich uncle that's feeling poorly, well... generally, they aren't the best news."

"Thanks all the same." Dave held a spare porcelain cup next to his tall thermos. "Care for some coffee?"

"Don't mind if I do." The tall man visibly relaxed. "Not too often that I get such a kind reception."

"You're a working man, same as us." Dave poured out a generous serving. "Well, at least for the moment, anyways."

The man nodded his thanks, and sat down on the iron bench in front the pump house.

Albert gave Dave another puzzled look.

"Albert, the only one knows we're out here this time of night is the Auburn Dam, and maybe your wife and my daughter. Which one of them, you think, sends us a note by Pony Express?"

The tall man chuckled and took a long drink, draining his cup. "Well, thanks for the coffee, Mr. Bailey." He smiled and stood to go. "And good luck to you, sir."

"You betcha. I wouldn't have it any other way."

Albert sat down on the bench and opened his envelope. Dave peered over his shoulder. After a moment, Dave opened his own:

Three Rivers Construction, Inc.

Thomas A. MacBride

Partner/General Manager

Due to unforeseen circumstances, staffing levels must be adjusted

on the Auburn Dam project. Please consider your employment

terminated, effective immediately.

We are grateful for your service.

"Well, you're welcome." Dave folded the envelope back into his pocket.

Albert kept reading his letter over and over again. He looked stunned. "You don't think they know what we were up to, do you?"

Well, of course they do." Dave laughed. "Or anyways, somebody does."

He pictured the burly supervisor from the last pump house inspection. They had a lively discussion about the uncertain future of the Auburn Dam.

"Mind your own business, Bailey," said the supervisor. "Just clean the pumps, and stay out of things that don't concern you."

"I surely will," Dave replied. "But they're making a mess out of this, I can tell you that much."

"And how would you know?"

"Seen it all before. St. Francis Dam in LA - that one tore up half the damn town. Lake Olympia... Hellhole in '64." Dave eyeballed the sneering man. "Progress, they call it."

"You bet it is." The man took a step closer, his double chin rising in the air above.

Dave stood his ground and snarled. "Tell that to the folks on the Rubicon.

These ol' mountains don't like being messed with. Some things are plain better off the way God made 'em."

"Don't be a fool, Bailey. There's real treasure in a dam like this." The big man pushed up against him, his face red in protest.

Dave paused for a moment to collect himself. He took a slow step backwards and smiled. "Yes sir," he replied. "I do believe there is."

The supervisor gave him an odd look and left the pump house in a huff. Dave wondered if he might have been a little too clever in his conversation.

As if it mattered.

He never thought they would finish the stupid thing. After the big quake at the Oroville Dam, the Auburn job site had slowed to a crawl; the same fault lines ran right by this canyon. The company had kept the pump house working, and that was all that mattered to Dave.

Everybody knew California was ripe for another big one. Let the politicians argue about the Auburn Dam for another decade. By that time, he and Albert would be deep in their golden years, fishing up on Lake Spaulding.

Dave looked at his watch and made a quick calculation.

"Like you said, Albert, they need to run these pumps no matter what. This here letter just makes it all nice and legal-like. But somebody knows." Dave pointed to the rumbling pumps. "And whoever that somebody is, he don't like us taking the lion's share of the meat."

"So, now what?" Albert stopped staring at his letter.

"We got six hours before the next shift. Let's open up every one of them pumps, and pull the stuff out by hand."

"Damn right, Dave." Albert's good humor had returned. "Fuck 'em."

"And the horse they rode in on." Dave pulled off his flannel shirt and clapped his old friend across the back.

"Come on, Al. You and me are gonna' get real dirty."

THE LONG RIDE HOME was pleasant and peaceful. Work would come and go. It always had and it always would, if a man was willing and gave a day's labor for a day's pay. He didn't think twice about the high-grading they'd done. It was a well-worn tradition, one that started long before his time in the mines.

Rich folk had their wealthy ways, but a working man had only his hands and maybe a little bit of luck to make a go of it in this world. And he'd always been lucky.

He thought back to the long nights in the Idaho-Maryland, to his old taxicab, to the day he left to join the Merchant Marine. He pictured the nightlights and the floating dance floor on Lake Olympia and his first dance with Becky. He thought about her sweet brown hair, the music in her laughter, and their long canoe rides on Lake Spaulding, pretending to fish for something beside the moment. Come summer, he'd go fishing on Spaulding again, this time with Albert Simpson. Maybe that would be the first official act of his old age.

He turned his truck off the highway and pulled through the open metal gate at the ranch. It was an hour before dawn, and only a single porch light lit his way past the corrals. The old black horse they had rescued from the stock auction nickered as he walked by, and he reached into the feed bin to draw out a sugar cube. Soon, he would be sixty; quiet reminders had shown up in his joints on cold mornings and in the short breath that came after any hard exertion.

He thought twice as he lit another cigarette, glancing at the warning label that the government had put on every package. *Mind your own business.* He decided once this pack was finished, to return to rolling his own.

A beacon moon was falling behind the hill, and he lingered for a moment with the old horse, inhaling the animal's moist breath mixed with his tobacco smoke. He let the cigarette burn down too far and it singed his fingertips, marking the time to go inside.

He opened the front door as quietly as he could and slipped down the hallway to the first bedroom. Watching his sleeping daughter in the silence, he considered how she wasn't much older than Billie when they first met. Standing there, it was hard to fathom just how much time had passed. It felt like so little, even with all the twists and turns. He listened to the rolling waves of his daughter's breath for a moment, and stepped outside into the night.

He had taken to sleeping in the same small room that his father had, alongside the front porch. He opened the door to the darkened room and stepped to the closet. Above the tiny alcove stood a long row of glass containers, their gleaming contents lining the heavy shelf. He added another full mason jar to the row. There were plenty more in the pickup, but they could wait until morning.

"WHEN WE OPEN UP the trailer, he bolts, Dad." Vicki was flushed with exertion. "We tried everything, but he just won't learn. As soon as I drop the ramp, he backs out at a run."

"How's he load?" Doc put his newspaper down on the kitchen table.

"He loads up fine, but we can't unload him. Not without getting run over."

"Oh, sure you can." Doc took a sip of his coffee. "Just use your head." He picked up the paper and looked at the front page.

His daughter clenched her jaw and went back outside on the porch. Her best friend had caught the black gelding and was holding it beside the trailer.

"What'd he say?" The tall blonde was feeding the big horse a piece of carrot.

Vicki called out to her girlfriend. "He says to keep trying."

Doc watched through the kitchen window as the two girls put the horse back in the trailer. They were two best friends trying to make a go of it in the horse business. He smiled at the thought of them making their own way in the world.

Once the horse was loaded, Vicki slipped the lead rope through the rails, then dropped the gate on the stock trailer. The gelding bolted backwards, nearly slamming into her as it raced out of the enclosure. She shouted and pulled the lead rope tight, barely keeping the horse from escaping.

Doc took his coffee cup and sauntered outside. He looked at the horse and then at the trailer. He liked this big black horse, it was well put together, and he figured it had a lot more sense than it had shown so far.

"Load him up again. Then take the trailer and bring it round to the pond." He pointed to the spring fed pond at the edge of the property. "Ass end to the water."

Vicki didn't argue. She knew it was pointless, where her dad and horses were concerned.

Once they got the horse loaded and the trailer repositioned, Doc walked out to the pond. "Back it up even further." He motioned for the truck to keep going until the trailer's rear wheels were nearly at the water's edge.

He pointed at the back gate. "Now, let 'er go," he said. "And don't hold on to that lead rope."

Vicki opened the gate and the horse bolted straight back, crashing into the pond. It sank on its hindquarters, turned over and thrashed to its feet, charging out of the pond and racing across the paddock.

"Now, go catch him and do it again." His daughter frowned at him, but she didn't hesitate. He smiled as she turned to go. She'd make a hell of a trainer someday.

Ten minutes later, the rear of the horse trailer was repositioned, and Vicki released the horse again. Once more, it crashed backwards into the pond.

As it ran away, she threw her ball cap down in the dirt. "That horse won't ever learn!"

"Maybe not." Doc said. "But we'll do it again anyway."

The whole process was repeated, and the result was exactly the same. Doc could hear Vicki and her girlfriend grumbling as they stalked off in search of the runaway horse.

"One more time." By now, Doc had brought a chair off the front porch and tucked it under the shade of the big Catalpa tree next to the pond.

After the sopping-wet horse was loaded, his daughter released the bolt and dropped the ramp. The horse moved slowly backwards, one careful hoofstep after another.

"Dad, he's on his tippy-toes," Vicki grinned as she watched the big horse come down the ramp, step by step, until he came to a full stop at the bottom. He nickered as Vicki came alongside him, relieved to be on solid ground.

"Now, put him away and feed him."

Vicki walked the horse over to the corrals. Ten minutes later, she came back to her father with a fresh cup of coffee.

"I think you taught him, Dad."

"I can't teach a horse nothin'." Her father looked over to the muddy pond. "But he can teach himself damn near anything."

Vicki laughed and offered him the cup. Doc took it and got up from his chair.

"You know, hon', people are the same way." He put his arm around his daughter and gave her shoulders a gentle squeeze. "I can tell you all day long how to do something, but till you can see it for yourself, feel it on your own, I might as well be talking to the moon."

T HAT HORSE WOULD get his feet up in the corners like that, and boy, he'd just be braced in there." Doc was laughing as he spoke, his sister joining in beside him. He and Wanda were like two 8 year-olds, giggling like they were both in on the same joke.

We were at Tommy and Wanda's house near the south shore, a brick red A-frame, well-constructed, with a single-story extension off to one side. We'd gathered in front of the house, at a round table built from an old PG&E cable spool. For the last hour or so, brother, sister and brother-in-law had been rewinding their adventures from beneath a shady circle of ponderosa pines. Tommy was re-packing his pipe as Wanda poured more lemonade from a Tupperware pitcher.

I was long since grateful that I'd placed my little tape recorder out on the table between us. ""Now, what? Tell me this again, he went where with that horse?"

Wanda laughed and threw her hands in the air. "Everywhere!"

"Like it was a dog?"

Tommy leaned back in his bent cane rocking chair. He'd been having some trouble moving around lately, a kind of gradual weakening that the doctors had found no good explanation for. I figured that was one reason Pop had decided to stop in Lake Tahoe.

"Well, he had a dog too, named Bummer." Tommy paused. "That dog was another character. That dog would go right up on the roof of that pickup." Tommy's arms crossed in a gesture of finality. "Stayed up there till Rendo came, then he'd jump in through the window."

I was determined to keep the wandering racecar on its track.

"And the horse, what kind of horse was it? Did he carry it to ride it, or...?"

"Mustang," Tommy said. "Rendo would just bring it with him. It was his horse and he liked it."

Dave chimed in, his memory now refreshed. "He got this mustang and he broke it. He was living off Pioneer Trail out here. I come to work one day, and he says he's got this mustang he's gonna' break. Next morning he comes in…"

"Man, he can't hardly move!" Tommy shouts. 'That son of a gun threw me! He done stomped on me!'"

Dave continued without a pause. "Several different times he come in there, saying that horse threw him or bit him or kicked him or something or the other. Finally, one day, he says, 'I got him broke'. And he comes by that day, and that's the first time I seen that horse in that pickup. Comes by with that horse, and I thought…" Doc passes the baton to his brother-in-law. "Well, you was there."

Tommy deepens his voice, in an echo from the past. "What the hell is going on here?"

"Here ol' Rendo comes with that horse in the back of that damn pickup," Dave was nearly shouting too. "No sideboards to hold him, nothing to hold him, he's just up in there!"

"He wasn't even tied down." Tommy shook his head in disbelief. "Didn't even have a rope on him!"

"But he broke that horse, you could do it." Dave was admiring the picture that was so well-framed in his memory. "Even after that horse got dumped out, he tells that horse to get back up in there and that horse would do it!"

I tried to imagine the situation. "And so, everywhere he went, he'd put the horse in the back of his pickup?"

"Yup, dropped the tailgate down and said, 'Get in 'er." Tommy took a puff off his pipe as if to seal the deal.

Dave slapped his thighs in agreement. "Rendo was going down Kingsbury one time, and he dumped that mustang off there. God, that poor horse rolled halfway down the mountainside. He goes on down to the next turn, "Come on now, you no-good-darn, get up in 'er!" And the horse jumps up in there, and he turns on over to the Indian camp, or to a bar somewhere…"

"What kind of truck was this?"

Tommy didn't hesitate. "'37 Dodge pickup. Regular pickup box."

"Like I say, that horse would brace itself in all four corners. That's the only way he could stand up!" Doc bent over and held his arms down and out as if he were the mustang in the truck; Wanda giggled wildly at her brother's antics.

"That was some kinda' horse," said Tommy.

"He lived up on a mountain someplace?" My curiosity was in overdrive.

Seldom did I get a chance to look at Pop's life from a different perspective than his own.

Tommy took a puff on his pipe, and a kind of calm descended. He seemed to gather strength from the memory of his old friend. "Rendo had a place over there off Cold Creek. He lived by Sierra House, an old, old place, with his dad. A log cabin that's been there a hundred years."

"Didn't Sierra House used to be a kind of a way station stop?" asked Wanda.

"Pony Express route." Tommy answered. "Wells Fargo stage."

"Now, how old was he, when you guys were doing all this?" I pictured the three men in civilian life after the war.

"34?" Wanda was counting on her fingers.

"Yeah, thirty-four, thirty-five." Tommy said.

"And you guys were the same age?

Dave nods in agreement. "Yeah, we're all about the same age."

"He was my best friend for a long time. Till he died." Tommy paused at something just beneath the surface. "He died young, too. He was probably forty, forty-five when he died."

"What killed him?" I asked.

"I have no idea," Tommy replied.

"I think probably his liver gave out." Wanda's diagnosis was sudden and precise.

Dave gave it a moment. "Yeah, he probably drank himself to death. His mother lived to be a hundred."

"So, he was a hard drinker?"

Here it was again. I couldn't seem to escape that line of thought, even when I least expected it.

"But do you know something?" Wanda spoke with genuine fondness. "I don't ever remember him being mean or anything."

"Oh, he could drink more booze than…" Dave gave his sister a wide grin. "You didn't think he was a hard drinker? Oh, I tell you, that sucker, Goddang it…"

Tommy had his own opinion. "We used to get drunk a lot, but…"

"Well, that's a hard drinker!" Dave exclaimed.

"We'd drink a fifth of whiskey apiece," Tommy spoke with some satisfaction. "But you enjoyed it!"

Dave and Tommy broke into wild laughter, cut short only by Dave's hacking cough.

"I used to see that man stand, and drink and drink and drink and never show it," said Wanda. "Rendo was so strong, right up until…" Wanda glanced at her husband, then Dave. She was bracketed on both sides by the two men she loved most, but for a moment, she had to look away.

It was silent, as if a stranger had been brought into the room. I said nothing and waited for the mood to change.

Tommy packed his pipe without a word, then scratched a kitchen match off the table and brought it to his bowl. He rocked back in his chair and let his hand fall on Wanda's arm.

"I remember Rendo was out there all winter, up at Cold Creek. During the big snowstorm, we used to carry out big bags of stale bread, that's the only thing we had. There was no hay in the whole damn town." Tommy blew a puff of blue smoke from his pipe and held the stem up at an angle. "Globin's store would give us all the old bread that was in the freezer, and we'd carry that 10 miles up and throw it in there for that horse. That horse lived off bread all winter long…"

Words turned to wind. I listened quietly and tried to make sense of the moments before. Once again, I was grateful for the tiny tape recorder, as I sank beneath the weight of my own thoughts.

ON THE WAY BACK from Tahoe, we took the Highway 20 cutoff across Emigrant Gap and down into Bear Valley. It was the same overland route that ten thousand weary settlers had used a hundred years before, winding around the pine hills as the elevation dropped from 6000 to 2400 feet. I wasn't all that anxious to get home, and a scenic overlook with a broad turnout made for a nice place to stop and rest.

"Let's pull over for a few."

"Ok." Pop sat up and pulled on his hat. He got out of the car slowly. It had been a long day's drive, and we were both tired. I took out a cigarette, watching as the more determined travelers passed us by.

"What ever happened to Angelo?" I asked.

We were sitting on a low rock wall that ran the length of the turnout; it offered a panoramic view across the canyon. The smooth granite barrier had been carefully laid by hand, transforming the remote rural highway into a perfect picture post card. In the '30's, the WPA had built dozens of projects just like it, putting desperate men to work crafting small monuments to the beauty that was still America.

"Ol' Angelo Manzenelli." Pop spoke his name like a song, his voice dancing on every syllable. He paused to think about his answer. "Last I heard, he might be up in Montana somewhere. He was a teamster, I think. I wonder if he's still driving."

Doc pointed to the other side of the canyon. "San Juan Ridge. Me and my dad used to fish right over there, on the fast creeks come down off the mountains."

"What ever happened to your folks?"

"Same thing that happens to all of us, I suppose. They died."

"You know what I mean."

Pop gave a nod and stood up. "After I came down to the ranch, Mom and Dad went back up to Grass Valley, to that little house on Union Hill. That was good for a while, but then it was the nursing home, and…"

His voice grew quiet, almost to a whisper. "My sisters tried to help." Pop turned away. He looked at the ground around his feet. "Well, let's just say they'd been together for so many years, there was no way they were ever gonna' be apart for long."

Pop turned back to me, his eyes moist. "You got to be ready for whatever comes next, Bill. This ol' world don't care what you think. It cares what you do."

I didn't want to press him. We sat quietly and smoked, the light fading into a dozen pastel hues, the occasional car passing behind us on the highway. I thought about the last time I'd seen my wife and kids and wondered what love was like when it wasn't all tangled up with regret.

Doc looked out across the dark valley and spoke in a full voice. "It's a great life, if she don't weaken."

* * *

WE WERE SITTING at the green formica table. No one had said anything for three or four minutes. That was something of a record for Pop and me, especially with a cup of coffee between us.

"Where is she now?" he asked.

"She's gone to her mother's place in Oregon." I found myself stirring the coffee in my cup for no particular reason. "She took the kids and left yesterday."

"Probably for the best. You two won't do each other any good right now, and you can do a lot a damage to the children."

"I suppose you're right."

"Ain't no doubt." He spoke quietly, as if about the weather. I let the thought settle in. Pop knew her as well as anyone, maybe better than I did now.

"I didn't see it coming."

He gave me a knowing smile. "Most folks never do. Leastwise, I never did, and boy, I had plenty of warning."

I suppose I did, too.

The curtain of silence descended again, broken only by the sound of a spoon turning in a half-empty cup.

U-Name-it Ranch
Nevada County, California

"DADDY, THERE'S A COP AT THE GATE." His daughter looked flustered and a little bit frightened.

"I'll take care of it, honey. Just stay inside."

Doc peered through the kitchen window and wondered what the bubbletop was doing out here this time. He looked around the house, noted the general condition of his son and some of his friends, and slowly walked out the front door. It was his daughter's birthday, and she and the boys had been celebrating for most of a day and a night. Rusty had just gotten out of the Army. Dave had to step carefully over one of his high school buddies, still sleeping on the front porch.

A deputy sheriff stood by his car at the closed metal gate, some 50 yards away. Dave could see him clearly. He watched the deputy flash his lights and siren.

Doc took a rolled cigarette from his pocket and lit it. He savored the rich grey smoke, then stepped off the front porch and moved deliberately up the gravel drive. The deputy flashed his lights again.

"I saw you the first time." Dave stopped five feet away from the gate. "What can I do for you?"

"We've had some complaints from your neighbors at the top of the hill." The deputy looked down at his clipboard. "Loud music going on, all day and night - they say there might be underage drinking, said they could smell marijuana smoke."

"There's no one here underage that's not with their momma, and you can hear for yourself how loud the music is." Dave looked the deputy right in the eye. "You smell anything?"

"No, sir, not from here."

"Well, you're a damn sight closer than that asshole up on the hill. And if you don't have a search warrant, I don't expect you'll want to push that."

"Well, Mr. Bailey, we're just doing our job."

"I'm sure you are." Doc tossed his cigarette to the ground and crushed it with the toe of his boot. "You know, I've spent half my life dealing with people like that. Tell that son-of-a-bitch to come down here himself and speak to me directly." He took the creased straw hat off his head and wiped his brow with the back of his hand. He tapped the hat against the side of his jeans.

The deputy recalled an earlier conversation with his boss, after they'd gotten the call at dispatch. "Don't push him," the Sheriff had said. "That man's from another century. Dave Bailey would just as soon shoot you as look at you."

The young deputy observed the older man across the gate. He measured his response carefully. "I'll pass that along, sir."

"Tell him it's my daughter's birthday, and my son's back from the war, and this party will last just as long as we like, thank you very much."

"Well, just keep it down, if you would." The deputy opened his car door, took a deep breath and turned around again. "How long do you think that might be?"

"You know, I really can't say for sure." Dave leaned against the wooden gatepost and tucked one thumb into the pocket of his jeans. He smiled broadly and pushed the worn straw hat back on his forehead.

"I think the last time I threw one, it went for about 30 days."

THE WINTER OF '98 was cold and wet, soggy with the kind of red mud that filled the creek beds and made the roads around the ranch slippery and dangerous. There were flash floods in Yuba City, and the check dams in the high country threatened to overflow their banks.

I'd been sober for two years. Things got a lot harder for a while, but after a time, a whole lot easier. I finally got the good sense to stay home and raise my kids, even if it was only three days a week. There were no more trips on the open road, and Betsy was as likely to be seen in San Francisco as she was in Grass Valley.

Dave Bailey was trapped in the final stage of chronic emphysema, slowly drowning in his own phlegm. As his lungs filled up, his heart struggled to pump enough oxygen to supply his brain. He had finally given up smoking, but the decision had come far too late and couldn't make up for sixty years of tar and nicotine.

Over the summer, word came that Tommy Johnson had ALS, and like Lou Gehrig, he was playing in a game that he couldn't win. After he heard about Tommy, Pop took to his post at the kitchen table, there to quietly await his own fate.

I visited him on the day before he died. He sat in the house that he and his father had built, attached to an oxygen tank. He could only speak a few words at a time, his shallow breath barely keeping enough air in his lungs to sustain him. We spoke briefly about life, about his favorite keno numbers, and the old coffeemaker in the kitchen. I told him that I loved him, and thanked him for all the good times we had shared.

"Don't get old, Bill."

"You never did."

With his breath lost, Dave's eyes said everything. He was ready for whatever came next.

Morning

THERE WERE TIMES when his calamity would pass
like smoke through the branches. He would disappear
into the past, standing in the searing sun at a medicine show,
the barker hawking cures with the utmost confidence
while he and his friends watched the desert scorpions dance
to the death in the hot sand. The crowd gathered round for
the spectacle, no victors, only spoils, empty shells left
to bake on the hardpan. The music sang and the people
circled, fathers, mothers, ranch hands clapping in a two-step
rhythm at the bottom of the barn. Spinning bodies swirled in
the breeze, drifting leaves across the rough floor of the cabin.
Dust flew in through an open window, his back turned
against the darkness into a wide sea. The light was rising,
a crack at the edge of the ocean, bright like the sheen on
the coat of lean black horse. The windows rattled with a chill
winter wind, an ice-cold night in Tonapah. He dove down
deep in the blankets, searching for that last warm spot,
far away from the storm.

Billie was there.

MORE THAN TEN YEARS would pass before I traveled south again. My kids were grown now, and I had learned to treat my ex-wife as the mother of my children. I'd started to put some of Doc's stories down on paper, but there came a time to put aside my pen and head for the desert.

Betsy had retired to her parking spot beside the barn, but I had found another old car that spoke of the open road with the same soothing voice as the big '56. And it had air conditioning. This time, I traveled to Arizona on Interstate highways, with all the windows closed.

Beside me was a battered silver thermos, a bag of beef jerky, and an ornate pipe tobacco can. I'd kept some of Pop's ashes in that can, determined to deposit them in Wellton. It was a long drive, and when I got lonely, I would play one of Doc's tapes, the old stories rendered perfect by the sound of Betsy rattling around inside the silent sedan. The ashtrays in the German car were empty. I had given up the cigarettes with the booze a dozen years before. They still called to me when things got complicated.

The trip to Wellton was uneventful. It was too early for flowers on the Mojave, and the swift Mercedes seemed to bypass all the places where Doc and I had lingered. This time, Bakers Tanks was marked on a map, and the dirt track that led out to it was fairly well worn.

Someone had built a concrete block roundhouse for campers. There were four burn barrels and three cooking stands with iron grills, and a sign put up by the Boy Scouts that read 'Please carry your trash out with you'. A grey seagull pecked at the remnants of a plastic bag while another one circled in the warm air currents above. I guess they came to Bakers Tanks with the tourists.

I walked down to the tanks. There had been no rain for some time, and the cracked ground had given way to brown dust. The mesquite tree was still there, older, thicker, and heavily calloused. Scavenged for firewood, it was holding its own against time and the Boy Scouts of America.

The edges of the tanks were littered with fallen leaves and milkweed. I stood silent for a moment, sensing the finality of my farewell. The tobacco can opened easily enough. I sprinkled Pop's ashes over the granite, watching as they drifted down, dissolving into black water.

I tried to say thank you, but words failed me. The tanks were still there, but he wasn't. Once again, like so many times since Pop had died, I was lonely.

All I really wanted was a cigarette.

The car started on the first try, just like Betsy had. I made my way out to the main road, careful to dodge the sharp fronds of ocotillo and the growing ache in my gut. Once on the highway, I opened all the windows and floored the old Mercedes, flying down the road through a wave of hot, desert air.

I thought about how easy it would be just to take off and go. *Disappear.* Nobody knew where I was, and no one would know where I was going.

A couple of miles down the road, I spotted a little store with a single gas pump, a spare remnant of the old highway. The small adobe building was littered with beer signs and the colored light bulbs that passed for neon in the new century. The pump was padlocked and dusty, like almost everything I'd seen that day.

I parked next to a stack of broken clay bricks and closed my eyes, stopping for a moment to watch my breath and let the urge for a cigarette pass. A collarless yellow dog circled my tires and lay down in the shade. I opened the car door and went inside.

The store was cramped and small, stocked with items that only a place far from any shopping mall could be. The floor was covered with cases of water, sacks of rice, and standing racks of tortilla chips and candy. Long wooden shelves were dotted with mixed goods: bread, jelly, toilet paper, batteries, some dusty cans of Sterno. Straw hats hung on the wall next to a pair of garden shovels and a plastic umbrella. At the end of a long counter sat an ice chest full of half-frozen popsicles. An old coffeemaker stood behind the counter, its contents black as motor oil.

The glass-door refrigerator hummed with the low-throated growl of a compressor that had never seen a day's rest. Tall bottles of Corona and Miller Lite stood silent sweating frost, waiting for the chorus to begin. I thought about how good a cold beer could taste on a hot day.

Packs of cigarettes lined the wall behind the cash register, my old brand prominent in the middle of the rack.

I was thirsty in a way I hadn't been in years.

Something caught my eye. I glanced at the container by the fridge. Someone had recycled a glass pickle barrel and filled it with jagged pieces of what looked like burnt brown leather. A cardboard sign on the front read:

Jerkey
$1 dollars each

The dark man behind the counter noticed my interest.

"Barbecued burro. *Hecho por mi Madre.*" He pointed to a framed photograph of an older Mexican woman. "Homemade. You want to try a piece?"

I felt a smile over my shoulder. *It matters what you do.*

"I believe I will, sir. And that coffee looks pretty good, too."

I bought a creased straw hat. Maybe the desert would be in bloom on my way home.

- Ø -

AFTERWORD

This novel is a work of the imagination, but most of the details come
from a series of recordings made over the course of a decade. In reconstructing
Doc's life, I relied heavily on those conversations, and the wealth of information
available in newspapers and scholarly journals.

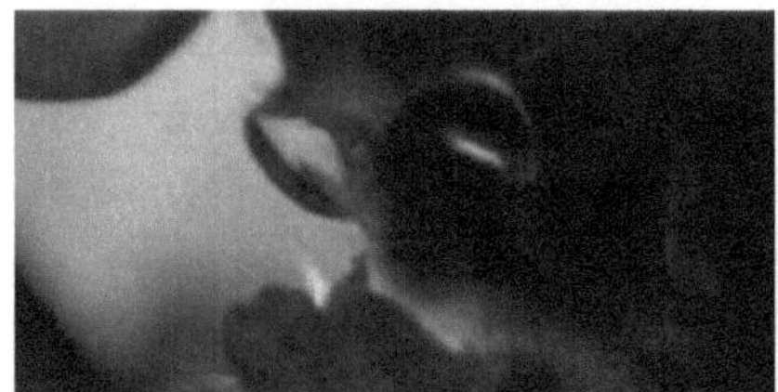

There is never a perfect recollection of any story, nor a perfect life,
but I'd like to think we're still learning.

To hear and see some of those films and recordings,
visit ADesertInBloom.net

WILLIAM LANDVOIGT BAYNE grew up in the South, lives in the West, and was educated on the roads somewhere in between. As a young man, he hitchhiked across America, drew comic books, and ran away to join the circus. That didn't work out long term, so he moved on to advertising and television, using the same skills he picked up shoveling manure with the Ringling Brothers. He has a lot of shiny statures from those filmmaking days.

Writing fiction is a lot more fun than shoveling, so that's what he does now.

COYOTE FILMS EDITION

Finished reading? We hope you've enjoyed *A Desert in Bloom.*
Please be sure to share your thoughts with friends. We'd love to read your review
on Goodreads, Book Riot, or anywhere else you'd like.

Or write us at: info@adesertinbloom.net

We'll be sure to reply.